T0354333

ALSO BY JONATHAN ROSEN ────────────────

Novels

Exhumed
Dead People I Have Known
Time and Tide

Non-Fiction

Senioritis: a guide to what ails the aging

DISPLACED PERSONS
BY JONATHAN ROSEN

iUniverse, Inc.
New York   Bloomington

This is a work of fiction. All of the characters, names, incidents,
organizations, and dialogue in this novel are either the products
of the author's imagination or are used fictitiously

iUniverse books may be ordered through booksellers or by contacting:

iUniverse
1663 Liberty Drive
Bloomington, IN 47403
www.iuniverse.com
1-800-Authors (1-800-288-4677)

ISBN: 978-1-4401-4731-9 (pbk)
ISBN: 978-1-4401-4735-7 (cloth)
ISBN: 978-1-4401-4734-0 (ebook)

Printed in the United States of America

iUniverse rev. date: 8/26/09

To my patients, for whom I have always tried to do my best.
And to my wife, Linda, who has always done hers for me.

There is no greater sorrow on earth than the loss of one's native land.

—Euripides

CHAPTER 1 ───────────────

Asher knew he was precarious. But only after the incident in the mortuary did he realize how far out on the ledge he teetered.

That particular Sunday in mid-March, nine years after starting out medical practice, Asher should not have been surprised by the call from Tolmisano's Funeral Home. He had spent the morning diving into a cauldron, simmering with nurses, patients and hovering relatives. Having surfaced intact, he still anticipated some emergency would arise from some random source that would prevent him from making it back home until well after suppertime. Yet, he held out hope that the extraordinary might occur–nothing else would happen that day and he'd actually sneak home before nightfall.

The day was bitter cold, bone-chilling—winter could not decide whether or not to finally give up—blustery as hell, with a bright, blue sun-sparkled sky. A day best spent sitting by the fireplace, hanging out with Mandy and the kids, watching the leafless trees bend forward and back while praying for spring. Taking a break in the hospital cafeteria over a plate of yellow glop they called chicken-ala-king, Asher's brief moment of comfort was interrupted when his beeper went off for the thirty-second time that day. He dialed the answering service. Sheila, the operator answered in her unmistakable, cigarette-afflicted voice, "Sorry again, doc. Tolmisano's Funeral Home in Talcott wants you to give them a call."

When Asher dialed the funeral home, a soft-spoken woman answered. "Dr. Asher, thanks for calling back so quickly. Usually you all take hours to get back to us. We just received one of your patients, a Mrs. Lockhart, Martha Lockhart. A neighbor found her passed away in bed after not hearing from her for a day. The EMTs were called, but she must have expired over twelve hours before they got there, so they brought her directly here."

Asher conjured up an image of Mrs. Lockhart from her last office visit—her eyes receding into her skull, the pungency of uremia wafting off her like a mist. She'd developed kidney failure after cardiac bypass surgery and, at eighty-one, had fared badly with dialysis. "Has her family been notified?"

"Her daughter's already been by here. But, as you know, we need someone to pronounce the patient. Would you be able to come by so we can begin working on the body?"

After hesitating a moment, since that task was not in his job description, Asher agreed. Usually, the town medical examiner handled these situations; ultimately *he* was charged with deciding whose death was natural and whose was not. But Asher thought of a lifeless, already decaying Mrs. Lockhart lying on some slab in the morgue, recalled the homemade pumpkin cheesecake she had brought him last Thanksgiving and surrendered.

When Asher called Mandy to tell her he wouldn't be home for a while, she responded, "So what else is new?" He couldn't help but detect the weariness in Mandy's voice from years of hearing "Sorry, hon" at the beginning of a phone call. Another seven hours of another Sunday watching their wired, nine- and seven-year-old daughters by herself would only multiply their problems. After hanging up, he imagined Mandy slumping into the family room chair, allowing her fatigue to overtake her for just one moment before throwing her hair backward and then jolting her slim frame up in defiance.

Only three or four times before in his career had Asher been called into the community to pronounce a patient. Eight months earlier, he'd had to visit a patient's home for that ordeal. One early summer Saturday evening, a police dispatcher had contacted Asher to inform him that Sandor O'Reily, a fifty-four year old patient of his, had dropped dead in his kitchen. Those bare facts hardly matched the reality.

When Asher had arrived that night at a small Cape Cod house on a pot-holed, cracked-sidewalk street in South Dover, he found a police cruiser idling in the driveway, its flashing lights sending strobes of red alarm onto the home's worn wooden siding. A youthful officer stood guard at the door, looking apprehensive and sweating profusely. As he passed by, Asher handed the officer the cold can of Coke he had just bought, "You look like you need this more than I do." The surprised officer said, "Hey, thanks, Doc. Sorry to disturb you. You're not going to like what you see in there."

By then Asher figured he had seen about everything. Undaunted, he headed into the living room. Immediately, he was assaulted by the sight of clots of fresh blood splattered all over the house, pulsating and throbbing in concert with the cruiser's flashing lights. The sickly, cloying scent of a butcher shop thickened the already stagnant air. Asher tracked a trail of blood through the living room and into the bedroom to the bathroom, where the tub was also filled with blood. Streaked red handprints decorated the walls like souvenir Manson wallpaper. Asher trudged on, following the trail back through the living room and into the kitchen, the congealed blood sticking to the soles of his shoes, making another path of gory footprints. There, on the yellowed, vinyl floor lay Mr. O'Reily, whiter than porcelain, collapsed in a heap, still clutching the kitchen phone to his chest, a towel wrapped as a tourniquet around his left thigh.

Asher bent over, inspecting his exsanguinated patient. Upon careful scrutiny of Mr. O'Reily's left leg, Asher finally found the bleeding source. A pinpoint opening in his mid-shin outlined a tiny calcified artery that had eroded through his skin and then pumped Mr. O'Reily's entire blood supply out onto the floor of his home. Asher recoiled as he imagined his patient's desperate attempts to halt the hemorrhaging, when all he'd needed to do was apply some direct pressure until help arrived.

"What a waste," Asher muttered.

The cop hovering nearby asked him, "What was that, Doc?"

"Nothing," Asher replied. "Just talking to myself." He ripped the latex gloves from his hands in frustration. For a moment, he felt like collecting the scattered blood and reinjecting it back into his patient. Finally, Asher did answer the officer. "One damn thumb. That's all he needed. A thumb, a forefinger, even a fucking pinkie. This happen to you or yours, just put some damn pressure right on the wound. You'll stop the blood in no time. OK?"

"Sure, Doc. No problem. Thanks for the tip."

As Asher watched the officer turn away, he thought to himself, "Dumb. Why take it out the poor cop who must forever be on the downhill side of all the crap people send his way?"

Before leaving, Asher took one final look at Sandor O'Reily and his bloody trail. Never again would this man walk the earth. His particular genetic make-up, his history, his loves and losses, his temper and temperament would never again be duplicated. Whether a coal miner or carpet layer, his life and soul were unique. What purpose could it serve to have that soul spilled senselessly onto his own vinyl kitchen floor?

*

Thank God Asher would not have to face similar philosophical misgivings on attending Mrs. Lockhart. She had overdrawn her account a while back and, though dialysis had temporarily delayed the inevitable, everyone, herself included, knew she was living on borrowed funds. Still, driving over to the funeral home, he registered a pang of sorrow at the death of another of his patients who, as was so often the case, had been struck down by a series of progressive body-wasting insults for which the pomp and paraphernalia of modern medical science had no adequate response. Everyone these days seemed to die piece-by-piece— failing organs, followed by crenated cells, followed by cascading chemical disarray.

Asher waited at a light as a late-sixties mustard-yellow Plymouth Valiant pulled up next to his six-month-old Lexus. A series of almost sculptured dents lined the relic's sides, while a pair of Rasta men sat in the front seat, grooving to a blaring Bob Marley and sharing a joint. When the driver spotted Asher staring at him, he smiled a huge, yellow-stained grin at Asher and held out his joint, offering a toke. Asher smiled back, but shook his head and faced the road ahead. At that moment, a ten-year-old kid in an oversized sweatshirt and Red Sox cap walked directly in front of Asher's car. The kid looked just like Tom Mallory's son, Jake; maybe it was Jake. Asher ducked his head and covered his eyes until the boy had safely moved on. Two weeks after Tom's death, Asher wondered once again how much longer he'd be hiding in shame. As the light turned green, out of the corner of his vision, he caught the Rasta driver laughing at him.

At the side entrance to Tolmisano's, Asher rang the buzzer, waited thirty seconds, then identified himself to the disembodied intercom that finally responded. He stood on the concrete side steps, shivering in the white lab coat he had forgotten to take off, waiting for that voice to let him in. An isolated snowflake surprised him as it blew by, since the frigid winter sun was still framed by the bright, blue sky. Quickly though, that snowflake was followed by a dozen others and then a dark, smothering cloud engulfed him in a sudden winter squall. Finally, a woman in her early thirties opened the door, then stepped back as the wind blew Asher into her foyer. Ignoring the crucifix on the wall, he could not stop himself. "Jesus Christ! That storm came on so quick, I thought it was aimed just at me."

The woman almost smiled but chose to ignore his non-greeting. "Dr. Asher, I'm Heidi Garnett. Thanks for coming over. Hope I didn't ruin your weekend."

She was a good foot shorter than Asher, had light brown hair, an unadorned, heart-shaped face framing cheeks too well-scrubbed. With her knee-length gray skirt, man-tailored stiff white shirt and stylish pumps, Asher speculated she could just as well have been cast as a saleswoman in the ladies' shoes department at Nordstrom's as a funeral home director. "Don't apologize. If you hadn't called me, inevitably someone else would have." He reached down and shook her hand, transmitting a slight shock through them both, as if each emitted charged particles.

"Dr. Asher, you probably don't remember me, but we met once at the hospital a few years ago. You took care of my stepfather, Carl Thompson, when he had pneumonia. Unfortunately, he died inside of ten hours after he got there. I suppose you did your best, but the walk-in clinic had misdiagnosed him a few days before, so by the time you got to him, I guess it was too late."

Asher stammered an apology. "Yes, terrible tragedy. He was so sick By the time he was admitted, we couldn't do much. Sorry." He remembered well that day he spent trying to revive Mr. Thompson. For months afterward, he had worried that he would be pulled into the lawsuit he was sure the family would file against the walk-in clinic, but had heard nothing since. Asher did not, however, recall Heidi's part.

Heidi repeated, "I'm sure you did your best." Then changed the topic. "Follow me. Mrs. Lockhart is in the morgue downstairs."

As he trailed her, Asher tried to distract himself from this reminder that there was likely a sizeable coterie of people out in the community who had feelings about him of which he was oblivious. Instead, he chose to focus on the funeral home's beehive of quiet activity. They stepped silently through three formal parlors, each holding a smattering of family members huddling around open caskets; then past an ornate, packed sanctuary with a sobbing congregation engrossed in a mournful eulogy; and finally past a side room packed with empty caskets, waiting for future occupants. Asher bent over and whispered to Heidi, "Busy day, I guess." Heidi merely smiled back, whether in agreement or in satisfaction, Asher could not tell. As they headed down the stairs to the morgue, Asher followed a curious black and white photographic exhibit, hanging on the stairway wall, of the various hearses this funeral home had used over the prior fifty years.

In the basement, amidst large porcelain sinks and multiple bottles of pungent formalin, Mrs. Lockhart rested on a metal table, covered with a white sheet. This time there was no blood to be seen. Whatever exact terminal circumstance had led to her death was not apparent. When Asher uncovered Mrs. Lockhart's face, she seemed more relaxed in death than she had ever been in life. He engaged in the formalities of looking into her eyes, one of which refused to close, then listened to the absence of sounds in her heart and lungs. He brushed his hand across the fistula used as access for her dialysis, aware of the now absent thrill—that once vibrating sensation of blood flowing from artery to vein—signaling the end of her circulation. Asher neglected to cover Mrs. Lockhart back up, suddenly aware that Heidi was hovering a foot away, watching him intently. He moved away, trying to put some distance between them. "Poor lady. At least she's at peace now. She suffered enough at the end."

Heidi hesitated, then answered cryptically, "Isn't there some old proverb, 'Better to suffer injury, than injure others'?"

Asher was taken aback. Did Heidi still harbor resentment toward him, or maybe doctors in general? Now, intent on getting out of there as quickly as possible, he asked Heidi for the death certificate. She handed Asher the red-bordered, flimsy paper and stood over him while he filled it out, a task he had completed dozens of times. Usually, he took his time with these official documents, taking seriously his role as the determiner of when where, why and how his patient had exited. In this instance, though, he hurriedly scrawled "Renal Failure" and his name and address. He rose and handed Heidi back the paper, face-to-face with her now, trying to end the encounter with caregiver's banter. "Well, I guess that's it. Another loss for our side. Seems by the crowds you've got upstairs, business is booming."

Heidi answered, and for months afterward, Asher wondered whether she was merely being flip, whether she was she trying to provoke him or was she giving voice to her poorly disguised hostility. Because her comment triggered a reaction that neither of them could possibly have anticipated and was so out of character for Asher, he wondered afterward if he had imagined the entire episode.

"Well, Dr. Asher, if you did a better job, maybe I'd be less busy."

The half-grin indicating Heidi was kidding that should have followed her remark might have staved off Asher's immediate response, but none came. Instead, reflexively, his arm spring-loaded, Asher's right hand jerked upward, slapping Heidi across the face, leaving an irrevocable, five-fingered stain on her cheek.

They both froze in place, neither able to believe what had just happened. Heidi slowly brought her hand to cheek as if to convince herself the sting she felt had a true physical antecedent. Then she tore upstairs, running into an office and slamming the door shut. Asher ran after her, the door almost striking him in the face. For the next five minutes, he tried to apologize through the closed door, listening to Heidi's sobs on the other side. Finally, he gave up and left the funeral home, trailed by the image of Mrs. Lockhart's unblinking eye, the sole witness to his crime.

CHAPTER 2 ————————————————————

Asher drove away from the funeral home, engulfed in a squall that had morphed into a whiteout, just matching the storm swirling in his own head. Simultaneously, his beeper and a police siren broke into his oblivion. For a moment, he couldn't tell if the discordant sounds were real or were resounding from his brain's turmoil. Then, as the siren intensified and approached, Asher felt his face flush and the sweat bead up on his forehead. Could Heidi have called the police? Would they have identified and tracked his car down this quickly? What possible story or excuse could he offer? He was under great stress? He was provoked, had an out-of-body experience? What would the police care? He had assaulted a virtual stranger. His white coat would not protect him.

Pulling over to the side of the road and watching the approach of flashing lights in his rearview mirror, Asher agonized over how he could have committed such an act. He had never slapped anyone in the face before. He'd never hit anyone, anywhere. Not Mandy, not the kids, never so much as a spanking. His sister must have provoked him ten thousand times when they were kids, but hitting just wasn't in his repertoire.

One time, his father had struck *him* in a similar manner. Asher had just turned fifteen. He had forgotten what time Thanksgiving dinner was called for, hanging out at a friend's and arriving home twenty minutes late. He had rushed into the dining room, thrown his coat on a nearby chair and found the family, with half a dozen relatives at the table, already eating. His father rose quickly, blocking Asher from making it to his chair. They'd stood face-to-face. Asher, still a good half-foot shorter than his ramrod-straight dad, had mumbled an apology. His dad answered, "Pick up your coat and wait in the kitchen till everyone's done and then you can eat your meal alone."

Asher looked his dad square in the eye, hesitated, then committed one of only two acts of defiance toward his dad in his lifetime. "Pick it up yourself."

Asher heard the sting of the slap that followed before he felt it. He touched his cheek, just as Heidi would years later, and then bolted upstairs to his bedroom, locking his door; no Thanksgiving meal for him that year. Asher had never forgotten the sting of pain and humiliation from being struck in such a way. How he himself could have perpetrated such an act was beyond comprehension.

The rise and fall of the police siren echoed off the walls of his skull, making Asher wonder if a squad of cruisers was heading for him. He imagined a half-dozen officers springing from their cars, guns raised, pulling Asher out of his car and spread-eagling him against the hood while they handcuffed him. As Asher sat awaiting his fate, in a miraculous reprieve, the cruiser overtook him and then shot on by. As the siren's shrieking faded, then disappeared, Asher felt his shirt drench, his stomach clench, amazed at both his good fortune and his sudden grip of paranoia. He staggered out of the car and vomited green bile on the white snow, then squatted in a heap on the sidewalk until he could gather the strength to move again.

Asher finally made it home that night after several more hours in the hospital, caring for three new admissions while wandering around the halls in a trance. By the time he got home, the girls had already gone to sleep and barely stirred when he kissed them goodnight. Mandy was engrossed in a *Masterpiece Theatre* episode of *Jane Eyre*, evidently in an after-dealing-with-the-kids-all-day veg mode. She gave him a preoccupied kiss and a preoccupied, "Hi hon. Hope you're not too beat. Dinner's in the microwave. Set on three minutes and you're ready."

Relieved she had asked no questions, he answered. "Thanks, hon. Sorry so late. Kids give you a hard time?" She shook her head no and waved him off.

Asher was surprised Mandy had not noticed the distress evident on his face that he found when he stared at his distorted image in the bathroom mirror. How a grown man, a physician no less, could strike, with no provocation, an innocent woman was beyond him. What manner of madman had he become? And who do you tell about such a deviation, who would possibly not be revolted by it? Certainly not Mandy. She'd reasonably become afraid of him herself. What kind of husband would do such a thing? What would stop him from hitting the kids? After eating, he slid silently into bed next to Mandy, convincing himself confession was not an option.

CHAPTER 3

The following day, a world-weary, beaten Asher, back in his office a hundred yards down the road from the hospital entrance, had little success putting the incident at the funeral home out of his mind. The first thing he did that day was send Heidi a card, along with a bouquet of flowers in apology, trying to explain the unexplainable, undo the undoable. He had little hope for a reply, or for forgiveness.

His self-recrimination was interrupted that afternoon by an encounter with one of his few blind patients. Anthony, thirteen now, had been blind since birth, a victim of retrolental fibroplasia, the byproduct of prematurity and a twelve hundred gram birth weight. This visit was for a routine school physical. On two prior encounters, Anthony and his mom had seemed so comfortable with his condition that Asher, despite having only a few completely blind patients, had also quickly taken Anthony's sightlessness for granted. While performing the routine exam of Anthony's ears and throat and listening to his heart sounds, Asher asked how Anthony was adapting to school, how his piano lessons were going and how he was getting along with his sighted identical twin. Just as Asher finished giving Anthony a kick demonstrating his patellar reflexes, Anthony interrupted him.

"Dr. Asher, mind if I examine your face for a minute? Helps me picture you when I leave."

Asher hesitated, always uncomfortable when his facial appearance came up, "Sure, Anthony. Not fair that I'm always the one examining you."

With Anthony's mother seated nearby, Asher patiently stood still while Anthony's sensitized hands surveyed his features. Always, Asher had been self-conscious about his own physical appearance. At three, an Ear Nose and Throat surgeon, removing a cyst from Asher's parotid gland, had traumatized Asher's right facial nerve, leaving Asher forever after with a weakness of that side's facial muscles, rendering his face asymmetric, forever warring. Despite growing to over six feet tall, acquiring a square jaw, a firm brow and penetrating dark eyes, Asher felt he was forever after defined by this resulting quizzical look. He sensed others could never be sure whether he was in the midst of a half-smile or half-frown, surprised or confused, intensely interested or rudely preoccupied. Asher was an enigma to others and, forever receiving mixed feedback, an enigma to himself.

Sightless Anthony, though, sensed none of this visible schizophrenia. His hands gently scrutinized Asher's discordant features, the slightly stubbled, squared-off jaw line, and the deep cleft in his chin. Instead of the queries Asher was used to hearing, Anthony merely proclaimed, "Gee, Dr. Asher, you have a nice, kind face." And for the only time that week, Asher broke out into a broad smile that circuited through Anthony's fingers into a similar reaction on Anthony's face.

That evening, Asher drove back to his house, his mind swirling, unconsciously ducking his head whenever he passed a police cruiser. The number of people Asher had begun avoiding appeared to be multiplying. The driveway to his home was unlit, so at first Asher didn't spot the clumped shadow lying between the garage doors. He clicked on the automatic garage door opener and if not for the fact the garbage can had been left outside, he might have missed finding Trotsky lying on his side on the tarmac. At first, Asher wondered why no one had thought to let the dog back in the house when it was clearly too cold out even for the well-insulated black lab. Then, when he moved the garbage can, he realized the dog had not jumped up to greet him and, as he looked closer, the dog was not moving. A sudden catch came to his throat. Asher bent over and realized Trotsky wasn't breathing. He shook the dog and felt the unnatural, cool fur, then spotted the stream of drool pooling under his mouth. For a second, Asher feared he might have struck Trotsky on the driveway, though the dog was clearly not in his car's path. Then he assumed someone else must have hit him. But Asher could find no sign of trauma—no bloodstains, no evidence of broken bones, nothing at all.

When Asher stood up—thinking how would he tell Mandy and the kids, wondering what to do with Trotsky's body, wondering how they would fill the void left behind after having their dog with them for ten years—most of all, he wondered how divine retribution could unleash judgment on him in such a dramatic fashion? Since when did God intervene in these direct and manifest ways? Murderers went uncaptured for years. Rapists, thieves, scoundrels, and hypocrites lived in serene obscurity with no punishment until their deaths and then who knew what became of their souls? Why had he been singled out for immediate sentencing?

Before he went inside to tell his family about their loss, Asher felt an overpowering desire to scrutinize Trotsky. He stooped back down, the medical detective in him taking over, wanting to know the cause of his pet's death. Something natural, something rational must have ended Trotsky's life. Not just the unseen hand of an all-knowing being sweeping down and snuffing him out. Inspecting every hair and limb, palpating every organ, even retrieving his stethoscope from the car and trying to listen to an unbeating heart gave Asher no clue to the cause of Trotsky's sudden death.

Asher dragged himself into the house, weary beyond words,

finally finding Mandy and the kids upstairs, in the midst of their bathing ritual. Mandy was sitting on Emily's bed reading *Stones from the River*, not far from the kids, who were splashing and carousing in the tub. Mandy read so intently, it took several moments before she noticed Asher in the dim hallway. He gestured for Mandy to come out of the room so the kids would not see him.

Mandy rose up and greeted him, with no attempt to hide his presence from the kids. "Hey hon, you finally made it. Sorry we couldn't wait for dinner. You must be starved and exhausted. You want to shower or eat first?"

Asher was amazed the twin burdens he now carried had not changed the rest of the world's normal functioning. He gestured again for Mandy to come into the hallway. Mandy instead went to the bathroom doorway and said, "Kids, dad's home. Finish up your bath and come give him a hug."

In unison they yelled out, "Hey dad. Come see how high we got the bubbles this time." Trapped now, Asher went into the bathroom and plastered on a smile, "Wow, great job kids. You made a bubble elephant on the wall. Nice graffiti-ing. Someday you'll make some subway wall proud. Let me talk to your mom for a minute, then I'll come help you get into your PJs."

In the hallway, Asher got to the point immediately, though practice had told him it was best to lay some crepe first before spelling out bad news. "Mand, have you seen Trotsky lately?"

Now catching on to his secrecy and his tone, Mandy paused before answering. "Yes, I put him outside after dinner. Why do you ask? Did he break through the invisible fence again and run away?" Seeing Asher hesitate, she said, "Don't tell me something happened? He didn't run into the road and get hit did he?" Her voice rose, "Don't tell me that, Miles."

Finally, Asher answered, "Well, not exactly, hon. But he's lying on the driveway, cold-stone dead. I can't for the life of me figure out what could have done him in."

Mandy's hand came to her mouth and tears welled up in her

eyes. "Oh, Miles, what are we going to do? What will we tell the kids?"

"I was just trying to figure that out. Trotsky's just lying out there. I guess we could call the vet, but what's the point now? It sucks, though. Couldn't have been more than three weeks ago we had him over to Dr. Paulson and he gave Trotsky a clean bill. Blood work perfect and all. Shows you they're no more reliable than we are, I guess."

"I've got to see this myself, Miles." She pulled him down the hall. "Please hold my hand."

Together they went down to the driveway. Mandy's hand turned ice-cold before they even got outside. The driveway light struck Trotsky's body at such an angle to spread his shadow across the asphalt, making him appear like a dark wolf on stilts. Mandy crept over to where the dog lay and extended her hand to barely graze his fur. Then, she pulled back in revulsion and began weeping. When they got back inside, Mandy said, "I guess we have to tell the kids. They should have a chance to see Trotsky and say goodbye to him."

"No way. We can tell them he ran away or that he's sick and I had to bring him to the vet or that we gave him to a farm in the country because he was getting allergies. Anything we can make up would be better. Emily's just stopped having nightmares about my mom's death. We don't need to get those started again."

Mandy voice stopped shaking. "You know we can't do that, Miles. The kids have to know the truth. They've got to learn about these things just like we did when we were kids. You can't lie to your loved ones to protect them or to protect yourself. You should know that, Miles."

Guilt now added to remorse, Asher silently shook his head in agreement and went upstairs. At the least, he would tell his girls this truth.

Three minutes later, their ears still reverberating from a chorus of wails, the Ashers huddled around their now-stilled family spark. Emily clung to her father's neck, while Stacie sat on the ground, her arms wrapped around his left leg. From behind Asher, Mandy clung to them all. There they stood rocking in time to an internal dirge, tears streaming down their faces. Finally, Emily, just seven, wiped her sleeve on her dad's cheek. "Don't cry, Dad. Trotsky's lying down here, but I bet in heaven he's running on clouds chasing butterflies." A slight smile broke out onto each of their faces at that thought. They headed inside for the night, moving together in an eight-legged processional.

CHAPTER 4 —————————————————————

The next night, all four stood around the makeshift grave Asher had spent had spent an hour digging in penance after he came home from work. Each pick, as it pierced through the crust of the barely-thawed earth, jarred his bones and sent a needed jolt through his spine straight to his skull. He hoped this toil could also jar some sense into his head. Not sure what to do with Trotsky's remains, Asher had double-wrapped the stiffening corpse in plastic garbage bags, then placed it in a beaten leather suitcase. Mandy and he knew some ad hoc ceremony was necessary for both the kids' sake and their own.

With a quarter moon on the horizon and the distant porch lights eerily casting each of them in shadow, the family formed a semicircle around Trotsky's resting place. Asher had no precedents to guide him, so improvised. "We are gathered here to mourn the death of our wonderful pet and remember the joy he gave us over the years. Trotsky was a friend, a playmate, a helper, a supporter and a comfort. He was more than our pet; he was one of our own, Stacie and Emily's brother. We will all miss him greatly." Then Asher recited a semi-accurate version of the *Yisgadahl*, while all bowed their heads.

As Asher began shoveling dirt over Trotsky's remains, Emily

stepped forward. She pulled from behind her back her forever companion, "Blinky," the once-white rhesus monkey that she'd been clutching and tripping over from day one, the same stuffed animal that her parents had been unsuccessfully trying to wrest from her for the past two years. Then she said, "Here, Trots. You need Blinky for company more than I do." And tossed her remaining best friend onto the top of Trotsky's suitcase coffin. Asher's eyes met Mandy's just as a tear formed in the corner of hers, perfectly mirroring the one falling from his own.

*

The next evening, after struggling to focus on the problems of each of the thirty-two patients who faced him that day, Asher drove home, his mind sucked dry, seeing nothing before him on the road, thinking no thoughts, not sure if he was up to pretending good cheer with his family. When he entered the foyer, the house was still—dark and silent, palpably dogless. For a second, the irrational part of Asher wondered if somehow Mandy had become fed up with his recent detachment and passivity, taken the kids and left him. Then, he remembered the kids had gymnastics that night and he'd been left to fend for dinner himself.

Relieved on several counts, Asher hesitated a moment at the ceramic sculpture of his two daughters sitting on the mantle of his fireplace. By habit, he found himself stroking their heads, almost able to feel their true silken fibers instead of the kiln-hardened clay. A few years before, Asher had decided a lifelike bust of his two daughters would be a perfect gift for Mandy's thirty-fifth birthday. He had little appreciation of the pain he would inflict on the girls and on himself by asking a six- and a four-year-old to pose quiet and still for five separate hour-long sessions on consecutive Saturdays that winter. Not to mention the machinations he had to undertake in order to convince Mandy he was taking tae kwon do lessons with the girls. After buying them white pajama-like uniforms, Asher choreographed a series of misdirected, synthetic contortions for them to perform after each session that he couldn't believe even a guileless soul like Mandy could accept as tae kwon do moves.

For the first two excruciating sessions, Asher bribed Emily and Stacie into marginal cooperation by promising them sundaes of their choice at Friendly's post-posing. Those sojourns ended when Emily, the four-year old, stuffed just one more Oreo cookie into her mouth, then proceeded to puke back up her ketchup-laden hot dog plus her triple-scoop mocha sundae all over the not-so-Friendly waitress who had just arrived to clean off their table. The last three sessions, Asher had pathetically tried to entertain the girls while they fidgeted in front of the sculptor who, despite his obvious artistic talents, had no clue how to garner cooperation from two antsy schoolgirls. Asher spent each hour in gyrations and pyrotechnics to amuse his kids. He first tried a frightening imitation of Michael Jackson moon-walking; the next week he produced a more successful laser light show on the studio wall; then the final *pièce de résistance*—a reenactment of a half-dozen scenes from *Toy Story* in which Asher simultaneously played the parts of Woody, Buzz Lightyear, and even Mr. Potato Head, though, ultimately, his imitation of Don Rickles' voice left the girls unimpressed.

On the night of Mandy's thirty-fifth, Asher and the girls blindfolded a reluctant Mandy and led her into the living room where the life-sized intertwined ceramic replicas of her gorgeous daughters sat on the fireplace mantle. Stacey and Emily pulled off the sheet covering the bust at the same moment Asher untied her blindfold. "*Ta da!*" they shouted in unison.

Mandy stood for a moment, too stunned to speak. Over the next ten minutes, she silently caressed the hair and features of her daughters while the tears streamed down her face. Finally she unstuck her tongue, "Miles, girls, how could you…? How did you…? When did you…? And Miles, how the heck did you manage to get the girls to sit still for this? I can't get them to sit for dinner for seven minutes."

Holding his arms out in a gesture of triumph and hugging Mandy, Asher replied, "When a man has talent, nothing can stand in his way." He then proceeded to reperform his pathetic moon-walk across the living room.

The girls rushed at their dad, toppling him over, then landing on top, followed by Mandy piling on and shouting, "here comes the syrup," in their patented stack-of-pancakes collapse. Later on, Mandy extolled him. "I can't believe you pulled this one off. You might as well stop gift-giving from here on; you'll never top this one, Miles. Especially considering our first date."

Leaving that memory and his amped-up remorse, Asher went to the kitchen and heated up the left over macaroni and cheese, a dish the girls loved to help prepare. Just as he was about to take his first bite, the evening news masking his home's silence, Asher's pager went off. Where previously he might have been ticked off at another interrupted meal, since Tom Mallory's death, Asher eagerly answered the page, hoping for a serious problem that might send him hospital-bound in atonement. Instead, the nurse on 7 East merely wanted a renewal on Mr. Granderson's fluid IV. Asher finished his meal that now tasted like cigarette ash.

CHAPTER 5 ——————————————————

At some point during her pharmacy internship at Bellevue Hospital, thirteen years earlier, Mandy had become aware of Asher's ubiquitous presence. One quiet Saturday afternoon, at the cash register of the hospital cafeteria, she sensed a hovering, dark-haired figure behind her on line, staring at the back of her head. When she turned to him, he stammered, as if he'd been rehearsing, "You should try the moo shu pork. Amazingly genuine. Must have bussed a chef up from Chinatown."

Instantly, Mandy linked the slightly askew, familiar face with the voice she had heard a dozen times over the past month. One of the first-year residents had become a frequent pharmacy visitor and inquirer of late. Asking about doses of meds one would have thought he learned in his second year of med school, bringing back expired IV fluids that the aides usually conveyed, and, once or twice, stopping at the half-door to the pharmacy for semi-lame conversation about how many hours they seemed to be working. She was intrigued as much by his reticence as by his doggedness. By mid-year, Mandy had developed a well-honed mechanism to deflect the barrage of self-impressed, cocksure residents who had taken to hitting on her. But Asher's dark persistence and shy, puppy-dog ingratiation had piqued her interest.

At Asher's comment, Mandy arched an eyebrow, looking down at her low-fat Dannon peach yogurt, "Not exactly my taste. Watching my grandmother snap the neck of our Sabbath chicken every Friday night when I was growing up turned me into a vegetarian."

Asher recovered from the moo shu swing-and-miss. "Sounds kind of gruesome. Guess I can't blame you. But you know, they say pork is the new zucchini. Had the notion of becoming a vegetarian myself along the way. But I couldn't shed the suspicion that fruits and vegetables had feelings too."

Mandy chose not to be skeptical, "Oh, do they now?"

"I guess. I keep thinking back to this dieffenbachia plant my roommate in college kept in his room. He named her Sirena. Every time I passed by, I could feel her wave to me, almost beckoning. Could never shake the idea that she really preferred me to him, but just couldn't express herself adequately."

Mandy could not suppress a grin. "Alright, enough. But, sounds like you're taking this tree-hugging movement a bit too literally."

After paying, Mandy hesitated a moment, wondering if more might come, almost feeling Asher's mind churning for what appropriate comment came next. He managed to extend his hand, saying, "Miles. Miles Asher. I've seen you around, haven't I?" Mandy refrained from answering "Yes, like a lawyer around ambulances." Instead, she introduced herself and headed back to her office, tray in hand, feeling his eyes follow her out the door, wondering how much more of the initiative she would have to take.

That same night, a half-block down from Bellevue's ER entrance, Mandy again passed by the sidewalk sculptor she had seen creating instant ceramic busts of passers-by. Her dad in Tucson had a birthday coming up. Mandy knew he hated being three thousand miles away from his only daughter and could think of no better gift than a life-sized replica of herself. After her shift in the pharmacy, Mandy, seeing that the sculptor was unoccupied, decided to stop.

The slick, black-haired Hispanic sculptor jumped at a possible customer, saying in a thickly accented voice, "Ah, *señorita*, I have seen you pass by here many times and have prayed you might stop and allow me to capture your splendid beauty for all posterity."

Not at all taken in by his spiel, Mandy nonetheless had seen the quality of his work and acquiesced. About twenty minutes into their session, with dusk tinting the glassed storefronts and sidewalks, and the world at large a rosy hue, Mandy again felt a presence over her right shoulder, and identified the pink reflection in the window facing them. Without looking up, she said, "I hope you're not here to tell me I gave you the wrong concentration of potassium chloride again."

Asher answered, half his face grinning, "No, not this time. And I'm not stalking you, I promise." Then, under his breath, "Though that wouldn't be such a bad way to spend my off time."

"Pull up a chair and join me. Don't get the wrong idea here. I'm not some flagrant egomaniac. My dad lives in Tucson and I know for Father's Day he would love a three-dimensional me to keep him company."

"Well, I sure can't fault him for that." Asher looked more carefully at the emerging sculpture. "Wow, and this guy is good." Then, holding his hands outstretched, framing a picture, "Though I'm not sure he's captured the idiosyncratic beauty of the line of your nose."

The sculptor looked up, bristling. "Look, gringo, there's no charge for watching. But if you criticize, you beat it, *comprende?*" Then, staring more closely at Asher, he added, "I'm just grateful I don't have to sculpt you. I'd need double sets of hands, to match your *loco* lines.

Mandy looked up at Asher, feeling as much shame on her own face as she detected on his. She stared at the deep wound she suspected opened up each time someone noted Asher's dissonant features. Without thought of boundary or consequence, Mandy reached up to soothe the pain in Asher's face, gently stroking his features until the warring elements finally relaxed. She felt him break into a huge grin that channeled into one of her own.

*

About a year into their marriage, when career pressures were starting to mount, the day after a nonsensical but lingering argument, Asher passed an arts and crafts store and decided to stop in. That night, when Mandy came home from work at Pelham's Pharmacy, she found on the foyer table a piece of soft clay molded into the imperfect but unmistakable shape of a heart. Mandy's melted. From then on, the couple used that two-dollar lump of clay to express their feelings about the day they had just had, or about each other, or about life in general. Mandy, clearly the more artistic of the two, might fashion a beach umbrella planted in sand if she needed a vacation, or a Chinese takeout container if she didn't want to cook that night. Asher once, when his patients were driving him nuts, made a reasonable facsimile of a head with a hatchet buried in its center. Another time, when he felt amorous, Asher created a decent representation of a busty, spread-eagled woman lying on a bed.

In a similar vein, Mandy, one night pre-kids, when she was in the mood, had left an almost-exact replica of an erect phallus on the foyer table, setting off a raucous night of the hot and heavies. However, these more risqué sculptures ceased when a UPS delivery man came by the next morning and was unable to stifle his laughter on seeing the makeshift phallus.

Some ten years later, Asher revived the memory of their first date by having a sculpture made of their kids, the sculpture that still rested on their mantle.

CHAPTER 6 ———————————————

Asher discovered at an early age that he had a heightened sense of suffering. He felt the pain of others almost viscerally, which rendered his assault on Heidi even more deviant. His first encounter with death, at age three—a crushed squirrel lying in the middle of the road—had given him nightmares for weeks. Watching a kindergarten classmate weep over the loss of a pet rabbit brought tears to Asher's eyes, tears he quickly learned to hide from the rest of the class. At about ten, a friend's father died of a heart attack. Asher had not heard of the weeklong custom of sitting Shiva until then, but felt obligated to spend every waking moment that week with his friend.

Later, once he realized everyone else possessed a more controlled sensibility, Asher wondered about the origins of his hyperacuity. Perhaps, he speculated, like someone born with an overly developed sense of smell or perfect pitch, he'd been born with an intensified sense of empathy. After years spent trying to harness this gift, Asher wondered if someday a researcher might discover the locus of that trait in the brain, like Broca's area for speech or the amygdala for anger. Given the choice, Asher thought, would he choose to have that sensibility either surgically or chemically dimmed?

From day one of preschool, Asher was fated to go into medicine. His dad had been a renowned ophthomologist at Lenox Hill Hospital in Manhattan, serving for years as the hospital's chief of staff. When Asher was thirteen, babysitting for his ten-year-old sister, she had fallen off her bunk bed and dislocated her thumb. Despite her screams of protest, within minutes Asher had reduced the dislocation and made a makeshift splint for her thumb with kitchen utensils. He could not wait for his folks to return home to see his handiwork and ingenuity.

When their folks did return, both kids were contentedly sitting on the sofa watching *Bewitched* and eating ice cream. His dad, as always, focused on the problem instead of the solution. "Are you not responsible for your sister when we are gone? Isn't that why I am paying you a babysitting fee? Not to sit on your duff and watch drivel, but to make sure nothing happens to her."

Asher tried explaining. "Sorry, Dad, Becky was jumping on the bunk bed and slipped. It was an accident."

His dad's face lit up a warning red. "An accident! There are no accidents. The only real accident happens when you walk outside your front door to pick up the morning newspaper on a perfectly bright, sunny day and a lightning bolt strikes you. That's an accident. Everything else is preventable. If Becky's jumping on the bunk bed, it's your job to stop her before this so-called accident happens. Get it?"

A cowed Asher replied, "Got it, sir." Over the years, he heard that same philosophy when he borrowed his father's Jaguar and a Manhattan parking lot attendant smashed it up, when his wallet containing $250 was stolen in Grand Central Station just before his senior prom and when he unknowingly bought a textbook from another student at NYU that turned out to be stolen. All were non-accidents in his father's worldview, non-accidents that Asher had to pay for in one form or another.

Later on, Asher's career decisions had further rankled his father. Asher had scorned the paved path to success his father had laid out for him. Instead, he had entered the fringe field of family medicine and, though he could have had a ready-made upscale practice in midtown Manhattan, chose to fend for himself in the obscure town of Dover, Connecticut.

Like many small cities in Connecticut during the mid-nineties, Dover had struggled with the necessity of expanding from a manufacturing, blue-collar economic base to one more diverse. More than its neighbors, Dover had succeeded—new businesses had come into town, and its surrounding hills had developed a suburban, bedroom-community feel. Yet Dover's genial small-town character endured, mainly due to its location in a valley between a few low-level mountain outcroppings that passed themselves off as ski resorts. To Asher, Dover's insularity and permanence were its greatest attraction.

Growing up in the indifferent anonymity of Manhattan, Asher found the warmth and intimacy of Dover nourishing. Somehow the town had melded first- and second-generation French Canadians, Poles, Blacks, Russian Jews, Hispanics, a few Vietnamese, Pakistanis, and a strong contingent of Italians into a close-knit community—everyone seemed either to be related or to know each other and no one's offspring ever seemed to leave. Meeting someone you knew at every market or newsstand fascinated and buoyed Asher.

Being the family doctor to many of these residents immersed Asher in their lives. Not two months before the incident with Heidi, around Christmas, Dover still felt like a safe harbor in a disinterested world. Asher was shopping in the local Wal-Mart with Mandy, wandering around in the toy aisle. Often, Asher encountered his patients around town. Initially, they seemed surprised to see Asher in the real world, as if, for them, he existed only in the eight-by-twelve foot room in which they had gotten to know him. But then they became effusive, introducing Asher to their friends and relatives, inquiring about Asher and his family in ways they never did in the office.

At the Wal-Mart that day, Asher had spotted out of the corner of his eye, two brothers, six and eight, whom he had seen in the office for asthma the week before. The older, Todd, on seeing Asher, rushed up and grabbed him around the leg, balancing on his shoe. Asher noticed the younger one, Mack, shyly holding back. He dragged a still-clutching Todd over and bent down to Mack's eye level. "Hey, Mack. How's it going? Sorry about that shot the other day. Couldn't let that mean asthma monster keep grabbing your chest so you couldn't breathe."

Asher then pulled out of his pocket a couple of Spiderman stickers he kept for just such occasions and pasted them on Mack and Todd's jackets. Mack smiled and gave Asher a hug, too. Neither one was then willing to let Asher go until their mother came and apologized while dragging her kids away. In his adopted home, Asher felt like a politician who had no need to solicit votes and no axe to grind.

But since Tom Mallory's disastrous death, Asher found himself skulking about town, rarely making eye contact, going out of his way to frequent stores and service stations outside town. Making rounds at the hospital, he took care of his patients, then disappeared as quickly and quietly as possible. Who knew when he might run into one of Tom's students or, even worse, Tom's wife or sons? The nurturing small-town atmosphere that used to invigorate Asher had now turned against him. He believed Dover's instant lines of communication were filled with news passing from colleague to colleague, relative to relative, neighbor to neighbor, all repeating the tale of Asher's malfeasance. Asher's sanctuary had become his prison.

A couple of weeks after Tom's death, Asher was sitting in the dictation room at Dover General, hidden from view in a corner. The soft light from the half-shaded window had almost lulled the sleep-deprived Asher into nodding off. But Stanton Meisner, a pulmonologist, entered the room speaking to another physician. "Yeah, since I've been on the hospital risk management committee, I can't recall us having the number of lawsuits we're now facing. Scarier still, if those suits all go against us, our rates will increase so much that we may have to shut our doors. Plus I just heard about another preventable case that Miles Asher had with a young guy dying of sleep apnea that's sure to go to court." He hesitated a moment, then went on. "I can't figure out what's up with Miles these days. That's not the first case of him screwing up lately."

The other doc, whose voice Asher could not identify, merely responded. "Yeah, heard the same thing. I wonder if he's drinking or something. I hope we won't have to deal with him on the impaired physician committee." Asher slunk down in his chair, holding his breath until Meisner and his associate finally left the room.

Several days later, Asher had just left his tennis club when he passed Fred Williamson, with whom he had played twice a week the prior summer. A few years before, Fred had lived on the same street as Asher and the Mallorys and, like everyone else, loved Tom. Asher had not seen Fred since Tom's death and, suppressing the instinct to duck his head and move on, stopped him. "Fred, haven't seen you lately. Terrible about what happened to Tom."

Fred stared at him for a long second, then nodded. "Yeah, really tragic. Poor Irene." He hesitated, "Sorry we missed you at the funeral."

Asher felt his face redden and stared down at his feet. A group of sweaty tennis players sat at the wooden table nearby, sharing a few beers after their match. How much info had circulated around? How much did everyone know? "I felt terrible. But we were out of town. Still having trouble getting over this myself."

"Yes, well, we all are. See you around." Fred headed quickly out the door, leaving Asher with a long, hard view of his back.

*

The day after his encounter with Fred, upon arriving at work, Asher got a needed boost. Planted on his desk, rising like a twisted alien statue, sat a lone flowering orchid of such delicacy he thought it must be silk. A quick caress of its wooden, coiled stem, its diaphanous flower and a whiff of its subtle fragrance convinced Asher that the orchid was the real thing. Resting under the orchid was an ivory envelope with a handwritten note inside.

Dear Dr. Asher,

I am Colleen Swenson, Darla Carlotta's daughter. I just wanted to express my eternal gratitude to you for taking such wonderful care of my mother. As you know, she was in agony for months, seeing doctor after doctor with no help until you discovered her spinal abscess. Now that the abscess is drained and she's off all those narcotics, she's back to her old self again. I know how difficult she can be and I cannot thank you enough for sticking with her.

I raise orchids and this one has won prizes three years straight at the New York orchid show. Please remember how grateful we are each time you look at it.
Sincerely,
Colleen

Asher smiled at the phrase "how difficult she could be." He had been dealing with Mrs. Carlotta's pains for almost a decade when this particular incident cropped up. On that Wednesday morning, Asher remembered standing outside the exam room perusing volume three of Mrs. Carlotta's mammoth chart. The triage nurse had written as her chief complaint, "Back and neck pain for one year."

He had entered the exam room warily, not sure what to expect since he had not seen her in that intervening year. Asher found an unchanged Mrs. Carlotta sitting on the exam room table—shock-red, brushed back hair, framing a pale, oval face with white orbs for eyes that forever appeared on the edge of terror—imagine Little Orphan Annie being chased by Freddy Krueger. Asher mustered a smile. "Well, Mrs. Carlotta, haven't seen you in about a year. Last time we met, I had sent you over to the pain clinic to try to get some relief for that chest pain that just would not quit."

Mrs. Carlotta answered in her mega-soprano voice, always ten decibels too loud, with every sentence ending on a high-pitched whine, like some dissonant Lily Tomlin character. "Yeah, well that one they finally shot-gunned out of me. Docs in the clinic said something about nerve pain between my ribs. And then they shot me seven or eight times like throwing darts at my chest 'til the pain finally was just a dull roar. Dull roars, I can take as long as they keep my pills going. But that pain's nothing compared to the pain I got now. My neck and back have been killing me day and night so's I can't sleep, walk, talk or eat without agony."

Asher sucked in a breath, not pleased to hear they were now confronted with a whole new problem. "I wasn't aware this was going on, Mrs. Carlotta. When did this pain start?"

She gave one of her patented tangential answers. "Well the pain's there all the time, like when I'm shopping or eating or sometimes when I'm on the phone calling my sister-in-law. Even she doesn't want to hear about it, so she makes an excuse that her pop-tarts are burning or some such and gets right off the phone. Told my brother not to marry her, such a cold-hearted B…But I can show you better than tell you. Come here a second, will you, doc?" She grabbed at Asher's hand.

Asher let himself be pulled toward her. "Doc Asher, turn around so I can show you." He complied, while Mrs. Carlotta jabbed a finger into his mid-back, then traced a path. "See, doc, the pain starts here 'bout the middle of my back, then shoots up my back to the neck here, then travels around my neck here 'til it hits my throat, then ricochets back again to here. I feel like a bunch of tiny torturers have been hired to electric shock me twenty-four-seven. You've got to help me, Dr. Asher. You always have before."

Smarting some from her jabs, Asher sidled away and tried

again. "I get the idea, Mrs. Carlotta. So the pain's been there about a year or so?"

"Maybe about year, I'm not sure. I know last summer I was at a barbecue with the family and my Uncle Charlie, who's always such a pest, asked me to bring around the charcoal briquettes. He said the fire was dying down and he still had a dozen hot dogs to grill and picked me as his workhorse. Me, of all people. So I dragged what must have been a ninety-pound bag over to him, but he didn't even say thank you while he was showing off how perfectly he was grilling each hot dog, wanting Cousin Janie to take his picture, the master chef in his white..."

"So you hurt your neck bringing over the bag, did you, Mrs. Carlotta?"

"No, not then. I was getting to that. I was surprised that time it didn't hurt, cause it seemed every other time I did anything the pain was tremendous. But this time, no pain, which struck me as very strange and made me think of maybe lugging ninety-pound bags all day just to keep the pain away."

Suppressing a grin, Asher said, "OK. Then I guess we're talking at least eight months. And during that time, by the records here from other docs, it looks like the pain clinic sent you to an orthopedist who sent you to a neurosurgeon who sent you to a physical therapist and then you landed back in the lap of the pain clinic doctor."

"Yup, you've got it right, that's what happened. Then the darned pain clinic said they couldn't take care of me anymore, 'cause my insurance changed and they didn't take my new one. I think they were just sick of me. So they dumped me back on you."

"Sorry about all that shifting around. I guess no one could find what was wrong. It says here you've been warm sometimes. Have you had a fever?"

"I would say so! I wake up in the middle of the night with waves of heat so I got to throw off my blankets and rip off my nightgown and lie in the altogether for the whole world to see 'til it passes. Of course all the other docs say it's just a forty-eight-year old woman's hot flashes, but what do they know?"

"Well, have you taken your temperature or had the chills?"

"Who owns a thermometer these days? Last one I had was the butt one I used on the kids twenty years ago that broke all over the bathroom floor so my three year-old had the most fun playing..."

Asher interrupted again, knowing no further useful history might come from this torturous inquisition. "How about I take a look at you, Mrs. Carlotta?"

On examining Mrs. Carlotta, he found that she had dramatic weakness of her right wrist, and, when he felt her neck, she had pinpoint tenderness over her sixth cervical vertebrae. He felt around the area several times to convince himself she was truly tender in that one spot and not merely hypersensitive. Two days later, after her white blood count and sed rate came back sky high, Asher ordered a repeat MRI of her spine. He was as surprised as anyone to find out from the radiologist that Mrs. Carlotta had a large abscess in her cervical spine that was probably set off by one of the injections she had had in her ribs. He had to remind himself that even difficult and/or nutty patients get sick too. You can't ever get sucked into the temptation to dismiss someone as a crock. That's when you're most likely to get burned. He allowed himself a moment of pride that he had not taken the well-trod road of writing off Mrs. Carlotta as the other docs apparently had.

Asher carefully placed the orchid on his bookshelf, not sure if he had any idea how to care for such a fragile-looking plant, but resolved to try.

With such a lift, Asher approached his patients that morning with some of his old gusto. He found himself bouncing between rooms, listening to his patients with interest—cleaning a wound on Ron Holden's leg, draining a cyst on Karla Sheehan's back, scheduling a stress test he was sure would be positive on Don Carlisle—then answering half a dozen calls from nurses in the hospital and another dozen from patients calling in from home. Once again he felt like Fast Eddie Felson dancing around a pool table. All these activities he had conducted with pride and skill for the prior nine years since entering practice. But, at this juncture, they had become but a source of stress and uncertainty.

Two days later all unraveled again. On his desk *that* morning was a note written by his nurse, Denise, paper-clipped to Ella Gengras' chart. "Mrs. Gengras called. She is transferring her care to another doctor and wants her records released. She says you failed to diagnose her pancreatic cancer soon enough and now she has less than six months to live. She sounded pretty upset."

Asher slumped to his chair, again reminded of the fickleness of his patients, of disease, and of life itself. He had known Mrs. Gengras was upset with him. She had had vague belly pain for a couple of months that could have been from thirty-two different causes. When he finally ordered the CAT scan of her belly and told her the results, she was inconsolable. The problem with pancreatic cancer was that it almost never causes symptoms until it's too late, that there's no good treatment and virtually no one survives no matter when diagnosed. None of those facts provided an iota of consolation to Mrs. Gengras. Hence her message. Deflated, Asher struggled through the day, not sure whether next to expect high praise or condemnation.

CHAPTER 7 ————————————————

The first time Asher Met Tom Mallory, he knew he was the real deal. Five years before Tom's death, the Mallorys moved into the neighborhood and Asher's girls had become fast friends with their two boys, almost exactly the same ages. One Sunday morning, Tom appeared on Asher's front door with his five-year-old Travis sheepishly hiding between his legs. The men ignored the fact they were both still in pajamas. Tom's pair, adorned with spouting whales and floating octopuses, testified to his unresolved desire to remain a kid. Standing at the front door, his face dominated by a bushy graying moustache, his pony-tailed hair reflecting an ongoing commitment to the sixties, Tom was a breathing, ambulating anachronism. That was everyone's first impression— Tom was born out of time. But once you got to know him, you realized that Tom reckoned it was time that was out of step, not him.

Tom had run his family's hardware store in Dover until the opening of another Home/Wal/Depot/Mart finally forced him out of business. Before that particular modern injustice, when anyone came into Tom's store, they not only got personalized service, but also a history of the origin, development and current status of whatever object was on their shopping list. Most times Asher visited the store, he would find Tom immersed in a discussion on some obscure detail of his products.

One visit, Asher overheard Tom spend the better part of an hour relating to a customer the infinite variety of birdseeds available in the world, which ones were preferred by which birds, which were best at what time of year, and even which was likely to produce the most desirable quantity and quality of bird poop. Another time, when Asher needed to paint Emily's room, Tom gave him a dissertation on the handles, bristle sizes and density of the brushes in stock and their intimate relationship to the type and size of the surface being painted, the consistency, color and type of paint, the scope of the job, and even their relationship to the style of hand motion, forearm strength and height of the painter. Tom was a living, breathing fossil from a time when knowing the product you sold and the customer you were selling to was the purpose of being in business, rather than a perk the world could no longer afford.

Instead of feeling like the world had left him behind, however, Tom's attitude was that he was so far ahead of the curve, everyone would sooner or later return to his way of doing things the "right way." Why would anyone settle for less? So, instead of being disheartened and disenchanted when he had to close the doors of his family's eighty-year old store, Tom didn't kink his hair. He said the change gave him the chance to do something he had always wanted to do. He went back to college, got his degree in two years and became the best damn industrial-arts teacher Dover High had ever seen.

When Tom appeared at the Ashers' doorstep that Sunday, they had not yet met. "Doc, sorry to bother you all. I'm not sure if Travis here has some kind of doll-envy thing going on, but I think this must belong to one of your girls." He handed to Emily, who was lurking behind Asher, the Barbie Doll the Ashers had spent the past evening tearing up the house searching for. "I hope our kids can keep on playing together. They seem to have hit it off real well. More than that, I am hoping this incident won't cost me five years of psychotherapy for Travis, trying to iron out his sexual identity conflicts."

"No problem. There's a couple of married cross-dressing shrinks living down the block on the cul-de-sac who can fix any gender problem imaginable."

After that day, when the two families had become so close, Asher reluctantly had taken the Mallorys all on as patients. He discussed the issue with Mandy one night over dinner, after the girls had gone upstairs. "You know the Mallorys are a terrific family. The kids get along so well. But I'm just not sure it's such a good idea taking care of them as patients. They might feel awkward about calling me off-hours or stopping me to ask a question. Most of all, I worry if something happens, I will feel doubly bad. Plus, taking care of patients I'm close with is bound to cloud my judgment. During residency, they kept reminding us about keeping an emotional distance from your patients. In real life, that's not so easy."

Mandy answered while clearing the table. "I know how you feel. But I must say, it kind of rankles when you balk at taking care of *us*. You're even afraid to look in the kids' ears when they have an earache. I understand you don't want to screw up. The guilt is ten times greater. But I'm sure you can use your judgment, it's always so good in these situations."

"Right. So far, at least. It's just hard to be objective when your family's life is on the line. With friends it's easier. But still not ideal. Let's just hope nothing serious ever happens to any of them."

*

Sitting in his study that night, three weeks after Tom's death, Asher once more asked himself "Should I have had someone else care for Tom to begin with? Or in this instance, at least, referred him to another physician? But sleep problems. I've dealt with dozens of them. Why this screw up this time? What was different about Tom? Why him? Why then?"

Asher stared at the dark, invisible world outside. His left hand rested on a glass of red wine, half-empty, perched precariously on the desk by the computer. The glare from his computer screen cast an eerie glow on the white-walled, otherwise unlit room. He held his right hand in front of the screen, watching the light shine through his translucent flesh, illuminating the bones of his skeleton like a radiograph. The night's blackness pressed upon the bank of windows to Asher's right, trying to overtake the room. Asher took a sip from the glass and remembered how at one time he felt good.

It had not been that long ago. By all externals—by finances, possessions, reputation, by comfort, shelter, and sustenance, by respect of peers and patients, love of family, and fortune of health, by the luck of the draw and the luck of the ages, by any measure he could name—Asher was a success. Not that he often counted those blessings. But he did maintain a fundamental hum in his subconscious, reminding himself of them. He did not take them for granted, nor pat himself on the back, nor bask in his achievements.

Nor did Asher forget the relentless misery he dealt with on a daily basis. The comfort and ease of his life were conveniences—either by God's grand design or by the forces of fate—trappings that permitted him to support others in their suffering. His patients were a continual reminder of where, but for the grace of God, he too might end. If Asher were forced to explain his philosophy, this was its core. His comfort, intelligence, talents, and sensitivity were on loan, permitting him to help the less fortunate. He was no saint or martyr. He was like Joe Hardy dealing with the Devil—if you got the benefits, sooner or later you might have to pay the price. Dedicating his life to the ill balanced his debit sheet and let him live in peace. He could keep his comforts, but never forget what enabled them.

At least it had always been that way. But now Asher no longer had that foundation. If those who had nurtured him were mere smoke-and-mirror illusions; if his battles to stave off death and disease always failed, if he immersed himself in the delusion that what he did made a difference but even in that delusion he screwed up, what was the point of fighting? No answer was forthcoming. Nor, it seemed, was any other message visible that night in the silent sky.

CHAPTER 8

Maybe because Asher's career in Dover began with a thunderbolt, he felt fate had drawn him there. Perhaps if Asher had explained some of his mystical connection to the town with his father before his dad's death, maybe his dad would not have felt such eternal disappointment about Asher's moving there.

While a family practice resident at Bellevue ten years before, Asher had occasionally done a weekend ER shift to earn some extra bucks at one of several small hospitals in Connecticut. One foggy spring Saturday night in June, he was driving to Dover General for just such a shift. He was just a couple of miles along Route 8, already almost nodding off, wondering how he would be able to stay awake for the shift on just five hours sleep at Bellevue the night before. Suddenly, the Volvo wagon just ahead of him swerved to the left, crossed the yellow line of the two-lane road, screeched its brakes and smashed into a telephone pole. In the dense fog, Asher's headlights lit up a stationary deer standing in the middle of the road that finally unfroze itself and bounded off into the woods.

Asher pulled over and rushed to the Volvo, wrenching open the crushed driver's door. He found the bulky figure of a barely conscious, middle-aged man slumped in the front seat, a dark stain of blood filling his right pants leg where a piece of plastic from the center console had penetrated his leg. Later on, in the ER, Asher discovered the victim was a prominent banker named Zigfrid Zantay, something of a local folk hero.

Heaving with all his strength, Asher maneuvered the drenched, sweating hulk out of the car, his face inches from the man's own bleach-white countenance. Just as the stranger lost consciousness, he whispered in a deep, thickly-accented voice, "I vas just trying to avoit the deer in the road. Sorry to haf to bother you." After dragging the dead-weight figure onto the side of the road, Asher looked up and down the dimly lit road, searching for another car to flag down, but found none headed his way.

Asher stood immobilized in the middle of a road, lit and shadowed by the headlights of both cars bouncing refracted rays of light off the glistening trees. In the ethereal fog, the crushed car smoking near the prostrate body of the near-extinguished life lying on the ground created a shimmering, otherworldly tableau much like the opening scene to a Stephen King movie. Asher knelt back down and felt the victim's pale, diaphoretic skin and thready pulse, and realized he was in shock. Ripping open the patient's pants, Asher was struck in the face by a shot of fresh arterial blood pumping out of a deep gash in the thigh. He rushed to the trunk of his car and grabbed his virginal medical bag.

Frantically searching the open wound with a penlight and absorbing the pulsating blood with wads of gauze, Asher finally located a small, severed artery pumping blood out from the leg wound. He grabbed a suture kit out of the bottom of his bag and, while holding the penlight in his mouth, Asher's shaking hands somehow managed to tie off the bleeder, halting the flow of blood.

After getting a handle on the bleeding, Asher sat back on the cold tarmac, his hands dripping in blood, his heart pounding. He glanced up at the still figure before him, only to realize his patient's breathing had stopped entirely. Asher then grabbed at his arm, feeling the cold, clammy lifeless skin and now absent pulse. He tore at Zantay's jacket and shirt and listened with his stethoscope for a heartbeat. Hearing none, Asher pounded twice on Zantay's chest and listened again. Again nothing. Panicky now, Asher stood up and once more searched the dark, silent road for help, with only miles of emptiness staring back. He knelt back down and tried CPR for several minutes, breathing twice into Zantay's mouth, then pumping his chest up and down eight times, then repeated again and again until he fell back in exhaustion.

Coming to the sickening realization he had only one option, Asher went to the trunk of his car and grabbed a pair of jumper cables. He rushed to the hood of his car, lifted it and quickly attached the cables to the car battery. With the car still running, Asher bent over Zantay's moribund body, holding the other end of the cables in the air. He hesitated, wondering if this desperate act had ever been attempted. He knew he had never read or heard about it. Just prior to proceeding, Asher wondered if this moment might end his medical career before it could even begin. But with no other alternative, Asher lowered the cable's metal tips, barely grazing the sides of Zantay's chest, igniting a sudden spark into the air that jerked Asher's arms and head backward. Emboldened, since neither Zantay nor he had been electrocuted, Asher recontacted Zantay's chest, this time holding the cables firmly in place for three seconds. The cables made a loud thump and sent an arc of electricity across Zantay's chest, singing the skin. Zantay's entire body jerked half a foot into the air.

Asher tossed the cables backward and pressed his head to Zantay's chest, his nostrils filling with the odor of singed flesh. This time, he heard the loud, regular pumping of a vital, forceful heartbeat. He watched the color of life fill up Zantay's cheeks, followed by several deep gasps for breath, and then even, regular respirations.

Asher fell back, amazed and exhausted, staring at the black night and thanking the stars. Just then an ambulance with siren blaring came speeding up to the accident. Asher stood up, his hands and shirt drenched with blood and told the EMTs what had happened. With barely a "thanks, mister," they shunted Asher aside and hustled Zantay off to the hospital.

By the time Asher made it to the hospital, washed up, changed into surgical scrubs and headed down to the ER, he found that his first real life saved had already been taken up to the OR. Asher explained to the head of the ER whom he was replacing that night why he was late. The doc replied, "Was that you? We heard some Good Samaritan saved the bank president's life, but I had no idea it was you. Great job, man!"

Asher answered, "Just happened for once to be at the right place at the right time. Another ten minutes and he would have been a goner. I hope he won't lose the leg. That was some wound."

With a half-grin, the doc said, "Well, if he's got a chance, it's thanks to you. But the EMTs said something about jumper cables and a battery. You might not want to advertise that part of the rescue too much. We don't want it to get out into the public that we're practicing auto-mechanic medicine here at Dover General." Asher grinned back, embarrassed at even having attempted such a crazed act.

Asher was busy the rest of the night and, since he had to be back at Bellevue the next day, never got the chance to go up and see how Zantay had fared. He did hear, however, through an OR nurse, that the operation had gone well and Zantay was stable in the recovery room, right leg intact.

Several weeks later, in his mailbox at Bellevue, Asher found a typewritten note on formal white stationary with Dover Community Savings Bank engraved at the top. It read:

Dear Dr. Asher,

Sorry it has taken so long to get back to you to thank you. It took me awhile to find out who had saved my life and to track you down. Please accept my eternal gratitude for your timely help, for your kindheartedness, and for your superb

*skill. The surgeon who operated on me said that without
your help I surely would have lost my leg and possibly even
my life. My wife also extends her grateful thanks and hopes
my burnt chest hairs will soon grow back.*

*Next time you are in Dover please stop by my bank and
meet with me. We would like to have you to our home for
dinner to express our thanks in person.*

Yours in gratitude always,

Zigfrid Zantay

Despite being thrilled to receive such a note of appreciation, Asher was reluctant to pursue Zantay's invitation. It was his job to save lives. Hopefully it would be one of many. Was he to pursue a personal relationship with each success? Where would that leave his failures? Despite his decision to keep Zantay at a distance, Asher realized, even in medically impersonal America, saving someone's life established a special bond, conferring a mutual obligation neither party could ignore.

A month later, Asher received a similar note on the same stationary, this time handwritten.

Dr. Asher,

*I appreciate that you may not have had an opportunity
to allow me to thank you in person. However, if I might
extend an offer to you such that when you are completed
with your training, you might think about us here in Dover.
It is a wonderful town and I am sure we could use a talented,
young physician like yourself. I guarantee my bank will help
finance a startup for your practice with better terms than you
will get anywhere in the state. Think about it and call me.*

Your grateful patient,

Zigfrid Zantay

That offer, Asher did roll around in his head for a good while. Connecticut was a great place to raise a family; he was becoming

tired of the incessant city and he needed to get some distance from
his father. He ran it by Mandy, who agreed. When he finished his
residency, fending off his dad's wishes, he contacted Zig, who set
Asher up with his loan officer, who in turn offered Asher a loan
that was almost a gift. On the first day Asher opened his office,
Zig sent a huge floral arrangement with a note saying,

> *Just remember to keep your patients first and foremost in
> your mind and you will do great good.*
> *Your friend and first Dover life saved, one I am sure, of
> many to come,*
> *Zig with a Z.*

Asher reminded himself daily that he had to live up to Zig's faith
in him by caring for his patients as well as he possibly could. He
chose to believe that he had been destined to save Zig's life, in
order end up in this particular locus on the planet.

Though neither of them deliberately avoided the other,
amazingly, in the years he'd been practicing in Dover, Asher never
directly ran into Zig. Early on, Zig sent Asher sporadic notes of
encouragement—once when he had seen a letter of thanks in the
newspaper to Asher from a grateful patient; another time when
he heard a compliment from an acquaintance for whom Asher
had cared. A few times, Zig sent him a note asking Asher to see a
friend or relative as a favor. But up until the present, they'd never
again met face-to-face.

CHAPTER 9 —————————————————

Asher was nearing the end of his residency when his dad died suddenly in an accident. The last time they had seen each other was about a month before the accident, when Asher had finally succumbed to his father's wishes by doing one rotation on the neurology service at Lenox Hill. Having his father as chief of staff of that NYU-affiliated hospital had sent Asher scurrying around town to a dozen other venues for his electives. But his dad convinced him to at least try one rotation at *his* hospital; it didn't have to be on the ophthalmology service if Asher didn't want special treatment. But their neuro service was one of the best in the city. "We can even have lunch together sometime," his father had remarked, as if that prospect alone would be adequate enticement.

That lunch they never had. But they did have one sit-down conversation during that month, when his father tried to convince him to give up the idea of entering the low-respect, low-paying field of family medicine.

His father's secretary summoned Asher to the office, a huge suite atop Lenox Hill Hospital with the panorama of Lexington Avenue and the Upper East Side on display outside eight-foot windows. Asher sat in the plush leather chair in front of his dad's polished mahogany desk, wearing his bloodstained short, white coat with note cards and medical paraphernalia spilling out the pockets, his eyes bleary from being awake most of the previous night. He once again felt like the eleven-year old he'd been when first planted in that seat, getting reprimanded for breaking his sister's tricycle by riding it into a tree. A brass and wood name plaque atop the desk, reading "Richard M. Asher, MD, Chief of Staff" stared back at him. Asher tried to avert his eyes from the wall full of diplomas and awards and honorary degrees. But the other wall to his right was just as packed, this one with pictures of his father posing with the variety of celebrities and notables he had treated throughout the years. He even had a picture in the center of the display with Francis Albert himself, bearing the inscription, "Thanks, doc, for letting these 'ol' blue eyes' see again. With eternal gratitude, Frank Sinatra."

Asher could not blame his dad for showing off. Asher had been the envy of his eleventh grade class when, one night, his dad had taken him backstage to meet Bruce Springsteen. They had gotten free front-row tickets when Asher's dad had removed a sliver of glass from the Boss' eye the night before. His dad had endured the entire blaring concert without complaint. He even let Asher bring a date, who, for the next three months, prefaced every one of their conversations with, "Your dad is so cool." On the ride home from the concert, after dropping off Asher's date, his dad had stated "You won't ever forget I did this for you, will you?" A statement Asher took as a command, not a wistful suggestion.

Behind his desk, Asher's father held court, imperious as always, his temples graying, his ramrod posture never deviating. Only the presence of a slight tremor in his right hand, one that Asher had never before noted, signaled any change over the prior twenty years. "Well, son," his father began without looking up, after making Asher wait for several minutes in silence while he stared through his bifocals at the pile of medical reports on his desk, "it seems as if you have arrived at the end of your third year of residency. I know you've made some tentative decisions about your future." Tentative! Asher had an office lease, financing, was getting married and moving to Dover in less than 3 months. "Although you have chosen not to carry the baton of becoming an eye surgeon thus far, I might still maneuver you a position in our ophthalmology program, if you so desired. Even though your board scores and recommendations are not as stellar as the residents we usually accept, I still might have enough influence to secure you a position." At that comment, his father finally looked up, peering over the rim of his glasses at Asher across the desk.

Asher stared back, trying to control himself, his second cup of coffee that morning accelerating his edginess. "Dad, you must have forgotten. I'm not going into ophthalmology. I'm finishing my family practice residency, then setting up a practice in Connecticut."

"I can't believe you're still holding onto that childish notion about family medicine, even at this late stage in your education."

Trying to be patient, Asher reiterated, "Believe what you want dad. That's the facts. I want to care for my patients like whole people, not just some isolated organ system, amputated from the rest of their bodies. I know it sounds Pollyanna-ish, but I like the idea of following my patients throughout their entire lives, maybe become involved in their lives and, in some ways, a part of their families."

His dad snorted, "General Practitioner, jack of all trades, master of none. You could at least sub-specialize. Or even become a general surgeon, if you like. But a GP, that is too much. Or should I say, too little? At least stay in Manhattan where I have a whole network of contacts. Set up your practice here in our office building. I'll make sure you have a steady flow of patients so you'll never have to struggle to establish yourself."

"They're not called GPs anymore, Dad. We have far more training than they used to. Plus, I want to achieve this on my own. You handing me a practice on silver platter won't feel as if

I've accomplished anything. Sorry, Dad. I'm sure you mean well, but my mind is made up."

Looking up again, this time in disdain, his father gave in, acting as if Asher had chosen to become a missionary in Kathmandu. "Fine. If that is what you choose, it's your problem. I wash my hands of the issue. But just be aware, I cannot help you with any of those people. You are on your own. And when you see your income about a third of what you might have expected in another specialty or another location, don't expect me to support your restricted lifestyle. You've made your bed."

"Fine, Dad. I never asked for or required your support. I'm sure I'll get by."

And Asher for once got up without being dismissed, turned, and started to walk out. His father as usual got in one final word—curse or prophesy, Asher could not tell. "A final comment, Miles. When you realize you can't become all things to all people, when you have trouble mastering the entire scope of medical knowledge required to be competent in your chosen field, when you find that no matter how hard you try, you will never be able to satisfy everyone, you will come to regret this decision."

Several weeks later, prior to finishing up his neurology rotation, while standing at a nurse's station, Asher overheard a conversation between two of the residents nearby in the doctor's chart room. One of them, a bearded Iranian who had been particularly hard on Asher, was commenting, "You know that hack botched another one. I don't know how they can keep him as chief of staff when he has to be rescued from surgical mistakes all the time." The other resident replied, "Yeah, I know. Deadeye Dick has struck again. Lucky this patient only lost the vision in one eye and has another good one. How much this one's going to cost the hospital, I can't imagine."

The Iranian cocked his head in Asher's direction. "Shh. That's his kid over there." How he can be here with a father like that, I can't understand."

Asher hunched over his chart, pretending not to hear. Could

they really be talking about his dad? 'Deadeye Dick'? Where could that have come from? Thank God he had only two days left of his rotation at this hospital. And just a few months more before he could head out of his father's realm for good.

CHAPTER 10 ——————————————

A few months later and three weeks after his father's traumatic death, Asher and Mandy were sitting at a table across from each other at Hoagy's Place, a hangout in Soho they frequented. The owner of the eleven-table storefront restaurant was Hoagy Carmichael's nephew who had plastered the walls with black-and-white autographed pictures of his uncle posing with a variety of celebrities. Neither Asher nor Mandy had ever heard of Hoagy Carmichael till they had ducked into the place looking for shelter one rain-drenched Sunday afternoon. But both were immediately struck by the burning-wood fired smell from the oven behind the counter, the worn brick walls, and the shimmering copper ceiling. Most of all, they were captivated by the beat-up, black player piano in the corner that spun out a continuous run of songs they were familiar with, but had no idea all came from the same composer. "Stardust," "In The Still of the Night," "Georgia on My Mind," and "The Nearness of You" all lit up the room from the magically moving keys of the unmanned piano. On top of that, any random patron or employee who had the urge and a good enough voice to tackle the classics might be inspired at any moment to burst into song. Mostly, a waiter would be the star of the moment, since each of the waiters was apparently a Broadway hopeful. But at times, even a customer, who Asher always figured for a plant, might give such a stirring rendition of "In The Cool, Cool, Cool of the Evening," the always-filled restaurant would break out in applause.

A few months before, Asher had been in a funk about losing a patient to acute leukemia who died less than twenty-four hours after hitting the ward. Later on that day, drained and discouraged, Asher wandered by the restaurant On that bleak afternoon, there was but one other customer sipping coffee at a corner table. Asher hesitated at the entrance, then spotted someone uncharacteristically sitting at the piano. Taken in immediately, Asher spent the better part of the next two hours watching a wizened, chocolate-colored, gray-haired, wrinkly man named Isaac—tuning fork in one hand, left ear almost touching the keyboard—painstakingly try to retune that relic piano. Asher sat two feet from the piano, mesmerized by the syncopated rhythm of the tuning fork's ping, followed by the piano keys' resonant ring, measured in time by the rise and fall of Isaac's extraordinary ear. As he dragged himself away from his immersion in this time-honored ritual, Asher could not help but feel buoyed that another world still existed outside the white-tile, sterile confines of his grief-filled hospital.

But this particular evening, sitting across from Mandy at a corner table, even such a mood-rich atmosphere could not raise Asher out of his funk or encourage more than perfunctory attempts at conversation to break their silence. With his father's sudden death leaving their relationship now eternally unresolved, added to lurking questions about the exact nature of his dad's accident, Asher's personality had changed. He had morphed from someone sporadically intense, but basically easygoing, into a brooding recluse. He knew this was taking a toll on Mandy and *their* relationship, but seemed powerless to change.

Even before sitting down at their candlelit table, they had exhausted the topic of their upcoming wedding, several months away, plans unchanged despite his father's death. They had already scheduled a five-day honeymoon in the Bahamas before the move to Connecticut where Asher was setting up practice and Mandy had a job lined up in the pharmacy department of Hartford Hospital.

Trying to break the awkward silence, Asher reintroduced the topic of Mandy's upcoming six-week internship at Northwestern Hospital in Chicago, due to start the following week. He placed his hand on top of hers. Mandy withdrew hers to take a sip from her water glass. "You sure this is such a good idea, heading out to that huge, unfamiliar city on your own in the dead winter of freezing Lake Michigan?"

Staring across at Mandy, the flickering light dancing off her dark eyes, the music fading into the background, Asher once again was stunned. In the candlelight, Mandy's beauty was subtle, like a sketched lithograph whose lines danced and wavered, hinting at the whole composition but needing the mind's eye to complete. Her glacier-like, coal-black hair framed her full cheeks, her thin, slightly off-center nose, and her diaphanous, silken skin. She walked with a ballerina's grace that, when she entered a room, drew every eye to her slim form.

Asher reminded himself that Mandy's physical fragility masked her core toughness. As a twelve-year-old, while her friends were phone-gabbing or boy-chasing, Mandy had spent every afternoon walking the three miles from school to White Plains Hospital to watch her mother disintegrate from metastatic breast cancer. One hundred and seventeen days of that ritual finally ended with her mother's passing, after which Mandy was drafted into the role of mother, teacher, drill sergeant, and doter for her seven-year-old twin brothers, in addition to that of surrogate spouse to her devastated father.

Asher had heard from at least a dozen of Mandy's relatives at different times over the prior year since they had been together about her younger brothers' Bar Mitzvahs. Lucas, the twin older by 11 minutes, had breezed through his part of the ceremony, oblivious and confident. Daniel, the younger twin, who would grow up to become a pediatric oncologist, was another story. He had insisted on being the one to read the elegy his mother had composed just prior to her death, written specifically for their Bar Mitzvah. Daniel had overridden his father's suggestion and his mother's instructions that their father handle that task.

Despite his heartfelt intentions, Daniel had broken down on the *bimah* after just one sentence. Seeing his distress, Mandy climbed up to the *bimah* and took over for Daniel, suppressing her own tears, while the congregation all produced handkerchiefs. Only eighteen herself, Mandy read her mother's message of love for her husband and her kids, her regrets about leaving them all too soon with too little time together, about her grief at not being able to see this memorable day, not able to watch them grow into manhood, or dance at their weddings and never to have the joy of holding *their* children in her arms. Afterward, tears streaming down her face, Mandy embraced Daniel and Lucas and their father, who clutched a framed photograph of his wife and their mother while all of them, along with the other two hundred-odd congregants, broke into inconsolable sobbing.

One evening soon after Mandy and Asher began dating, they were speaking to a new acquaintance, a social worker named Eileen at a dinner party. When Eileen heard about Mandy's mother, she boldly asked Mandy whether losing her mother had made her softer or harder, more disciplined or more hedonistic, more likely to have children of her own or more fearful they would lose *her* or she would lose *them*. Asher held his breath, waiting for Mandy's response to such an intrusive question. Mandy hesitated but a second before responding with a succinct "Yes and no." Then offered no elaboration. But Asher thought he understood. "Yes and no," she was both softened and hardened, sometimes disciplined, sometimes unfettered, at times wanting kids, but at other times terrified she would lose them or they her. Conflicted about all that can ever conflict us all. But still neither daunted nor paralyzed.

Asher realized in his heart that it was not Chicago that now

55

discouraged her, but that *he* was the problem. Yet, he also knew Mandy did not give up easily on her attachments. He could not suppress his doubts, though, whether their fragile young relationship could withstand a six-week separation.

To his question about heading out to Chicago, Mandy answered, "Don't worry about me. I can deal with the cold. It's a great opportunity to learn at a terrific hospital. And I can't wait to spend some time with my cousin Lisa. Rooming with her will feel like finally getting the sister I've always wanted." Then she tried once more to broach the topic they had been avoiding. "Miles, I still feel so bad about your dad. It's almost a month after the accident and I can't stop thinking about him. What a terrible way to go."

Asher stiffened. "Listen, Mandy, I know you mean well. But he's gone and it's best we move on. He barely communicated with me when he was around and, when he did, it was mostly by instruction manual. We've got a thousand things to do and a whole life to live ahead of us. He's gone. Whatever happened, happened. Time to move on."

That non-answer silenced them both as they sat listening to the piano play a mournful rendition of "When Love Goes Wrong," this time with no vocal accompanist willing to breach the spaces between the slow sad notes.

*

During her time away, when they spoke on the phone, Asher could sense Mandy's growing distance. The last call before she was to return east, Asher spent trying to convince her to let him drive her back from Chicago. She had offered, "I'll just take a plane and ship my junk back home to follow me."

But Asher had insisted, trying to reestablish some control. "Nope. Not a chance. I want to help you pack and all. The drive out to Chicago will clear my head. And on the ride back we can catch up."

That venture did not start well. After a painful, unscenic drive west, barely able to keep his eyes open from being on call the night before, Asher had arrived in Logan Square where Mandy was rooming with her cousin in a third-story walk-up. Catching sight of Mandy waiting for him on the landing at the top of the stairs, some of Asher's trepidation abated. She looked spectacular and simple, wearing a plum-colored cashmere sweater, and a pair of tight jeans with her hair swept back in a casual ponytail. Their reunion kiss was certainly passionate enough to allay his fear that Mandy might have accelerated her reservations.

But when Asher tried to help with her luggage, their quick cocoon of comfort began to unravel. Asher insisted on carrying all three pieces of bulky luggage at once and, of course, refused Mandy's attempt to help. About halfway down the second flight of stairs, the latch came loose on one of the suitcases, sending an avalanche of clothes cascading down the stairs. In his attempt to grab and rescue some of the items, the cosmetic case in his other hand went flying down following the clothing. The sound of shattering glass echoed off the narrow stairwell walls and froze Asher. When he was able to summon the courage to look up, he caught only a glimpse of Mandy's disgusted expression before she disappeared into the bathroom for the next twenty minutes.

On the road, it took almost an hour of the dead silence that followed Asher's seventeen apologies before Mandy spoke again. However, Asher was buoyed when Mandy began almost warmly with, "Miles, you really rescued me last week with that resident who was giving me such a hard time. He thought I was nuts when I told him his toxic patient probably had serotonin syndrome from taking antidepressants. Then, I showed him the articles you found for me. I became something of a star on the wards after that. They thought those SSRIs were totally harmless. Thanks for the help."

"No problem, Mand. I've been telling you all along that we make a great team."

Although that beginning broke the tension, the conversation

still flagged. Even talking about the house on which Asher had put down a deposit for them couldn't breach the widening chasm. Finally, an hour and a half out on I-80, just past South Bend, with Asher feeling almost desperate, he took a turn north off the highway. "You know we're not far from Battle Creek. Always wanted to visit there."

Sounding incredulous, Mandy answered, "You mean Battle Creek, Michigan? Cereal-land? You have some kind of previously unexpressed, unresolved attachment to Frosted Flakes, Miles, do you?"

"Don't tell me you haven't had a thing for those Rice Krispies gremlins all these years. Come on. It should be fun"

Skeptical, Mandy said, "OK, what the heck. But don't try to weasel out of that nice dinner you promised with some surrogate sample cereal boxes."

An hour and a half's detour later, after getting lost three times, they passed through the eccentric, multi-colored, Tony the Tiger-adorned gates of "Cereal City, USA." Plunging ahead on an unplanned, self-guided tour, they wandered past two-story high boxes of Sugar Pops, Cocoa Frosted Flakes, Rice Krispies, with flaked sweetened samples of crunch being thrown at them from all sides. They passed a gaggle of screaming toddlers swimming in a huge bowl of simulated Fruit Loops. Somehow, during their wandering, Mandy separated from Asher. While searching for him through the maze of cereal paraphernalia, she encountered a seven-foot Tony the Tiger hoisting kids onto his shoulders and running them up and down the aisles. On seeing Mandy, Tony launched down the aisle, barreling right at her. He grabbed her in a furry embrace, announcing, "Yerrrr Grrrrreat!!" Trapped in his warm but unbreakable grasp, Mandy tried pushing Tony off of her to no avail. She searched around for a rescuer, and, with none to be found, began calculating where on a tiger suit a kick should be aimed. Then Tony ripped off his mask revealing a sweaty-headed Asher, grinning ear-to-ear. Mandy grabbed his tail and pulled him off his feet, while a hysterical Asher explained he had given the real Tony $20 to let him wear the uniform.

Just then, two preschoolers with Cocoa Krispies hanging from their hair wandered by and spotted Tony flailing on the ground with his headpiece off. They pointed at Asher and started crying that Tony the Tiger wasn't really a tiger, just a person in a tiger suit. Asher rushed over to them, and, while offering them fistfuls of Frosted Flakes said, "Gee, kids, sorry. The real Tony came down with striped fever today and is laid up in bed. So he asked me to fill in for him." Asher gave them both huge hugs and they padded away placated.

On the road back from Battle Creek, Mandy couldn't quit laughing. "I will forever carry that image of you thrashing on the ground in your tiger suit, trying to comfort those poor disillusioned kids. They'll probably stop believing in Santa now, too."

Asher merely grinned in response.

She sidled close to him in the front car seat, linking her arm in his. "You know, you scared the shit out of me. A giant tiger assault is not a minor crime."

"A guy in a fluffy orange tiger costume scares you? How'd you survive the concrete jungle of Chicago? Lucky you have me back to protect you, even if what's threatening you is only me to begin with."

Asher then announced, "Every Step You Take," and changed the radio station. Ten seconds later Mandy proclaimed, "Sultan of Swing" and also changed the station. They had resumed their long-standing contest wherein whoever first identified the name of the song playing on the radio gained control of the dial. And their period of uncertainty—the wall that had been separating them—vanished like the border between two countries that exists solely on a map, and can be crossed if one only has the will to do so.

59

CHAPTER 11 ———————————————————————

One week after assaulting Heidi in the funeral home, Asher had once again had hunkered down. At the office, he answered questions only when necessary and then only in monosyllables. He exchanged pleasantries with no one. He took lunches alone with paperwork for company. By the end of his workweek, he needed a break. Seeing some hundred and twenty patients in his office each week usually served to distract him from personal concerns. Not this week. Plus, home no longer felt like the sanctuary it had been. He found that avoiding the truth was akin to lying and, as a result, began steering clear of Mandy and spending an inordinate amount of time reading stories to Stacie and Emily.

Wednesday evening that week, the dreaded had occurred. The incident was so quick, for a moment, Asher thought he had imagined it, since he had conjured up just this possibility multiple times. He was standing at the checkout of the local CVS on the way home from work, picking up some cold medicine for Stace. He felt a breeze on his shoulder as a figure blew past him. Asher turned to see a disappearing Irene Mallory, who had hesitated just long enough to leave one sentence hanging in the air, a sentence that lingered with Asher for weeks.

Asher had known Irene as one of the most easygoing, down-to-earth women possible. She was born to be a kindergarten teacher, though burdened with an incongruous, husky, frog-like voice from taking a wayward football in the throat as a child that had permanently damaged her vocal cords. When they first met their new teacher, Irene's students must have been frightened by that voice until one unabashed four year-old started calling her Miss Kermit. Such a label might have hurt another person's feelings but Irene had laughed more than anyone and accepted being called that forever after.

At the CVS that day, Asher recognized Irene's voice before he had time to turn and see her disappearing body head out the door. "Sorry you chose not to say goodbye to Tom at his funeral. He would have been disappointed." She darted out, giving Asher no chance to respond. Though he mustered the courage to call her several times that evening, leaving a message on her answering machine, Irene chose not to call back.

*

Other than rounding on his seven patients in the hospital the following Saturday morning, Asher was free for the weekend. Yet he resisted the pull of heading directly home. Figuring he might have a potential hospital admission down in the emergency room, he took the three flights of stairs down to see if one of his patients had crumped and might need hospitalization. While winding his way through the obstacle course of wheel-chaired patients, preoccupied nurses, and rushing EMTs, he almost tripped over a stretcher in the hall, heading over to X-ray. He came face-to-face with a deeply jaundiced, sunken-cheeked image he thought he recognized.

But his attempt at recollection was interrupted by the sight of the forlorn figure of one of his patients, William Cassidy, sitting alone in a row of otherwise empty chairs in the ER waiting room. From the other side of the room, Asher stopped and stared, not sure what Mr. Cassidy was doing there, not sure if he wanted to find out. There was less than thirty feet separating them, but it was thirty feet filled with two wailing babies, a Hispanic couple in the middle of an argument and, above the clamor, a World Wrestling Federation match blaring on the TV.

When they had first met, and every time since, Mr. Cassidy asked Asher to call him Hopalong—after the ancient TV cowboy—as apparently everyone else had done for the past sixty years. But Asher was not in the habit of calling his patients by their nicknames and felt, by this stage in his life, Mr. Cassidy was deserving of a bit more respect. He was just past eighty. His hair had all but vanished save for a few isolated white threads springing out here and there. His face was weather-beaten and scaled from too many days gardening hatless under a fierce sun. His upper body was bent forward at a thirty-degree angle—a legacy of the two back surgeries he'd endured over the prior seven years. When he walked, he shuffled ahead six inches at a time— pure torture for someone who, when younger, had to be lassoed to be slowed down. But Mr. Cassidy's mind remained intact and he still gripped Asher's hand in a tight, almost challenging way when he shook it.

Therein lay the ultimate insult. Mr. Cassidy's mind was willing; his body was not. Over the past two months, Asher had watched Mr. Cassidy disintegrate from a vital, active senior citizen into a barely mobile, agitated, off-kilter enigma. Asher had ordered every blood test in the book, an MRI of his head and neck, a spinal tap and EEG, all yielding no diagnosis and therefore no treatment. Asher had finally sent Mr. Cassidy off to Hartford for consultation with a specialist on movement disorders. That had been about three weeks before and Asher had heard nothing from either patient or consultant since.

His curiosity piqued, Asher headed over to Mr. Cassidy. He sat down in the adjacent chair and for a few moments said nothing; he was now close enough to Mr. Cassidy to be shocked by his appearance. For Mr. Cassidy seemed to have aged another ten years since Asher had last seen him. A wheeled-walker had replaced his cane. He had lost any hint of life's rose in his cheeks. Asher noted the wasting of Mr. Cassidy's temporalis muscle, a cardinal sign of major internal degeneration. The thin wisps of hair that had previously clung to Mr. Cassidy's scalp were now entirely absent. In their place at the back of his bent head, Asher noted a raw red scab, he immediately identified as the remnants of an ulcer that could only be produced by lying in bed, immobile for long periods of time. Asher wondered how he could have been unaware of what must have been Mr. Cassidy's prolonged hospitalization.

At the same time, Mr. Cassidy was absorbed watching a curly-headed Hispanic boy playing with a couple of action figures. The boy, also oblivious to his surroundings, was busily using his figures to mimic the body slams and headbutts of the wrestlers on screen. Since Mr. Cassidy was too preoccupied to acknowledge him, Asher dove in. He leaned over and asked in the amplified voice he knew Mr. Cassidy's failing hearing required, "How's it going there, Mr. Cassidy—you OK?"

Mr. Cassidy looked Asher's way, blankly staring for a second before he recognized him. "Doc Asher! I was hoping I might run into you sooner or later. How's it going with you? Nice tan, doc. You been on vacation?"

Asher face reddened even more, considering the circumstances of his vacation. He merely answered, "Good to see you, Mr. Cassidy. What brings you to my neck of the woods?"

That simple inquiry managed to open up the floodgates. "More tests. What do you think? Those Dr. Jekylls over at the big medical center got a half dozen more blood tests they want to check out. Already took so much blood while I was there for two weeks, they had to lend me a few pints from some other poor sucker. Damn near killed me, those chop-shop carnies. But they're not done with me yet. They say they've a bunch of questions they still need answered. Me too. It almost took me a lasso and a gun to get one of them to sit still long enough to give me the answer to my one question, what the heck was wrong with me?"

Asher interrupted, "Yeah, I haven't heard myself what happened to you after I sent you to that neurology specialist in Hartford."

"Well, you're gonna want to hear this then." And Mr. Cassidy pulled in as much of a deep breath as he could muster and took off. "I finally got to those supposed pros you sent me to at the medical center and, before you can say Aloysius T. Cornpone, they threw me into a hospital room with three other saps, hooked me up to half a dozen tubes, punctured me full of more holes than a streetwalker's dress, X-rayed me till I glowed crimson, then spat me out the other end worse off than I started. Said they were going to find out what was wrong with me if it killed them. Them? What about me? After all their tests, one of those tubes they stuck up me must have been hiding some mean germs, because before I had my butt sat back down in my car to get back home, I started shivering so hard my skin nearly split."

Asher shook his head, knowing that every hospitalization could almost as likely kill you as cure you. "Sorry to hear that, Mr. Casssidy. What did they say you had?"

Mr. Cassidy's voice was gravel-dry, his words separated unevenly by heaves and gasps as he tried to catch his breath between each one. "A day after they set me free, I ended right back up in that torture chamber they call a hospital with a hundred and five degree fever. This time they tied me down for a week, pumped me so full of antibiotics some bugs must've dropped dead in Indiana. After all that, a bunch of them white coats came by grinning ear-to-ear and said I was all cleaned up, cured and ready to go home. But by then I was weaker than a guppy— couldn't walk, barely could get a spoon from bowl to mouth. I couldn't complete a sentence without spitting up a huge honker. But they said I was ready to go. So here I am, someone who looks like me, talks like me, acts like me, but I got to say, someone who just no longer *is* me."

Asher was shocked into silence. After a long pause, he said, "Well, I've got to admit, you do look a bit worse for the wear,

Mr. Cassidy. I was at least hoping that neurologist would find out what the heck was wrong with you, 'cause I sure couldn't.'"

Mr. Cassidy took out an already-moist white handkerchief from his back pocket to wipe some spittle from the corner of his mouth, then kept the handkerchief in readiness on his lap. "Do me a favor will you, doc? Call me 'Hopalong.' Well, I tell you that was the final butt-kicker. I'm all dressed up and ready to leave the place, happy I'm not going out the back in some leather bag, when it dawns on me, I still don't have a clue what the hell is wrong with me. So I ask the only nurse in the place who ever paid two cents worth of attention to me if someone could please explain to me what the heck was wrong with me to begin with. And she says, 'Oh' and she'll come right back.

"An hour later she returns with some rookie in tow who, I remember, was hiding in the background that first day I got to the hospital. Kid looked like he wasn't old enough to be invited to the junior prom. He comes up to me all apologetic, saying he was sorry, he didn't realize I was in the hospital. But then, this one is rich, doc. He says he has good news for me. They know what's wrong with me. They figured it out. He's busting with pride, like he'd just invented Twinkies or something. He says I've got 'ain't my trophies' or some such mumbo jumbo. And there are many things they can do to help. So even though it's incurable, I should stay hopeful.

"Well, I must not have been as thrilled as he expected, because after his little speech of triumph, I didn't say a word. I just sat there staring at him, because all I really heard was the incurable part. The rookie starts to sputter and stumble and backtrack some. He says, 'you must have heard of it—ain't my trophies in your skivvies.' You know ALS—Lou Gehrig's Disease—you must have heard of that?'

And then the light *does* go off in my head. 'Cause that one I've heard of. And that one, I know, only means one thing—I'm a goner. No matter how sick I've been, I'm only gonna get sicker. Then, the kid walks out of the room and I feel a little bad I wasn't as thrilled as he wanted me to be. But sometimes you just can't please everyone, you know, doc?"

That was one long rendition for Mr. Cassidy. Between coughing and honking up phlegm, wiping his mouth, blowing his nose, and pausing to catch his breath, between rubbing the scars on the back of his head and arms, and smacking Asher with his walker for dramatic effect, took a good fifteen minutes to get out. By then both he and Asher were exhausted.

Asher thought to himself, "Crap. ALS! I should have thought of that. But the early signs are always tough to tease out and he had so many other things wrong with him. In any case, he's right. He's a goner. And it doesn't matter when he was diagnosed, no treatment is going to help."

Asher and Mr. Cassidy then sat side-by-side silently for a while, both victim and perpetrator shaking their heads in amazement at their roles. Asher was unhinged by the sight of Mr. Cassidy, and even more so by the audacity of his chosen profession. He could not even bring himself to offer the standard "sorry" he doled out to patients in apology for the insults both the medical profession and life heaped upon them.

Just as Asher was about to leave, knowing there was little left to say, a nurse popped her head out from behind the blue ER curtain by the triage room.

She scanned the room searching for someone. "Mrs. Zantay? Mrs. Zantay, are you here? Mrs. Zantay?" When no one responded to her summons, the nurse repeated her call. She shook her head when again there was no answer, then disappeared behind the curtain.

Both Asher and Mr. Cassidy sat there silently for a few minutes more, apparently thinking the same thought. Finally, Mr. Cassidy said "Zantay, hmm. I thought that guy heading down the hall in the stretcher looked familiar. 'Course seeing him now'd be hard for even his mother to recognize him, the state he's in. Poor bastard. Somehow, I was worried he might be dead by now. Guess not, though. Remind me to tell you sometime about him. Zigfrid Zantay—now there's a story. There was a man!"

Asher said nothing, now also recognizing that shell he had passed by at the ER entrance. He too was remembering the same Zigfrid Zantay, struck numb by the ghost that memory had become.

CHAPTER 12 ———————————

Three days later, as Asher left his office twelve hours to the minute after he had arrived, he found Mr. Cassidy waiting for him in a banana-yellow, antique Jeep Cherokee. Somehow Asher was not surprised, as if he'd run into his old college roommate at the Burger King one day during lunchtime. He *was* surprised Mr. Cassidy had gotten up enough energy to drive over to his office and moreover, to wait for him, since who could predict when Asher might finish up for the day? With a weary sigh, Asher followed his feet to the old man's car and found that Mr. Casssidy was asleep in the front seat.

As he walked around the back of Mr. Cassidy's car, he scanned the parking lot. Since most of the time he left out the back door into the rear lot, Asher rarely got this view of his office from the front. They say if you want to get a real picture of whether to trust your doctor, you should spend an hour in the waiting room. Watch the receptionists and nurses greet the patients, see how long you have to wait, notice how much dust has accumulated on the chairs, note the anxiety on everyone's face; that will give you a good idea what you can expect once you meet the doctor himself. Asher wondered if his parking lot might provide the same type of clues. He found several crushed old plastic Poland Spring water bottles strewn about, more than the expected number of potholes in need of repair and on the ground right near the stairs to the front door, a used condom. Not an image Asher might have chosen for his office. He resisted the impulse to pick up and dispose of the condom.

Asher rapped on the Jeep's window, waking Mr. Cassidy, who gestured for Asher to come around and sit in the passenger seat. Weary but curious, Asher complied. Despite his nap and the encumbrance of his illness, Mr. Cassidy seemed buoyant, as if he had purpose to his life again.

On settling himself, Asher asked, "What brings you around to my neck of the woods, Mr. Cassidy? And do you really think it's a good idea for you to be driving in your condition?"

"Now you're sounding like my old lady, doc. It's barely three blocks. I've got to have some way to get out of that prison of a house besides going to the doctor or getting more tests. Anyhow, I wanted to catch up with you and didn't know when we'd run into each other again. You weren't about to come over to my house for a visit if I had asked, were you, doc?"

Asher shook his head no, knowing that such a visit would be unlikely. He stared at Mr. Cassidy a moment, his clinician persona taking over. With Mr. Cassidy's diagnosis now a certainty, Asher could categorize his clinical symptoms more easily. He noted Mr. Cassidy's upper-extremity spasticity and rigid, inconstant muscle movements that obeyed orders from somewhere besides his own brain. He noted the head bobbing due to weakness of the neck muscles, the insistent pool of mucus forming at the corner of the mouth that gurgled his speech. He noted the fasciculations—those worm-like muscle twitches so characteristic of ALS—of Mr. Cassidy's brachioradialis muscles, making his arm jump, at times bouncing off Asher's. Were these signs new, or had Asher missed them? Either way, Asher was amazed Mr. Cassidy still had the stamina and tenacity to venture out into the world. Ninety-nine percent of those with Mr. Cassidy's degree of disability would be homebound. But his brain and thankfully, so far, his speech had not been affected by the unrelenting illness.

As soon as Asher was seated, Mr. Cassidy started right in as if they had never left off from their last meeting at the hospital. "Doc, I've got to tell you, this guy Zantay was something else. After you left the other day and I was done with my tests, I headed up to see my old friend Zig in his room. He looked like crap. You saw. But he was still with it. Knew me right off. Was tickled almost pink to see me, though you could only really call him tickled yellow.

"But he's just a shell of the extraordinary man he once was." Mr. Cassidy stretched 'extraordinary' into six syllables and punctuated the thought with a soft whistle. He shook his head back and forth, apparently mesmerized by the scenes playing inside his head. "Didn't realize you knew him too, Doc, until he told me the other day. But I guess if you've spent any time hanging around this town, you've had a chance to be helped by Zig."

"That's what I hear, Mr. Cassidy. I got to know him almost the first day I set foot in Dover."

But before Asher could embellish, Mr. Cassidy rumbled on, "Well, I met the guy right in the ER, maybe even right in that seat I was in the other day. Must have been about twelve, fifteen years ago, can't exactly recall. Time seems kind of difficult to figure right now. But he was a different person then. I was pretty different myself. Time has a way of sucking the juice right out of you, leaving you all dried out and pruned up.

Asher settled in. He could tell he was in for the long haul. But he found himself curious both about what had brought Mr. Cassidy out to see him and what that had to do with Zig.

"I think I was in the emergency room that time waiting for my wife. She slipped in the shower and broke a couple of ribs. Boy, she was a handful to care for then. Couldn't lift a muffin without cringing. I had to do everything for her, even brush her hair. Now I guess it's payback because she's been waiting on me this past year like I'm the King of Siam.

"I was sitting in the waiting room that day when Zig hobbled in. He was wearing a pair of green shorts and leaning on some kind of tennis racket, so I knew right away the most entertainment I was going to get out of him was guessing how far up his leg the nurse was going to wrap his ankle. Even so, I immediately wondered about him. He was pretty imposing. Judging by his size, I didn't figure him to be playing some namby-pamby racket game. I figured him more for a middle linebacker or maybe a weightlifter. Zig was at least as wide as he was tall—not fat, just solid like one of Lombardi's Seven Blocks of Granite. With his shorts on and all, I could see he had these pillars for legs that looked like they were four-by-eights. Later on, I heard tell that despite his size, he could wipe the floor with any challenger at racquetball. He'd just stand in his position in the middle of the court and let the other fleas bounce off him. Couldn't budge him an inch. Heard he lost maybe once over a ten-year span before he took sick."

Asher again tried to intervene, hoping to get Cassidy to the point. "Yeah, I can sure vouch for his heft. Had to lift him once. But you're here to tell me something, Mr. C?"

"I'll get there, Doc. Have some patience for an old man, will you, Doc?" And he rambled on, "But, Zig's face didn't match his body one bit. On top of that marble block of a body sat a round pillow of cushy softness. Zig had these pink, puffy marshmallow-like cheeks that made small slits of his black eyes whenever he smiled, which was most of the time. Sitting on top of his head was a pile of jet-black hair that looked like it had lost a war with itself. One Christmas, Zig showed up in a Santa Claus suit to give the kids in the hospital gifts and I guess I realized I always saw him that way—a Santa out of costume, 'stead of the other way around.

"Well that day, Zig plopped himself down right beside me like I was expecting him. Maybe come to think of it, I was. Most everyone else, when they'd walk in the ER entrance, would find himself as much space as he could, trying to separate from the rest of the patients. Who knew what kind of disease or how much grief might be sitting just two feet away from you. Best to keep your distance. Not Zig, though. Either he right away recognized I was no patient—no carrier of bad germs or bad news—or he didn't much care. Even with some twenty-odd unfilled chairs scattered throughout the room, Zig picked the seat next to mine to settle into."

During Mr. Cassidy's monologue, Asher found himself entranced, lulled into passivity. He felt like he was sitting next to a fireplace, listening to one of those old console radios as a gravelly-voiced actor narrated a tale filled with intrigue and suspense.

"Then Zig's deep voice boomed out an accent I couldn't quite lay my finger on, but I was sure came from some place like Yugoslavia or Albania or maybe even Russia. Sounded like Count Dracula had just entered the room. Right off, Zig started talking not like the strangers we were, but more like he was starting a conversation that would go on for years to come. Like we had plenty of time to complete the story down the road and we were starting off in the here and now to end whenever and wherever, who knew.

"'You tell me what I was supposed to do, please,' Zig said. 'Was I supposed to refuse people like them? People from town who had worked all their lives here and had dedicated themselves to this town? Who better to support and back up than those people?'

"Zig stared off into space for a moment then came back to the present. Must have dawned on him I hadn't the foggiest notion what the heck he was talking about, 'cause he backed up and parked in my driveway for a minute. 'Sorry, got myself lost there for a second. I know the receptionist at the desk over there. Laura Petrofsky and her husband Walt, too. Fine people they are. My name is Zigfrid. Zigfrid Zantay. People call me 'Zig with a Z,' or just 'Zig.'

"I returned the intro. 'Cassidy here. William Cassidy.' For some reason I didn't ask him to call me Hopalong that day. Maybe I knew this fellow needed a nickname far more than me. We shook hands. He grasped my right with his right, then placed his left on top and rested it there for a moment like he was the Pope blessing me. Then he went on.

"'What, might I inquire, should I have done when this family came to my door asking me for help? Should I have sent them away, turned them down, as so many banks had done before? Should I have let their lives' work and the sweat from their brows run down the drain like sewage? These people came to me not just for my help, but also for my belief—my belief in them and their ability to make it in this country. Wasn't that why my bank was formed? Wasn't that the reason for our existence? Not merely to make profits for those already-too-rich investors. And for sure not to satisfy the rules and regulations of a federal banking system that had no idea what it was doing.' Then Zig gets even more fired up. 'Goddamn it! I would do the same thing again if they ever give me the chance. Even after all was said and done, for the Petrofskys and a hundred others, I would not change one solitary loan I made. And screw those bureaucrats. I had enough of those sniveling, rodent-eating government bastards to last me a lifetime back in Europe. How they weaseled their way into this country, I'll never understand.'

"Well, Zigfrid with a Z was so wound up that day, I just sat and listened for the better part of an hour. Later on, he turned out to be one of the calmest, most easygoing guys you'd ever want to meet. But that day, when we first met, Zig was hotter than griddle sizzle.

"Zig's troubles with the bank was in the eighties, when all those bank failures sent the feds out investigating everyone left and right. They lumped the good ones in with the bad and assumed everyone was on the take. Zig ran the Family Loan and Savings Bank then—had worked himself up the ladder, one of those Horatio Alger stories. Started out with nothing; put himself through college, busing tables, and then through business school at that fancy one in Philadelphia. Then he started lowest rung on the ladder at the Dover National Bank, working his way up until he became president. But some stuffy old Brahmans on the board thought his foreign accent wasn't the kind of image they wanted for the bank, so they dumped him with some trumped-up excuses."

At that moment, both Cassidy and Asher jumped about three feet into the air when they heard a sharp rap on the passenger side window. They had been so immersed in Cassidy's story, the sudden intrusion from the outside world sent both their hearts pounding. A huge woman in a tent dress they somehow had missed on her approach stood at the passenger door. Asher rolled down the window. She almost shouted at him, "I thought the pharmacy over there was open till nine on Wednesday nights. They seem closed." Asher looked over at the darkened, locked-up store. Not sure what she expected him to do about the situation, he merely shrugged. Seeming miffed at his indifference, the woman galumphed back to her car, gave them both a dirty look, and then drove off.

Mr. Cassidy winked at Asher and said, "I guess it takes all kinds and all shapes, Doc. Hope she's not one of yours."

"We take all comers, Mr. Cassidy, regardless of race, creed, color, or dress size. But go on," replied Asher, hoping to move things along.

Mr. Cassidy resumed his story without a dropped syllable. "When the bank dumped Zig, he didn't blink an eye. He went out on his own and formed a brand-new bank with a bunch of guys who had been war victims or immigrants like him. That was the thing about Zig; he tried to make money, yeah, but he did it to raise everyone up, 'stead of stepping on them while he climbed up the ladder alone. He and his new bank set out to help first-generation, ambitious folks with zilch when they got to the States—ones who were willing to work their butts off to get more, if given half a chance. The bank was doing great till the economy bottomed out. They'd put a bunch of money into that eyesore of a mall downtown that went under. Then things really hit the fan.

"The IRS came in and pored over Zig's bank records, looked over his personal finances, and decided to prosecute him. They closed down the bank and Zig hit the skids. About then, I started to see him more and more often. He had a heap of time on his hands, so we started to meet for lunch or to play rummy at the Polish Club downtown."

Asher broke in. "You're right, Mr. Cassidy. Zig was something else. You'll never believe how I first met him." And Asher went into the tale of finding Zig bleeding out on the road about ten years before, and how Zig had set him up in practice.

"Wow! That sure beats my story, Doc. Now I'm almost as impressed with you as him. But let me finish my point here, before I lose it."

Asher sighed and looked down at his watch. "Mr. Cassidy, it's getting late; maybe we could finish this another day. I've got to get home to the family. As it is, I'm kind of in the doghouse there anyway."

"Well, OK, Doc. I guess this story can wait a few more days. Though I can't be sure which one of us might buy the wooden box by then. Your generation just has not learned patience. Always rushing off somewhere else. You already know that Zig started to get sicker and sicker, so I had to visit him at home or sometimes I would head to the hospital to hang out with him while he was getting this or that test. I always thought it was those damn IRS agents who revved up Zig's illness, even though he told me it was only a matter of time before that virus got him.

"Damn thing was, the guy never bitched about his fate for one second. I mean, his whole life, he had been tossed on the ocean this way and that like he was a one-masted sailboat in a typhoon, but he always stayed even-keeled and calm. I guess when you've seen the worst of life as just a kid, everything you get afterward is bonus time. And Zig had some bonuses. He had a great wife and kids—I'm talking like he's already had the dirt poured over him—a terrific career. But nothing can make up for what he went through as a kid during the war. Nothing. But maybe we can talk again in a few days?"

Asher answered half-heartedly, "Sure, Mr. Cassidy. Stop by again when you get a chance. But you're right. Zig's quite a guy. Feel bad he's so sick now. Plus, I heard he's lost most everything—career, wife, family, the works. I wish I could help *him* somehow."

CHAPTER 13 ─────────────────────────────────

Five days later, Asher again found Cassidy's beat-up Cherokee in the parking lot. A sigh and the knowledge he was late for dinner did not stop him from heading over to Cassidy's car. Dusk was settling on the parking lot. The timed anti-crime floodlights loomed twenty feet above the lot like alien surveillance cameras. Asher once again found Cassidy asleep in the front seat and wondered how long the old man had been waiting. As Asher stared at his patient, he realized Cassidy was not moving a muscle. Then, he couldn't tell if Cassidy was even breathing. He knocked on the window three times hard, like the obese woman had done several days before, then tried the door. Locked. Imagining breaking the car window with his shoe, dragging Cassidy out of the car and starting CPR, Asher rapped one more time and Cassidy jolted upright, almost knocking Asher over in shock. He rolled down the manual car window. "Hey, Doc. Why so jumpy? Been waitin' for you a while. How come so late?"

Then, without waiting for an answer, he gestured for Asher to join him in the passenger seat. By the time Asher had opened the door, settled in his seat, and begun to tell Cassidy that he had to head home, Cassidy had launched into his monologue, starting where he had left off a few days before. Asher was neither sure what kept sucking him into Mr. Cassidy's story, nor what was the ultimate point of Cassidy arriving at his doorstep these nights. But he found himself looking forward to hearing out Cassidy, perhaps just to escape from his own concerns for a while.

"Maybe you can explain this better to me, Doc. Zig told me all about it, but either I'm thick or this medical mumbo jumbo stuff is too tough for us normal folks to grasp. Can't seem to get Zig out of my head these days—watching him waste away feels kind of like looking in the mirror, I guess."

Asher said, "I know you feel like crap, Mr. Cassidy. But don't go hoisting up the white flag just yet. You've still got some fight in you." He didn't sound convincing, even to himself.

"Doc, don't worry about it. I know what the cards have in store for me. Sooner or later we'll all be sleeping with the worms. Anyway, a few years back, when he was starting to go downhill, Zig told me he picked up some virus that was killing his liver. Said the doctors figured he caught it from a transfusion he got when he first came over to the States. Must have been about twelve or thirteen then and almost as soon as he hit New York, he had to be hospitalized nearly a month.

"Zig said he was spewing up blood. The docs never saw a twelve-year old with an ulcer like that. In those days they didn't mess around with a bunch of fancy tests and whatnot, they took you right to the cutting room. Inside of a day, they had sliced out a good part of Zig's stomach. Later on, it didn't seem to affect his eating habits much, seeing how in his prime Zig must have weighed near two-fifty. Once or twice, he pulled up his shirt to show me this angry red scar winding its way down his stomach, kind of like the Mississippi emptying out at his bellybutton. Bragged about his scar like it was some kind of war wound, 'stead of the end result of a heap of neglect and malnutrition. I caught a glimpse of Zig's belly one time as he was wasting away and the flesh hung from his bones. The scar had shriveled more into a thin, squiggly worm crawling down his belly, by then looking more like some flesh-eating parasite sucking up what was left of his reserves."

Mr. Cassidy paused a minute to catch his breath. He had a coughing fit that sputtered on until the flush of excited speech drained from his cheeks and he turned a ghost-like white. Asher felt his own pulse quicken and wondered whether one day, or even right then, he might have to throw Mr. Cassidy down on the ground and pound on his chest and breathe some life into a body no longer willing or able to go on. But Mr. Cassidy gathered himself and continued. "Sorry Doc, can't get that damn phlegm to get up and go and stay gone.

"Anyway, somehow this virus must have been hitchhiking along with one of those transfusions they gave him, then hid out in his system till about forty years later it started to eat up his liver. Zig got weaker and weaker and sicker and sicker, till now he's turned yellower than an overripe grapefruit, with a huge belly that I guess is now full of some kind of fluid and seems about ready to pop. And that scar of his I saw last week, when they wheeled him in, is now stretched so tight it might unzip any second and shoot a fountain of whatever the heck's inside of him straight up to the ceiling."

Asher interrupted. "Yup, Mr. C, you're right. When your liver's shot, you're pretty much a goner. But I know most of this. I gotta get going, Mr. C, family waiting."

"Hold on, Doc, hold on. Almost through. 'Cause, after seeing Zig in the ER the other day, I decided I should go up and visit again; doesn't seem like he has a heap of time left for me to say my goodbyes. We got to talking and I mentioned I had just run into you that day. He knew you were taking care of me and felt bad no one could figure out what the heck was going on with me. He once said to me, if *you* couldn't figure out what I had, then either my disease hadn't been invented yet or it must all be in my head. That's how much he thought of you.

"Then he said he had heard you were having some trouble. One time while waiting for a CAT scan, he overheard some doctors in the hall talking about it. Didn't have a clue what he meant but hope it's nothing serious, Doc."

Asher reddened, but remained silent.

"So just before I was ready to leave, Zig says, 'Do me a favor. I've been meaning to talk to Doc Asher for a while. Ask him to stop by and see me. I've got something for him.' So, I'm back here today delivering the message. Go visit Zig before he can't be visited anymore." And Cassidy began another coughing fit, which he could interrupt only long enough to wave his hand, dismissing Asher from the scene.

CHAPTER 14 ———————————————

The next morning, on rounds, Asher decided to do just what Cassidy had suggested—visit Zig.

He checked the hospital computer registry and found Zig's room, 712, then headed straight there before he lost his courage. He was not sure why meeting Zig again was daunting. Maybe his reticence stemmed from having only seen him face-to-face that one time, and Asher was reluctant to view the decimated waste Cassidy had described. But, no, Asher had seen decimated times seven hundred before. More likely, Asher feared Zig's disappointment, knowing that he was aware of Asher's recent disaster. Overcoming those concerns, Asher headed to room 712. He nodded at two nurses standing outside Zig's room, knocked on the door and, hearing no answer, entered. Asher was disappointed to find an empty bed and no sign of Zig.

He surveyed the room. There was still enough evidence of habitation that Asher felt sure Zig hadn't passed on. A pruned, empty plastic bottle of D5W hung limply from an IV pole next to Zig's unmade bed. On the sheet right below the IV, an inkblot of pink suggested his IV, at some point, had leaked around the insertion site in his arm. Below the crumpled top sheet, Asher saw a familiar stain of brown surrounded by a yellowed ring, testifying at least to Zig's limited mobility, if not also to his loss of bodily control. However, the stack of books resting on Zig's brown laminate tray table asserted the persistence of an active, inquisitive mind. Stendhal, Ken Kesey, and a couple of Stephen Kings. Incongruous, but interesting. A veritable greenhouse of flowers erupting below the TV and maybe 30 get-well cards tacked to the walls showed that the rest of the world still cared.

As he was about to head out and ask the nurse where Zig had gone, Asher was stopped by a beat-up briefcase resting on the vinyl chair in the corner. On top of the briefcase, stuffed to the hilt with paper, rested a white envelope with the words "Doc Asher" written on the front. Asher hesitated, not sure if he was reading correctly. He picked up the unsealed envelope and removed a single handwritten page that, though somewhat shakier, Asher recognized from ten years before as originating from Zig's unmistakable hand.

> *Dear Doctor Asher,*
>
> *Still, ten years after our first encounter, our lives may once again intersect. I find myself in an inevitable, perhaps predestined decline. You too, I have overheard, may have reached a nadir. Though for me redemption is unlikely, you still have much more good to accomplish, many more lives to help, another lifetime to lead.*
>
> *I have accumulated this disorganized narrative over the years, hoping to assemble it in my anticipated, tranquil decline. Now that future will never materialize. Perhaps, though, you may make some sense from my ramblings. More so, perhaps the example of my trials may inspire you to persevere. Travails and disappointment follow us all, throughout our lives. You, I know, have the courage and tenacity to rise above yours. I hope my tale will help you do so.*
>
> *Your ever-grateful patient,*
> *Zigfrid Zantay.*

Asher read the letter three times. He stood transfixed, staring at the bulging briefcase. Then he snatched it up, turned and quit the room, ignoring the nurse still outside who, looking at him quizzically, said to his back, "Mr. Zantay's down in X-ray getting another abdominal CT. I'll tell him you were by." Asher merely waved his hand and headed down the hall.

Before leaving the hospital, though, Asher decided to check out what exactly Zig was dealing with to have made him so pessimistic. First, Asher went to one of the computers, tucked into a corner of the seventh floor. He surveyed the registry of patients admitted to that floor till he again came to "Zantay, Zigfrid" and highlighted that name in order to review Zig's lab results. The lab, more than any narrative, often revealed how soon a patient with liver failure would pass on.

Asher scrolled down: White count—22,300, Hemoglobin—8.3, Platelets—34,000, Total Bilirubin—8.6, ALT—467, INR—4.6, Albumin—1.6. Zig's liver was faring poorly on all counts. Whether these numbers were an improvement on an even more dire state or a midpoint in an inevitable descent, Asher could not discern.

He headed right to the lineup of old records arranged on a musty shelf in the doctor's dictation room. Asher nodded hello to Dr. Sherman, who was droning a rote discharge summary on a patient with CHF, then pulled out the chart from the slot of Room 712, Bed 2. It took Asher two hands to maneuver the huge chart down to the desk, where it landed with a loud thud, startling Dr. Sherman. Asher mumbled an apology, then sat down in front of the chart.

Over the years, Asher had pored over a thousand old medical records, over the endless, fading white pages recording the accumulated misery of a person's life and, not infrequently, his death. He had scrutinized the reams of hastily scrawled doctor's notes, barely able to decipher every third word. He had scoured the daily record of vital signs and accompanying nurse's notes, detailing a patient's minute-by-minute suffering, their ins and outs, the color and consistency of their stool, urine, and vomit, their cries and their whispers. He had perused the endless stream of lab results and X-rays, chronicling modern medicine's attempts to inscribe the narrative of the dying with a rationale and an order no death really possessed. For Asher, the process had all the emotional impact of reading a newspaper.

This time, though, Asher felt stirred. His stomach knotted as he realized the accumulated pain and suffering represented by the mere magnitude of this volume. For once, he recognized the dimly noted fact that each page signaled a distinct chapter in the suffering of its subject. Each page signified another IV inserted, an additional hour spent lying on the cold-slab of an X-ray table, another needle stuck into the patient's belly to draw off excess fluid. Each entry chronicled another aide cleaning this person's soiled sheets, another respiratory tech suctioning mucus from the back of his throat, another dressing placed on his sacrum to prevent his skin from further breakdown. Each page recorded another stanza in the non-lyrical, epic poem on the life and death of one man and on the life and death of us all.

So Asher took some extra time and care in wandering through the chart of Zigfrid Zantay. He focused on the hundreds of nurse's notes, honing in on references to belly pain, confusion, abdominal distention, agitation, nausea, vomiting, soiling, retching, twitching, seizing, staring, wasting, hallucinating, howling, wandering, and wailing. He scanned edema, jaundice, dehydration, tremor, aspiration, distension, wheezing, grunting, congestion, confusion, coma, and crusting; plus maceration, ecchymosis, scabbing and scaling, incontinence and incoherence, terminal care, and even terror. He surveyed the doctor's notes, which lapsed into the medical secret code he, too, took for granted. Asterixis, ascites, effusion, icterus, hemangioma, varices, portal hypertension, and encephalopathy. Then the abbreviations, shrinking complex diseases into portable packaging—AMI, CRF, TIA, CHF, SBP.

Asher marveled at the variety and ingenuity of vocabulary

available to detail the decline and fall of the human ecosystem. Like the American Indians of the old West who had ten thousand words to describe the differentiating characteristics of their horses, we have developed ten million others to eulogize our own suffering. And each one captures a moment, or an hour, or a lifetime of deterioration and demise from which none will ever escape.

Finally, Asher ended his subterranean exploration of Zigfrid Zantay's woes. He closed the chart, leaving exposed the green cover page. Absent-mindedly, he glanced at the page, his thoughts elsewhere. One item, though, refocused Asher's attention. At the onset of every hospitalization, a clerk in the admissions office typed up a cover page detailing the patient's vital statistics—his name, address, next of kin, occupation, insurance, etc. Asher zeroed in on an item on Zig's cover page under "Country of Origin" and the response: "Unknown." Asher then thumbed through the chart to investigate the entry during prior hospitalizations. Again, on each and every green sheet, the answer to that question was "Unknown."

Asher wondered what manner of human or computer error had instigated and perpetuated this non-information. Who would have given such an answer to begin with? Not likely Zigfrid himself. Could the person who answered the questions—Zig's wife or some other—have been ignorant of Zig's place of birth? Had each clerk simply copied down the prior hospitalization's information without inquiring anew, such that the original ambiguity was just repeated in perpetuity? Or was it Zigfrid himself who was unaware of his birthplace? Had no one told him the circumstances of his birth and upbringing? Might he have forgotten? Or possibly the question, "Country of Origin?" implied a connection and bond with one place that Zigfrid had never possessed. Might the place of Zigfrid's birth be no country at all? Could it be some unidentifiable tract of land that had never claimed borders, a language or a government to call its own? Some *terra incognita* that forever nurtured an identity crisis in its children.

The squeaking wheels of an occupied stretcher being pushed down the hall from the elevator by an aide prompted Asher to look up in time to identify the stretcher's occupant by the deep shade of yellow of the arm, hanging limply down as it passed by, like a flag in a parade. And had he any doubt, the white, sheet-covered dome of Zig's distended abdomen rose skyward like a biosphere. With the chart splayed out before him and what was left of Zig's life rolling by, Asher promised to find answers to those questions and, perhaps, a litany of others.

*

That night, after barely making eye contact with Mandy over dinner, Asher again retreated to his study. The girls were at a birthday party of a friend. He knew the excuse of being paged to call back a patient was transparent to Mandy. Yet she acceded without complaint. Asher also knew Mandy was troubled by his behavior, and biding her time before she would become impatient with him. But he was drawn toward his desk in the study where Zig's musty, cracked briefcase lay. Asher sat down across the room staring at the bulging briefcase, its latch unsnapped, allowing a clear view of several hundred yellowed, dog-eared pages. A full moon outside sent a beamed spotlight through the window, landing directly on the briefcase, rendering it luminescent, almost incendiary. Finally, with the sudden memory of the first time he had taken scalpel to flesh, he rose and split open the case, the pages bleeding out.

UZ ŠĪS ZEMES ES ESMU TRĪSKĀRŠI DZIĻŠ

Uz šīs zemes es esmu trīskārši dziļš. On this earth, I am three deep.
I am me in the here and now—my present self. I am me as I once
was—time spent and time lost. Third, I am me as I will too soon
be—destined for a future I can well surmise.

I am neither philosopher nor metaphysician. How could I be
either, raised successively on three languages, unable to tap my own
subconscious, much less that of others? Moreover, I am split from my
own body—the healthy always at war with the diseased, the diseased
now barely staving off the immortal.

My homeland likewise is thrice rent. Sited with a geographic
destiny more compelling than race, character, or sentiment. As it is
with a lamb born in a lion's den, the irrevocable accident of my
home's situation has sealed its history for all time. Trapped as it has
been, as it is at present, and as it may be forever. Tossed between two
great and terrible forces like a child pitched between two adults in
a game where each despises the other and the child itself is a prize
only to be exploited. Or perhaps like a horse that each side claims
ownership of, uses for a time, until the other captures the creature
for his own—each party branding the horse's hide, leaving scars from
their whips, sapping the horse's energies, and draining its spirit.

But for brief times, between the folds of history, my land escaped
all outside influence and—eerily, tantalizingly—controlled its own
destiny. And that becomes the final curse, as well as the sole promise.
Trapped between the ego of Russia and the mania of Germany, never
linked to either, at rare moments freed to imagine itself as it never
was allowed to be.

Latvija. Latvia. That name is its one constant. Throughout all
the turmoil of its history—through wars and famine and great shifts
of population and fortune—that solitary plot of orphan land has
maintained its name and identity. Refusing to yield this one claim
to individuality and autonomy. Linking that name to a distinct and
rich language and then to a unique folklore such that, when the three
combine, it forges a unity and a personality separating it from the

rest of humanity, allowing it a pride and a hope too enduring to be mere folly.

How to tell this tale? And moreover why tell it at all? Surely our suffering is not unique. Our turmoil and trauma has been duplicated or surpassed over the centuries by others. Even during my own lifetime, our distress pales when matched with others living right in our own backyard. Why repeat a tale that has been a dozen times told or can be found in the eyes and minds of countless suffering souls standing on any street corner you might choose?

And even more so why suffer my particular saga? Why, other than self-indulgence and grandiosity? Matched against millions of others in the same era, most would choose my fate in a heartbeat. Unparalleled torture and mayhem, sadism, and cruelty beyond belief—how to compare mere grief and pain against such a landscape? Can ordinary suffering have a place next door to cataclysm? When the prerogatives of millions are usurped by the indifference and disdain of the few, what weight can another body heaped on the pile of wasted flesh add?

Let me respond by relating an old Latvian parable my grandfather once told me. That day, must have been early 1943, he sat me on his lap, we were already several months since deported to Germany, displaced from our homes, separated from all we knew and loved; I just six years old. We had been transported there to live, not completely as prisoners, but certainly not as free people. We were treated at times like caged curiosities, at others like objects of derision and easy local scapegoats. But always—no matter how we were viewed by others—in our souls and our hearts, we carried a terror we could admit to no one, much less to ourselves.

I cannot be certain, yet I juxtapose these two events. I was in the schoolyard in second grade one day, only two or three months into my German experience. My German was weak and rudimentary. Class had not yet begun that day, so I lingered by the chain-link fence, clutching it as if I were truly a prisoner, not the student they pretended I was. I looked outwards through the fence, awaiting the arrival of my only friend in the school, also Latvian.

I suddenly became aware of the presence of several others in the corner of my vision. Turning, I found myself surrounded by a group of older, larger boys, maybe three or four of them, pointing at me and laughing. They were speaking German, pointing at my feet, asking me a question I could not decipher. Repeatedly they pointed at the wooden shoes I was forced to wear to school, ridiculing them. Finally, they must have grown tired of the game or maybe classes were to begin, for they turned to leave. Before moving on, however, the largest of the group, clenched his fist and struck me as hard as he could in the solar plexus. I doubled over, unable to move or breathe for minutes after.

When finally able to catch a breath, now on my knees, I glanced skyward, searching for a sign from heaven or maybe merely to bemoan my lot. I spotted high above and far off in the distance, a flock of small, dark birds appearing on the horizon. The birds quickly grew larger, approached, and roared louder and louder. Soon they began releasing ladders of arching metal toward earth, the ladders erupting into huge explosions upon hitting the ground. In the distance, I could see flames rising from buildings and smoke lilting skyward. In procession, the birds, trailing their ladders of metal and smoke and fire and noise, drew a path toward me as if I were their final destination. As if they were sent solely for me—either to rescue me or to destroy me, I could not tell.

And despite my desire to see and feel and know what was coming, I had to cover my head and my ears and hide from the knowledge. I had to cry like the helpless child I was and let whatever this onslaught was carry me away. Amazingly, when I uncovered myself minutes or possibly hours later, I was unchanged. I had not a scratch or a nick, not a smudge of dirt anywhere.

As I looked up, however, I saw that my school had been reduced to rubble. Small fires smoldered throughout the ruins. Strewn about were scorched and singed bodies. Screams reverberated in my ears. My teachers, my one friend, my torturers—had all vanished. And I alone was left, alive and abandoned.

When I reached home that night, I burrowed into my grandfather's lap. While I tried to hide from the reality of what I had witnessed, he told me the following tale. Did he recount the story to console me for the loss of my friend? Or to comfort me in my shame that I had been spared? Or to assuage my guilt, for I had wished for the destruction of my tormentors and that wish had been realized? Or, perhaps to explain all that was unexplainable? I know not. But throughout the years that followed, I have returned to this story as to a well—for solace, while attempting to fathom the unfathomable and for strength, to endure the unendurable.

As he has on every Saturday morning of his life, a country farmer awakens before dawn to bring his produce to market twenty miles away. He sets out in his cart pulled by his two beleaguered horses, his mind, as always now, fixated elsewhere. For the farmer spends all of his waking moments and much of his subconscious life dwelling on the loss of his wife and children. The year before, his family (his wife and four children) had been taken from him within a week of each other, all victims of an outbreak of dysentery. For the last year, he has lived in a fog, trapped in a nightmare—tending to his crops, going about his business—but his unjustifiable loss never for a moment left his mind.

As the farmer heads down the rutted road on wooden wheels, the horses rotely leading, he is shaken from his reverie by a sight some twenty yards ahead. The horses instinctively pull up beside a heaped-up pile of fur that the farmer now recognizes as a dead lamb laying by the road. Climbing down to inspect the lamb, the farmer notes a huge gash in its skull. However, as he searches the scene, he can find no offending instrument—no rock or tree branch—that might have caused such an injury. Thus, to the farmer, the death of the lamb seems almost supernatural. He slowly climbs back onto his cart, again overcome by the mystery of a universe that eradicates life on a whim.

All the way to the market, while quickly discharging his produce, while barely picking at a snack of honeyed bread and coffee at the town's tavern, while heading back to his isolated farm, the farmer cannot remove the imprint of the lamb's shattered and exposed brain from his own.

Ahead of him, on the ride home, at the exact point on the road where the dead lamb had lain, the farmer again spots an object. This time the object is taller and more upright. To his amazement, the object seems to move. As he pulls alongside, standing at the exact spot where he had found the slaughtered lamb, the farmer sees, tethered to a stake in the ground a live, breathing, oblivious, grazing lamb. He searches around the empty pastures and hills, scanning the horizon to see who might be playing such cosmic tricks on him, but finds no one. Then, without hesitating, the farmer untethers the lamb from its stake. He leads the lamb over to his cart and hoists it onto the cart's wooden flatbed, then heads on home.

Somehow, the farmer sees the lamb as a message from above, reaffirming life. He reacts not with bitterness that the Lord has provided him with this mute animal as a poor substitute for the comfort of his loving wife and children. Instead, he recognizes that all tragedies and traumas are possible in the world. Anyone, anywhere, anytime may be struck. But all types of miracles are possible, too. And these miracles may not be the ones we chose or wish for, yet they exist. And from all that, the farmer took solace. He endured.

Es ari zagis tragedija. Es ari zagis brinums. *I too have seen tragedy. I too have seen miracles. And up until now, I too have endured.*

CHAPTER 15 ⸻

Instinctively, Asher latched onto Zig's scattered memoir as if it were the solitary raft in an endless ocean. He could not explain what he hoped to gain from this immersion, but the convolutions in the text itself and the machinations required to find time to attack his task only spurred him onward. Zig's random scribbled messages, his interspersed German and Latvian colloquialisms, the scattered conglomeration of images, dreams, and nightmares only made the challenge more real and immediate. Asher found himself thrust into an unplanned odyssey that absorbed his energy and even tested his sanity. The fact that the quest was undertaken in the warm confines of his home made the endeavor no less real and the threat no less immediate.

Had he been less absorbed, over the several weeks of his obsession, Asher might have noted Mandy's increasing frustration as he headed upstairs night after night directly after dinner. Into the second week, just as they were clearing the table, Stacie, the nine-year-old, tore into the house, hysterical after scraping her knee falling off her bike on the driveway. Asher barely glanced at the wound on her leg before sending her off with a pat on the head and the reassurance that it wasn't so bad and would heal in a few days, then retreated upstairs. Mandy said nothing to Asher, but instead followed their weeping daughter into the bathroom to comfort her.

However, the next night when Asher again headed upstairs, muttering an excuse, Mandy finally erupted. "You're going where to do what again? I don't think so, buster. We're not spending another night alone down here while you flee from the family and me, leaving me to wonder what is so much more vital upstairs than letting us know you still exist."

The suddenness of her outburst that night not only surprised Asher and the girls, but Mandy herself. To Mandy, Miles had been distracted and remote ever since their Disney cruise, and she now had little patience for him. She had spent the prior seven years out of the workforce, caring for the girls until they reached school age. Two months before, she had taken a job at the University Hospital pharmacy, half an hour away. She needed to resurrect her career; otherwise her training would have been for naught. But caring for house and kids in light of Miles' inconsistent schedule while maintaining a full-time job was more burdensome than she could have imagined.

Running every which way but where she herself wanted to go and feeling guilty about doing nothing well enough might sound like an *Oprah* episode, but it had become Mandy's reality. That very day, her supervisor had told her, since she was the most junior pharmacist on staff, that she would be required to work at the hospital every other Saturday for the next three months. Looking back on her contract, nothing spelled that possibility out; then again, nothing seemed to prohibit it. With just an ounce more provocation—noting the slight smirk on her tenured, doleful letch of a department head's face as he delivered the news—she might have smacked him. But neither that nor an appeal to the administration was going to circumvent this particular burden. She could take the added load, or leave the job altogether. It might have been OK for her husband to have a midlife crisis when she was less stressed. Right now, he could suck it up and give *her* some support for a while.

At Mandy's outburst, Asher quickly yielded. "Sure, no problem, hon. Didn't realize I was spending so much time up there. I'll hang out and help the kids with their homework." Mandy allowed herself to be mollified.

Later that same night, she woke after midnight to find her husband again among the missing. She wandered down the hall to the study where she found him kneeling on the floor, a single light illuminating shocks of his disheveled dark hair, the spill of yellowed pages erupting from Zig's cracked leather case and cascading in heaps around him. Mandy stood at the threshold, silently staring. Either her footsteps were so soft as to be undetectable, or Asher was so focused on his papers that he failed to sense her presence for some time.

Despite her frustration, a wellspring of emotion rose up in Mandy as if she were watching one of her kids babble to herself in her playpen. What was going on with Asher? Might she have to stand aside and let him work himself out of this funk? She was reluctant to accept such passivity without making some effort to breach the gap. Mandy took a deep breath and plunged ahead, trying the jibing route first. "In search of the Holy Grail, are we, bud?"

Asher jolted up. "Mandy! Didn't hear you standing there. The Holy Grail? Nope, not quite. Just can't make out a lot of this scrawl and confusion."

Mandy stepped forward. "Need some help? Looks like a mountain of muddle."

She crossed her arms and waited while that offer bounced around in Asher's head like a pinball that hits a few bright lights but ultimately scores little and rolls irretrievably into the recycle bin. He looked up from his kneeling position, surrounded by a thousand pages of barely decipherable text, aware that it was nearly two AM He had been at this pursuit for almost three hours. He saw himself now as Mandy must see him—hunkered down on the floor in sweats, holey socks, and a ripped T-shirt, his past-five o'clock shadow darkening rapidly in the dimly-lit room, poring over a mass of esoterica that had overtaken his real world.

Help? Asher pondered that question. Well, he sure had needed some help reading Zigfrid's scribbled messages, written over a five- or six-year period with no apparent temporal order in mind. Asher could have used a linguist, a decoder, a Baltic historian, and a semiologist all rolled into one. He might have hired the entire staff of the New York Public Library and kept them occupied for a month.

In spite of these obstacles, Asher had taken on his task with the intensity of a starving prospector digging for gold. He had divided the papers into sections, trying to establish some temporal order to Zig's fragmented messages. Hence, the seemingly random piles. Pages he could not categorize, he had taped up on the walls and bookcases to have at hand should he find the appropriate sequence. He had enlisted both Latvian and German native speakers from among his patients, sending them sporadic phrases or whole segments to translate. Surprisingly, when he was able to arrange the pages, sort through all the translations, ignore random scribbles on the side of pages, the story that emerged became coherent and compelling.

Asher had sought out help from these disparate sources, but Mandy's involvement would provide no such non-judgmental anonymity. He tossed around her offer in his head. She sure was organized enough, he thought. And she could probably make out Zig's scrawl a whole lot better than he could, having ample experience with his own hideous scribbles. Plus, she had a flair for languages. So why had he not already asked Mandy for her help?

Part of him was ashamed of his self-indulgence in spending hour after hour, night after night, holed up in his computer room, exploring cyberspace, the life of some distant, dying soul, and his own muddled psyche. And he suspected Mandy, as open as she seemed at the moment, might have already begun searching her address book for the number of a couple of shrinks they knew back at Bellevue.

Just the night before, the same night Stacie hurt her knee, around midnight, Emily, barely seven, had appeared at the threshold of his study. "Daddy, I'm scared," she said, her eyes half shut, the strap of her Pooh Bear nightgown hanging off one shoulder, clutching the stuffed zebra that had replaced Blinky. Asher looked up, ignorant of how he must have appeared to his seven-year-old daughter—holey socks and holey shirt, darkening beard, sinking in an ocean of papers.

He had pulled himself up with difficulty, unratcheting his locked knees, and picked her up. "Bad dream, honey?"

Emily wrapped her arms around his neck, clenched her legs around his waist, and pressed her smooth cheek against his sandpaper one, attaching herself to him like some parasitic alien life force. "No, daddy. Bad awake. I couldn't sleep."

"Something got you worried, Em?"

She nodded her head up and down slowly. "Daddy, are you going nuts, like Mommy says?"

Asher flinched. "Mommy said that? No, honey. I'm not going crazy. It's just that I'm working on a project that mommy doesn't quite understand." Then, as much to himself as to Emily, "Come to think on it, I'm not even sure I understand it myself. But it doesn't mean I'm going nuts. Just a little confused. I'm normal, like always. Everything will be fine, hon, I promise." And he gently placed Emily back in her bed, rubbing noses good night with her like always, but not mollifying her much and not convincing either of them he was even in the same galaxy as fine or normal.

So, as he looked up at Mandy the next night, he hesitated. "Crazy, I'm not," he thought. "But Mandy believing I'm going nuts might be better than what she'd think if she knew everything." He hadn't told her the truth about Tom and Irene, or his incredible behavior in the mortuary… was he ready to answer the flurry of questions and veiled accusations sure to follow? He thought not.

So, in an act of self-preservation and maybe cowardice, Asher merely shrugged and replied, "No, thanks anyway, Mand. I'm OK. I know this seems odd. But if I can just get through these papers, I know I'll be all right."

Sensing Mandy's disgust with that response, grasping at air, Asher tried to plea bargain. "Mand, do you remember a few years ago I missed the Valentine's Day dinner you made for me because I got stuck in the hospital. I walked in four hours late. Must have been the third year in a row I did the same thing on Valentine's Day."

"I remember, Miles. I vowed to myself you'd next get a home-cooked meal when termites learned to talk."

"Well, thanks for breaking that vow. But, before you stormed off to bed, I tried to give you a Valentine with that story I had written for you. You know, the one about Tao-Li, the inventor of fireworks whose one true love disappeared in a puff of smoke. You were so pissed, you took the Valentine and without even bothering to give it a glance, ripped it up and threw it in the trash, and then stormed off to bed. I spent the night pulling the pieces out of the garbage and taping them all together. The next morning, after you read the story, your eyes filled up with tears and you gave me a huge hug. That tear-stained, mutilated card is still in a shoebox in our closet somewhere, right?" Asher was emboldened by her reluctant nod. "Mand, trust me on this one. Sooner or later, I promise, I'll tape this torn heart back together again, too."

Mandy nodded her head again, then answered grudgingly. "OK, Miles. Maybe you'll learn one day, I'm here for you. All you have to do is ask. I'm here." Mandy once more retreated.

Asher stared at the vacant doorway. Mandy's shadow seemed to occupy the carpeted hallway long after it should have disappeared. In frustration with himself, and the world at large, Asher picked up Zantay's tattered, decaying briefcase and threw it against the wall, knocking an old tennis trophy off the bookcase. As he picked up the trophy, he spotted a small, dark, glinting object on the carpeted floor that had fallen out of the briefcase. Bending over to inspect the smooth, almond-sized article, he found himself examining a translucent, rust-colored stone. He held the luminescent object up to his desk lamp, watching the rays of refracted light prism through it, goldening the white walls. On further inspection, Asher found a small pinhole at the apex of the stone. Without thinking, Asher grabbed a spool of yellow thread from a desk drawer and deftly wove a double-strand through the hole. Then he placed the amulet around his bare neck and slid it inside his shirt. He headed back to the pile of papers on the floor, feeling, for once, more resolved, more purposeful.

MANS TĒVS

*If I have answered satisfactorily—at least in my own mind—why I
should exhume my distant self in order to record my history, I leave
still the question, why now? After fifty years, three lives, no external
provocation or pull from the past, why dredge the river of remnants
now? Why drain dry what life left me, pouring more tears into this
waterwell of sorrow?*

*Can it just be that I now have little left to lose? That—having
lost my livelihood to the state, my family to my stubbornness, my
health to the microbes, my youth to the jackals, my heritage to the
Huns, and finally, my soul to the deities—I have nothing left but my
memory. With no future ahead, can I only now sip from the past,
tasting the bitter and the bilious? Yet do I not also hope to recall some
of the sweet juices, the mellowed wine that at times filled my life? I
cannot know. At this juncture, I can only do.*

Un tagad es sākšu. *So let me begin.*

*When I was three or four, I learned a poem. For years afterward,
I replayed that poem in my head like a litany. Often, I tapped my
fingers on a desk or a table in time with the poem as if I were playing
the piano. Frequently I tapped on the wall while lying in my bed
at night to soothe myself to sleep, to empty my mind. Later on, I no
longer consciously recited the poem, merely tapping my fingers as if
the rhythm conjured up the words and calmed me. In Latvian, the
poem was thus:*

Es sēžu tētiņa krēslā.
Es lieku galvā tētiņa cepuri.
Tētiņa cepure ir ļoti liela.
Man trūkst tētiņa gudrības.

*I am sitting in my daddy's chair.
I am putting on my daddy's hat.
My daddy's hat is very large.
I lack my daddy's wisdom.*

Long after my mind's image of my father had faded, I retained my memory of his appearance only through a wallet-sized, cutout photograph I kept these many years. This picture of him, frozen in time as a young man, no older than my son now—a black cap resting on a shaved head, his eyes staring out boldly, dancing behind black-rimmed glasses, an unbearded, smooth face, and the bare hint of a smile curling his mouth upward—a disembodied image I attached to the huge torso fixed in my mind, with hands the size of my head. All composed a larger-than-life, mythic figure with maybe no connection to the reality. But even more than that aging, dog-eared photo, throughout all the intervening years, I clung to those few lines. Those stanzas became, for me, a litany and a prayer to a long-lost and unattainable god.

Many years later—before my health had fled, before I lost my bank, before my consumption—I returned to Latvia. I stood on the Riga Bridge overlooking the Daugava. It was mid-November and the chill of winter was cooling a darkening sky that threatened to yield a torrent of snow at any moment. Riga itself had little changed from my memory. Of course, my memory from age five was limited. Yet I still recalled the city's foreboding stone fortresses, the church spires piercing the air, and the statue, Minas, the sole monument to liberty that still exists now. Once again, Riga's flat, bleak landscape, buffeted by winds from off the gulf punished me. That wind, a tactile memory imprinted on me from a hundred generations past, again penetrated to my very core.

During my visit, fifty years after my father had been snatched away, I was most struck remembering all of the street names. When I was no more than three, after supper each evening, my father walked through the city with me resting atop his shoulders, feeling as if I towered above the stone edifices we passed. Each street we passed, my father would recite its name. Atop a green-painted pole at each corner rested a street sign my father hoisted me up to, lifting me high above his shoulders. I would touch the sign and try to read the letters he had identified for me on prior walks. Elizabetes Iela, Kalpara Iela, Raina Bulevara, *the Russian duo*—Turgenev Iela, Puskin Iela.

If I named them correctly, my father would reach up to my face and so gently stroke my cheek, a butterfly's wings might just as well have grazed them. Lifting me thus, caressing me thus, I felt his strength and gentleness at once, so that I believed he was the embodiment and essence of both.

Standing back on that Riga Bridge those many years later, staring down at the flowing river, the moment years before when I had escaped to that selfsame spot as a five-year-old flooded back to me. I could see that serious, dark-haired boy's reflection staring back up at me like a rebuke. A rebuke to the aging, self-satisfied adult I had become. A rebuke to the promise I had made to wait at that very spot as long as it might take until my father returned—to wait a lifetime, if that is what it would take. A rebuke to my sloth that allowed me to delay these fifty years until this moment to finally attempt to discover the fate of my father—mans tēvs.

*

That day long ago, when my father disappeared forever, I was sitting on the kitchen floor playing with matchboxes. Frequently alone, I would concoct elaborate games, using the collection of matchboxes my father kept to light his pipe. I often divided the boxes into three separate armies who defended positions, staged ground attacks, and conducted sudden strikes against the invading enemy. My preoccupation involved deploying the matchboxes throughout the kitchen in various states of armed readiness. Always the Latvian forces were overmatched, always seemingly helpless against the coming onslaught. Yet, the Latvians in grand and daring maneuvers outflanked the sluggish Germans or Russians or even both at once, always to emerge victorious. I could spend whole afternoons making the world safe for Latvia, orchestrating the defeat of the Huns.

That one Saturday in November 1941, on a day similarly bleak and gray as on my visit these many years later, a neighbor rushed up to our house and pounded on the door. I went to the doorway of our kitchen and saw our bearded neighbor, Janis, gesturing wildly, whispering at first, pointing out the door, then almost shouting for all to hear—maybe loud enough for the entire household, the neighbors, even the entire city to hear—that he had seen the Nazis march my father across the Riga Bridge not ten minutes before.

On hearing our neighbor's words, my mother became hysterical, inconsolable. No reasoning or comfort anyone could offer brought my mother solace. Such wailing continued unabated for the entire day. The sounds of my neighbor's shrill alarm, my mother's molten panic, my grandmother's shrieking, all collided inside my head, resounding for hours. I held my hands over my ears, buried my face under cushions, drummed my litany on the floor in vain, unable to quiet the roar.

Finally, unwilling to endure the tempest any longer, I decided to venture forward myself. Simply sitting inside weeping would not restore my father; prayer alone would not bring him back. What if he was lying wounded, bleeding on that bridge, unable to rise and return home? I would go discover him. I would rescue him and become a hero in the process.

I slipped out just at dusk, slinking down the stairs, turning the doorknob ever so slowly, trying to time the creak of the opening door with the heaving sobs of my mother. Escaping, then skulking through the city as I imagined spies would do, clinging to walls, jumping over shards of light, I was a boy on an adventure. I was unaware, though, of the real danger lurking everywhere—Nazi soldiers, only recently in possession of our homeland, marched all over the city. I learned later they had no qualms about shooting children at will, as an example of their iron fist.

Excited, heart pounding, fearful yet exhilarated, I ran through the dark streets and alleys until I approached the rushing engine of the swollen Daugava. I was familiar with the river, having gone fishing a dozen times with my father and my cousin. On these outings, my task had been to break the worms and carefully pierce their rust-colored bodies with the sharp hooks. I was the supply officer for the assembly line of fishing—my cousin, Stanis, would take the hook and attach it to the line—my father and he fished while I searched for more worms. Eventually after a successful catch, I would grab the still-writhing fish and smack him over the head with a mallet, then place him in our wire basket, while the river water formed puddles on the ground beneath. That past spring, my father had given me my first fishing pole for my fifth birthday. This was my greatest thrill. From then on, I was not just the wormer or the pounder but, with everyone else, took turns fishing and pounding and worming. And I was just as they were, a man.

I was not always so bold. I recall the first time my father took me fishing. At the first fish he caught, he made a demonstration. He brought me to the side of the river and told me to hold the fish in my hand. With the fish still alive and squirming in my grasp, he took his knife and severed the fish's head. Blood poured onto my hands, but I was obliged to hold the now-still body. My father then sliced lengthwise down the fish and reached his hand into the cavity, pulling out a fistful of black roe. He licked the roe from his slimy fingers stating, "Fresh fish roe—nothing in Latvia finer." Then he offered me some; I resisted. He held my head still with his powerful hands and forced me to lick the black and red briny mess from his fingers. "Beidz raudāt!" "Stop your crying," he told me, "You will grow to love this as all true Latvian men do." But he was wrong. Never again could I look at the prized black caviar native to my homeland without recalling the black and red slime my father made me swallow as a four-year-old and without the taste of the salty mixture of roe mixed with blood and my own tears once again burning my tongue.

But on that day of his abduction, in search of my father, the sound of the flowing river coupled with the fading light held little fear for me. My wooden-heeled shoes clacked against the cobblestone street as I approached the bridge. Quickly, though, that sound multiplied times fifty. I believed my ears were playing tricks on me. Soon I realized the clatter arose from a troop of marching Nazi soldiers, heading over the bridge directly toward me. I had only a second to jump down an embankment beside the bridge and hold my breath while they passed, my heart now pounding in rhythm to the march, my fingers playing out my poem on the wet grass beneath me. I held fast in my position for more than an hour, afraid that at any moment another troop of fierce, armed soldiers would approach. I waited while the last light of day faded, till I was sure the darkness would afford me enough cover. Then I slowly stood up, ready to search for my father, now merely a frightened, solitary boy desperate for his dad.

I sneaked silently back up the cobblestone path, hugging the side of the stonewalled bridge. My eyes, now accustomed to the darkness, sought out every nuance and shadow on the bridge, trying to see if my father was similarly hiding out, perhaps also afraid to venture from his own cover. I dared to whisper aloud several times, hissing out 'tētiņa, tētiņa' sure that the words would make him appear, just as 'abra cadabra' had done in the magic show I had seen that summer in the park. My words merely bounced against the bridge's stone walls and echoed back in mockery. All of a sudden, I became aware of a host of other night sounds—the owl's hoot, the roar of a distant train, an occasional shout in the distance; one time I was sure I heard a flurry of gunfire. Fear rose up inside me like a flame. As if I myself was on fire, my impulse was to run, to run anywhere, to submerge myself in some blanket of comfort, to escape.

But instead I held fast. I clutched at the stone wall as if it were my mother's apron skirt, holding tight to my hope and to my mission. There, I must have fallen asleep. At the base of the bridge, clinging to a pillar, curled up in a stone enclave, I must have slept for hours. For when I woke with a start to the sound of a horse-drawn cart clambering over the stones, the first light of dawn had broken.

A whispering, gray fog rose up from the river like a creeping shadow that shrouded the world, so I could see my hand stretched out before me but nothing else. The stranglehold of fear grabbed back at my throat. Even at five, I realized I had failed. But more so, I was now trapped in some otherworld—a world I had seen in a picture book where gnomes rose up from the steam of the earth and snatched little boys, bringing them underground for a feast. This time I did run. I ran with a pounding in my head and a fist in my heart and a fear that I possibly have never lost. How I ended up home in my bed later that night I do not recall.

*

Common it may have been in that era to have a loved one disappear, never to be seen or heard from again. For my mother, though, and for my father's parents who lived with us, the event was cataclysmic. One month later, my mother still had not made my father's side of the bed or touched his pillow so as not to mar the impression of his body. My father was the center of our universe, a man of uncommon abilities and strength. He could repair virtually anything—broken engines, radios, wounds, ruptured emotions. As his parents described him to me in my youth, my father held almost mythic abilities. His calmness in the face of distress, his stoicism in case of pain, all contributed to an image I carried of him that colored how I saw the world. If such a man could be snatched and vanish from the earth, then nothing was permanent, nothing could be trusted.

Over the years, my solitary mission to rescue my father took on larger-than-life proportions within our family lore. When I recounted the tale of my quest, perhaps embellished by a child's imaginings, my family soon replaced their anger with awe. I became my father's anointed successor, destined to perform acts of courage and strength just as he had. The episode spawned iterations and reiterations through the family tree that, with embellishment, had me circumventing legions of Nazi soldiers, nearly rescuing my father along with scores of other persecuted Latvians. I did nothing to inform the rest of the family of their misperceptions. Why would I, when I was given a respect and rank no prior youth had ever been accorded within my family circle?

However, my mother's reaction was much different. She held no illusions about my courage. Over the next five years, through uncounted trials and traumas—through fearful train rides in the night, through narrow escapes down unlit streets, repeated losses of our home and possessions, poverty and hunger, sickness and sorrow— my mother never again treated me the same. For those next years, she never hugged me, never clutched me to her breast, sharing our fears. Never tousled my hair just to feel her fingers run through the locks, never spoon-fed me early tastes of her flanken soup to tell her if it was just right or if it needed a dash of salt or a pinch more fennel. She never again came into my room in the night to recite from her storehouse of Latvian fables, memorized from her own mother and grandmother; she never in her lilting high-pitched voice sang the folk songs of her youth.

The night when I returned home, I remember finally being safely tucked into my bed, my parched tongue moistened by drink, my empty belly sated, almost drifting off to sleep. My mother tiptoed into my room and stroked my forehead. Over and over she chanted, my eyelids fluttering in time to her words, "You were dead to me, you were dead to me." I drifted off to sleep. I was dead to her. But she never followed those words with "And now you have come back alive."

I always wondered after if something had snapped inside her. Somehow that day she had mourned for the loss of her husband. Perhaps she had accepted the truth that she would never see him again. When she found out I was missing, she must have mourned for the loss of her only child, even though he returned to her less than twenty-four hours later. But during those twenty-four hours, she may have walked through the stages of grief for me too. Maybe she could not bear to grieve more than once. Maybe her sorrow overcame her love. Maybe she went a little insane.

After that episode, I recall my mother staring at a framed picture of me at age two that she kept on her bedroom dresser. Often, even when I was sitting on the floor not five feet from her, doing a puzzle or playing with my figures, I would hear her exclaim, clutching the picture to her chest, "Tas Zigrīds, kāds gan skaists bērniņš viņš bija." That Zigfrid, what a beautiful baby he was." As if the real thing right next to her was invisible—a figment. Perhaps she was correct. Part of me was forever lost that day.

Finally, standing on the bridge in Riga, those many years later, I vowed to recapture that missing piece, to resurrect my quest, and, at last discover the fate of mans tēvs, my father.

CHAPTER 16 ─────────────────

Asher was halfway through his final year of residency when his director called him into his office to tell him that his father had died. Asher had been looking through the teaching head of a colonoscope while the attending gastroenterologist was removing a malignant polyp from a seventy-six-year old's intestine when his beeper went off, telling him to head to his director's office "stat." Asher knew this summons could not be trivial. In his three years as a resident, he had never before been similarly beckoned.

As if he were in high school being called to the principal's office, Asher sorted through situations that might prompt such a request. He thought about the patient the week before who'd required hospitalization after his biopsy site would not stop bleeding during one of Asher's first solo colonscopies. But Asher rationalized, virtually every gastroenterologist he knew had similar difficulties, that the patient had recovered uneventfully, and the mistake was unlikely to have earned a formal reprimand. He wondered about the incident several weeks earlier, when a radiation oncologist had left their mutual patient on a slab-like stretcher for an hour in his cold waiting room. The oncologist had been really pissed when he overheard Asher ask the patient if he was getting "the proverbial runaround." That comment might have prompted the oncologist to go to the top to protest. Even though Asher was in the residency version of senior slide, he hated to have any further demerits that would surely wend their way back to his father's desk.

When Asher arrived at Dr. Lorenson's office, the secretary simply said, "Please, Dr. Asher, go right in. Dr. Lorenson is expecting you." Her lingering, sad-eyed stare made him wonder more broadly what this meeting might be about.

Dr. Lorenson pulled open the door before Asher could gird himself any further. "Come in, Miles. Come, sit down. Sorry to have to pull you out of your procedure like this. But I could not allow this to wait." Since Dr. Lorenson had never before called him Miles—it was either "Dr. Asher" when he was trying to be collegial or "Asher" when he was upset—Asher's antennae were further raised.

Physicians have to deliver bad news to their patients often enough that they develop an individual style. Some deliver the news cloaked in a barrage of information detailing the steps that led up to the final verdict, the subsequent implications, therapy, and prognosis, all wrapped up in medical jargon. As a result, patients might come away with some appreciation of the complexity of their case, but no emotional connection. Other physicians will drop the bomb straight out—"I'm sorry. You have terminal cancer. Therapy will not help much." Still others will evince such empathy, emote so intensely, the patient might find it difficult to tell who is suffering more, his doctor or himself.

Maybe being a residency director limited Lorenson's personal experience in such matters, since his technique most resembled the last. Even this method he botched. "I cannot tell you how sorry I am to have to tell you this, Miles. Life at times delivers unexpected, undeserved blows to each of us, testing our mettle and our resolve. I myself have been victimized by similar circumstances and have endured. My own child only just out of infancy, the victim of a terrible accident. Still, seven years later, my wife and I have barely recovered. To have to be the bearer of such a horrible verdict such as the one I am about to tell you unearths all of those terrible feelings I myself have suffered and brings tears to my own eyes."

The entire time Dr. Lorenson gave this uninformative speech, he stared not at Asher but rather into the ceramic coffee cup advertising Paxil that was nestled in his palms, as if the grounds at the bottom contained a teleprompter scrolling his lines. Asher could not believe such a preamble was necessary. But the pounding that had begun inside his head shut out any rational sense of what was acceptable and what not.

Finally, Dr. Lorenson came to the point. "Let me not beat around the bush any longer, Miles. I really do not know how to say this any plainer. There has been a terrible accident. Your father—your superb model of a father, an example to all of a committed, involved, admirable life, your personal icon and an icon to all physicians everywhere—has met with a horrendous tragedy. Such a vibrant unquenchable spirit, I know this seems impossible. This morning, on his way to work, your father fell onto the train tracks and was struck by a Metro North commuter train and killed instantly. I am sorry to tell you, Miles, your father has died."

And with those words, tears began streaming down Dr. Lorenson's face. He rose from behind his desk and picked Asher up from his seat to embrace him in a bear hug from which Asher could not escape. So astonished and uncomfortable was Asher, he had no ability to react. His mind was a roaring tunnel of non-thought.

After several moments in that awkward embrace, Asher was able to extricate himself and backed away toward the door. In his haste, he backed right into the doorknob, which struck him squarely on his right kidney, doubling him over and, in the next few days, producing an almost perfectly circular bruise and some transient hematuria. Bent over in pain, Asher was barely able to open the door and hobble out of the office, ignoring Dr. Lorenson's pleas to wait while they both could digest such news and also ignoring the secretary who stood up at attention and clutched at Asher to offer her condolences as he rushed by. Asher was not about to be stopped. He wanted out as fast as he could.

Finding the nearest men's room, Asher locked the door behind him. He drenched his face in ice-cold water, then soaked his head, trying to freeze his thoughts and the now-insistent drumbeat that had replaced them. He stared in the mirror at his wild hair and his crazed, distorted facial expression, wondering who this creature staring back was. He brought clenched fists to his eyes, first to shut out his own image and then to halt the flow of tears.

While leaning over, Asher's reflex hammer fell out of his pocket into the sink. He stared at the heavy, silver-plated, engraved hammer for a moment before picking it up. He reread the inscription engraved on the handle, one he must have read forty times when he first received the gift at his graduation from med school but had ignored ever since. "Miles, Sorry I could not be at your graduation. Congratulations. Your Father."

Asher could recall verbatim his father's explanation during a broken phone call from across the ocean the night before graduation. "I know you understand, son. Being the keynote speaker at the International Society of Ophthalmology meeting in Brussels is a once-in-a-lifetime opportunity. We'll celebrate when your mother and I return in a few weeks." On opening his gift, eating dinner alone on graduation night, Asher was not amused by the note his father had attached titling his gift "Miles' Silver Hammer." Asher had resisted tossing the hammer into the garbage.

This time, tears clouding his vision, resentment and grief clouding his judgment, disgusted by the wild-eyed image staring back at him, Asher flung the hammer at himself, shattering the mirror, shattering his reflection, but failing to shatter his now-permanent, glassed-wall cell of regret.

*

Asher spent the next week sleepwalking through a fog of mourning rituals, through funeral arrangements, through his mother's and sister's shared hysteria, through a thousand condolence calls, through a standing-room only funeral, and finally through a week of sitting Shiva, with barely a memory of any of it. He *did* retain the information that, while rushing to catch the 9:12 train at the Dobbs Ferry station, his father had tripped and fallen directly into the path of the onrushing train. He had been killed instantly. Asher and the family had all chosen not to look at what they imagined was the unsuccessfully reconstructed, shattered remains of their loved one lying in his casket. Asher never asked his mother why his father had taken a train leaving two hours later than the one he had taken for the previous thirty years.

Asher's only other indelible memory of those days was from day five after his father's funeral. Asher's mother had asked him to wake up early that morning because Sol Kaplan, the insurance agent who handled his father's life insurance policy, wanted to speak with him. He had already spoken with his sister Becky and his mother while Asher was making funeral arrangements. In response to Asher's questioning look, his mother commented that it was just a formality.

The next morning, before nine, Asher awoke to the sound of the doorbell ringing. By the time he washed up, threw on a sweatshirt and jeans and headed downstairs, Mr. Kaplan and his mother were already sitting at the kitchen table, having a cup of coffee. Asher recognized Mr. Kaplan from seeing him at synagogue on high holy days, but up until then had had no idea what he did for a living. Mr. Kaplan rose to offer his condolences. After Mrs. Asher excused herself, the two men sat down at the butcher-block kitchen table with Mr. Kaplan's large manila folder—presumably a file about Asher's dad—resting between them. He opened the folder and spent at least five minutes silently looking through the papers, often shaking his head back and forth. Then he began asking questions without explaining exactly what he was after. "Miles, do you mind if I call you Miles instead of Dr. Asher?"

"No, sure. Dr. Asher's my dad. Or at least *was* my dad. But, anyway, go ahead."

"Miles, had you noted anything unusual in how your dad seemed to be feeling or acting of late? Had he been down in the dumps at all? Had he been less interested in his work?"

"Well, Mr. Kaplan, you know I've been pretty well immersed in my residency and planning for next year and the wedding and all. I don't live at home at all and have seen my dad for maybe two days out of the past sixty. But no, he seemed fine. My mother would know better." Asher felt his synapses start to fire. "Why are you asking? What are you implying? This was an accident. My dad sprained his ankle a few weeks before. He was on crutches and stumbled onto the train tracks. What more do you need to know?"

Mr. Kaplan pulled a handkerchief out of his back pocket and began to mop his brow. "Yes, yes, I know. This is merely a formality. But the home office insists on these questions being answered. I volunteered to ask these questions as a friend of the family. I know if they sent some stranger, he would not understand. Please forgive me. But I just have a few more."

Asher grudgingly nodded his assent. Kaplan rushed onward then, the impetus of a lifetime of such inquiries spurring him. "Do you know what medication your dad was taking for his Parkinson's disease? Did he tell you how he felt about not being able to operate any longer?" Kaplan continued despite the rising voltage Asher was giving off. "Were you aware your dad had two multimillion-dollar malpractice suits pending?"

Asher was too taken aback to even sputter a reply. Parkinson's? How had he missed that one? Asher *had* noticed a slight tremor last time they were together, but it was so subtle that it seemed inconsequential. Then he recalled a few months back, during the entire evening of their last dinner out as a family, his dad keeping his left hand in his pocket. Plus, he was an ophthalmologist. No tremor is inconsequential when it comes to eye surgery. What kind of observant doctor was Asher supposed to be? Thoughts began to click together and link in ways totally unacceptable.

His ire rose in response. "Look, Mr. Kaplan. I know nothing of what you're talking about. My dad was in fine shape. And if he couldn't operate, that would have been OK with him. He ran a hospital. He taught students. He had paid his dues for thirty years, operating on anyone who came his way, rich or poor. Every eye surgeon has to hang up his scalpel sooner or later. My dad knew that. And doctors get sued all the time. Especially world-famous eye surgeons. They're like sitting ducks for the scumbag lawyers. Do me a favor and take your routine questions and your sly insinuations back to your home office and shove them up your boss' ass."

That ended the conversation and any further inquiries. But Asher was not about to calm down. After slamming the door shut on Mr. Kaplan, Asher took off after his mother. "Mom, what the hell is going on here? Did you hear what this guy was asking? What he's insinuating? That dad offed himself? And why didn't either of you tell me about some of this stuff. About his Parkinson's and his operating and all. How could you keep all this from me?"

Asher's weary mother tried to placate him. "Calm down, Miles. I know Sol was forced to ask those questions. Insurance companies, you must know by now, hate to part with their money. He reassured me everything would be fine. And the Parkinson's was just a slight tremor. Your dad was planning to stop operating soon anyway. He was over sixty. We're at our wits' end with your father going like this, Miles. Please stay strong for all of our sakes." With that his mother began to sob uncontrollably again. Which, at the time, was enough to shut Asher up.

A few months later his mother called to tell Asher that the insurance company had paid out on his father's policy. There had been no further questions or insinuations. Asher felt then and for the ensuing nine years that the case was closed. He dismissed any absurd thoughts of his father being suicidal.

Not long after, Asher's mother told him that his father had discussed helping him finance his new practice. She was sending a check for fifty thousand dollars right off to him. But based on that conversation with his father just before his death, Asher knew this was not true. He politely declined. "I have financing arranged, Mom. Don't worry about me. Use that money to start a new life for yourself." Asher hoped—with his move to Connecticut, his new practice, and his impending marriage—he would be able to do the same.

DZINTARS

What defines a people? What unique blend of characteristics—physical traits, language, culture, history, bonds and pride—allows a disparate group to stand before the world and proclaim in one voice its identity? What compels the world to listen and give credence to its plea, to allocate precious turf to its cause, to permit that group voice and sway in the conduct of its own business and in the business of other nations?

Throughout history, force and military might have been the arbiters of that debate. Cultures and peoples did not request control over their land and destiny; they seized it. In lands not fortunate enough to reside in remote geographies, not bounded and protected naturally by oceans or mountains or vast expanses of unpopulated territory, the rule of sovereignty has forever been defined by the rule of might.

Only in recent times has the world coalesced enough to allow politics and influence, autonomy and moral righteousness to enter into these decisions. Therefore, in result, Israel is born from the will of a group of men in discussion and debate inside a building in New York five thousand miles away. Halfway around the world, an assembly of politicians decides the thirty-ninth parallel ought to divide a formerly unified country.

Even more magically, seven states secede with the world's blessings from their Russian jailer with nary a bullet fired or a body wounded. On August 23, 1989, one million Estonians, Latvians, and Lithuanians literally joined hands from Tallinn through Riga to Vilnius. Throughout the city centers of eastern Europe, cranes operated by workers and students and government officials alike removed huge statues of Lenin, tying metal-cable nooses around his neck and consigning him to oblivion.

So, miraculously, unexpectedly, unceremoniously, Latvians were set free. Liberated. Freed to make our own destiny and charter our own course. Yet we remain ever wary; for we know whatever the force of politics and pressure can birth, those same forces can as easily destroy. What mankind for the present makes sense, can, in an instant, be made non-sense. We know in our hearts that the rule of right may again be usurped by the rule of might. But for now, we bask in the sunlight of our days and in the glow of our full moon, hoping against hope we will not again be eclipsed by the huge planets in our geographic solar system. Such was not always the case.

In antiquity, we had one defining resource. Our people valued one prize, birthed in our homeland, above all others. We had sparse arable land, few native game, and the barest comforts. However, one unique attraction drew both adventurers and opportunists to this barren, cold, landscape. That one prize—dzintars—amber.

The land itself held little magnetism—our flat plains and unfertile soil, the frigid unending winters, the Baltic winds, and glacier-packed swamps offered minimal competition to the warm Mediterranean sands to the south. My people's history traversed a circuitous path to arrive in such an unwelcoming tract. Harsh circumstances attracted a thick-skinned and likewise harsh settler. The initial visitors to Latvia—an area bounded on the north by the Gulf of Finland, to the east by Lake Pskov and surrounding the Gulf of Riga—traveled a variety of routes. From the Urals, around 5000 BC, came the Ests, Livs and natives of Finland, the Ingrians. The Letts and the Lithunians came from White Russia around 2000 BC; the Kurs and the Sels likely migrated from as far away as India. This conglomeration of peoples and cultures lived in apparent harmony and isolation for three thousand years with that sole attraction— dzintars.

Later on, toward the end of the first millennium AD, the pull of commerce and religion brought a series of opportunists to the lands of the eastern Baltic. First, they hoped to find an easy access to the furs and pelts from interior Russia. German fur traders from Lubeck poured into the area then termed Livland. These traders, like Germans throughout history, imprinted on the land and the architecture the stamp of Teutonic culture. To this day, the architecture of Riga, Danzig, and Stettin mimics the high towering church spires and gabled merchant houses that prevail in Lubeck, the German capital farther west down the Baltic coast.

Early in the second millennium AD, the Catholic church began to exercise its expansionist inclinations. As with the Crusades to the south and east, the Church seized any opportunity to purify souls, this time focusing on the heathens in northern Europe. What often began as a peaceful desire to convert the uninitiated, when met with resistance, soon became a religious battlefield. In 1199 AD, with the support of Pope Innocent III, Albert von Buxhoveden, a German bishop, led twenty-three vessels, each carrying one hundred knights, to Livland. His charge was to inspire or, if necessary, impel the resident heathens, who worshiped dozens of gods, to acknowledge the one true God. In a pattern to be replicated dozens of times over the next millennium throughout the civilized world, the Teutonic invaders, this time with the cause of religious purity propelling them, embarked on the Drang nach Osten—*the push to the east. Their ferocity of purpose, their murderous exploits, their* Furor Teutonicus *resounded in the land for centuries after. This invasion established Germanic dominance on the soils of the Baltics, building feudal fiefdoms that endured for the next eight hundred years.*

In 1201 AD, Bishop Albert founded Riga and was proclaimed by the Pope, "Reichsfurst"—Prince of the Holy Roman Empire. The precedent for German domination and self-proclaimed moral superiority had been set. My homeland and the world would never again be the same.

These conflicts, played out in the legends and tales passed down from generation to generation, are still the source of much Latvian culture today. Our prototypical Latvian epic, Lacpelsis, the Bear Slayer, tells the story of an invincible hero who journeyed throughout northern Europe to battle foreign forces, only to be defeated when the German Black Knight cut off his ears, rendering him powerless.

However, before the practical horrors of trade and religion branded their imprint on the landscape of my homeland, one object of beauty—unique, unblemished and unsullied by corruption— dzintars—drew thousands to the region. One value we trade and treasure to this day. What the Greeks called rays of sunset or hardened tears, produced from millions of years of nature perfecting the fossilized resin from trees. These brilliant, smooth stones of yellow-brown, polished through the ages, were claimed to be possessed by mythic spirits and imbued with powers to heal and nurture. The ancient Greeks made necklaces of the "stone of the sun." Roman ladies carried it to cool their hands. In the 1600s, amber was used to treat coughs, nosebleeds, gonorrhea and even hysteria. An object like none other—durable, irreplaceable, undeniable—a reflection of the people who cherished it.

I myself have preserved an example of that rare item, passed down through the centuries and then miraculously rescued by me during the war. Through research I have come to realize the vital role this amber jewel has played in my ancestry. My mother told me her own mother told her that her own mother claimed that this red-brown amber jewel I now hold in my hand has been passed down over ten generations. Its smooth, curved edge outlined a likeness of the profile of my grandfather ten times removed—Andrejs Vajeiks. How much credence to lend the tales surrounding this stone, I cannot tell after hundreds of years of oral history. The mere fact of the tale's endurance and the existence of my amber amulet is sufficient for me to record the legend.

My ancestor Andrejs Vajeiks' family lived and worked the same plot of land just south of Riga on the banks of the Ogre for nearly two hundred years. They survived as serfs on the estate of Hofzumberge under a series of German barons in the von der Pahlen lineage. The barons were a long line of autocrats, ruling their fiefdoms in manners ranging from casual indifference to benign paternalism, though often extending to sadistic slavery. The Baron Peter von der Pahlen evidently fell into the latter category.

Just barely past his teens, Andrejs had married a flaxen-haired beauty from a neighboring farm named Natalie Kuiva, whom he had coveted from childhood. With the idealism of youth, they had roamed the fields hand-in-hand, fallen in love, then married and settled down together. After celebrating the birth of their first son, they should have suspected their idyllic life could not be sustained in such harsh and hostile circumstances.

During his reign, the Baron Peter had exercised his prerogatives on a series of peasant women throughout his fiefdom. As a matter of course, the Baron would have heard of the lovely, fair-haired young woman residing in his domain and, though purportedly over sixty at the time, he showed no sign of abandoning that venal course of behavior. When the Baron sent out a representative to the Vajeiks' household to bring Natalie to his household as a servant, the soldier met Andrejs' unyielding resistance.

However, resistance in those days was not an option for a peasant. Soon after, the Baron sent ten "representatives" to accomplish the task. Andrejs was prepared this time with his cousin, several pitchforks, and a knife; but their efforts were futile, and resulted in Andrejs' quick demise. Natalie was spared to service the Baron. Their son, Rudolfs, after whom my father was named, was also spared, though forced to live with a neighboring family until Natalie was used up and released. This pitiable story permeated our multi-generational consciousness like a red stain on the family quilt, forever sealing our hatred of the Germans.

Over the years, I have imagined this scene dozens of times in my own head.

I imagine Andrejs, a tall, strapping, black-haired man just blossoming into adulthood, his dark hair and darker eyes flashing in the wind as he waits outside his front door for the cadre of soldiers on horseback. He has heard their hoof beats maybe five minutes in advance, but has known for the prior three days, since the first messenger left, that more would soon follow. He has listened stoically and unyieldingly to the pleas of his wife, that he release her to live at the manor house for however long it takes for the Baron to tire of her. She is sure that this course is their only option for resuming a normal life at some point in the future. But Andrejs will consider none of that.

Andrejs' cousin, Artis—shorter, squatter, and more powerful— has volunteered to help, knowing if one household in the fiefdom can be pillaged, all can be. They stand outside Andrejs' doorway brandishing their rusted weapons, while inside Natalie pleads with them. Ten soldiers ride up the rocky path to the Vajeik's two-room stone farmhouse and slowly come to a stop when they spot Andrejs and Artis. A smile comes over the armored leader of the band as he surveys the situation. He has had dozens of similar encounters, dispatched by the Baron as his enforcer. Most are routine, boring, and distasteful events with a pathetic husband sobbing inside the home while his whimpering wife succumbs dutifully to her fate. The knight himself is forbidden to indulge in the wife's favors until he returns her used, many months later. At least, he can take some modicum of pleasure imagining that encounter further down the road.

But what the knight truly anticipates with gusto is the odd heathen who refuses to yield so easily, who puts up a fight for his honor and the honor of his wife. That's when the knight's special training and unique talents reach fruition. For this knight was not chosen as a vehicle of transport, but as a messenger of mayhem. He has been selected not only to fulfill his mission with purpose and speed, but also to convey to his victim the foolhardiness of his chosen course and to warn any other like-minded peasant the price paid for insubordination.

The knight stands for a moment in front of the determined duo, gathers himself, then erupts. He nods his head slightly and a second knight in back rides between the two men on the ground, separating them. Almost at the same instant, the leader raises his sword and in one swipe decapitates Artis. Blood spurts, a head rolls, hysterical screams from Natalie fill the air. If Andrejs has second thoughts or appreciates the helplessness of his position, it does not deter him. In a swift lunge, he drives his pitchfork into the chest of the horse holding the second knight. Horse and rider tumble to the ground and Andrejs in one second slices the knight's throat before the rest are upon him and in control.

For control is just their aim at this point. Now, they have no need for haste or dispatch. Andrejs is theirs to do with what they choose. And what they choose to do—with Natalie standing in the entryway, clutching her infant son in horrified hysteria, pleading for mercy—is to each take a slice. They tie Andrejs to stakes in the ground, then in single-file line up and, with their steel-handled knives, each takes a cut. First a toe, then a finger, the next a foot, a hand follows—each slice so deft and practiced they may have created an art form. The second-to-last knight makes great ceremony out of castrating Andrejs, but gets no screams as reward from the unresponsive youth, only a bloody sack to hold to the sky in triumph. The leader then removes his cape to prevent blood from sullying it and, almost bored now, lops off Andrejs' head. He then places it atop the pitchfork he has planted vertically in the earth.

As he rides off with the now-unconscious Natalie slumped over his horse, the captain directs another knight to inform a neighbor to come collect the babe. He orders the peasantry to leave Andrejs' head in place for a fortnight or the rest will suffer a similar fate.

Maybe I am too morbid in imagining this scene. Maybe its accuracy is suspect. Or maybe the hatred, nurtured through my youth, had a Jungian precursor housed in my unconscious, harboring such a scene. But regardless, thus birthed my people's contempt and revulsion for the Germans. A universal revulsion that makes my father's ultimate capitulation all the more inexplicable.

CHAPTER 17 —————————————————

Spending another night entrenched in his study, Asher once more held the smooth, golden gem in the palm of his hand, inspecting it in a new light. He raised it up to the moonlight shining through the window to watch the refracted, yellow rays scatter off the stone, gilding the desktop and white walls. Gently holding the amulet between thumb and forefinger, he moved it about, allowing the sunlight to scatter through its prism and break into golden streaks. He pill-rolled the fluid gem no larger than an eyeball between his fingers, flattening his fingertips until they too felt like glass. Then, he rubbed the stone between his palms, half-expecting a genie to pop out, ready and willing to grant him three wishes.

One more time, Asher held the stone up to the light, rotating it until he could identify the outline of what might be inferred as a profile. A straight forehead, strong nose, just indented mouth and square chin could be construed from the topography of the stone. Linking this image with that of a long dead, persecuted eastern European, Asher left to the imagination of others.

Asher walked to the bathroom and stared at himself in the bright light reflecting off the mirror. Who was this unfamiliar person now sporting an ancient talisman on his bare chest? Was he honoring the past, the sacrifices of history's martyrs? Was he some dislocated soul, hoping to latch onto a history and a past he could not claim? Or was he merely an interloper, treading on hallowed ground he had no right to occupy?

*

The next day, Sunday, during lunch—on one of Asher's brief interludes outside his study—Mandy noted the new ornament around his neck. "You're sporting some jewelry?" she asked with a casual tone. "Haven't seen that around before."

Asher brought his hand to his neck. "This, you mean? It's kind of a good luck charm. No big deal. I found it at the bottom of that leather briefcase full of papers you wanted me to chuck. It's amber—must be hundreds of years old."

Asher paused, looking out on the horizon, focusing on some invisible point in the distance before he continued. "Hard to explain, but it gives me a sense of peace wearing it. Like I'm linked up to some greater history than my own feeble one. Did you know amber has been around for a million years? In Europe, during the Middle Ages, it was coveted about on the same level as diamonds today. It's made from fossilized tree sap that nature has molded over centuries into this smooth, glistening, transparent jewel. Take a look at it through the light."

Asher held it up toward the window with sunlight slashing through the blinds, pouring amber onto Mandy's hair. Mandy stared at the stone, then slowly brought her eyes up to her husband and gave him a puzzled look, as if she was having trouble recognizing him.

Asher went on, ignoring the worried look on Mandy's face. "Pretty amazing, no? People used them as good luck charms or family heirlooms or to speak to their gods or even to cure their illnesses." Then, almost to himself, "Sometimes I can see the outline of a man's face when I hold it just right. He looks troubled when tilted just this way, like he can't quite figure out how his life has gotten away from him." Again Asher held the amber up to Mandy for verification. "See what I mean?"

Mandy squinted her eyes at the stone, her head resting on his shoulder, as if she were trying to see the world from his vantage. "Yes, I guess I see what you mean," she responded. "Very lovely, Miles. And certainly unusual. I've been meaning to ask you about that journal. What seems so fascinating?"

Asher hesitated, not sure if he was ready to uncap this gusher. But he was spared the choice when a screech arose upstairs from Emily. "Mom, Stacie smacked my head with Pumpkin."

Asher quickly headed upstairs, shutting off the dialogue. "I'll take care of it. At least Stacie's using stuffed animals as weapons." He heard but did not see Mandy slam a glass into the sink, breaking it.

*

The next night, Mandy, with a cut on her index finger from the broken glass, could not so easily restrain herself. They had just finished dinner, the girls heading upstairs to do their homework while Asher cleared off the table. Dinner had again been tortured, funereal. The girls, picking up on the ambient mood, gave monosyllabic answers to Asher's attempts to ask about their school and social lives. They wasted no time finishing their meal to get back to their room. Likewise, Mandy could feel the lure of his stacks of paper pulling Asher upstairs to his study. After wiping the kitchen table, he said, "Hon, I really have to get to work on our taxes. The paperwork is in shambles and they're due at the accountant next week."

Mandy balked. "Let *them* sort through the mess. I thought that's what accountants are paid to do. I promised Stacie you would help her with her math. She's having a devil of a time mastering fractions and I told her you would be thrilled to explain them to her. She said that you'd probably be too busy again to help her." She placed her hand firmly on Asher's arm, trying to root him to the spot. "Even your adoring, oldest daughter has noticed your absence, Miles."

Anxious to get back to his papers, but knowing he was trapped, Asher gave in. "Okay sure. I can get to the taxes later, after the girls turn in."

Within twenty minutes, Mandy rushed up the stairs, having heard enough of high- and low-pitched shouting followed by a wail of tears. She found Stacie at her desk, sobbing, and Asher standing in the doorway, throwing her math textbook onto the carpet in disgust. Emily crouched in the hallway, looking scared.

Before Mandy could start, Asher defended himself. "I'm sorry, Mandy. This stuff is just not that complicated. One-half you divide stuff in two. One-quarter you divide into four. One-half of one-quarter is an eighth. Mandy, we did pies, we did money, we even divided up her dolls. She's being deliberately dense." Stacie began wailing again. Hearing these words spill out of his mouth and remembering the phrase 'deliberately dense' that his own dad had thrown at him dozens of times, Asher's face fell. He stormed out of the room, knowing he had blown it, but unable at that moment to stop to admit it.

Mandy hurried after him, not about to let him get away. Even though they were out of earshot of the girls, she whispered harshly. "Look, Miles, I don't know what has gotten into you, but you either start treating us like your loved ones around here, get yourself some professional help, or move your goddamn ass out. I won't have you dumping your depression on those who love you." Mandy stormed off, not waiting for a reply.

She spent the next few minutes hugging and consoling Stacie. "Dad's been in a funk lately and we have to cut him some slack. You remember, Stace, when your best friend Angela all of sudden started ignoring you, because you were invited to Louise's party and she wasn't? You were mad at everyone in the world and didn't talk to anyone except to complain. Well, Dad's feeling that way too. I think mostly about work and his patients. So we have to help him feel better by understanding him and letting him know we still love him. OK, hon?" Stacie nodded and dried her tears.

Later on, when he had composed himself, after making a round of apologies to the girls, Asher headed over to their bedroom, to Mandy. But his attempt at the same with Mandy fell on an unsympathetic audience. "Just get your act together Miles. I said my piece upstairs. I'll make excuses to the girls for only so long. You're not going to subject me to another year like the one we had after your dad died. I know this sounds harsh, but either move on or move out."

Asher nodded in assent, feeling the heat radiating off his wife. He inched closer, hoping an embrace might cool her down. Shrugging his hand off her shoulder, Mandy turned her back. "Don't try to hug your way out of this one, Miles. Just get better or get some help."

He headed upstairs to Zantay's story—the only source of help he could think of at that moment.

ATMINA

Any recall of my early life is a patchwork of half memories, fantasies, post-fact presumptions and illusions—a series of fractive images, jumbled and scrambled in my mind's eye. When I delve into the hodgepodge of impressions muddying my early youth, I retrieve a tangle of coiled yarn. One strand, my house on Cemetery Street in Riga, the only real home I ever had, the street name a sad omen of our life to come. That house, clustered among a dozen other similar stone edifices, imprinted on me the image of a huge welcoming face: the gabled roof—a crown of slate hair neatly parted, the two upstairs windows—open welcoming eyes, the pale wooden front door—a smiling mouth ready to receive all visitors.

A second strand, Stiene, the town where we hid out for months in an old farmhouse owned by my uncle Stefan. That town, dominated by its ancient crumbling castle with overgrown vines and huge untended hedges, surrounded by a muddied moat—those foreboding images might have been the source of the serial nightmares with which I was plagued as a child. Another strand, our unending treks, enforced marches from the familiar toward the unknown, repeated endlessly with no apparent order or reason. A fourth strand, the Schwabisch Gmund, *the German refugee camp where we were sent after the Germans took over Latvia. And finally, the DP camps in Germany, where we were taken after the war.*

Most of all, those treks still haunt me; those never-ending days of trudging through mud or snow or dusty roads, interminably heading this way or that, never knowing whether the march would take an hour or a week. During those marches, I recall foremost in my mind my feet, for that is where I must have concentrated my line of sight and my attentions. I spent hours on end staring at these two abused and battered appendages. Surrounding me, there must have marched a tumult of like trudgers—wearied, starving, decimated families toting their hastily-packed, precious possessions, rickety carriages pulled by aging, wasted mares, orphaned children, wailing babes and already beaten-down teens, waddling pregnant women and barely-mobile, shriveled elders, an occasional cow and scavenging dogs, wives without husbands, children without parents, suitcases and trunks filled with valuables that soon were painfully discarded along the road, along with people dropping from exhaustion left to die, and others being trampled by a convoy's right-of-way. Despite all this surrounding chaos, all I chose to concentrate on were my feet. Nothing else endures in mana atmiņa, *my memory.*

I had three distinct coverings I recall—the first was a pair of shoes I clung to most fervently. They may not have even been truly a pair, since in my mindsight they do not match. Each was a lace-up, ankle-high, black leather boot with the laces long since vanished so the tongue flapped upward with each step I took. The right side clearly had five distinct pairs of holes for a shoelace, the left but three; the right sported a buckle strap at the ankle that had lost its buckle and therefore incessantly flip-flopped back and forth. The left had no such adornment.

I recall believing all pairs of shoes were made thus singular, that no pair was identical so each must therefore signify a contrasting message. I felt the discrepancy in lace holes mandated a distinction in how many steps were allowed with each foot and found myself attempting five right steps for every three left. Such awkward movements left me clumsy and often lagging, such that my mother frequently squawked at me and grabbed me by the arm, jerking me forward, destroying my rhythm and making me compensate for the untimed gait by trying to recount how many left versus right steps I had been forced to make, hurriedly trying to make up the difference.

Oftentimes, while marching after a rainstorm, my shoes would sink into the mud-bathed road, allowing molds of mud to cake my trousers and crawl into my feet. At such times, my lower legs would become single forms like brown stolid pillars, such that I could imagine myself a huge lurching monster like the Frankenstein I had seen on movie house billboards. My footprints, stretched behind me as I turned back to look, seemingly not my own, but some larger more powerful other, as if I were being carried by him along the road, rather than trudging isolated and insignificant.

At other times, I remember being supported by a cork-soled shoe, light brown with a cloth cover that I assume now must have been some type of canvas. Early on, wearing these on my mandated marches, I felt light-footed, as if I could float along the road effortlessly, my feet barely touching the ground. These served me perfectly for this journey, for I frequently bounded ahead of my mother and grandparents, which allowed me time to stop and pick wild flowers or chew on pieces of grass as I had seen the cows do. But when used later on in the winter, these shoes instantly filled with ice and snow, freezing my feet insensate. At such moments I would cry out and my mother might finally heed my pleas and stuff old newspapers into the shoe, mollifying and insulating my feet.

Most of all, though, I recall a pair of shoes that were not shoes at all. Perhaps under their cover, a remnant of a true pair provided some protection for my by then raw and macerated feet. But I merely recall the outer casing that I was forced to stare at day after trudging day on a road that seemingly never ended. And each step I took, whether I stared at my feet or not, reminded me of the hopelessness of our journey and, most of all, of the painful absence of my father. For my mother had chosen to wrap my macerated and swollen feet in the remnants of the arms of my father's last white shirt.

Before he disappeared, my father owned one stiff, starched white shirt, which he wore only to church on Sunday, laundered during the week and then wore again the following week. When, after several years of wear and tear, the shirt frayed at the collar and sleeves, he would head back to the finest haberdasher in Riga and replace his white Egyptian cotton shirt with a new one. I can still recall the sensation of sitting on my father's lap after church and Sunday dinner, enveloped in his huge arms and smothered in this great white shirt while he read me a story. He read until a full belly and two glasses of wine stilled his deep voice and sent him into a deep, sonorous sleep, heaving me up and down with his respirations, so I felt as if I were on a ship riding the gentle and soothing waves of the ocean. I can, even now, recreate the scent of his stiff white shirt, redolent with the perfumed soap powder and starch used to clean it, but harboring a deep, dusky, earthy undertone that must have been my father's true essence.

My mother's use of the last of my father's white shirts to cover my feet represented for me a tormenting defeat of the worst kind. Perhaps she believed the thickness of the cotton doubled over as insulation and the stiffness of the cuff would protect my fragile, abused feet from inevitable disintegration. The psychic decimation my spirit took, however, left a far greater and lasting scar than any endured by my feet. For, each step I took, each forward motion resting on my father's remnant, each layer of dirt added onto the formerly white surface, each rent in the fabric equally rented my soul and stomped out any hope I had of ever seeing my father again.

*

My first memory predates those enforced marches by several years. I realized this five years ago when I made my lone pilgrimage to my homeland. After a week sifting through the stored memories of my hometown, Riga, I ventured out to the countryside. I traveled by train the hour-and-a-half from Riga to the Gauja National Forest, staying in nearby Cesis where we had lived years before after moving from Riga. There stood the remains of a medieval castle built by the Germans in the thirteenth century. The castle was partially destroyed three hundred years later by defenders against the onslaught of Ivan the Terrible. These stalwart defenders chose to blow up their garrison and themselves rather than be captured by the Russian invaders. Later, in Cesis, the flag of Latvia was designed to commemorate that battle, patterned after the image of a fallen soldier lying bleeding on a white sheet, his blood seeping into the sheet's fabric. To this day, the Latvian flag remains a solid maroon background bisected by a white-stripe.

During my visit to the city where we had lived for three years prior to the war, walking through a park near St. John's Church, following a narrow path leading to a pond, I was struck immobile. A series of stone statues of fully armored and armed knights lined this narrow path, guarding it like sentinels. They memorialized the knights who had sacrificed themselves to protect the city during that battle. But, what stopped me was the sudden recall of having seen these knights in my childhood. I could not have been more than three, for I was being wheeled in a stroller down this pathway when I stared up at these huge, impenetrable stone monoliths. That image of this wall of warriors remained intact over some fifty years, though I had thought it had been a fantasy.

Karavīri un statujas, soldiers and statues. Often, I had conjured up those knights, both in dreams and in my waking life, as protectors and fellow warriors against the evil Nazis or, more often, as allies against my childhood tormentors. But, at other times, those stone-faced figures arose in my fantasies as unrelenting pursuers coming after me. I must have been confused as to the nature of my enemies and the character of my supporters—a confusion clearly warranted. That day fifty years later, upon confronting these same images, my fear and vulnerability flooded back into me with a paralyzing jolt. I stood transfixed in the pathway for upwards of an hour until another stroller, trying to pass by, finally jostled me out of my stupor.

*

I am not sure it is possible to assemble a chronological reconstruction of my childhood. The images meld and diverge in an unplanned collage. Which dirt-stained wall supported what four-by-eight foot room while I was lying on what pile of straw, listening to how many foreign dialects in which of a half-dozen hovels? At what point in time was I forced to place my lone crust of bread for the next week inside the filthy lining of my cap to protect it from the ever-present band of rats? Where were we living when my makeshift bunk of plywood nailed to the wall came crashing down onto the bed below, only missing crashing onto my mother by inches?

My attempts to piece together my early life depend most upon the grudging contributions my mother has been willing to make. But she has steadfastly refused to share with me details of our life in the years during and after the war. These years spent in hiding, in work camps, in detention camps run by the Nazis, or in DP camps organized by the Allies—all the while in a state of almost unbearable anxiety as to the fate of my father—are, for my mother, topics best left buried.

Often though, through design and practice, I have been able to connive information from her. With subterfuge, I have pieced together enough details to enable me to make some sense of our tribulations during a time when the entire world seemed to have lost its senses, a time that more souls than just my mother has chosen to forget.

Frequently, I would begin a likely scenario, casually mentioning during dessert, "Milots, do you remember that Albanian living next to us, it must have been in Esslingen, the one who could not have bathed for the entire 6 months while we lived next door to him? Nu ir gan smirdoṇa! What a stink! Ugh, I still cringe my nose every time I think about passing by him in the hallway. It is fortunate he did not live with us but instead that Polish couple who at least cleaned themselves now and again. In any case I swear I saw him last week in Philadelphia after a class of mine. I ran after him shouting his name, Alexis—but he moved on so fast onto the bus, I could not catch him."

And my mother, in an off-handed, absent-minded way, with an uncanny recall that likely stored ten thousand other such thoughts and memories, answered, "First, the Albanian you are remembering was not Albanian but from Rumania—his name, Stanis. And not in Esslingen, but rather in the DP camp just before in Rakwitz, probably 1945." She would scratch her chin and muse on, perhaps in a reverie to herself, "But yes, you are right. The Polish couple living with us was at least neat, but they stayed for less than a month out of the total four months we resided in that stinkhole. They got dragged away, if you remember. And you could have not have seen Alexis at all, for he is dead. You must recall the great scandal when Alexis was found dead in the outhouse—clubbed over the head by our Polish roommate, Jorges. Alexis was advancing on Jorges' wife and then he was dead and then the Poles were both dragged away and that was the end of them all. Such a waste. But what could you expect from such uneducated heathen? And what else might you expect during such times when people of all nationalities and all languages were thrown together in tiny, filthy hovels and everyone was starving and everyone was frightened and no one knew whether they would be in the same place or even on this earth for another day or another week. "Uz ko gan citu tu vēl ceri?" "*So what else do you expect?*" *And then my mother returned to adjusting her full head of perfectly coiffed white hair in the mirror.*

In such a way, I recovered bits and pieces of my childhood and, like a jigsaw puzzle, interlocked them with other pieces, finally making a more complete picture. Yet that picture, as a matter of course, has gaps and cracks and several large canyons that, at this juncture, will never be filled.

One night, when visiting her—I must have still been in my twenties—while she combed and preened her beloved shih tzu's hair, I slipped up, not yet fixed on how I should approach my mother with these sensitive topics. I was truly curious and forgot for a moment my tactics of information-gathering and asked, "When, exactly, and how did Grandma die leaving the old country? I remember Grandpa took sick and died of consumption while we were still in Germany. I know Grandma died on the ship crossing over from Europe, but I forget what exactly happened to her."

My grandmother, despite being almost seventy by the time we were placed on the ship, "Krakow", that transported us to the States in 1950, had survived the trials and tribulations of the war with remarkable resilience. She was the "lime," the glue that held my family together. After my father disappeared—while my mother spent long hours holed up in her room mourning for her lost husband, her lost home, and the loss of her life's expectations—my grandmother persevered. She pushed us to keep our most precious belongings each time we had to pack up and move. She forced us to eat whatever was available, when the smell alone of the meager offerings given us was enough to make us retch. She pushed us to walk just another step farther, then another step again when we were so exhausted we believed that the next step would truly be our last and we would collapse in a heap, never to move again. I suspect that each family that ultimately survived the tribulations of those days must have had a Grandma Miklah to spur it onward. Naturally, at some point, I would be curious what circumstances finally overcame that spirit.

But I should have realized questioning my mother on such a topic was taboo. Hearing my question, with a sudden fury I still cringe from, my mother threw the dog off her lap, almost cracking its skull against the wall of her living room. "You forget! You forget what happened to your grandma? Have you turned insane? Did she mean so little to you such that you can forget the atrocity of her death? Did her sacrifice mean nothing? I am sick that you, her only grandson, the light of her life, her only reason for living should have such little gratefulness." And she stormed off into her bedroom, not speaking to me for the next two days.

Finally, when she recomposed herself and once more would speak to me, she ventured, "Well, I assume you were very young when your grandmother departed and possibly you did not understand all that happened that night. But that night for me still pounds in my brain like it was yesterday. At least once weekly, I still awaken in the midst of that night, dreaming of the horror as if it was still happening before my very eyes. And for you, after these many years, to not remember, to not kiss the memory of your departed grandmother for each minute you are still alive, it is a sacrilege, svētuma zaimošana. It brings tears to mine eyes and a retching bile to my lips."

And that was her sole explanation to me. In result, I have never discovered how my grandmother was killed on the ship we took to America. I have nightmares of darkened steel hulls and shifting clumped bodies, of evil eyes and terrorized women. In my dreams, I see a crushed bleeding skull, hear a screaming cry of outrage. But I can piece nothing together, nor separate childish fear from grim reality. That limbo world of uncertainty without doubt will remain with me forever.

CHAPTER 18 ⸺

After the first panic attack of his life, Asher realized his standard fallback position of denial was not succeeding. In the middle of office hours that afternoon, exactly a month after his meltdown in the mortuary, his secretary knocked on the exam room door while Asher was checking a patient's blood pressure. Ellen, having no idea of the impact of her message, merely related, "Dr. Asher, sorry to bug you, but someone from Tolmisano's Funeral Home named Heidi Garnett is in the waiting room. She says she has to speak with you."

Asher's heart quickened, instantaneous sweat poured off his brow. Sensing his patient's and his secretary's eyes boring into him, he quickly excused himself, asking Ellen, "How long has she been out there?" Without waiting for an answer, Asher hurried to his office and closed the door behind him.

Asher had heard nothing from Heidi in the intervening month. His apologies had gone unanswered. He hoped she had put the incident behind her, but half a dozen times he had imagined the police coming to his office or home and arresting him for assault. Once, a sheriff *had* shown up at his office to serve a subpoena and he was sure this was the start of a lawsuit against him. Instead, Asher was merely being called to testify on behalf of a patient who had been injured in an auto accident.

He now imagined that Heidi must be there to subpoena him in person or, at the least, to announce to the world how he had humiliated her. A pulsating, rhythmic pressure began behind his left eye, keeping time with the thumping in his rib cage. Not sure which might burst first, he rushed out the back door of his office, ignoring several open-mouthed patients and his medical assistant's querulous look.

Ten minutes of deep breathing outside finally slowed his heart and allowed his legs to regather beneath him. Asher resigned himself to accept whatever he might encounter and his deserved punishment. He headed to the waiting room, hesitating only a moment at the threshold to observe Heidi Garnett, looking unchanged from her appearance at the mortuary—same grey skirt, white shirt, black shoes—seated calmly, legs crossed, a leather portfolio on her lap. Asher opened the door and gestured for her to follow him back to his office. Heidi arose, ignoring his outstretched hand, avoiding eye contact. In his office, he asked Heidi to sit down, then, having little choice, let her control the encounter. He detected a slight tremor to her facial muscles, synchronous with his own, hoped she could not hear his trip-hammering heart and waited.

Without expression, Heidi said, "Dr. Asher, sorry to disturb your day. You may not have heard that Elaine Bilsocz died last night after her long bout with lung cancer. The hospice nurse wasn't authorized to sign the death certificate. Would you mind doing so?"

Asher stared at the tremulous hand, now handing him the familiar red outlined paper, not believing that this simple task alone precipitated Heidi's visit. Realizing what courage it must have taken for her to come to his office like this, he said not a word. He hurriedly filled in the areas for cause of death and his ID information, trying to disguise his own shaking hand, then handed the paper back to Heidi without comment. Heidi thanked him, this time allowing herself to shake the offending hand. She gave him a brief fixed stare, seeming to indicate that this was all she wanted of him, all she ever would want of him, that she had conquered her fears, and she now would leave him with his own burdens. Asher again tried to apologize, but Heidi marched out the door without a look back, her shoulders square, her head up. He took ten minutes to calm his heart rate and regain some measure of composure before attempting to care for his afternoon patients. Later on, he was unable to remember a one of them.

*

The same night, Asher came home to a whirlwind of turmoil. He heard shouts and crying even as he approached on the driveway. So weary on the drive home, Asher had been forced to stop on the side of the road and had fallen into a brief, mind-swirling sleep. He had awakened with a sudden, sharp stinging on his face, so sure his father's hand had struck him from the beyond that he searched his face in the rearview mirror for fresh wounds.

He should not have been surprised to find a tempest stirring inside his house when he arrived home. By the time he reached the kitchen, the house had fallen silent. Only the intermittent sound of Mandy drumming her fingers on the kitchen table and an occasional whimper from upstairs from Stacie broke the quiet. Seeing that the storm had died down, Asher hoped he could escape into the bedroom, loosen his tie, and maybe catch a scotch on the rocks before being assaulted by the details of his home in crisis.

But Mandy would have none of that. "Before you scoot away again, Miles, you might want to ask your daughter about her encounter today after school."

"Can't this wait, Mand? I'm just beat up, whipped. Maybe after dinner, OK?"

"Not OK, this time, bud. You've been avoiding this one too long."

Now alarmed by her tone and her resolve, Asher asked, "What do you mean? What's going on?"

"Ask Stacie. She'll let you in on what happened at her soccer game."

Realizing he would get no further with his wife, Asher headed upstairs to Stacie's room where she lay facedown on her bed, sobbing into her pillow. Her muddied soccer shoes and shin guards lay scattered about on the carpet next to a couple of soccer trophies knocked off their shelf. Asher felt pulled to her side, his paternal instinct to comfort kicking in.

"Stace, hon, what's going on? Why so glum?"

The pressure of her dad's hand on her shoulder ratcheted up Stacie's sobs into full-blown weeping again.

Asher waited for her to calm some while stroking her soft black hair, matted with sweat. "Take your time, hon, and tell me what happened. Maybe I can help."

Between her sobs and deep breaths, Stacie managed to blurt out, "How can you help? You're the problem."

Asher was taken aback. How was this about him? "What do you mean, Stace?"

Stacie sat up then and looked him square in the face, the torment of pain and disappointment written on hers. Then she let loose. "Dad, did you kill Mr. Mallory? I saw Travis at the soccer field today. When I ran up to give him a hug cause I hadn't seen him in so long—our team was playing at Coopersville—he practically pushed me away. He told me to get away from him. He said, 'Stay away from me. Your dad killed my dad.' And then he ran away. What did he mean, dad? How could you have killed Mr. Mallory?"

At Stacie's first words, Asher had pulled away. Then by the end of her sob-laden queries, he was almost out the door, his total body tremors from that afternoon returning in an instant.

Asher took a couple of steps back into the room, trying to

steady himself. "Stacie, hon, you know I wouldn't ever want to hurt anyone." He quickly composed an explanation that would suffice. "As a doctor, I take care of sick people and, sometimes, sick people die. No matter how much I try to help them, there are times I can't. That's what happened with Mr. Mallory, Stace. I couldn't help him, and he died."

Stacie looked up at her dad again, questioning this time more than accusing. "I thought Mr. Mallory wasn't really sick, was he? But he died anyway."

Trapped, Asher replied, "Well, sometimes people are sick, and they don't seem like it and don't even realize it." He added, feebly, "That's what happened to Tom Mallory. No one knew how sick he was, and then he died. But it wasn't exactly my fault and I sure didn't mean for him to die. I'm sorry Travis blames me and took it out on you. That must have felt terrible, Stace." Approaching her bed and again touching her shoulder only intensified her crying. He left the room with one final, pathetic, "Sorry, Stace. When you get older you'll understand." The heart-rending sound of Stacie's unabated weeping followed him down the stairs.

Mandy stood at the bottom of the stairs, arms crossed, a steadfast frown fixed to her face, saying nothing, but blocking Asher's way.

Asher slid by her, saying "Mand, I know you've got more questions, too. But I'm wiped out now. I can barely move. I've got to catch a nap. Have dinner without me. It's the weekend. We'll talk tomorrow." And he escaped without waiting for Mandy's inevitable protest.

Jonathan Rosen

CIVILIZĀCIJA

A seventeenth-century philosopher named Kleinstadt said true civilization begins the instant you are born. Prior to that, all seems primitive, boorish, primal. As for my life, the opposite is true. One might be moved to say civilization ended with my birth. For I was born on July 17, 1936, the day the Spanish Civil War began. 1936 was also the year that birthed the Rome-Berlin Axis and the Japanese-German Anti-Comintern pact. These alliances sealed the forces that, over the next decade, would enflame the planet in conflict and unleash the spirit of the Antichrist throughout the world—and most notably in eastern Europe.

Not that the previous fifty years were models of deportment and carriage. Eastern Europe, and most assuredly Latvia, was the setting of some of the most horrific atrocities ever imposed by one man upon another. Battles, strikes, skirmishes, conflagrations, tortures, and torments such that one can only hope the world will never again witness. So perhaps it is not fair to postulate that civilization ended with my birth, but rather the kinetic energy that was to culminate in civilization's demise coalesced that year.

From the beginning of the century until the time the Russians took control during World War II, Latvia was a dented and bloodied ping-pong ball smacked back and forth by the mighty—grabbed by Russia, then stolen by Germany, then turned back twice over. In example, in 1905, when the Russians dominated Latvia, Latvian workers protesting against the brutal Tsarist government called a general strike. For retaliation, the Russians slaughtered thousands in the streets. Six months later, seeking to quash efforts to democratize the Latvian government, Russian 'punishment brigades' executed over two thousand Latvians and sent thousands of others into Siberian exile.

Later on, during the early part of World War I, the Russians raised eight battalions of Latvian soldiers to battle the Germans, who had already overrun half of Latvia. But by 1917, the Germans overwhelmed the weakened Russian and Latvian forces and took

Riga. Before Germany was defeated, the Brest-Litovsk treaty in early 1918 between Russia and Germany ended their conflict, and ceded Latvia to the Germans.

But one year later, after the German surrender to the Allies, Latvian nationalists declared Latvia an independent state. Over the next two years, in a three-way tug-of-war, both renegade German forces and Russian Bolsheviks staged continuous battle against the nationalists for control of the land. Russia unilaterally declared Latvia a Soviet republic. But even after World War I officially ended and Germany had surrendered, Germans continued to stake claim to the land. Ernst von Salomon, a German general, saw his role as a protector of "Aryan interests" in Latvia and laid waste to the landscape. Later on, he described the fighting. "We hunted the Letts (Latvians) across the fields like hares, set fire to every house, smashed every bridge to smithereens, and broke every telegraph pole. We dropped the corpses into the wells and threw bombs after them. We killed anything that fell into our hands; we set fire to everything that would burn. We saw red; we lost every feeling of humanity. Where we ravaged, the earth groaned under the destruction. Where we charged, dust, ashes and charred balks lay in place of houses like festering wounds in the open country. A great banner of smoke marked our passage. We had kindled a fire and in it was burning all that was left of our hopes and longings and ideals."

Rudolf Höss, in later years to become commandant of the Auschwitz extermination camp, was a young German soldier fighting the Latvians during this battle. Afterward, he too reflected on the brutality of that era. "The battles in the Baltic were more wild and ferocious than any I have experienced either in the world war or in the battles for liberation afterwards. There was no real front; the enemy was everywhere. And when contact was made, the result was butchery, to the point of utter annihilation. The Letts were especially good at this. It was there that I first encountered atrocities against civilians. The Letts exacted a terrible revenge on those of their own people who had hidden or cared for German or White Russian soldiers. They burned their houses and left the inhabitants to burn as well. Countless times I saw horrible images of burned-out cottages along with the charred or smeared corpses of women and children. When I saw this for the first time, I turned to stone. I could not believe that this mad human desire for annihilation could be intensified in any way. Although later, I had to face more horrible images repeatedly, I can today still see, perfectly clearly, the scorched cottage with an entire family dead inside, at a forest's edge on the Dvina River. In those days, I could still pray and I did."

Brutality begot brutality. Höss learned his lessons well. Later on, during the second World War, the Germans were to take pride in the efficiency of their killing, their dispassion, their ability to remove the emotional consequences of their acts from the reality.

Thus, we were both the victims and the perpetrators of carnage. We learned from our oppressors the lessons of mayhem and destruction, turned those lessons back upon them and upon ourselves. We became one with our enemies, perhaps the only rational alternative available to us. To justify our behavior, we claimed the moral high ground, the nobler motives. Our efforts for freedom and democracy over the next fifteen years are testimony to that idealism. But, inescapably, we must come to terms with our own savagery and brutality. Perhaps war dictates that we all behave as destroyers. Perhaps under similar circumstances, we all flay open our sanquinous entrails.

Finally, in January 1921, under the Treaty of Riga, Russia agreed to recognize the independence of Latvia; the world followed suit. For the next twenty years, for perhaps the first time in its history, Latvia operated as an independent, free state, with neither German nor Russian domination and, during that brief period, flourished.

Throughout the rest of the century, though, Latvia became a microcosm of the instability, the unrest, the unleashed brutality, the hopes for peace and for freedom, the rage and the barbarism that dominated Europe. What lessons we drew from this exposure to the naked underflesh of human nature, I can only speculate. Whether this was mankind's last gasp of savage inhumanity in a history strewn with similar events, or another in the unbroken line of mayhem to continue on into perpetuity, only time will tell.

*

I was born in the army hospital in Riga, the capital of Latvia. My father had earned a degree in mechanical engineering from the Riga Technical Institute but, unable to find suitable employment, had joined the Latvian Army in his early twenties. For technically skilled people, military pay was excellent. That decision, reasonable at the time, made in innocence and out of necessity, was likely directly responsible for my father's ultimate fate.

At birth, I was over six thousand grams, about thirteen pounds, and, although my mother was not a small woman, she required eighteen stitches and two months to recover from the ordeal. She utilized the army hospital, though medical care there was substandard. Subsequent to my birth, my mother developed an infection that kept her at more than arm's length distance from me for our purportedly critical bonding period. I have never held much support for the belief that those first few minutes and hours after birth are a crucial juncture in developing the relationship between mother and child. As everything else in America, isolated incidents and minor deviations are accentuated far out of proportion to reality.

However, I have often come to wonder if those first few months when my mother was either maintained in the hospital or convalescing at a distance from me in our home were responsible for much of the detachment that over the years has characterized our relationship. Surely, as her only child, one would believe she would have clung to me with a fierceness that might have been paralyzing. Especially considering the times and evanescence of relationships, property, and home, one would expect her to have latched onto me with a vengeance. Not to say that my mother did not love me or that she does not continue to love me still, even as now, at the age of eighty-one, her capacity for all human sensation begins to fade.

Yet throughout our lives and especially during my early years, I felt a barrier or veil between us that, though intangible, was real enough. It was not that she did not fondle and hug me the way I saw other mothers do, though I must say those moments were rare. Nor was it that she did not applaud my accomplishments and comfort me in my failures. Mostly, I believe our distance came from a sense that my mother was more observing me than relating to me, almost as one might observe the daily habits of a neighbor as he walks his dog each morning or the comportment of a student in one's class while he is taking a test. The behaviors of either might be interesting, and in their way compelling, but lack the emotional connection required for true empathy.

I suppose such detachment was necessary in those days and quite possibly a standard adaptation to the unpredictability of all relationships defined by that era. In result, though, I suspect I may have felt judged as much as loved, a symbol as well as a son. The pain of not knowing the whereabouts of my father was immense. Often, when saying goodnight, while we still had hope we might reunite with him, she would instruct, "Be sure to dream of your father tonight. I know that I will. He must know through our thoughts and dreams that we have not abandoned hope of ever seeing him again."

Not knowing how to control my dream life, I often awoke in the morning in guilt, either not remembering my dreams at all or aware I had dreamt something frivolous and inconsequential in comparison to the loss of my father. In either case, when asked by my mother, I would lie and state, "Of course I dreamt of him. We were back again at the river, fishing and laughing, always throwing back the small fish and smacking our lips at the larger ones." Afterward, I felt ashamed on all counts, aware I was failing at once both my mother and my father.

In example of my mother's manner with me, I recall one telling incident. Again during one of our multiple escapes through the war years, we were hurriedly departing one of the refugee camps. I cannot verify if my memory serves me correctly, but possibly this episode occurred in the spring of 1945, when I was nearly nine, for I know we were fleeing the advancing Russians. We had spent some months in a Polish-controlled camp in Rakwitz, with food that bordered on the inedible, but at least a decent roof over our heads. Suddenly, we heard through the refugee pipeline that the Allies had ceded this area to the Russians.

Within the hour, we would have to board some cattle cars to be transported back to the west and hopefully, to safety. Whenever the Russians occupied a territory, we were told, the inevitable consequence for refugees would be transport to Siberia or possibly worse. We had one hour to collect whatever belongings, foodstuffs, and personal effects we could carry. The Poles were happy to assume whatever property we left behind, so my mother was intent on carrying the maximum she, my grandmother, and I could carry.

My grandmother managed to secure a cart on which we piled suitcases and boxes of whatever, while my mother pushed a bicycle similarly laden with our possessions. So encumbered were we, my mother wore twelve layers of clothing in the hot May sunshine.

Embarking on our journey, I vividly recall being reproached by my mother for thinking only of myself. I held clutched to my breast, my fingers white from grasping, a small box of toys—the only possessions I regarded as important to me. With my mother's stern rebuke to not waste our precious space with such inconsequentials, I carefully set the box down in a ditch, crushed that I had let my mother down. In tears, with all my strength I pushed the bicycle the several miles to the station. I so wanted to be strong and unselfish.

In later years, my mother denied such an event had ever occurred. She even insisted on her tolerance of my ongoing possession of a straw pony that she says I transported from place to place as if it were my brother. I myself do not recall possessing such an object. I did have an excessive preoccupation with all matters involving cowboys and Indians, so I presume clinging to such a prized possession was possible. In any case, I believe the stress my mother felt during those years obstructed her from seeing me as a child, and moreover, as her child. I have long since forgiven her. My God, who could not react similarly under such provocation?

Yet, I digress. Around the time of my birth, my father was invited by the Latvian military to join the equivalent of Officers' Training School. Discovering he could make more money if he instead trained as an instructor in weaponry, he declined. Again, a tragic decision. Taking that position, he was transferred with us to the town of Cesis, the home of those guardian statues in the park.

The next three years, though they had no way of knowing it at the time, were the happiest of my parents' life. Among the officers and instructors living on the military installation at the time, there were many gatherings and excursions and official dances. My parents were active participants. Plus, they doted on their at-times precocious son, able to walk at ten months, to read sentences before he was three. How little prepared they were for the carnage to follow.

In August 1939, Germany and Russia ratified the Molotov-Ribbentrop Pact or what became known as the Hitler-Stalin Pact, ostensibly a non-aggression treaty. However, a secret supplementary protocol assigned "spheres of influence" within eastern Europe and essentially divvied up our territory. The Baltic states—Estonia, Latvia and Lithuania—were assigned to Russia. Immediately, Russia sent Soviet forces within the borders of these previously independent nations purportedly for "security" purposes. Less than a year later, on June 17, 1940, the Red Army proceeded with outright occupation of all three states. They held sham elections and the USSR illegally annexed the Baltic lands.

In the process, Moscow installed puppet governments, nationalized all transportation facilities and industries, seized control of all bank accounts and other valuables, controlled and censored the press, suppressed societies, associations and religious worship, deported national and local leaders (often never to be heard from again) and purged army officers, police officials, school teachers, professors of higher education and other intellectuals, many of them imprisoned or sent to slave labor camps, and still others executed at the hands of NKVD secret police. Ultimately these efforts escalated into mass arrests and deportations of Balts from all walks of life, resulting in a systematic campaign of "Russification," designed to transform the Latvian way of life into the Russian way.

My father, possessing a much-needed military skill, was spared these debasements. He was immediately conscripted into the Russian army as an armaments specialist. Fortunately, that position did not involve direct combat. We were moved back to Riga, back to Cemetery Street.

Early in the war, the Germans were an irrepressible force. By mid-1941 they began taking control of extensive territories to the east of the Fatherland, completely ignoring their "pact" with the Russians. Fearing the occupation of Latvia by the Germans, the Soviets began confiscating what natural resources they could marshal. One of the principal resources available was the people. Free labor, supplemental soldiers, women and children—all were considered exploitable for Soviet military efforts. Village by village, the Bolsheviks packed up Latvians into cattle cars to be transported to Siberia.

In early July 1941, we went to bed, already having moved from Riga to my grandfather's house in Stiene, dressed and ready to be transported the next day to certain hell in Siberia. The village next door had been decimated the week before and we knew we were next. Amazingly, at the last moment, the Germans arrived first, forcing the Russian army to flee. We were saved! Or so we thought. We should never have been foolish enough to hope the Germans would be more humane than the Russians had been.

During the chaotic Russian army retreat, much to my mother's surprise, my father managed to flee the Russians and, within the week, rejoined us. To this day, I can, at will, recapture the sounds of joy and relief, the overflowing tears and shouts at our sudden, all-too-brief reunion. Before a fortnight had passed, however, the Germans heard tell of the availability of an armaments specialist who had collaborated with the Russians. They apparently had multiple uses in mind for such a man. And if any scruples restrained the Germans from seizing this person and his talents, his cooperation with the hated Russians overcame them.

My father was taken from us on the afternoon of August 2, 1941, never to be seen or heard from by his family again.

CHAPTER 19 —————————————————————

About one AM the same night as Heidi's visit and Stacie's meltdown, unable to sleep any more, Asher once again snuck out of bed, and headed back to what had become his sanctuary. At this juncture, Asher realized he had few choices. Shrinks were worthless. He didn't need drugs but rather, absolution. He had a long-term friend, Stan, who would likely understand, but would understanding help? He thought of confessing to Tom Mallory's wife, Irene, but she had made her feelings about him clear and did not need the additional burden of absolving his guilt. Only Mandy's judgment and forgiveness would do. More than that, she deserved an explanation. She deserved to have a husband and father back in the house. This time, instead of diving back into Zig's increasingly coherent narrative, Asher opened up a blank Word file in his computer and began typing.

Mand,

I know you've become more and more frustrated and bewildered by my behavior these past few months. Don't think I haven't been appreciative of the restraint you've shown in not smacking me upside the head or, as I know you've felt like doing, kicking me out of the house. You've been especially tolerant considering how much increased pressure you've been under, working full-time now while still running the household.

I'm writing you this missive partly as an apology, yet more as an explanation. I can't really say there is a direct cause-and-effect between my behavior and the events I'm about to tell you about. But, since I can't stop thinking about them, I suspect they must be related... Self-diagnosis apparently is not my strong suit.

You, of course, remember hearing about Tom Mallory's death after we returned from our cruise (which I again apologize for essentially being absent from) and then being puzzled and disturbed by Irene's reaction. Well, I was more involved in Tom's death than I ever let on. In fact, I cannot escape the conclusion that my actions were directly responsible for his passing. Practicing medicine since then has become an increasing stress and drain on my energies, instead of the joy and satisfaction it once was.

Why have I not related this to you before? Shame, embarrassment, pride, fear of the loss of your respect for me all come to mind, yet none of them may be adequate explanations. In any case, here it is.

About a week before our cruise, almost two months ago, Tom and Irene showed up in my office for an appointment. The day was pretty much indistinguishable from any other. I had my usual quota of about thirty patients scheduled, with an assortment of complaints ranging from a college student's depression to Mrs. Norman's follow-up after finishing chemotherapy for her lung cancer. (As you may notice, having obsessed over that day, I can recall the details with ease. I've even gone over the records of every patient I saw that day to see if I made any other screw ups. Thankfully, none that I could detect.) When I saw the Mallorys on the schedule, I felt pleasantly surprised, having not seen them for over a year. As you know, since Tom's store closed and they moved out of the neighborhood, we've kind of lost track of them. I've always loved Tom and our kids used to be inseparable, so I've regretted we didn't hang out more with them.

Anyway, I remember standing outside the door to the exam room, reviewing Tom's chart. His last visit over a year before had been for an elbow tendonitis he had gotten from training too many students

149

how to turn too many bolts. His last physical was about five years before and at that time, Tom was in great condition. He evidently frequented doctor's offices about as often as I visit hardware stores.

Just as I was about to knock on the exam room door, I watched a mother chase her two-year old son down the hall while she scrambled behind him, tissues in hand, trying to snatch up the little rabbit turds he was dropping out of his diaper onto the floor. I was still grinning at that sight as I entered the Mallorys' exam room. I had to consciously regroup my uncooperative facial muscles in an attempt to match the Mallorys' expressions, because, at first glance, they looked as if they were in an airplane that had just free-fallen six thousand feet.

Irene's face in no way matched that serene, unflappable expression she carried with her always. She barely managed to manufacture a smile. Moreover, her usual immaculate grooming was in major disarray. She had thrown on a wrinkled, faded UConn sweat suit and not a trace of make-up. Her usually perfectly arranged hair flowed in a tumble of misdirected strands. Her damaged voice sounded even five octaves lower than usual, like a poorly tuned cello string.

I could tell they were in no mood for pleasantries, but couldn't suppress the impulse to catch up with them. As usual, they were accommodating and fell into their natural sociability. I asked about Jake, since I had heard, even at 9, he was tearing up the soccer fields, scoring more goals than any other kid in the league ever had before. I said something like, "Sounds as if Jake could be on a sure path to a college scholarship."

They relaxed some, talking about what their kids were up to. Tom was sitting on the exam table, dressed in khakis and a plaid flannel shirt, looking nowhere near as disheveled as Irene and, for that matter, looking not much changed over the five years since we had first met. His bushy mustache may have been a bit grayer, the corner of his eyes wrinkled a bit more. But he still had that constant flush on his cheeks and a bounce in his voice that was unmistakable. While we were making small talk, I said to myself, "Tom doesn't look too sick, maybe I misread their fears."

"Yeah, the kid's a natural," Tom replied. "Thank God he doesn't take after his klutz of an old man. And a college scholarship sure would be nice. Two teachers' salaries will barely cover the cost of their backpacks. Of course, we could always fall back on our plan to heist the town wishing well." Tom produced his usual wry, crooked grin, but Irene couldn't manage even a half-smile. Then he asked how the girls were doing. I said something about Stacie already becoming a phone/e-mail/rap music guru, plus my usual plaint about being overwhelmed by estrogen-hysteria every few weeks.

Maybe that was where our visit began to go awry. Maybe their relaxation, their quick recovery of easy manner and affability made me relax, too. Maybe my familiarity with them allowed me to forget too quickly their initial apprehension and panic.

Finally, I got to the topic at hand. "So what brings you two here? Doesn't seem by the chart like I've seen you in over a year, Tom. What's up?"

Tom started to speak, then cleared his voice and began again, "Well, Doc, Irene seems to think I'm having some problems with sleeping. She says I fall asleep, and then keep jerking myself awake all through the night. I don't remember a thing… It's kind of hard to describe." He paused and looked over at Irene, who was not at all reluctant to speak. She couldn't stop her voice from shaking when she took over. "What it really is, Miles, is that Tom's been having problems not just sleeping, but, more so, problems breathing. *Mostly at night—especially last night. He's been stopping at times while he's sleeping and I watch him for a while and sometimes he starts on his own and then, sometimes, I have to shake him till he gets started, like he's forgotten or something."*

Tom grinned again, kind of embarrassed. "At my age you begin to forget a lot of things. Why should breathing be any different?"

I must admit, at that, I relaxed even more. I'd heard this story enough times not to be too concerned. I responded, "Sounds like sleep apnea. Does he snore a lot?"

Irene again took the lead. "Snores! Like a tugboat on a foggy night he snores. But he's been doing that for years. I almost can't sleep myself anymore unless I've got his wood-sawing in the background. But this was different last night. He wasn't just snoring last night. And he didn't stop breathing for just a few seconds. He really stopped!" Irene picked up steam and her words became rushed, her face flushed. "I shook him and yelled at him and even slapped his cheeks. But he would not start breathing. Finally, I called 911, but before anyone arrived, Tom suddenly started up breathing again." She got panicky then, reliving the moment. "I have no clue what got him jump-started. But, he picked up breathing and then he woke up and opened his eyes. He asked what the big deal was, like nothing at all had happened. When the ambulance got to the house, which seemed like an eternity, we were sitting at the kitchen table and Tom was having a Coke. And I couldn't stop shaking. I thought I might have a seizure then and there myself.

"The EMTs came in with all their paraphernalia, looked at us sitting there and they seemed kind of disappointed the emergency had petered out. They asked a few questions and took Tom's blood pressure and listened to his heart and said, 'Well, he checks out OK now.' They asked if we wanted them to take him up to the hospital and get him looked at some more. But by then we felt kind of silly. And Tom said, 'No, what the heck. I feel fine now.' As they were going, they suggested we get Tom checked out today. After that, it must have been three AM, I was not about to go back to sleep. Inside of ten minutes, Tom was back sound asleep, snoring his head off. But there was no way I was going to take my eyes off him for one second. Naturally, he was fine the rest of the night. I never want to go through a night like that ever again." And having gotten all that out, Irene wiped her eyes and kind of imploded—her face fell, her chest sagged; the pressure of that night had sucked the life out of her.

Tom was still sitting up there on the exam table, grinning, embarrassed at the big fuss. But I could tell, he was listening with rapt attention to the story, as if it had happened to someone else. I too became transfixed, listening to Irene. The sounds of the office—the ringing of phones, other doctors speaking to patients in other exam rooms, the rhythmic sound of whooshing air as a nurse outside the door took someone's blood pressure—all faded into the background. I remember hearing the sound of crackling exam-table paper underneath Tom as he fidgeted.

Then, Tom held his hands out palm side up and shrugged. "Can't take care of everything, you know. I'm a busy man, what with lesson plans and after-school hours and fixing up the house and then picking Jake and Travis up after their practice. Man's got a lot on his mind. You expect me to also concentrate on breathing 24/7? Give a guy a break."

His grin even made Irene half-smile for a second. But then she got dead serious again. "No jokes please, Tom. You scared me half to death. I swear I don't know if I'll ever get a good night's sleep again in my life." She turned back to me and said, "Miles, you've got to do something. This cannot be normal."

Asher was startled out of his writing trance by the lone, blaring wail of an ambulance-siren crescendo, seeming to come right to their front door and then fading into the distance. He looked up, listening to the quiet of his home, ignoring the usual sounds of rumbling furnace, humming refrigerator, whistling wind. Stacie's voice suddenly penetrated the walls, though the deep rumbling, resembling a cow's inconsistent low, reassuring Asher that she was once again sleep-talking. Although she no longer suffered from night terrors, when particularly agitated, she still would carry on prolonged dialogues with herself while asleep. Asher tiptoed to her bed, quietly sat near her head and once more stroked her sweaty, dark hair until she settled. He returned to his study and resumed typing.

Mand, I sat facing the Mallorys—Tom in denial, Irene in an overcompensating panic—the way I have to face fear from every patient. I always try to balance out the intensity of the problem and the level of the patient's concern against my knowledge, against the odds of serious pathology, and also against my gut instincts. Though mostly subconscious and subliminal at this point, I ask myself, "How sick does he look? How worried is he and his loved one? How serious a problem are we dealing with? What's the worst possible consequence if this problem goes untreated? Does he need hospitalization? What tests would be appropriate? How soon can I get these tests done? Should I refer him to someone else? Is there something I'm missing? How truly worried am I?"

The answer to that last question usually tips the scales. If the patient seems fine and my internal alarm system doesn't register anything, I'll do whatever necessary to reassure the patient and his spouse. On the other hand, if the patient is blasé about his or her symptoms, yet presents a problem that churns my gut, I'll pursue the patient's complaints regardless of any pushback he gives me. In the past, that internal alarm has always served me well.

But somehow with Tom and Irene sitting before me, my alarm malfunctioned. Maybe my desire to reassure Irene outweighed my sound judgment. Maybe I had become too used to relying on the odds—most patients get better no matter how you treat them. Maybe this particular failure represented the culmination of a series of deteriorations I had never noticed before. In any case, Mandy, I blew it.

In my defense, though, I did not dismiss Tom's problem out of hand. His dramatic symptoms didn't jive with my experience of a typical patient with sleep apnea. Yes, they stopped breathing, but not usually for long. Sometimes it was difficult to rouse them, but not so you have to hit them over the head with a sledgehammer. To ease my own mind as well as Irene's, I sent her out of the room and went about giving Tom a thorough going-over. I examined Tom from head to toe, including a full neuro exam, an EKG, and a pulse oximetry with not even a glimpse of pathology. Tom looked great. Healthy as a hippie in heat. But then what else would I expect? Tom was not experiencing any symptoms at the time. I really had to catch Tom during one of his spells to be sure his problem was caused by sleep apnea. The only verifiable test that would then determine his treatment would be a sleep study in which Tom would spend a night in a sleep lab, where he could be monitored for signs of decreased oxygen or arrested respiration or arrhythmias. The problem was these tests always had a backlog of at least a month before they could be arranged.

Though I had never heard of anyone actually passing away from an episode of sleep apnea, I was concerned. I could hospitalize Tom for observation, but the HMOs would inevitably hassle me. Plus, the odds were pretty slim Tom would have one of these spells while in the hospital. Tom could stay in there for five nights and never turn a hair, and where would we be then. The sleep lab was what Tom needed, not the hospital. I got on the phone myself and made the sleep lab tech put a rush on the study. One week later was the best I could get.

I went back to Tom and Irene. "Guys, I managed to twist the sleep lab tech's arm into getting your study next week. It really sounds like you've got sleep apnea, Tom, which, though scary, isn't fatal. I know Irene is worried you're going to pass on any minute. But the odds of anything happening as bad as last night are pretty remote. In the meantime, I'll send off some lab tests, and if Tom has anything like another episode, give me a call right away."

And I sent them on their way. Was Irene mollified? Reassured? Her parting glance suggested not totally. But she trusted me. We had been neighbors; our kids were like cousins. Surely if there was anything else to do, I would do it.

The question is Mandy, was I satisfied? Had I done all I could and should have done? As they headed down the hallway, watching the Mallorys walk out the door to the office waiting room, I remember Irene's last lingering glance back, seeing Tom clutch her hand and pull her along and out. I had this visual hallucination, watching them telescope down in size as they headed down the hall. They looked just like those pictures in art primers that teach you to draw perspective by making figures smaller and smaller, in order to appear farther and farther away. Likewise the Mallorys, leaving the office that morning, slowly shrank away from me, till they vanished completely.

Since that day, I've avoided reliving that moment. Now I realize, at that instant, my alarm system may actually have triggered. But this time, for whatever reason I still cannot fathom, I dismissed that

155

omen, that premonition. And that dismissal has been haunting me ever since.

The next day, along with a hundred other patient problems, a pile of unfinished charting on my desk, a nurse having a meltdown because her dog ran away, an irate patient on hold because I failed to return her call pronto, I did take a moment to think about Tom. As usual, the night before and up until that incident, I slept fine. I wondered if Tom's night had been similarly uneventful.

I assume I was afraid to hear any bad news directly, because I asked Laurie, you know the nurse who's been raising sheep in her barn, to call the Mallorys and see how Tom had fared overnight. An hour or so later, as I was engrossed in a phone conversation with a cardiologist, Laurie dropped a note on my desk. "Irene says Tom did fine overnight. No problem at all. She did not sleep much, but he did great. They thank you for asking."

In the midst of the phone call, the degree of relief I felt might have surprised me, had I the time to dwell on it. But with that reassurance, I put Tom on the back burner in the category of "Dealt with for now. More to follow later," and moved onto my next problem. The thing is, Mand, that day, although I screwed up, was only a fender-bender compared with the head-on collision that came later.

Asher stopped the almost-frenzied rattling of his typing, by then mentally exhausted. He had endured confessional enough for that night. Knowing, however, that he would not be able to sleep, his sensibilities revved, Asher's eyes fell back onto Zig's magnetized pages.

JO GERMANU

After all my people, my family, and I have been through, you might ask, do I hate the Germans? From the time my father was stolen in 1941, until settling in Massachusetts nine years later, from age five though fourteen—the entirety of my youth—we had no home. We had no money, no jobs, no friends, no predictable meals, no security, and no comfort. We had no knowledge whether or not the next day or the next week we would be moved to a new location, under whose predatory thumb we could not guess. We slept in wooden barracks, makeshift tents, barns, ditches in the road, wagons, and on top of each other. We walked in blinding heat, torrential rain, and brain-numbing cold.

We had a saying that applied both in Latvian and in the German. Kas to lai zina? Wer weib? *Who knows? For we never knew. They say uncertainty breeds frustration and leads to violence. For us, uncertainty led to passivity. We arose when told to, we walked where directed, we ate when fed, we emptied our bowels when allowed. We were mute animals led around by contemptuous masters.*

For the first year after my father's capture, we stayed in the relative comfort but fear-laden confines of my grandfather's home in Stiene, forty miles outside of Riga. My only memory of this small farm was my lone friend—a baby chick hatched right before my eyes in our tiny hen house. I immediately adopted him as mine. "Calis," chick, I called him for want of any imagination. I slept with Calis. I forced my mother to accept him at our dinner table. I walked everywhere with him resting in my pants pocket. I cried inconsolably six months later when told after the fact that we had just eaten him.

At age six, I had no idea we were living in perpetual terror, that we might be dragged away at any moment. The only clue I had arose out of my mother's insistence I keep a packed suitcase at the foot of my bed at all times. After a year of such uncertainty, we were finally sent to the camp in Leipzig that I have described in the incident at the school at which all but me were blown up. This transfer set off a series of movements I have difficulty dating and which, having no explanation or order, I cannot distinguish. But each moment we were under the thumb of Jo Germanu, *every second, we felt like insects. Grubs, sometimes to be noticed, at other times to be ignored and occasionally to be squashed. Even a six-year-old knows when he is seen as dirt, and that humiliation brands the soul.*

One incident during another of our forced marches, near the war's end, I still recall as if yesterday. How long we had been marching, I have lost. Where we were going, I am sure I never knew. By then, the Germans guarding us along our trek may have been exhausted themselves. They may have been the dregs of society, the last vestige of a warrior culture whose betters had already been spent. Or possibly they were merely typical exemplars of the fruits of hatred and malice. Perhaps all of Hitler's hordes were always just dregs.

Predictably, along our march, the weak and the weakening fell by the wayside. Most often they were left on the spot with no notice by the guards and no aid from their fellow marchers. This day, several meters ahead of me, a scarecrow-thin, bearded man collapsed on the road. The day was bitter cold. The man fell into a mound of snow, a mist of steam wafting from his body. Later on, when they had removed his body from that spot, I recall thinking that the linear red stain surrounded by white snow where he had lain reminded me of the Latvian flag.

As usual, after the prisoner fell, everyone proceeded on without notice; except this time a teenage girl stopped to help. She began crying out for assistance, for someone to please help her get him up. No matter how she pushed or pulled she could not get him to budge since by then he was too weak to stand. Again, as usual, no one paused to even look.

Hearing the commotion, one of the guards, in this case a lieutenant, came over to the scene. In crisp German he said to the girl, "Move along now. Get going. No stopping. Leave the old man there or I will have to shoot you both."

The girl screamed out, "But he is my father. Please help him, we've come so far. Please, someone help me get him up." No one budged.

Then the lieutenant stooped over the prisoner, staring at him for a moment, as if thinking about possibly helping. Quickly, a dark veil enveloped him. I can still recall the image, like an evil mask had been placed over his face.

"Help? Help this animal? This is Jude! Drekin Jude! How could a Jew have escaped our grasp?" Then standing and pointing to the man on the ground, "Do you all see the Jew? Who else could have a nose like that? A bastard Jew. He must have lied all these years pretending to be one of us. Eating our food, coveting our women. A Jew taking the food out of our babies' mouths, stuffing himself while the rest of us suffered." I could see his words spit out of him and frost up in the cold air as if the words themselves could freeze the heart. At the time, the word 'Juden' had no meaning for me. For all I knew, he could have attacked me next with the same accusation.

"You need proof?" he said to no one in particular. "Watch." And then without hesitation he pulled down the pants of this barely-struggling man in order, I realize now, to expose his circumcised penis. "You see, a Jew, right down to his privates. I will teach him for cheating and lying and stealing. He thought he would escape German justice. Well, I will show him German justice."

And the lieutenant pulled out his knife from his side holster. "I will show you what happens to Jews who lie. A nose such as this never lies. It will expose them every time."

With the prisoner's daughter screaming for help and all the rest of us standing helplessly watching, the officer grabbed the man's nose and tried to slice it off. Only at that point did this wasted human summon enough energy to struggle. He twisted and turned his head, blocking the knife's attacks with his hands. The knife drew deep gashes in the man's hands and arms, but he managed to protect his face while the lieutenant became increasingly frustrated.

During this entire scene, my grandmother's hand tightly clutched my shoulder to stop me from intervening. Perhaps she sensed that even at eight, my impulse was to run over to the torturer and knock him over. To beat my fists into his face. To rescue the prisoner and his daughter. And if that were my impulse, was it not also everyone else's who witnessed this abomination? Did not all have to restrain themselves? Or had that impulse been gradually subtracted from everyone's soul? Had the war and a thousand similar abuses erased any semblance of humanity from the group? Had it sucked out our guts, leaving behind mere shells of our former selves? On these matters, I offer no answer. I merely stood stock-still in the clutches of my grandmother. I looked up to the sky and once again was struck by the fact that birds no longer flew overhead.

Finally, in his frustration, the lieutenant screamed out to his other guards, "Don't just stand there, you fools. Come help me. What are you doing just standing around, dein kopf uben Arsch? *Help me!"*

Three guards standing nearby hesitated. They looked at each other, none of them wanting to make the first move. Maybe they had lost the taste for such mayhem. Maybe by this stage of the war, they were afraid of the consequences of further atrocity. But above that fear, they must have been most afraid of their superior's wrath. Because, with a silent nod to each other, they stepped forward to help. Two held the prisoner's arms, while a third steadied his head for the lieutenant. A fourth held still the prisoner's screeching daughter. Then, with a flourish and a triumphant shout, the lieutenant sliced off the prisoner's nose. A torrent of blood shot from the old man's face. The lieutenant stood up brandishing the nose for all to see. "This will remind all of you. Never try to deceive the Führer and his followers. We will always find you. We will always punish you." He then stabbed his knife through the macerated flesh and impaled it onto the old man's chest.

What I recall most, even these fifty-odd years later, was not this sick, demented sadist who was allowed to flourish and thrive during the war. Though to this day, I still am able to invoke with ease the triumphant expression of victory on his face—his sick, gluttonous countenance, beaming at his feeble conquest. And I am nauseated by the image of the bleeding, fleshy appendage hanging from his dead victim's shirt.

But more than this, I am haunted by the memory of the four soldiers who helped the lieutenant complete his savage act. For rather than delighting in their task, as did the lieutenant, the four appeared reluctant participants. They knelt hesitantly, unsure of their options, looking for an escape. Mind you, there were no physical threats placed on them. The lieutenant coerced them only with the order, "Help me, you idiots."

Yet each accomplice permitted himself to be coerced. And at the moment of the atrocity, I watched, as each soldier—even the one holding onto the prisoner's daughter—at the critical instant averted his head. Not a one of them could bring himself to watch as the lieutenant completed the task for which he had enlisted their complicity. Without their help, he likely would have failed. With it, his heinous crime became simple.

So, I have hatred for the lieutenant —for his deeds, and his ability to thrive in an era when he numbered only one among a thousand like-minded, diseased creatures. But his underlings equally sicken me—their passivity, their collusion, their cowardice, and their secret delight that someone else other than them was the victim— sickened most of all that they remain to this day unpunished.

And thus, in answer—yes, I hate the Germans. Yes, they repulse me. But over and above that hatred, I find I can understand them. And, in my ability, and moreover my desire, to understand them, I discover I also leave some room to hate myself.

*

Throughout the war years and the years to follow spent in DP camps prior to our emigration to the U.S., only scattered events stood out from the predictable terror, turmoil, and monotony of our lives. For as in all children's lives, the inconsistency and mystery of the adult world precluded true comprehension. And without true comprehension, retention and memory often do not follow. How can any child understand what the universe of adults meant other than through those specific episodes that attacked his core? And what child could possibly grasp whether sense or lunacy directed the behaviors of his elders when mankind's compass no longer pointed north?

Even the seismic event of the ultimate victory of the Allies over the Germans in 1945 does not register in my memory bank. I suspect, for us, the unpredictability of still another conqueror having control over our lies precluded any celebration.

However, I will never forget that day in Mid-May, 1948, when we traveled to Stuttgart in search of my father's trail. We lived in Esslingen in southwest Germany in a displaced persons camp from 1946-1950. Our address was Weil Strasse 17, in a building formerly occupied by local Germans but which had been awarded to displaced persons in the American zone by the United Nations Relief Act of 1945. Though we were despised by the German youths who lived nearby and frequently the object of epithets hurled our way along with an assortment of bottles, sticks, cans, rocks, and even an occasional bullet shell or burnt-out hand grenade, we banded together as a cohesive group of Latvian youths. Often shouts of "Verfl'uchte Ausl'ander," "Damned foreigner" rained down on our ears. But such occurrences were rarely followed by physical encounters. The German youths were unlikely to prevail against us hardened and perpetually challenged refugee kids.

Although the living conditions were, to be kind, spartan, and the general animosity toward us palpable, we had, for the first time in my remembered life, the constants of a roof over our heads, plentiful though atrocious food, a dependable school, and most of all, no immediate threat of deportation, destruction, or dissolution. For the first year or so, until we became complacent, such a camp—which in other circumstance might have been considered nearer a prison than a home—was for us a heaven-sent palace. Even my mother became somewhat relaxed under these conditions. She never exactly wavered from her resolve to find her husband, but at least now engaged each day with a sense of purpose and even hope.

Painfully conscious of her inability, due to lack of general freedom and her responsibility for me, to venture outward in pursuit of her lost husband, my mother nonetheless devoted untiring energy to discovering his whereabouts. Much of her days were spent composing letters to various relief organizations and governmental offices, inquiring as to my father's fate. Realizing names were often confused in translations or altered in transport to other countries, she provided detailed description of my father in each letter, even extending to his peculiar quirks and mannerisms, which she assumed the chaotic world would note as easily as she. In the camps, my mother took up sketching in order to perfect her ability to copy one of the two pictures she retained of my father through all of our travels. We had no photo lab around the corner allowing us to copy these pictures and send them out, so had to rely on my mother's artistic ability and the good offices of overwhelmed bureaucrats to uncover my father's whereabouts.

Needless to say, such a dependence was foolhardy to the extreme. Nonetheless, my mother's perseverance and paradoxical optimism never allowed any possibility other than her eventual reunion with my father. Even to this day, she will speak of him as if he is about to enter her living room at any moment, clasp her to his chest, and express his undying remorse for leaving her in such difficult times and for such an extended period—an interval that is approaching fifty-four years. To my mother, it must appear as if my father has undertaken a prolonged sea voyage, filled with calamity, which has diverted him from a timely return to her arms. She knows with a surety borne of obstinace that he will inevitably return from his absence with great fanfare and celebration to regale her with gifts and tales of the great beyond. Thus the realities of the base degradation and savagery of those years seems to have been replaced in my mother's mind with the romanticism of a Greek tragedy.

Now that my mother's thinking is more circuitous and her reasoning tangential, I find myself frequently in the position of reaffirming my own reality to her. For she will often, upon my entry into her home, even if only from a brief absence within the same day, latch onto me with a cascade of hugs and greetings as if I were the returning hero she has long anticipated. In her mind, how can she not retain an image of her husband frozen in time by all evidence, despite our age difference, resembling me? When I reorient her as to my true nature and the persistent unavailability of her husband, how can I not reproach myself for the cruelty of my message? What harm would I perpetrate, should I allow her fantasy to prevail? What manner of ethic dictates that I continue to hold truth and reality above my mother's ultimate release? Yet I persist in reminding her of who I truly am and the constants of the here-and-now, as if my pretending to be her husband would violate some natural order.

Upon discovering the truth about my father's destiny now some three years ago, I spent many a sleepless night in debate, wondering whether I should inform my mother. Ultimately, I opted for the path of silence. What purpose could I possibly serve by replacing her rich fantasy and island of hope for the stark substance of my father's final resolution?

Inevitably, the passivity of launching untold messages into the vast ocean of uncertainty yielded to more dynamic action on my mother's part. In response to her barrage of inquiries, we received form letters that initially provided random flurries of hope. Such hopes were quickly dashed and consumed what remained of my mother's patience. Most of the return letters neither mentioned the individual whose loss had instigated the request, nor noted the desperation of the petitioner.

The government of the People's Republic of Poland recognizes the disgorgement of vast numbers of citizens due to the criminality of the Nazi regime. We have undertaken official efforts to identify and categorize those persons. Their ultimate fate upon discovery will be reported to the Polish Central Registry on Missing Persons, which you may visit or correspond with as befits your convenience. As in all matters of state security, we will retain information and persons as necessary to ensure government safety.

I cannot of course recall such responses verbatim, nor was I privy to many of them. They were usually written in the language of that particular government and therefore a mystery to both my mother and me. Within the camps, I became a courier of these cryptic messages, scurrying about seeking interpreters who might help to decode their content. The messages' translated meaning never failed to disappoint my mother, first for their impersonal nature, yet more so for the implied persistent claim of the government to ownership of these lost souls.

One of my mother's newfound fears was that my father might have miraculously survived the machinations of this terrible strife and now was in the control of another sinister and arbitrary government that considered all people within its purview merely resources. How else to explain his persistent absence? Were he alive—which the contrary she could not for a moment consider—why would he not be seeking his son and her as desperately as she was seeking him? Over the prior two years, she had advertised her whereabouts on every bulletin board and with every potential agency and office on the European continent. Were her husband alive, there was no reasonable way he could avoid finding us. Unless of course he was now in the grip of another malevolent menace, directing all his actions and controlling his movements.

Once again in Europe after the war, the rights of the individual were in conflict with the prerogatives of the state. (As you may note, I have done no small amount of research over the past few years on the fate of Europe's homeless.) In 1943, well before the end of the war and even before the establishment of the United Nations, the Allies set up the United Nations Relief and Rehabilitation Administration. Although its mandate did not specifically dictate refugee relief, UNRRA was created to assist in the relief and rehabilitation of the vast European diaspora. Toward the end of the war and in the early postwar years, UNRRA assumed the leadership in providing emergency assistance and aid to the hordes of homeless refugees wandering through Europe's decimated cities.

Much of UNRAA's initial efforts went toward repatriation— transporting displaced citizens back to their original homelands. From May to September of 1945, UNRAA assisted in the repatriation of some seven million people. Of these, two million were Ukrainian or Baltic state citizens, most of whom were returned against their wishes. Since the agency was not permitted to operate in the Soviet-controlled territories, I will be generous and allow that UNRAA may not have been aware of the exact nature of the governments and conditions to which it was consigning these already-damaged wanderers.

After all the devastation and destruction of natural resources, property, industries and structures wrought by the war, what remained intact and exploitable still were people. Individuals with their bent backs and gnarled fingers and broken spirits remained the one natural resource yet available for governments to exploit. What more convenient means could a government have of clearing the war's rubble, replanting the fields, reconstructing the shells of industry than the hordes of reclaimed humanity it could conscript?

Thus, during the postwar years, Europe again became a battleground—this time not for territory, but for bodies, for human labor. The issue of forced repatriation versus an individual's autonomy became the focus of a new conflict between East and West. No longer were weapons the tools of the conflict, but politics. And no longer was land the goal, but rather control of the populace.

Ultimately, the U.S. withdrew its support for UNRAA's policies, believing repatriation only served to strengthen Soviet control over eastern Europe. After 1947, with U.S. backing, the United Nations formed the International Relief Organization. The resolution that chartered the IRO held two contradictory though ultimately liberating principals. The main objective of the IRO was "to encourage and assist in every possible way the refugees' early return to their country of nationality or former habitual residence." However in forming the organization, the General Assembly of the UN resolved, "No refugees or displaced persons with valid objections shall be compelled to return to their country of origin." At long last, the world endorsed a formal declaration of the autonomy of the individual. Despite the objections of the Soviet Bloc countries, within the next five years, the IRO assisted in the repatriation of a mere seventy-three thousand people, while helping to resettle over a million refugees to the U.S., Canada, and South America.

In the early postwar years, my mother was held captive by dual terrors. First, as I have indicated, she feared my father had been one of those early on reclaimed by the Latvian puppet government. Therefore, he would be under the control of the Soviets and thus likely a slave laborer in Siberia, from which no communication ever escaped. In such a scenario, my father would never be heard from again. Equally, my mother was tormented by the possibility that should she call significant attention to herself, the responsible powers might likewise see fit to return her and me to our former homeland. We would then become the slaves ourselves, with no choices or ability to seek out my father.

Thus, my mother was in continuous internal conflict between the options of stirring as much ruckus as possible to uncover her husband's whereabouts or remaining still, silent and passive in the hope if we "sat tight" then ultimately we would be discovered by him. Finally, she could settle on neither choice, constantly wavering between the two. She spent weeks immobile, writing no letters, phoning no agencies, agonizing the entire time whether she was taking the correct posture. These pauses she would follow with a flood of activity during which she could no longer restrain herself. She then would pour out a veritable tidal wave of requests, messages and pleas, all ultimately to no purpose.

One day, I was returning to our room in Esslingen after my clarinet lessons. At nine, my spare time outside of schoolwork often consisted of soccer games or rehearsing for stage plays or with an unseemly devotion to the clarinet. Somehow, my camp had latched onto both an ancient battered clarinet and a recording called The Sounds of Benny Goodman. *I must have played that record incessantly on the community gramophone till the grooves wore out and the sweet sound of "Fascinating Rhythm" became a mere screech. After school, I would light up my licorice stick for hours at a time.*

This one afternoon, I came bursting through the door to our room ready to show my mother the new "Moonlight Serenade" rendition

I had learned. Though tiny, maybe eight feet by ten feet for the three of us, the room was no longer unadorned. My mother had lined the walls with photos cut from a pile of old issues of Life *magazine she had found in a closet of the camp school. On the walls, she hung only photographs of nature. No people, no buildings, no instruments of war, nothing man-made would she allow to decorate our sanctuary. We awoke to visions of Canadian geese winging southward, fields of poppy flowers, huge redwood trees anchored in ancient forests, remote volcanic islands resting peacefully in the vast ocean, a snow-capped unscalable mountain. All these images insulated us from the reality, from the sickness and sorrow of the world we knew was lurking outside our door.*

Upon throwing open our door that day, I stopped dead in my steps, finding my mother sitting on the wood-slatted floor next to her bed. This event in itself was apbrīnojami, *amazing, since my mother could never be found resting on this wooden platform that covered the concrete floor of our room. All night we were forced to listen to the sounds of rats scurrying under the platform, driving my mother to distraction. She spent countless hours chasing these despised creatures with broomsticks, frying pans, poisons, and ultimately shouts of frustration, all in vain. To find her resting so near to the rats' freeway was unimaginable.*

She clutched a white piece of notepaper I immediately surmised to be another official letter of inaction. This time, however, my mother's response was overwhelming. She was alternating huge heaving sobs with shouts and cries of anger, lacing her outburst with a series of Latvian and German curses such as I had never heard escape from her lips—ones to which I myself was completely naïve. "Dirsēji, sūdlaižas, kuces bērni!" Assholes, shitheads, bastards!" When she had simmered down enough for me to understand her cries, in her thickest Latvian she wailed. "This whore, this despicable excrement of a human, he writes me back. He returns my letter after ten thousand of my requests for information get ignored. Some sick thief of a shithead in the government of Stiene gives my letter to the worm Meken. This bastard who tried to assault me when I was just a girl of fifteen. He is now the town commissar. He now runs my home for the bastard Russians.

"He wants to welcome us back to our homeland. To return to the home of my fathers! Ha! Tas ir pretīgi! That is an abomination! He says the people now occupying my father's home, he will remove in an instant if we return to our home to tend the fields and work for the Soviet and people's rights everywhere. A pile of pig dung. A spew of cat piss. He must be mad.

"No, he has no news of my husband. He is sorry to find we have become separated. But nonetheless, in his generosity, he will welcome us home. Young men like you, Zigfrid, he says, will be needed to bring our homeland back to its glory. I retch in disbelief."

Between sobs and curses and cries and wails of frustration, my mother repeated one phrase over and over until the words echoed in my ears, implanted themselves in my brain, tunneled into my psyche. First in Latvian, "Es nekad neatgriezīšos!" "I will never return! I will never set foot in that godforsaken place to again be at the mercy of those bastards. I will not allow my children to ever return there. I will not return." And then in the halting German, which she must have picked up along the way but which forever as long as I knew her she refused to utter: "Ich werde nicht antworten." "I will never return." Then in broken, hesitant, yet loud and defiant English that I had no idea she was even studying or considering, she repeated over and over again, "I will never return. I will never return."

And all I could do at the time, while standing in the doorway clutching my clarinet, was stare at my mother and feel afraid. While watching my mother melt before my eyes, while some part of me accepted the fact that we would never see my father again, while I wondered where on earth could we ever again find a place to call home, while a ten-year-old's imagination dug itself a hole into the earth, I found myself blanketed by an unnamed and unadulterated fear. For if we were never to return home, then where could we go? If not there, then where? If there was no back, what was forward? Those were the thoughts that swarmed through my brain. But these were thoughts I knew better than to give voice. And as such, remaining unspoken, they could maintain their power unchecked.

*   •

By 1948, with the official abandonment of repatriation, my mother had little reason to worry that if she shook the ground too much, the tremor would be felt in Latvia and we would be sent back. No one else in the camps had suffered such a feared event so she felt more comfortable loosening her restrictions.

Such an increased confidence must have occasioned our trip to Stuttgart. When I had just turned eleven, I awoke one springtime Saturday morning to my mother's voice. "Zigfrid, get dressed. Put on the clean white shirt we've been saving. We are going to the city." As if that were not an exciting enough prospect, she added, "Perhaps we might be able to find a more suitable instrument for you than that cracked, wailing stick of wood you've been clutching these many months."

I jumped out of bed excited yet somewhat fearful. Although the city of Stuttgart was not more than twenty miles away, in the two years we had been living in Esslingen, we had never ventured there. We had heard warnings about official corruption and the inability of the American occupying forces to control the population. And worse, we heard of German attacks on foreigners, especially DPs, even one riot that had taken place the year before protesting our presence. In result, we never ventured out to what should have been a natural magnet for us.

Stuttgart was a city about the size of Riga and had something of the same international flavor. Ultimately, that day we were ignored by the bustling, preoccupied, and possibly depressed populace. Nonetheless, the simple act of undertaking such a venture for my mother and me represented a considerable act of courage and determination. Whether or not our fears were founded did not detract from the intimidating nature of our endeavor.

During our visit, we were shocked by the degree of destruction evident even three years after the war's end. We learned that firebombs had destroyed over sixty percent of the city in the last two years of the war. Though Dresden received the most notoriety for these incendiary bombings, Stuttgart also suffered the desecration of most of its landmarks. By the time of our visit, it had made little recovery.

But the unconquerable rubble and the rumors of potential danger held no sway over my excitement and pleasure in venturing out of our camp for the day. My mother's mission was to meet with some German official in charge of identifying foreign nationals who may have worked in the concentration camps during the war. The Germans had been pointedly protective over disclosing much of the activity surrounding the camps. However, they were being forced by the Allies to turn over many of the records they had not yet destroyed. My mother hoped one of those foreign camp workers might have been my father.

The Germans' catalogued record of their genocide, when available, was comprehensive to the maximum. As in all else, the German bureaucrat was detail-minded and exhaustive. Much has been written about the violent nature of German character, of the Germans' inhumanity, their savagery, and their baseness. Based on the evidence, it is foolish to deny those sentiments. Hitler and his genocidal policy allowed those Huns particularly skilled in sadism and savagery to rise to the head of the class. The commanders and their underlings in the concentration camps flourished in that climate of torture and cruelty and many of those enforcers, as I have described, took no small amount of personal pleasure in their hellish tasks.

However, there was, in addition, a vast populace in Germany carrying out these psychotics' orders and directives who may have had no fundamental interest or inclination in the matters of sadism and malice. Their duties were carried out, as they would perform any task assigned, with efficiency, dispassion, and obedience. The German bureaucrat has no peer in the world. He questions not, he performs his duties, he forgets. The unpleasantness of the task, and even its conflict with his own sensibilities, do not enter into the equation. In fact, the more unpleasant the task, the more likely he is to perform it with increased efficiency. It becomes a matter of pride, of character, to overcome his own discomfort, to ignore his own fears and misgivings, to obey his orders and complete the job at hand as well, as efficiently as possible, no matter how inhumane the task itself.

These observations I have made based on my readings as an adult, as well as witnessing the Germans firsthand during my formative years. This is not to imply that the German worker, in enabling the Holocaust, was not evil. Or that he was unaware of what he was doing and somehow not responsible. Rather that his evil was convoluted. Not just banal, as Ms. Arendt implies, but circuitous and labyrinthine. A swirl of misdirected energy and misapplied loyalty packaged in a unique moral myopia, enabling him to see only what he chose to see. For the greatest sociopath of them all, Adolf Hitler, emboldened a coterie of lesser ones. And these were all supported by a populace of, in my term, "bureaucratic-maniacs"—people for whom upholding the dictates of their immoral government became their prime directive. Nothing else mattered, nothing else held sway.

The German's ultimate excuse for their final solution, "we were just following orders," ultimately was the truth. Their fatal flaw was that their obedience to the state was more important to them than their own humanity.

That day we journeyed to Stuttgart, my mother was aware she might encounter dueling Germans. Would she meet the compulsive character who would show her all the records potentially involving my father or instead the German criminal who would try to block any light from shining onto his crime?

CHAPTER 20

Almost exactly ten years after Asher's father had died, three months after his mother's death, nine weeks after Tom Mallory headed out of Asher's office, forty-nine days after the incident in the mortuary and just nineteen days after Asher had started in on Zig's memoirs, Mr. Cassidy died. His death, of course, was not unexpected. Yet, like all deaths, it took his family by surprise. And even Asher, experienced in these matters, was shocked. Their last visit together, though emotionally wrenching, provided Asher with no sense that Mr. Cassidy was on his way out.

Asher found out about Mr. Cassidy's death, as was often the case, by reading the obits in the *Dover Star*. Frequently, his patients—their medical care scattered, often transferred to distant nursing homes—passed on outside of his purview. While under Asher's watch, they may bounce a few steps down the stairs toward the morgue, but often some other caregiver escorted his patients to their final exit.

Asher's last visit with Mr. Cassidy this time was not in the parking lot but in the more usual setting of Asher's office. Up until then, with his visits to his neurologist, physiatrist, and physical and occupational therapists, Mr. Cassidy had not found the time or energy to see Asher. Yet he came this last time. That visit, disturbing as it was, had reminded Asher of the integral role he played in the lives of his patients and reaffirmed his value. Maybe it even helped stop him from taking down his shingle once and for all.

Asher took some time reviewing Mr. Cassidy's chart to get a better sense of his current status and what path of decline they might expect. Asher could almost always divine the state of a patient's health by the condition of his chart. The thicker, the more weather-beaten, dog-eared, faded and frayed, the more likely the patient was nearing the end. When the chart had to be split into two or three separate ones, Asher had an even surer sign. Mr. Cassidy still possessed one chart, but it was becoming unwieldy with seam-pressure from the accumulation of lab and X-ray results, consultations, and visiting nurses' reports.

First off, Asher tried to locate the start date of Mr. Cassidy's illness. He knew too well that patients with ALS had an average survival of 24-48 months from the onset symptoms. He also knew Mr. Cassidy was the kind of patient who might bluntly ask how much time he had left. Asher hated to prognosticate. But he saw it was now almost two years since Mr. Cassidy first presented to him with generalized muscle weakness and fatigue. If asked, Asher would have to inform Mr. Cassidy that he was already at least halfway through his disease; everything from here on in would be downhill.

For once, Asher felt no guilt about not making a diagnosis sooner. ALS was a complicated set of progressive neurological deteriorations that took time to develop and to be recognized. Even if diagnosed early, there was no adequate treatment to slow or stave off that decline. Inevitably, no matter when diagnosed and no matter how treated, ALS would result in the decimation of a patient's nervous system while leaving his cognitive function intact. How could it help to inform a patient sooner than later that he was going to have to watch his abilities to walk, move, eat, breathe, swallow, and talk disappear one-by-one, with no hope for adequate treatment?

Asher saw in a consultation note that Mr. Cassidy's neurologist had put him on the drug Riluzole, which might slow the progression of ALS, but which the neurologist acknowledged had little long-term benefit. He then surveyed in Mr. Cassidy's chart the comprehensive, exhaustive and exhausting work-up the neurologists had put him through. Three MRIs—head, cervical and thoracic spine—an electromyelogram and a nerve conduction velocity test, a swallowing study and pulmonary function tests, a lumbar puncture and a series of blood tests, including an SPEP, an ANA and a rheumatoid factor, anti-neoplastic antibodies and the more mundane thyroid function tests and metabolic profiles. A series of invasions and corporal insults that had two primary results—one, the diagnosis by the neurologist of "probable" ALS, and two, an exhausted and frustrated Mr. Cassidy. A physical therapist, writing the last note Asher read, must have been taken with Mr. Cassidy because she quoted him verbatim. "If you tell me one more time that I should watch my balance and posture, like I'm some tutu-wearing ballerina, I'm going to take my walker and toss that and the lot of you do-gooders and quacks right into the Connecticut River." Asher smiled at the image of a still-feisty Mr. Cassidy telling off some innocent, unsuspecting therapist.

By this juncture, Asher expected to encounter his patient in a major funk. Instead he found a serene Mr. Cassidy, a man who had come to terms with his illness and his mortality. His physical presence, though, belied that conclusion. When called from the waiting room by Asher's nurse, Mr. Cassidy took a full five excruciating minutes to maneuver on a wheeled walker the twenty feet into an exam room. His body tilted forward, his head bobbed like a marionette, his legs dragged fitfully behind. He wore the same outfit as always: a worn flannel shirt, a pair of suspenders that barely held up his now-oversized green work pants and a black cap that now almost covered his eyes. Mrs. Cassidy lurked nearby, struggling to provide clandestine support. Asher greeted his patient with enthusiasm, trying to mean it when he told Mr. Cassidy he didn't look too bad.

As usual, Mr. Cassidy was blunt and to the point. "Don't try to bullshit a bullshitter, Doc. I know I look like a can of refried beans left out too long in the noonday sun. But I hadn't seen you for a while and I figured it might be a good idea for us to catch up at least one last time before I hit the road for good."

Asher began to protest. "You don't look all that bad, Mr. Cassidy. Don't start divvying up your estate just yet. You still have some fight left in you."

"Maybe so, Doc. You never know. But a safe could fall on my head the minute I step out of your office." Mr. Cassidy's speech was surprisingly fluent, punctuated only by the sporadic sucking noise he made as he tried to recapture secretions that surreptitiously spilled out the side of his mouth. "I knew you'd be tickled to see me one more time. Just wanted to help you get the chance to squeeze another office fee out of me. Who better to use up my last few Medicare payments on than you, Doc?" Neither Asher nor Mrs. Cassidy could help but laugh.

"I knew there wasn't a chance in hell of getting one of you new-fangled docs to make a house call. So I came here. I needed to get out of the house anyway. Been stuck inside for so long, staring at four walls and at my sick-looking face in the mirror, feels like I've been committed to the loony bin. And the missus here's been doting and hovering and sighing and simpering so much, I've a mind to pop her one, assuming I could get up the energy to make a dent." Mrs. Cassidy, standing behind him, stiffened. "Don't get me wrong, Doc. She's been an angel of mercy for me. Florence Nightingale, Mother Teresa and Mary, Mother of God all rolled into one. Putting up with my sick old ass the way she has. If I were her, I'd probably be wishing the old man would buy the big one already and put us all out of our misery. But she's just not made that way."

Mr. Cassidy patted his wife's hand, knowing he had gone a bit too far and that his wife was likely to burst into tears. Asher looked up at Mrs. Cassidy and gave her a sympathetic nod, as if he knew what she was going through, but there was not much he could do to help.

Reading Asher's mind, Mr. Cassidy continued. "Look, I know there's not much you can do for me now, Doc. Only the good Lord can release this beat-up old body and set it free. And He sure is taking His sweet time in the process. Makes you wonder if He somehow doesn't enjoy this part of the show, watching the poor saps He created waste away into nothingness."

Asher answered half to himself, since he could tell Mr. Cassidy was about to get back on his soapbox, "Kind of wondered that myself lately. Sometimes seems like He's either preoccupied or left the scene altogether."

"Well, I've got to tell you, Doc, I'm done kickin'. When He wants me, He'll take me. And if He's not ready for me yet, well, that's OK too. I can put up with anything this rotting old carcass does to me. I'll tell you, it wasn't always so. When my health went south about two years ago, with my arms and legs acting like they were dancing to someone else's tune, I wasn't about to change for no one. I kept digging in the garden and hauling around thirty-pound bags of dirt and spending hours on my hands and knees weeding. No way was I going to give in to some weak bones. Then when I got so I couldn't garden anymore, I said, 'what the heck' and moved on. I dragged my sorry ass to the club every afternoon to play gin with the guys. Course, sitting around with all those old-timers puffing away on their cigarettes and cigars didn't do me a whole helluva lot of good. After a while, I couldn't take their smoking anymore and even had to give up the gin rummy."

Asher listened to Mr. Cassidy tell his story as he had listened to a thousand others over the years. Sitting across from his patients in this seven-by-ten-foot exam room, Asher plied his trade. An armchair for the patient, a rolling stool for himself, an exam table and a Formica cabinet the only furniture. On the wall hung a blood pressure cuff and ophthalmoscope, plus two pictures reflecting the schizophrenic nature of the setting. One picture, a close-up graphic of a patient's lungs and bronchial tree before and after the ravages of smoking. The other, a pot of roses sitting on a windowsill, painted by one of his patients and given to Asher as a present for his care of her dying husband.

"But maybe you already know this, Doc—people are pretty resilient. Some of us just can't be put down. You might be surprised how an old dog like me can still learn a few new tricks. Because I decided I wasn't going to sit on my ass doin' nothing but wait for the grim reaper to snatch me up. About three months ago, one of my kids bought us a computer and I've been online ever since.

"Damn thing's the most amazing piece of contraptionization I've ever set sight on. First month I had the sucker, I didn't know what the hell I was doing. I'd freeze the thing up or forget to type in this word or that word. I'd move the goddamn mouse the wrong way and conjure up a whole new screen, I couldn't find my way back if I had a compass and an Indian guide by my side. Finally, I got some computer whiz kid in the neighborhood to come out to the house and show me exactly what to do. He wrote down a whole mess of instructions so a five-year-old with an IQ of twenty-two could follow them."

Asher nodded. "I'm impressed. I still have difficulty with the damn things. I keep asking my nine-year old to rescue our computer from my bungling."

"Well, since this kid helped me out, I've done OK. For the past month, that computer has been all that's connected me to the real world. I would've been some forgotten soul out there floating by myself in the middle of the ocean if it weren't for the damn thing.

"I been e-mailing my kids and my grandkids and my daughters-in-law and a few relatives I haven't seen in over twenty-five years and some old friends and even some people on this online chess club. And they all must think I'm kind of nuts because I'm writing them these long-winded, run-on letters that never exactly seem to end and may not have much of a point but they sure seem important at the time that I'm writing them.

"I guess this must be my way of saying goodbye to everyone. And thank God I've got the chance. 'Cause even though my body's kind of a piece of crap by now, my mind is still pretty sharp. And if I don't tell everyone now how I feel about them and what kind of mistakes I've made in my life and how I think they all should run their lives, well, then when am I going to have the chance again? Most likely they'll think I'm just some doddering old fool, running off at the mouth. But maybe some of them will read what I've got to say and hear me and remember. And maybe somewhere out there in what they call cyberspace, my words will live on long after me and remind people that at one time I too passed this way."

During Mr. Cassidy's speech, Asher sat on his stool rapt. Mrs. Cassidy could not remain so fixed. About halfway through her husband's self-eulogy, Mrs. Cassidy's eyes filled with tears. She first ignored them, then wiped them with the tissue Asher quietly gave her. Finally, she could take no more and hurried out the door.

For Asher, the room seemed to shrink. The walls closed in, the air grew dense. Gradually, he inched his stool closer and closer to Mr. Cassidy, so by the end of Mr. Cassidy's speech one of Asher's hands rested on Mr. Cassidy's bony knee, the other on his shoulder. All he could offer at this juncture was physical comfort and an ear. Nothing else he had learned during his years of training would render one ounce more of aid.

While Asher sat with his hand on Mr. Cassidy's knee, staring into those rheumy, wrinkled eyes, he thought of his own father's sudden, unexpected end, an end that had left Asher in limbo, like a trapeze artist perpetually suspended in air, never to be caught, never to be rescued. Now Asher imagined a different end for his dad, an end more like the one Mr. Cassidy had conjured up. An end where the unexpected became foreseeable, where last thoughts and last desires and last hopes were realized. An end where you telepathed to your loved ones everything you'd neglected to say in life, where you knew they heard and understood and most of all remembered.

At the end of Mr. Cassidy's speech, Asher surprised himself by leaning forward and planting a kiss on the bald and weather-beaten head of his patient.

VIENS PATS

Before venturing to Stuttgart, my mother had spent over a year hoping to arrange a meeting with some German government official who would allow her to examine concentration camp records. It had long dwelled in her mind that her husband might possibly have been drafted into the service of one of these camps. He had skill with explosives. He had organizational and training abilities. The Germans were not likely to allow him leadership within the armed forces, but possibly they'd found other uses for his skills.

This particular May morning, my mother was finally granted an interview with a mid-level bureaucrat who was in possession of records from several Polish and eastern German concentration camps. The records not only included description of all workers in the camps, their country of origin, and other vital statistics, but reportedly contained photographs of many of them. The possibility of finding a picture of my father amongst those maltreated and manipulated unfortunates excited my mother into a frenzy.

We caught an eight o'clock train from the station in Esslingen, due to arrive in Stuttgart before nine. My mother was dressed in an overly bright blue dress with high heels, refusing, I conjecture now, to consider wearing a mourner's black garb or even anything remotely sedate. She felt the occasion called only for optimism. I wore the stiff white shirt of a grown-up, but was mortified when forced to don a pair of hand-me-down shorts from some older campmate that I felt too grown-up to be wearing. Plus, I hated the accompanying suspenders that were often the objects of snapping ridicule by other boys in the camp. Nonetheless I was thrilled by the adventure—the prospects of exploration, the freedom of escaping the camp, the possibility of finding a new instrument for my passion. If I was aware of the trip's profound objective, it did not seem to register.

Prior to the train trip, we had time only for me to wolf down a couple of slices of two-day-old bread accompanied by a cup of lukewarm water barely tinged with cocoa. The ultimate events of the day generated such excitement that I had no sense of hunger even though I ate nothing again until we returned home after six o'clock that evening.

At the train station in Stuttgart, we disembarked into a flurry of activity—scurrying people carrying packages or luggage, hawkers selling knickknacks or fruits and vegetables, shoe shiners, American and French military personnel, several street musicians, my first sighting of an organ grinder and his monkey accompanist—a compilation of visions such as I had never before seen. We hurried through the enormous station, rushing through the streets to the huge government office on Gehrlinger Strasse.

There my mother left me outside. She evidently did not want me with her during this interview, either because she felt I might be bored while she pored for hours over hundreds of records or because she did not want me to hear the results of any bad news she might encounter. Prior to leaving, she pointed out a park across the street with a pond and ducks and benches at which I could sit. She also noted several antique shops on the next street over, which we had just passed, that might sell used musical instruments. If I found one I liked, she would look at it when she was done. The huge clock above us struck ten o'clock and she promised she would be done by noon, at which time we would search out for a new clarinet in earnest.

For several moments after my mother left me, I stood stock-still on the street in front of the government building. Before me loomed this huge stone monolith, larger than any building I had ever seen, with rows upon rows of stone-corniced, barred windows. Behind one of them possibly contained my father's fate. On the street, the stiff winds blew dust and papers in a cyclone swirl that seemed to direct all debris to a rubble-filled remnant of a burnt-out building in the lot next door. Above me, an endless blue sky twisted and shaped clouds in double-time speed, leaving me dizzy and light-headed.

I realized for possibly the first time since my terror-filled night on the bridge in Riga, I was alone. Viens pats, alone. This time, rather than being fearful, I was exhilarated. As an eleven-year old, I could not recall one second during the previous six years when I had not been in direct view and oversight by another human being. Be they

Russians, Latvians, Germans, guards, relatives, teachers, schoolmates, fellow trekkers, or my ubiquitous mother, I could not remember a time when one or another did not lurk nearby. Moreover, their presence was not a passive coexistence, but virtually all had a claim and stake in monitoring my behavior. I did not realize until that very moment in Stuttgart, standing before the government building, that I had been in a cell-less prison all those years. Such sudden freedom and release were stupefying.

My gaze was drawn to the street corner intersection where a traffic director stood, moving along the cars. He was enclosed in an oval, caged, metal platform raised several meters above street level, a red and white-striped tin roof over his head. In this cell, the red and black uniformed guard directed the activities of the swirl of cars moving swiftly through the intersection. The guard engaged in a series of elaborate hand and arm gestures, body english and head-bobbing, hip swivels and finger-pointing, designed to guide the speeding metal autos safely through. Most remarkable though was the total lack of coordination of the guard's motions with the resultant behavior of the autos. A hand held before him signaling an auto to stop was answered with the oblivious continuation of the auto. When the director waved a car onward to make a left turn, instead the car turned right. All his actions appeared isolated, significant to him, but virtually ignored by the preoccupied motorists.

This scene, more than puzzling to me, was transforming. I found myself in sudden sympathy and alignment with this foreign traffic guard. Much of my life had been spent in exactly this dilemma. Always surrounded by others, always under the purview of a world of strangers, yet at the same time, always alone and ignored. I had forever been a floating island in the tempests of humanity, an object to be assailed but never touched. Not the calm in the center of a storm; more the anti-matter in the center of an atom, repelling all objects in its sphere.

For that brief interlude, standing in front of that monolithic building, I was liberated. I broke out into a run, speeding down the sidewalk as fast as my legs could pump. I tore down the street;

my wooden-soled shoes striking against the concrete pavement, each stride sending a jolt straight through my hips into my spine. I felt as if I was jarring myself free of encumbrances.

Ten minutes of such running, this time not away from any threat or danger, but toward an uncharted future, left me somewhere in the neighborhood which we had just passed from the train station. With my legs still aching, I stopped in front of a store window displaying a dozen gleaming musical instruments. Above, a sign read, "Abels Musikinstrument—neu und angeluendet, genhendelt oder eintauschen, repariert und auffricshen, erworben und verkaufte." Abel's Musical Instruments—new and used, traded or bartered, repaired and reconditioned, bought and sold. I had no idea such a place with such a variety of possibilities existed. The temptation was too great. I had to enter. Besides, had not my mother set me on the task of finding myself a more suitable clarinet?

Upon entry, I became mesmerized. In front of and above me, on the walls and hanging from the ceiling like low-lying stars, resided hundreds of instruments. Oboes and tubas, piccolos and pianos, violins, fiddles, guitars, triangles, drums and trumpets, all converging on my senses in a syncopated rush. Never before had I witnessed such beauty, such workmanship, such sheen. In our makeshift band at the camp, all instruments were worn to exhaustion, the wood scratched and chipped, the brass scuffed and dulled, the valves sticky and congealed. Here the instruments were objects of idolatry instead of the afterthought discards of an indifferent world.

My eyes gravitated toward a section in the back holding a series of dark woodwind instruments mounted on the wall. One ebony, smooth, and polished clarinet with gleaming silver keys, a reed still in place, captivated my attention. Moving toward the wall, I gently rescued the instrument from its resting place, trying not to notice its 10,000 Mark price tag. For a time, I just caressed the clarinet in my hands. I stroked its smooth, tapered body fanning outward to the bell, fingered the silent valves. I ran my palm over the mouthpiece, barely touching the brand-new wooden reed at its tip.

With such an instrument in hand, who could resist? Unaware of anyone else around me, I slowly brought the mouthpiece up to my mouth, wetting the reed with my saliva, tasting the soft wood on my tongue. Out of my soul sprang a rendition of Benny Goodman's "If Dreams Come True." Instead of the standard, up-tempo, driving version I had heard on our camp gramophone, I produced a sultry, measured version that just matched the quiet bliss I felt. Out of the clarinet sprang a sound with a resonance and clarity and pitch such as I had never before produced. The melody rose and fell, glided and sailed, peaked to the heavens and sank to the depths at the whim of my hands, my lips, and my heart. I felt free—loose and loosened, soared and soaring for the first time in my life. So foreign was the sound emanating from my instrument, I was sure someone else must have been creating this resonance. I turned around to see if I had an accompanist hiding behind me, echoing my music.

There, standing with her hand clasped over her heart, her mouth wide open in awe, stood a gnome-like woman in a print dress. She could not have been more than ninety centimeters tall. Were it not for her round, almost bald head jutting out from her dress, she might have faded into the curtain from where she had just emerged. At the end of my rendition, this creature, who looked plucked right from a Brothers Grimm's fairy tale, broke out into loud applause, wiping the tears from her eyes. Despite her otherworldly appearance, as I finished the last note of the song, holding it in the air for as long as my lungs would allow, I found myself smiling back at her. When I finished, she rushed from behind her cloak up to my side, embracing me. I recoiled in reflex for a moment. Then I allowed her to reach up and touch my shoulders as I stood a full head above her.

Ordinarily, I would have rebelled against the touch of any stranger, especially this alien-like one before me. Her ageless face was unwrinkled, her head two sizes too large for her body. But whatever fear her countenance may have held for me was mitigated by a three-inch colored mark on her right cheek that must have been a birthmark. It had almost the perfect form and color of a red rose. If I saw such a mark nowadays, I would swear it was a tattoo, so perfect was its outline.

With tears still in her eyes and her hands resting on my shoulders in a form of salute, she said in vibrating German, "Mein Gott! What a beautiful sound! Where did you learn to play so wonderfully?"

Unwilling to reveal myself yet, I mumbled, "Oh, I picked it up here and there. You have beautiful instruments here."

"Are they not? Come, let me show you. I am Greta. I have worked here all my life and since my father died and left the shop to me, I have been alone with my instruments." Greta proceeded to give me a guided tour of the wondrous shop, stopping at random instruments, describing their history, their prior owners, letting me feel the shiny brass or effortless smooth valves. She finally asked about me, my name, where I came from. Never before had I thought to trust an outsider, much less a German. Yet, I felt compelled at that moment, with this kindred isolated soul, to tell her about myself. When, I had finished, Greta's eyes had filled with tears and she had grabbed hold of my hand in sympathy. She said, "These instruments are like my children. When I hear a child himself, a likewise lonely heart such as you embrace one of my own, I cannot help but be moved. For it is as if one of mein kinder has now found another spirit to join with. Has found a partner and playmate or maybe even a lifelong soul mate to unite with forever. And my own heart soars."

Then, in an extraordinary gesture of kindness, an act I forever after have considered an attempt at reparation, my gnome said, "So take this lovely clarinet with you, my son. Know that in it you have found a kindred spirit and that its fate is linked with yours forever. Take it as a gift from a childless mother who births happiness in ways the world does not recognize."

At that moment, I found myself compelled to embrace this stranger before me, matching her tears with tears of my own, pouring out the same emotion I had unleashed in my music. I wept for the loneliness I sensed she must endure despite her kinship with her instruments, and also for the loneliness that had been an unspoken part of my entire life. Unable to verbalize the pent-up emotions I felt, I wept for the normalcy I had never known. I wept in the realization that all of life did not have to be filled with upheaval and turmoil. In some forgotten corners of the planet there was peace.

After our embrace, I realized I had to leave empty-handed. I replied. "Thank you for your kindness. But I cannot accept such a gift. My mother would not allow it. But maybe we could return today or another day so I might fairly purchase this wonderful present you have offered. Might you hold onto it until I can return and claim it?"

I handed Greta the clarinet, turned in place and, without a glance backward, headed past the rows of sheen and polish, brass and burnished wood and out the door. Without saying so, I had every expectation I would return that very day. I had no way of knowing, though I would think of them often, I would never again lay eyes on my gnome or my clarinet.

*

I wandered on down the road, my mind still residing in the wondrous atmosphere of the music store. A block away, I glanced up at a street sign on the side of another decimated building, reading, "Flatcher Strasse." This street held, as all of the rest, a series of burnt-out, debris-laden lots. However, one intact structure stood stoically in the middle of the block, unharmed. As I gravitated toward that building, I noticed it had not a defect on it—not a scorch mark from a nearby flame, not a dent in the facade, not a scratch on its massive stone columns. All around lay nothing but ruins and residue, yet this edifice rested undisturbed and enduring.

I stopped in front of this building, turning to face it with my hands on my hips. Before me stood a massive, concrete structure with ten three-story columns guarding the glassed entryway. Atop the columns at the peaked façade of the building there rested a carved, concrete frieze similar to pictures I had seen of the façade of the Parthenon. As I stepped back into the street, I saw the scene depicted a battle. An army of slain or stricken men flanked the central figure, a naked warrior on horseback. He appeared victorious, completely uninjured, raising his sword triumphantly in the air. I wondered how such an image might convince the gods to let this building remain unscathed, but by all evidence, convinced they had been. The huge stone-sculpted lettering below the battle scene read "The First Bank of Stuttgart." It seemed likely to me at the time that this must be both the first and the last bank of Stuttgart.

Before wandering off, I found myself compelled to look a bit further into this "First Bank." I climbed the twenty-two marble steps up to the glassed entryway and peered in through the massive windows. Inside stood the most spectacular room I had ever seen. A dozen marble columns rose up to an ornate copper ceiling ten meters above the ground. The floor was a still lake of polished marble. Five huge crystal chandeliers hung at a variety of heights from the ceiling. Even in the daytime these chandeliers were lit up, ricocheting light off each other, off mirrored walls, shooting scattering beams through the room. On the walls hung huge, scenic tapestries, depicting fields of flowers and dense, fertile forests. Massive mahogany desks were scattered throughout the room, flanked by deep-green leather chairs, resting atop ornate Oriental rugs.

My line of sight finally focused on the huge stainless-steel vault at the back of the room. The door to the vault was slightly ajar and I wondered for a moment what wealth might lie behind its massive doors. Suddenly a tall, almost bald man with a dark mustache emerged from behind the vault's door. I quickly hid behind one of the pillars, able to peer out while hopefully remaining concealed. For a second, the man stared out toward the space I had been just occupying, then turned away. He walked to one of the mahogany desks and sat down. I remember being impressed with the bearing and manner of the gentleman, and, most of all, with his attire. For he was cloaked in the formal wear (ascot on white shirt, greatcoat with tails, striped trousers) I had only seen in pictures of the participants in a wedding. He proceeded to pick up one of the dozen or so piles of Marks resting on his desk, rapidly count the total and place the pack into one of a collection of velvet bags. He similarly went through each pile, as I marveled that such wealth existed in this world. He then collected his velvet cases of money and retreated back to the vault.

Observing the banker, I thought, what better way to spend one's life—clothed in finery, amidst the most elegant trappings, engaged in the solitary task of preserving a community's wealth and security, while shielded inside an invincible structure. What better ambition? At that moment, I felt I had encountered a lifelong calling. Should I ever escape my constraints, I could spend a lifetime at a site such as this one.

I walked on, out beyond the antique neighborhood, passing decimated buildings, empty lots, clustered stores, transfixed in thought of my two encounters. How long I walked and to where I wandered, I had no idea. Perhaps in my preoccupation, I noticed no one else. But the Stuttgart I experienced that day was a world with virtually no other inhabitants. Outside of the train station—other than the two I have just detailed, and another whom I will describe shortly—I cannot recall encountering another soul. It seemed almost like these actors had been deliberately chosen that day to inhabit the stage with me, to the exclusion of extras or bit players.

In my trance, though, I was still able to sense the devastation that was Stuttgart. On street after street, once-proud buildings lay in heaps of rubble on the ground. In scattered spots, workers had attempted to clear some of the rubble, where an occasional lot contained more organized piles of debris—wooden pilings over here, cement pillars there, a mountain of refractive glass here. I could not tell whether the work had been abandoned a day or a year before. The charred concrete gave off an oddly sweet, musky odor, lingering in the air long after the original carnage.

In my more-than-limited view of the world to that point, I felt I had somehow arrived at its end. The devastation civilization had heaped on itself had resulted in this final common pathway. Isolated souls, reaching out to whomever happened by, amidst a rubble of destruction too massive to ever overcome. Perhaps these are just the retrospective musings of the declining spirit that I now have become, and not the perceptions of an eleven -year-old boy with his destiny still before him. However, I can still recall that boy's sense of the absence of humanity. That whatever agenda, whatever destiny mankind had been seeking was now abandoned, perhaps for some brighter future elsewhere. But at that spot, at that moment, humanity was no longer involved in its own resurrection.

I began to head back to the neighborhood through which I'd run, not far from where my mother had left me. Several blocks from the governmental building lay an area off Hemminger Strasse, hiding a series of narrower cobbled lanes, populated by antique shops. My steps slowed to a crawl as I passed by store window after store window cluttered with artifacts, I became absorbed in the spectacle before me.

Even at eleven, I recognized the import of these artifacts, though at the time I could not formulate a conscious sensibility on the matter. These windows held countless articles—dressers and candelabras, tablecloths and silverware, hand mirrors and dressing tables, ornate lamps and vases, umbrella holders and cigarette lighters, hairbrushes and untold numbers of books, Oriental carpets and more children's toys than one could use in a lifetime—all remnants from someone's past. All such objects, I could recall, had inhabited our home in Latvia those many years ago; we had one-by-one discarded them along the trail of our exile. And I recognized that each and every one of the articles populating these windows, filling these shops, likely bursting out of warehouses somewhere or other in Germany was the residue, the detritus of another person's life and comfort and hopes and dreams. Each one had had an owner, each had belonged to a family, resided in a home, had been bought or handed down or possessed by a life that had either been scattered or extinguished. Each was never again to be reunited with its rightful owner.

I found myself staring in the window of a shop called Einhorns die Antiquitat. *The window held dozens of objects. But my eyes fixed on a display of jewelry and necklaces, spilling out from a wooden box. The more I looked, the more I became convinced I had seen one of the necklaces before—a silver chain holding a solitary amber stone in the middle. I felt certain the necklace had hung around my father's neck. The stone had held intense fascination for me while I rode around on his shoulders, exploring Riga. Often I spent those hours twirling his necklace in my hand, turning the amber jewel this way and that, watching its light reflect the sun on my father's black, black hair. You might say all amber jewels looked the same. Why should this one be more outstanding than others residing in similar stores throughout Europe? I felt compelled to look more carefully, to discover if I was correct.*

Despite some trepidation, I entered the store, announcing myself with the jarring ring of a bell. I was immediately struck by the scent of the shop—a kind of musty old perfume I had never before encountered. In the past, on entering an unfamiliar building, I would be met by the odor of teeming humanity, of unclean sweat, cluttered bodies, poorly-disposed excrement, tin walls or rotting wood, medicinally-washed clothes, or harsh soaps. I had never before come upon this scent of comfort and continuity and woolen permanence. I found myself wanting to curl up in one of the large leather chairs standing sentry at the entrance and just inhale.

Presently, a gray-haired, mustached, crumpled man in a wool vest with a gold pocket watch in his hand shuffled out. He seemed not at all perturbed to find before him a boy with likely no resources for a purchase. In gravelly German, he asked, "Yes, young man, may I help you? Is there something here that might interest you? Are you perhaps interested in something for your mother? Or perhaps just something for yourself? That is allowed, too, you know. To just buy something for yourself."

Emboldened by my experience with the gnome in the music store, I answered in the passable German I had picked up, "Well, sir, I was hoping to see that necklace in the window over there." The shopkeeper followed my gaze toward the jewelry box. "Well, let's take a look, then." He walked over to the window and picked up the necklace I had been admiring, then handed it to me. "You have wonderful taste, my son. This necklace, over a hundred years old, was originally a possession of Kaiser Wilhelm, a gift to his daughter on her twelfth

191

birthday. I am afraid it is worth over 15,000 Marks, a sum I am sure too great for your means."

I rubbed my fingers over the amber stone, reacquainting myself with the sloped indentations that formed the outline of a face, unusual for a piece of amber. My father had been so proud of the distinctive shape of his stone that he repeatedly told me was an exact replica of the face of my ancestor, Andrejs, the one slain by Germans centuries ago. My suspicions of the stone's origins were confirmed. I resisted the temptation to reeducate the shopkeeper as to the true origin of the necklace. Years later, I often speculated as to what circuitous route this necklace must have traveled after it left my father's possession in order to end up at this particular corner of the planet, awaiting my arrival. Little did I know I would in time discover the answer to that question. Little did I know I would regret that discovery forever after.

Just at that moment, the doorbell rang again and an elderly man entered the store. The shopkeeper looked up. In a great show of pleasure and surprise, he welcomed the man. "Horst, my old friend. I have not seen you for almost five years. Where have you been all this time? You are like a ghost from the past. Come, sit down here. Tell me what you have been up to during our terrible ordeal." And the shopkeeper and the visitor sat together in a chair across the room, now oblivious to my presence.

In such a circumstance, I am sure any eleven-year old boy on the planet would have had a similar impulse to mine. To steal what is rightfully yours is not stealing. Had not the Germans robbed my family and me of everything we had ever possessed in our lifetime? Would not reclaiming this one small symbol of our loss help right some of the wrong we had forever been subjected to? But I told myself, I was no thief. My mother had beaten into me the awareness that we were not them. Their crimes against us should not justify our crimes back against them. In Latvian, the words for revenge and vengeance, for retribution and punishment, were just the same. No crime justified another. Yet clutching my father's amulet in my hand, somehow knowing that my possession of this object meant for *certain that I would never set eyes on him again, an eleven -year-old boy's heart pounding inside my chest, I did the unprecedented. I ran. I tore out of the store, slamming the door shut behind me, the bell ringing, the sound of the shopkeeper shouting "Halt!" in thick, guttural German also ringing in my ear. I ran and ran as fast as I ever had in my life. I ran, squeezing my prize in my hand until my fingers went numb. I ran until I reached the block of the government building, my lungs burning, my head throbbing, my heart bursting.*

CHAPTER 21 ―――――――――――――――――

At Mr. Cassidy's funeral, Asher sat in the back row. As Asher had predicted, Mr. Cassidy had not yet been ill enough to die as a direct result of his disease. Though Mr. Cassidy had said his goodbyes, made his peace, and was ready for his own terminal event, Asher surmised that he had *not* been ready for the manner in which his end took place.

Mr. Cassidy had been taking his daily trek to the mailbox the prior Tuesday morning, a fifteen-yard journey in his threadbare plaid bathrobe and glued-on tam-o'-shanter, a trek that by then took him the better part of an hour. He was not yet ready to give up this one remaining victory over his dissenting body. That windy day in early May, Mr. Cassidy stopped to rest on his walker at the end of his driveway, pooped from his effort, trying to summon the energy for the journey back. The motorist who hit Mr. Cassidy stated afterward that he had no time to react, the disaster occurring in a split-second. Mr. Cassidy opened the mailbox and reached for his mail. A gust of wind, a supermarket flyer soaring into the air, a jerking arm movement upward, a tumbled walker followed by a tumbling man, all occurred in the blink of an eye. Mr. Cassidy fell backward into the path of the oncoming vehicle, the front fender crushing his skull. The screech of brakes stopped the car too late, but brought Mrs. Cassidy rushing out to the road to find her husband's lifeless body sprawled on the street. Her echoing screams could be heard five blocks away. The EMTs made not even a cursory attempt to revive Mr. Cassidy.

When he heard the news, Asher was almost as relieved as he was shocked by the accident. Such a sudden, quick demise had to be preferable to the tortuous decline Mr. Cassidy otherwise would have endured.

The day of the funeral, spring had finally won the battle with winter; the air on this brilliant sunny Friday held none of winter's chill. Daffodils were starting to pop out through the layer of mud, and an occasional robin winged past Asher as he hurried up the church walk. St. Paul's Church on Federal Hill was of the ornate, hundred-year-old variety, rising above the town like a sentry. The masonry walls topped with intricate turrets seemed as likely to house archers and swordsmen as clergy and supplicants. Despite his many years in Dover, Asher had never been inside this local monument.

Asher had darted out of his office an hour before lunch break to make it in time for the funeral. Since the episode with Tom, any diversion, even a funeral, had become a welcome change from seeing patients in his office. By then, each patient represented a new potential screw-up. Each encounter might further demonstrate that Asher's previously flawless judgment was now suspect.

The parking lot was full and a parade of mourners somberly headed through the huge wooden doors. This final testament to the life led by Mr. Cassidy did not surprise Asher. He had been to more funerals than weddings in his life and could accurately predict which ones would have a sparse turnout and which ones would be packed.

It took Asher a few seconds to acclimate to the dark interior, coming in from the brilliant blue sunshine. As always, he felt uncomfortable surrounded by the icons and mystic paraphernalia that defined the Catholic Church. Though after his trip to

Venice—steeped in images of a pained, suffering, multi-wounded, exsanguinating Christ—Asher had lost some of his squeamishness with the more sterile American depictions of Christ's demise. This church had only three graphic carvings of a crucified Christ on the walls. None of them had blood spurting from the wounds on Christ's wrists or ankles, and none portrayed the huge gash in Christ's right upper quadrant so prevalent in Italy.

For maybe a year, Asher, with rare exceptions, had stopped attending the funerals of his patients. Prior to that, he frequently tried to catch the services for patients to whom he felt particularly close, or for those whose lives or deaths had touched a nerve. But after thirty or forty such events, he abandoned the practice. Partly, Asher gave up because he feared being accused of favoritism. Why would he pay respects to certain patients and not others? By that juncture, the deceased would not much care. But family members would. They were bound to be insulted if they found out Asher had snubbed their loved one by missing his funeral while attending others.

He had another, more convincing reason for his decision. Asher found that at funerals, the family was placed in the awkward position of comforting *him,* rather than the other way around. Upon seeing him on the receiving line, one of the mourning family members, after a prolonged hug, would offer, "So wonderful of you to come, Dr. Asher. My mother loved you so. She had such faith in you. We know you did everything possible to help her. It must be difficult for you to lose your patents all the time. Thank you for all your efforts." And Asher would be left with the feeling that, if conventions allowed, the next sentence might be "Of course your efforts were not good enough to save my mother, were they? Had you been a bit more conscientious or more capable, maybe she would be alive today." Thankfully, no one ever came up with that line.

And all Asher could ever offer in response to the spoken and unspoken was "It must have been your mother's time." Or,

"At least she's no longer suffering." A feeble explanation for the unexplainable.

Sitting at the end of a packed pew of silent mourners, waiting for the funeral to begin, Asher could not help but revisit his mother's funeral three months before. Eighty-three-year-olds, Asher knew, were prone to dying. But her death, coming so suddenly, without warning—even though he should have been accustomed to such misfortune—surprised Asher. If it had not been his own mother, Asher might have had to chuckle at the circumstances: while playing golf one Sunday, his mother's golf cart had turned over in a sand trap, fracturing her hip. After uncomplicated surgery, a fat embolus traveled to her lung, killing her instantly. Though angry that this complication seemed preventable, Asher in time accepted that, of all the torturous ways people died these days, his mother's had to be among the least traumatic. Right after her funeral, though, the shocking discovery of his father's ultimate fate overwhelmed any rational thoughts on the process.

If you spend ten years of your life unaware of a mystery, its resolution provides no comfort. Thus, an adoptee who discovers at age eighteen that the parents who raised him are not his natural parents and that his birth parents live across the continent, derives no sense of relief or closure at the revelation. Rather, such information unleashes a flood of new questions and doubts and causes him to reexamine his entire upbringing. Such was the case with Asher when, after his mother's funeral, he read the letter contained in her safe-deposit box.

For years, Asher's mother had been fanatical about reminding him of the location of her safe-deposit box at the Washington Mutual in Fort Lauderdale. Prior to every plane flight she'd taken for the last eight years of her life, she had called Asher to remind him that the key to that safe-deposit box was hidden behind the light-switch plate in her bedroom. What purpose hiding the key in such a manner served, Asher had no idea. As for the safe-deposit box itself, he assumed his mother had sequestered jewels and a storehouse of cash in the box. He had no reason to suspect that whatever was hidden there had any more emotional import than an heirloom bracelet.

On the day after his mother's funeral, after Mandy had returned home to be with the kids, Asher bemusedly freed the safe-deposit key from its hiding place, then drove to the bank, only mildly curious as to what he might discover. Passing by the aged, black security guard, handing the safe-deposit number and key to the officious clerk in the bank vault, being handed in return the surprisingly light box and sitting by himself in a closed cubicle, Asher suddenly found his heart pounding. After several seconds of silent conjecture as to the contents of the surprisingly light-weight box, Asher discovered that the sole occupant of his mother's long-sequestered treasure was a sealed, plain white envelope, inscribed on its face in his father's unmistakable hand, "For Miles, To be opened only when all is settled."

Asher headed out of the dark, cool, marbled bank into the stark, glaring Florida sunshine, clutching the equally inflammatory white envelope, his mind swirling. Merely the presence of such a document would have been sufficient to ignite Asher. The fact that his mother had kept its existence a secret for these ten years, the fact that she herself had been able to refrain from opening its contents, and finally the cryptic message on the envelope all aroused in Asher an eruption of suppressed emotions. Asher's first impulse was to head right back into the bank and bury this message from the beyond back in its time capsule for some future generation to uncover. But Asher's need these past ten years to hear from his father was irresistible.

In spite of his palpable curiosity, Asher managed for the next two days—while dealing with both his mother's accountant and lawyer, while sifting through all her personal papers, while returning her leased car, placing her condo on the market, disposing of most of her furniture, and then sorting through all her effects—to refrain from exploring the letter's contents. For those forty-eight hours, that letter sat on the kitchen table of his mother's condominium, at once an object of overwhelming enticement and intense trepidation. Finally, on the night of the third day after his mother's funeral, Asher awoke in a sweat, retaining the isolated dream-image of an indecipherable message written in his father's script engraved on twin stone tablets. He headed straight to the untouched envelope, ripped it open and began reading.

The letter was handwritten on his father's business stationery, the formal engraving of his name, degrees, titles and Park Avenue address counterbalanced by the blue, tightly-controlled swirls of his father's compulsive penmanship. Asher noted for the first time that these uniform swirls now contained an unmistakable irregularity, like the interference from a defective electrical outlet disturbing an EKG tracing. Underneath the letterhead, his father had written the date November 15, 1986—the date of his death.

Dear Miles,

If you are reading this letter it means that I have had the courage and fortitude to complete my intention and it is now some distant time from that event, when you have undoubtedly journeyed through a river of emotions revolving around my loss and your feelings about me in life and then in death. By the time you read this letter, you will hopefully have come to some peace regarding our often-tempestuous relationship and my sudden passing.

Which immediately brings to mind the issue of why I should write this letter at all, realizing it may disturb or even shatter that painstaking equilibrium you hopefully have achieved. My reasons are several fold and, in the end, may be inadequate. They may even ultimately lie in the selfish need of every man to explain his life and his decisions to those he leaves behind and also to himself. But selfishness is not my sole motivation. For I realize my sudden death may leave much unexplained and may never allow you to achieve that serenity of which I have referenced above. Perhaps our conflicts, perhaps my ongoing harsh judgments of you, my need to always spur you onwards and upwards, will forever leave you resentful of me and of yourself—leave you forever hypercritical.

The other reasons that I have debated emerge from platitudes and homilies and leave me still on the fence. The proverbial "The truth shall free you." Or Aristotle, "All men by nature desire knowledge." Alternatively, the platitude, "What you do not know cannot hurt you." And from the Bible: "For in much wisdom is much grief: and he that increaseth knowledge increaseth sorrow." No ultimate arbiter lay in these.

So my decision to write this letter, then to trust it with your mother to hold and protect until the proper time and finally to will it to you in full awareness of the explosiveness of this information, lies in the feeling (yes, the feeling and not the certitude of reason) that you have a transcendent need to be freed of me. That my model of perfection, which I have cultivated all of these years, that my assuredness and my attainments did not prevent me from being human, from being flawed. That though I set for you a goal to strive toward, you have it within yourself to exceed my achievements. The rationale of every taskmaster is that he acts solely for the good of his charges and, though that role may have been based on the only model for parenting available to me, such a posture may now, in retrospect, have been unnecessary. You would likely have achieved as much with less pain and less turmoil between us had I been less judgmental. Now I write this explanation to free you from such judgments. You no longer need to answer to me or to any man. I no longer judge you. You may now judge me.

I am sure you have heard and absorbed the information that I have contracted Parkinson's disease within the year prior to my death. Although it is a minor case, I have been on Sinemet to minimize the symptoms. I have tried to withhold the information about my illness from everyone possible, including you, since we travel in some of the same circles and I did not want to put you in the awkward position of having to reveal or hide family confidences from your fellow workers. As I know you must be aware, no case of Parkinson's is truly minor to an eye surgeon.

You likely have also heard that because of my illness, I have been asked to no longer perform surgery. I do not believe such a course is necessary, since to me my skills are undiminished. However, the powers that be in the hospital have decided otherwise.

Further, you may have discovered that I have several malpractice suits pending against me. In actuality, these suits involve cases when my symptoms were undetectable and moreover, in my view, involve complications that any eye surgeon might encounter. These cases, though, are the crux of my dilemma. Despite the complexity of eye surgery in general, despite the degree of difficulty of my particular practice—my reputation for handling some of the most complex diseases no other eye surgeon will touch—the hospital administrators as well as the malpractice insurance carriers have determined that my illness contributed to the regrettable loss of vision in the patients involved in these suits. In addition, they have concluded that I deliberately misled and concealed details of my medical condition from them, exposing them to greater liability. As proof—which I have no ability to dispute—they produce my last application for hospital privileges that ends with my sworn signature, stating that I have no medical condition that would impair my ability to care for patients. My malpractice application contains a similar affidavit.

These administrators and bureaucrats further maintain that such statements represent fraud and absolve them from financial responsibility in the conduct of the malpractice cases. In result, I am now left unsupported. After thirty years of untainted medical practice serving my hospital, after thirty years with no prior malpractice cases against me, after thirty years of impeccable care of my patients, I have been abandoned. The professional result of such a position is humiliating. The financial result is ruinous. Leaving me exposed without insurance, these cases could cost me personally over five million dollars.

You might ask, did I deliberately deceive the administration and, in result, my patients regarding the nature of my illness and the extent of my disability? Did pride and denial cloud my judgment, allowing me to continue to practice and thereby endangering those patients? Is my current dilemma justified? The evidence cannot be disputed. I misrepresented myself. But scrutinizing my motives in retrospect, I still can testify that I believe my illness, at that stage posed no threat to my patients. I believe those cases had nothing to do with my medical problems, complications which could have, and, in fact, have happened to every eye surgeon in the country. My opinions now though are meaningless.

Which leads to the final question. Is suicide ever justifiable? Is it ever a rational response to an irrational world to kill oneself? If you are reading this letter, then my response would have to be and must have been, yes. The professional humiliation I will endure, I can shoulder. The loss of my ability to operate, to further care for patients, to abandon my life's calling, I can survive. However the financial ruin we will sustain after a lifetime of struggle, I am not willing to accept. I will not see the fruits of my life's labor be tossed out with the morning garbage. I will not see your mother lose all of her accumulated possessions and watch our home being confiscated. I will not stand idly by while your painstakingly accumulated inheritance is snatched away by the wolves.

When I am gone, I am sure the hospital will settle these cases, not wanting to endure negative publicity or further scrutiny. Based on my careful arrangements, I am sure that my life insurance policies will be honored. I have justified my clumsiness by spraining my ankle a week ago, placing me on crutches. I have measured the most narrow part of the train platform to position myself. I have timed the event when the fewest witnesses will be present. Your financial futures will be secure. You and your sister and your mother will have some difficulty in adjusting to my loss. But, as all survivors and especially all Ashers have done throughout our history, you will go on.

Again you might ask, having absorbed these revelations, why do I insist on stirring up such memories? Why resurrect such pain? Why revise history in the name of truth?

First off, I ask that you forgive me. Both for the act I am about to commit and then for the revelation of this act in such a manner. You will no doubt curse me when you are done reading this letter, as I am sure you have cursed me so many times before. But I also ask that you now revise your opinion of me. That you see me not as the icon I have portrayed, but as a flawed seeker, not unlike you. That you see me as someone who believed he acted for your own good in driving you perhaps too harshly,; as someone who was motivated only by his love for you and concern for your future. Take this information and hate me for a while for giving it to you. But then use it to make your own life better. Don't adopt my role as your own harshest taskmaster, the memory of me still riding on your shoulders, whipping you to perform. Lighten up on yourself as I should have lightened up on you when I had the chance. And forgive us both, for the sins we have committed and more so for the ones yet to come.
Your loving father.

The morning after reading this message three times over, still bleary-eyed from his sleepless night, Asher retrieved the crushed letter from the garbage compactor, realizing that whether he disposed of it or not, its contents could not be erased. Although nagged by that one kernel of suspicion left by that insurance agent years ago, Asher had never believed his father capable of self-destruction. Now that one kernel had multiplied times a thousand, heated up, and each had sequentially exploded inside his brain. If his rigid, rigorous, unyielding father could annihilate himself, no matter how justifiably, who was not capable of such an act? If his father could not be depended on, then who and what on this earth could?

Rummaging through the garbage that morning, Asher conjured up an unwanted photographic image in his brain that thereafter he could never shake. He formulated a synaptic connection like the one you might unconsciously resurrect even years later on passing by the site of a flaming automobile of the indelible odor of burning rubber. Whenever he thought of this letter, then when he thought of his father at all and, finally, even when he thought of his own childhood, this one image dominated his mindset. His unconscious involuntarily generated the still-life snapshot of the distinguished, gray-haired nobleman who had been his father, adorned in his immaculate three-piece suit and glistening Italian loafers, suspended in mid-air above the train tracks, in the split second before being pulverized by the onrushing train, the expression on his face, as always, impenetrable.

*

The ornately dressed, somber priest who took the pulpit at Mr. Cassidy's funeral service rescued Asher from his musings, though the dark cloud hovering over his psyche lingered. At first, as in most Catholic funerals, there was a strange schizophrenia. The family members were steeped in a cauldron of misery and grief, wailing to the heavens and the devils for snatching up their loved one, while the priest left the deceased virtually unmentioned.

For fifteen minutes, after everyone had settled in their seats, the white-robed priest with his sequined headdress recited relevant passages from the Bible. Every reference to death was met with a loud wail from what Asher assumed was one of the children.

Thankfully, he did not recognize Mrs. Cassidy's voice among the wailers. Asher found mourning practices were much like those of childbirth. Some mothers and likewise some mourners endured their suffering in stoic silence, allowing virtually no cries to cross their lips. Others would cry and scream and wail till the room shook with their pain. Which helped more remained to be seen. For Asher, though, the silent sufferer made the experience much more bearable.

Finally, deviating from form, the priest made reference to Mr. Cassidy, unlocking Asher from his silent thoughts. "And we are gathered here today in sorrow and in sadness with a great heaviness in our hearts to share the loss of our beloved son, William Seamus Cassidy.

"William Cassidy, as all of you are fully aware, was a giant among men. He created a world around him that we can hold as an example for each of us. Beloved by all—family, friends, and fellow workers—he was no grandiose hero. Just a mortal man who made the most of his all-too-brief time on this planet. Though a hero he might have been, had he been born under other circumstances, for he had the principles, the steadfastness, and the bullish pride of one. With each forward step he took, he lifted himself higher and spiraled upward, bringing himself that much nearer the mount, just as the down-and-outer will let each defeat lead into another. And each of that poor soul's failures will lead him further and further from the truth and from the heavens, leaving him displaced from his true nature and from all that he believes. He will then spiral downward into nothingness.

"But William Seamus Cassidy would have none of that. He was an unrecognized man of greatness, unrecognized only because context dictates how we are all judged. A fish may rule in a pond or in an ocean, depending on where he was spawned. Thus William Cassidy will be remembered not as a leader of nations, but rather as a leader of his community and as a man who made the most of his life. His site of battle was here and his fellow soldiers were his neighbors. We have been blessed to have had him spend his lifetime fighting alongside all of us."

Listening to the priest's voice resonate through the church, mesmerized as much by the tone as the message, Asher picked up maybe every third word. But he came alert at the concept of one defeat leading into another. Two subsequent words penetrated his psyche: "context" and "spirals." For months, Asher had been searching for just these ideas. He concocted an image in his head, retrieved from a college calculus class in which those two words, "context" and "spirals," labeled the x -and y-axes of a graph. They plotted out a complex, derivative equation that corresponded to his jumbled thought pattern. And that equation would then describe a geometric form, a physical construct of his convoluted mindset. Irregular, uneven, inconsistent that form might be, but identifiable and mapable nonetheless.

Asher too had not been born of a time or in a site where great victories or grand failures would be played out on a worldwide stage. He was not to have the opportunity for monumental heroics or epic destruction. Rather he would be judged by the daily decisions he made in the one-on-one interactions he had with his patients and with his family. And while these judgments might not be earthshaking, nonetheless, they made up the stuff of each man's existence. Every one of us has his own limited view of the world, in which we feel our own pain and record our own triumphs above all else. Since these are all we have to cling to, of necessity we must make those moments of the same import as those who live their lives in the deepest pits or atop the highest mountains. All of us live and die, laugh and cry, celebrate and mourn in the context of our own lives.

That spiral the priest described lifting William Cassidy higher could just as well send another man to the depths. Each backward step may lead to another and another, until that is the only direction in which a man knows how to go. In the confines of his own life and expectations, Asher wondered how many steps backward he himself had already taken.

Before he left the cathedral that day, Asher took a moment to pray that he still had the ability and desire to reverse his own downward spiral, to once again strive for the summits. And to pray that his convoluted, descending geometric form might be transformed into a simple, algebraic, ascending straight line.

Jonathan Rosen

JO AVOTS

When I finally arrived on the street in Stuttgart at our designated meeting spot in front of the government building, the clock read nearly three o'clock, some three hours late. My mother was beside herself, agitated, pacing, pointing, garbling sounds and orders at the officials she had mobilized to search for me. It took her at least a full minute to catch sight of me, though I had spotted her while I stood still on the corner taking in the scene, not sure of how she would react, weighing my options. When her wild, searching eyes finally did hone in on me, my mother launched from her sentry spot and bounded toward me like a crazed gazelle.

With several potential responses available to my mother and with my guilt feeding on my imagination, I stood still, awaiting the inevitable tirade of fear-laced fury I expected she would unleash upon me. In such circumstances in the past, my mother had always allowed anger and fright to hold sway over love and relief. I expected no different a display that day, for during those years, she had lost to the Germans a husband and a home, a father and a life. The fear of losing her son, no matter how emotionally estranged, would be likely too much for her to endure.

But my mother surprised me. She reacted in a manner unexpected and out of character, which forever after caused me to reevaluate my perception of her feelings toward me, to revise my sense of the position I occupied in her life. For up to that moment, I saw myself in the role of an old trunk that she lugged around from place to place, one with sentimental value and holding a few sobering memories, too ingrained to be discarded, but also too cumbersome and unwieldy to be appreciated. After that day, I surmised I might be more akin to a limb—a leg or an arm—that has been damaged in some way. And this limb, though at times ignored and often a burden, when threatened with amputation, becomes the owner's sole purpose for existence.

My mother reached me in two seconds. She placed her hands upon my shoulders and for a moment gazed into my eyes, then

208

brushed her fingers across my face to assure herself this was truly me and I was truly there. Then she clutched me to her breast in a hug so fierce and long I hoped I would not smother in her grasp. In our prolonged embrace, I angled my torso away from hers, hoping my mother would not hear the jangling necklace in my pocket. But she was too overcome to take note of such subtleties.

Finally, she relaxed her hold of me, allowing me to move off to her side a bit. But instead of questioning me as to my whereabouts or scolding me for wandering off and being so inconsiderate, she merely clutched my hand to her side, keeping me no more than an arm's length away as we headed back to the train station. She did not glance back at the legion of uniformed or suited characters she had mobilized to help search for me. She did not speak a word about the hours she had spent in the smothering, unfurnished office, pouring over page after page after page of stamp-sized photographs to no avail. She merely towed me back to the station as quickly as possible, content to return home with as much baggage as she had brought, possibly, for once, not mourning what she had lost, but grateful for what she had retained.

On the train back to Esslingen, to the camp that now felt like a retreat, my mother volunteered not a word. She never spoke of the events in the government building that day, neither of the results of her search, nor of the pain she endured during the search. She never revealed if her efforts yielded any progress. But after that trip to Stuttgart, although I did not realize this until years later, she never actively pursued my father again. She never again wrote to officials, no longer harangued the German government. She made no further sojourns to explore farfetched leads. She no longer tracked the untrackable. Though I believe she also neither abandoned hope that my father would return, nor ceased praying for their reunion during every waking moment. But from that day on, she became the passive Penelope, holding out hope, but allowing life to proceed unobstructed.

Halfway into our train ride, while sitting across from her on the trip home, the darkened countryside whipping by our window,

I could feel her somewhere off in space, again taking an internal journey. Trying to return her to the here and now, hoping to rescue her from her morbid ruminations, I reached into my pocket and pulled out the prize I had rescued from the Germans. I placed it on the table between us, sure she would immediately recognize the amber necklace and rejoice in its recovery as I had. When she looked down at my offering, startled out of her reverie, she stared at the necklace for a moment before reaching for it. Then she picked up the object, stared deeply at the stone and felt the smoothness just as I had. "What a lovely necklace, Zigfrid. Where did you get such a treasure?"

I was prepared for her questioning and replied, "A shopkeeper gave it to me when I caught his dog running away from his store. The dog was running down the street away from his owner and almost jumped into my arms. The shopkeeper was so grateful to me, he gave me this present for you." My mother did not question this improbable explanation. But more puzzling, she did not acknowledge for an instant that this was the selfsame necklace my father had worn around his neck for as long as I knew him. And that it was the same stone that had been in our family for over ten generations. She merely replied, "Thank you anyway, Zigfrid. But having you back in my arms is gift enough. You keep the necklace for yourself. You hold on to it." And to this day I have.

*

I will now attempt to engage the history that depicts the discovery of my father's ultimate fate—the extraordinary circumstances that unveiled that discovery, the cataclysmic events themselves, and finally the life-altering effects of my discovery. The fact that up to this point I have discussed my findings with no one—not my wife, certainly not my mother—plus my belief that this story may be interred with my remains, spurs me to record it here, if for no other purpose than to verify to myself that all was not a subversive nightmare, that the events I shall describe truly happened.

First allow me an indulgence. I will not detail here the reasons I waited over fifty years before I pilgrimmaged back to my homeland and then to Israel. I will not delve into my unconscious or possibly even deliberate avoidance of the journey that permitted me in ignorance to indulge in a life of relative ease and comfort. I will refrain from exploring how the effects of that pilgrimage ultimately resulted in my cataclysmic spiral of decline. I will leave the analysis of these events to the psychologists, to the historians, or to my subsequent generations, should any chose to engage the task. Ļauj aizmigušiem suņiem gulēt. *Let sleeping dogs lie.*

I will however briefly speak to the direct results of that journey. For many would point to my decision to embark on such a quest as a fatal error. Surely by judging the subsequent events, they might be correct. I departed a successful banker with a wonderful home, a loving wife, two accomplished children, and my health intact. And within three years of my return, my children had scattered, my bank had failed, my wife had finally surrendered to my brooding silence, and my health had deserted me. The life of comfort, security, and community that I had painstakingly built over decades vanished in a blink. The fortress I had spent a lifetime erecting—built in a land insulated against tyrannical whimsy, designed to safeguard my home and my loved ones—suddenly evaporated into the atmosphere. My trip and these ensuing events cannot help but be linked as cause and effect.

Yet such characterizations I resist. Yes, my journey changed me. Yes, my life irrevocably was altered, declined, was subsumed. How could it not? My father was no longer the man I had enshrined. I could not be the same son of this altered legacy.

I have learned our lives too often are not the convenient results of cause and effect we would hope to believe. We may decide a course of action, execute that plan, expect to reap the fruits of those actions no šūpuļa līdz kapam, *from womb to tomb. But the deities or the devils, the aristocrats or the autocrats, the saints or the insane, all may have alternate visions. Their agenda most often does not coincide with our own.*

Though the bank was mine, I had little influence over the savings and loan debacle of the eighties that resulted in its ultimate demise. Though my health was likewise mine, parasites do not tend to obey the exigencies of their host. Though my marriage, too, was mine... well, on that count, I stumble. For I cannot deny, that failure lies solely at my feet. After thirty years of a marriage, of linked thoughts and emotions, I withdrew. I could not justify drawing my wife into my circle of shame. At least that is what I told myself while hiding in the anesthesia of alcohol. And I suffer the consequences of that decision and that failure most of all.

Yet as I sit here much closer to the dead than the living, I have few regrets. I have passed on a different legacy than the one handed to me. I have created a family and a life that will endure and flourish without the fear and subversion that has characterized my own. I have chartered a new course for my progeny's travels.

I have read the theory that man's ultimate purpose is to be the vehicle, the repository, and the temporary transport of his contained DNA. Over thousands upon thousands of years, we have passed on from generation to generation, virtually unchanged, our genetic information. Throughout history, these microscopic strands of chemical links fanatically dedicated to their own perpetuation have directed our bodies and our souls, our intellect and our abilities. Well, in my life, I can categorically state I have sheltered these compounds, preserved them, passed them on to a new generation who have every hope, opportunity and potential to pass their own chemical legacy on to a more secure and safe vehicle than that which I have occupied. I have done my part. No faltering steps, no reprehensible knowledge of the past, no shattered imaginations can alter that fact. I have done my job.

Surprisingly, when I did finally arrive in Riga—at age fifty-five, almost fifty years since I had been extracted from my homeland, (alone, since my proposal to my mother to join me on this journey was met with guttural disdain)—the experience was emotionally sterile. In retrospect, I should have realized my memory of places and events occurring at such a young age would be virtually eradicated. Though the names of streets, towns, landmarks, and sites held significance for me, no visual encounter with them ignited a flash of recognition or a spark of emotion. It seemed as if the hoped-for shrines of my childhood were plasticine recreations of my homeland, holding similar names to remembered sites, but devoid of context or connectivity.

Likewise the people I encountered held no sway over my sensibilities. My relations and their descendants had long since deceased or emigrated. They may have been dispersed by the vast postwar migration, interred in distant graves in foreign lands, or buried in local, unidentified crypts. The friends and neighbors whose names I was able to pry from my mother's locked memory banks had similarly moved on to other sites or to other levels of existence. Their remnants produced no sparks of recognition on either side, no flashes of shared enthusiasm for a past they all seemed desirous of repressing.

Plus the steady stream of pilgrims over the years—expatriates now residing in the U.S. or Canada or Australia, all possessing a saccharine picture of their homeland—had produced in the natives a jaded intolerance for the process. The besieged inhabitants had no interest in participating in another rite of emotional disinterment. They had their fill of being a showcase for a generation's sufferings, feeling pressured to simulate a sympathetic connection with distant relations that was hair-thin at best.

On my first day in Riga, I stood at the door of 21 Cemetery Street for the better part of an hour, gathering my courage. Hanging on the stone wall above the front door flew the flag of the new Republic of Latvia, the same white stripe on a red field that had been outlawed by the Russian occupiers, and now waved proudly in the breeze. Perhaps sometime over the past half-century my father had returned here, he too searching for his roots and possibly his family. Finally, seeing the window shade flutter and a face briefly appear, I managed a feeble knock on the door. After more than a few moments passed, an unkempt graying woman in a worn smock, whom I would have surmised was the housekeeper but for her reaction to me, opened the door. I stammered in hesitant Latvian, "Sorry to disturb you ma'am,

I am visiting from America. Once in my youth, before the war, I lived in this house."

Before I was able to utter another sentence, the woman scowled at me, resurrecting a phrase I had not heard for fifty years. "Noledets ebrejs. Fucking Jews. Wanting your homes back after being gone for half a century. You left us to suffer all that time with the Russians. Take it up with your government. Leave us alone." She slammed the door in my disbelieving face, leaving me speechless.

A week of similarly closed alleys climaxed on the final day of my travels. I have already alluded to this one seminal event in Riga when I stood on the exact bridge I had hidden under in my search for my father those many years ago. Knowing that this site of all places would spark my memory, I had avoided visiting it until the end of my trip. I had been torn between the desire for remembrance and the fear of recapturing the terror I had endured those many years before. Inevitably, I was forced to confront this charged location.

So one night at dusk, I again found myself standing at the crest of the Riga Bridge at the very spot at which I had hidden from the Nazis. The cobblestones under my black leather shoes still impacted my feet in the same way they had fifty years before. The sounds of the river rushing and the mist of the air still surrounded my senses as if I had never left. A church bell clanged in the distance. A man with a walking stick clip-clopped over the bridge and the stone walls resonated, multiplying the sound by a hundred times. I stopped myself from turning around for fear I once again would confront the legion of Nazi soldiers still ready to snatch me up. I peered into the swirling river waters, searching for a reflection of the man I had become, or the child I once had been, or the soul I hoped to recapture. And in response, I found a swirling torrent of rushing water carrying downstream, along with rocks and silt and hidden creatures, the tumult of my memories and the whirlpool of my imaginings.

Possibly at that moment, the virus finally took control of my senses, for there I stood, shivering under the gray sky with rain pelting my uncovered scalp. At that instant, I decided to finally research my history, to truly recapture my past. Here in my homeland—devoid of connection—alienated from it, this place monolithically indifferent to me, refusing to unveil its secrets. I realized I would have to search elsewhere. My thoughts jumped to one site, to no source on this earth other than Jo Avots, the original source—Israel.

Why Israel? Israel was not on my itinerary for this trip. I had never before even consciously thought of visiting this holy land. I had no relatives there. I was not sure I knew a soul who had ever lived there. I was not Jewish, had minimal connection to the Christ and his legacy memorialized in Israel, and had no attraction toward Islam. I could not fathom the compulsion.

On reflection, I confess to a more than usual affinity for the Jews. On some subconscious level, I suspect I have always identified with them. Their suffering has paralleled my own. Their path through history and through the continents has matched mine. When attacked by German youth during my years in Germany, following the hurled rocks were the hurled epithets: wilden, Juden hund, der schwine auslanders—*savages, Jew dogs, fucking foreigners. Always linked, always clumped into the same reviled dredges. Not that my suffering has matched theirs. Not that my people's Diaspora compares to theirs. Yet persecution by an unrelenting, multi-faced force, daily uncertainty, and pervasive powerlessness comprise both of our histories. It affords a kinship I have felt, but never truly identified.*

So perhaps my trip to Israel met the need for the pilgrimage I had hoped would have been satisfied by my travel to Latvia. Perhaps that is where I would link to my past and map out my future. I was unaware that the fulfilled quest for my father and the incineration of my past would also take place there. Had I known that, can I say I would have still made the journey? Useless speculation, I answer. No choice, no point. Kas padarīts, tas padarīts—what's done is done.

However, rather than the sanctuary of peace and contemplation I had imagined, for me, in late summer, 1992, Israel was an unfathomable Tower of Babel. A non-harmonic convergence of inconsolable elements. Others might have found challenge and stimulation in its contradictions and chaos; I only found contentiousness and circuitry overload.

First, even the topography rankled—three hundred-sixty square miles of irreconcilable differences. From sun-glistened ocean to crusted desert; fecund gladed forests abutting shrubless, scrubbed hillsides; endless mountainous vistas contended with ancient, stonewalled shrines; impenetrable fortresses beside sterile, glass-walled cities. Nothing jived, nothing melded. From Eilat to Masada, Tel Aviv to Jerusalem, the Dead Sea to the Jordan's West Bank, the Negev to Ein Gat, all dissembled.

The people likewise jangled—foreboding, caftan-clad Moslems juxtaposed with bearded Hasidim; fully robed and veiled Islamic women waded in the Dead Sea next to their nearly naked spouses; Bermuda-shorted, loud-shirted tourists toting cameras and camcorders commingled with bespectacled scholars and dark-haired, olive-skinned sabras; parades of nuns on pilgrimage, unloading from buses that would soon transport soiled peasants and their caged chickens. No wonder no one got along. No one was remotely like anyone else.

Most dissonant of all were the voices. A cacophony of languages, dialects, tongues, accents, idioms, and jargons all clanging against each other, never harmonizing. Perhaps the sound resonated too much in my mind with the reverberations I had heard years before in the DP camps, with a hundred languages spoken in a hundred different volumes by a hundred conflicting and conflicted souls. The memory was too close, too real, too sad. All around the air was permeated with elements non-synchronous, asymmetric, discordant.

There was one spot, I am almost ashamed to confess, where I did find solace in this multi-cultured labyrinth. One oasis in this distempered tract gave me peace and tranquility. At least for a few days. At least until I later plumbed its depths. That site was Yad Vashem. Yad Vashem—the Israeli Holocaust museum—became my one source of solace in this too-troubled and troubling land.

Just as I had no conscious intention of traveling to Israel, I had no plan to visit the Holocaust museum. I am not sure I was even aware the site existed. Certainly I knew of the one in Washington, though I had been loathe to visit there—the depicted horrors felt too close to home for me to voluntarily partake in the experience.

Yet some cosmic scheme seemed to draw me to this shrine, a kind of psychic divining rod.

Once there, I introspected for the better part of three days. The museum itself was multi-sensory and richly textured, a Dantesque wandering from heaven to hell and back. The noblest, most beautiful attributes of mankind coexisted with depictions of the most vile, obscene behaviors imaginable in a surreal greened and concrete setting—part sculpture park and part prison. In combination though, a site at which one could spend, at once captivated and revolted, a lifetime.

For the first two days, I wandered the wooded paths, rested on park-like benches, studied the awesome schizoid sculptures, and most of all, inhaled the silence. For nowhere else in Israel was quiet revered. Nowhere else did Arab and Jew, priest and rabbi, youthful and aged coexist in hallowed silence and quiet contemplation as in this memorial to man's most noble and ignoble nature.

The memorial held wonders at every turn. I wandered down the crushed stone, uneven paths through networks of open-air passageways and tunnels and tombs and shrines surrounded by honey-colored engraved walls of concrete honoring the thousands of obliterated Jewish communities throughout Europe. I walked down the Avenue of the Righteous, honoring those who risked their lives to help the Jews. I stood awed before the spiraling, six-branched candelabra memorializing the six million Jews who perished during the Holocaust. I wept before the glassed-in display of an almost infant-like, yellow stuffed bear that had been the sole companion of a four-year-old Dutch Jewish boy who had spent the war in hiding. He apparently had been tossed from Christian family to Christian family, hoping not to be discovered by the Nazis, his only comfort this tattered, decimated stuffed bear that miraculously survived the Holocaust along with its master. How could I not harken back to the day when I was forced to relinquish my shoebox of miniature toys while fleeing the oncoming Russians?

Only when I abandoned the ground's enlightened surface and became submerged in the nether regions of the Historical Museum and Archives did my too brief serenity perish like the canary in a coal mine. Have I ever recovered that serenity since? Will I ever recover it once again? I cannot say.

How to describe the next two days, which I spent immersed in the world's recent insanity and in my own personal humiliation? Clearly, those first days of tranquility spent exploring the memorial's outer layer were self-delusional. In retrospect, they constituted another subconscious attempt to avoid the inevitable. For whatever divine intervention had brought me to this particular corner of the planet had not intended for me to be merely engaged in generic pathos and humanitarian empathy. It had an entirely other agenda in mind. Yet, while wandering the shrine, I managed to convince myself just this end itself was adequate justification for my journey. If I never found a shred of evidence as to my father's fate, just steeping myself in this vortex of emotion seemed sufficient.

For if it is nothing else—not a shrine, not a memorial, not a work of art, not a tribute, not a lesson, not a hope, not a prayer for the future, or a eulogy to the past—Yad Vashem is, most of all, a warehouse for the truth. Nothing contained in these forty-five acres of buildings and sculptures, crypts and memorabilia, holds a candle to the vast irrefutable evidence catalogued in its core—its archives. And for those who dare to confront such accumulated horror, these archives stand silently, patiently waiting.

Contained in these vast stores of painstakingly itemized documents is the encyclopedic, exhaustive record of the greatest crime against humanity ever conceived. The sheer volume of information reposed in this site is staggering. Ten thousand photographs from Europe before, during, and after the Holocaust, two million pages of written testimonies from survivors detailing their personal horror, tens of thousands of recorded statements from around the world, culled from the surviving victims. At least fifty million original documents— personal documents of the Jews, passports, diaries, memoirs, lists of confiscated assets, deportation lists, and internal documents from the Nazi bureaucrats and their co-conspirators. All these combine to construct an irrefutable, sickening body of evidence detailing the enormity and the savagery of the Nazi sin.

And all combine to erode any faith or hope or misguided notion that man is a salvageable creature, or that somehow the nobility of our nature will in the end triumph over our baseness or over the core of our evil.

CHAPTER 22 ————————————

Once again in the throes of a mind-numbing sleeplessness, Asher returned to his letter to Mandy.

> *It's been almost a week since I started writing to you. Mr. Cassidy died. You know that old codger whose funeral I went to last week. I guess you can't help but become reflective at a funeral. That must be what they're for—you think about lost lives, loved ones who've gone, your own mortality, what you're doing with the time you're allotted. I know I'm screwing up mine, at least for now. But Tom's death and apparently my dad's are hanging over me like that cloud of thunder and rain that refused to leave us on our honeymoon.*
>
> *I've heard the notion that a man's life contains one seminal moment, one critical juncture at which he defines his true character. That, when all trappings, defense mechanisms, all his life's accumulated coats are stripped away, he's ultimately exposed. Maybe that's just male machismo. But it seems as if women tend to measure their worth not by such a singular, dramatic episode, but by a lifetime of devotion and dedication. Men don't afford themselves this*

luxury of accumulated worth. They are who they are when most focused and most stressed.

Most of the time, I suspect this moment tends to sneak up on you, catch you without preparation. You are forced to rely on your basic instincts, with no time for prevarication or forethought. If you're alone with no witnesses, maybe you can rationalize the conclusions; you could delude yourself that the moment itself was convoluted or confounded by other circumstances and make excuses. However, if another person witnesses your crime, you have no such refuge in self-delusion.

When confronted with a gun-toting assailant, you might instinctively hide behind your wife. Or you might be tempted by an open cash register in a convenience store with no one in sight. Maybe you see a gang attacking someone in an alley and turn away. All cast a spotlight on your essential nature. Afterwards, you might rationalize your transgression. But what if a newsman reports the next day that you were among witnesses of the mugging who refused to help? Or, if the security camera in the store shows you grabbing a hundred dollar bill from the register and stuffing it in your pocket? Or if your wife spots you duck behind her at that life-threatening moment. All your defenses are gone? Then you may no longer hide from the world's judgment of you or your own judgment about your true nature.

And that's my dilemma, Mand. Despite spending most of my life caring for others and despite my oath, when I was confronted with my moment of truth, I failed. I took a shortcut, an evasion that revealed the fraud that I am.

Exactly one week after Tom and Irene came to the office describing his brush with death, our phone rang in the middle of the night. I remember waking up startled, disoriented for a second, thinking, "I'm on call again? Felt like I was on call just last night." Then I realized I had been on call the previous night so could not be again. Maybe you remember that Thursday night before our vacation. I had spent three hours in the ICU from about three to six AM trying to revive a chronic lunger who didn't make it, despite a full frontal assault. The next day, I managed to slog through office hours only by anticipating our vacation, thinking how it was our first one in over two years and how much I needed it. That night, when I realized the phone call couldn't be about a patient since Darrell was on call, I relaxed.

I picked up the phone, fumbling before I got it to my ear. I remember the bedroom was lit up by a bright full moon sending a series of scattered rays through the blinds, striping the carpeted floor, and wondering how come so much light and noise wasn't waking you. It was Fred, that nighttime answering service rep who always sounds a little drunk and must average about three mistaken messages per week. Hearing his voice, I got ticked. I told him, "Fred, it's not me. Dr. Stiles is on call tonight. I was on last night and I'm on vacation as of five o'clock tonight.

Fred answered, sounding more lucid than usual, "Sorry, Dr. Asher. But this patient insisted I call you directly. She said you told her to contact you if there was any problem with her husband. Said she was a friend of yours. Irene Mallory?"

I answered him, now fully awake. "Yes, I know her. Go on."

Fred's voice quickened. "She said she used to have your home phone number. But now it's unlisted. So she told me to get hold of you immediately. Her husband is having another one of his spells. And you should come over right away. She sounded in a major panic."

I must have said, "Oh God!" or some such aloud, because you startled awake and gave me a look of fear, like you were wondering whether something happened to one of your folks. I waved off your concerns, then went into the living room so I wouldn't disturb you any more. I did some internal

*calculations: the Mallorys lived at least ten minutes away;
I wasn't even sure of the exact address. I had no equipment
that might really deal with an emergency. I was exhausted.*

*I answered, "Listen Fred, I am dead beat. I was up all
last night with a patient in the ICU. I don't think I can
move, even if I could do something to help him. Plus we
have to be out on the road to get to the airport by eight in
the morning." And at that moment, I made my irrevocable,
irredeemable, inexcusable decision. "Fred, do me a favor,
will you? Call Irene back. Tell her I'm away. Technically, I
am anyway. Tell her you didn't realize I would be gone for
the week and that Dr. Stiles is available. If she feels this is
an emergency, tell her to call 911. That's probably the best
course of action anyway." I hung up. Then I sat down on the
couch, drained, staring at the full white eye hanging in the
sky, boring down on me in judgment.*

*In the two months since that night, I've spent hours lying
awake at night trying not to think about that decision. I find
myself hovering over my own body, staring down at myself,
trying to observe my state of consciousness when I abandoned
my patient, my friend, and my oath.*

*Last night, while trying to catch some sleep, I recalled an
episode with my dad right after I got accepted to med school.
I decided to sneak into one of the classes he was teaching to
second-year med students, just to get an idea of what I might
have to contend with. I had never seen him lecture before. I
got there at the tail end, but still managed to enter unnoticed.
He stood ramrod straight, a suited centurion behind the
podium of a two-hundred-seat lecture hall. There were only
about thirty students scattered through the auditorium, not
a one of them occupying a seat in the first twelve rows. My
dad was just finishing up a lecture on the pathology of the eye
and as, most lecturers do, asked if anyone had any questions.
I noticed several students cringe and one or two snicker. But
one brave student halfway raised his hand, waiting to be*

acknowledged. Before doing so, my dad gazed around the room to see if anyone else was so bold. Finally, he pointed to the student who now had his hand barely above his shoulder, realizing his error too late.

"Yes, Bachman," my dad boomed while everyone in the room jumped a foot into the air. "Is there something I have explained to you or something in the copious notes I have painstakingly outlined for you so you barely need to think and certainly don't even need to come to my lectures and waste both of our time? Is there something that was not clear... something I can clarify for you?"

Trembling now, Bachman apparently could think of no adequate path of retreat, because he ventured on. "Well, yes sir. I'm really having trouble understanding the difference between open- and closed-angle glaucoma. Would you please run it by me one more time?" And my dad must have stared him down for a full minute, letting poor Bachman melt into his seat. Even I, via osmosis all those years at the dinner table, knew the answer to that one.

Finally, my dad threw up his hands, answering not at all. "Have I not already explained that to you in triplicate? I give up. I abdicate. My energies, my time, my efforts to teach you all are meaningless. From now on, you all will have to fend for yourselves. I will no longer hold your hands." And he once more repeated, "I abdicate," then walked away from the podium and, as far as I know, away from teaching that day and forever after.

I remember the resonance, the almost divine echoing of that voice, his majesty proclaiming, "I abdicate." And that's exactly what he had done at that class and then finally with his life. But what I thought at the time and ever since was that "abdicate" was his euphemism. What he meant was "I give up, throw in the towel, bag it." Abdicate, my ass.

Now I wonder if, at the moment of judgment when I too was faced with another demand I no longer could meet, faced with one more trial, I, too, quit. I too threw up my hands and gave up.

When I came back to bed that night after staring at the moon for a half-hour, you were still awake. You must have heard some of the conversation, because you asked, "What was that all about? Don't they know you're not even on call?"

Not wanting to face any more questions, I turned over toward the wall. "Darrell will take care of it. Get some rest. We have a long day ahead of us tomorrow." I could feel your clear eyes penetrate my back, but you said nothing, trying to spare me. Unfortunately, the next day, matters went from merely unacceptable to disastrous.

That morning, I arose from bed with a psychic hangover, in no mood for a vacation. I made a conscious decision not to inquire after Tom, figuring Darrell Stiles was responsible for him now. Like it or not, I was officially on vacation. You got the kids up and dressed, but their excitement put me in even a deeper funk. I used the excuse of having to run to the gas station to fill up the car for the drive to the airport so I could duck out. On the way to the 7-Eleven, my beeper went off. I thought it might be you reminding me to get something else, but I scrolled through the displayed message asking me to call the ER. Why couldn't they get it straight that Stiles was on call this weekend? I thought about not answering, but could conjure up no excuse to avoid the call.

Rita, the answering service coordinator, got on. I tried to restrain myself, saying jokingly, "You guys got your wires crossed again? Just got paged to the ER. Dr. Stiles is on call, not me. He's the victim."

Rita replied, "Sorry, Doc. It was Dr. Stiles who asked me to page you to the ER. I tried you at home, but the missus said you were out on an errand. Dr. Stiles wanted to talk with you stat about a patient there."

Now my dread returned with a thud. I sat in the car by

the pumps of the gas station, watching the Saturday bustle of patrons stroll in and out of the store, grabbing newspapers, cups of coffee, and stopping to chat with each other for a minute, all seeming happy not to be working and in no hurry to get anywhere. I remember the next person out of the store was a smartly dressed woman with a brand-new baseball cap reading "YALE" above the brim. I recognized her as the mother of a teen I had taken care of a few months back, who I had helped to recover from a case of mono quick enough so she didn't miss the start of her freshman year at Yale. Appreciative as her mom might have been, I was in no mood to exchange pleasantries and ducked my head.

Like a blind pianist, my fingers dialed the ER number by rote, while I felt like changing lives with the next person heading out the store. When the receptionist answered, I asked if Dr. Stiles had been looking for me. On hold, I ran a series of calculations in my head, trying to unearth any of a dozen possible problems Darrell could be calling about other than the obvious. What patient could have crashed or developed a complication such that Darrell would need input other than Tom? No one came to mind.

It was mid-January and mind-numbingly cold, and I remember being amazed to see a family of ducks waddle across the road right down the block from the store. The ducks had found the safest route back to their pond was directly on the white diagonal lines of the pedestrian crossing. Every driver on this busy street, who would not hesitate for a second plowing through if a person tried to negotiate passage, stopped and waited while the parade of ducks strolled across the road to safety.

Finally, Darrell Stiles got on the line, his voice shaky. "Miles, sorry to bug you like this. I know you're just heading out on vacation. But I thought you should hear about this. I was called down to the ER to help with a patient and the family said they were very close to you. You know them, the Mallorys?" An ocean roar enveloped my head. "Well, the husband, Tom, apparently had another of his spells last night. His wife, Irene, was pretty hysterical when I spoke with her. She said you were working him up for sleep apnea. Hadn't had his sleep study yet, she said. Everything was fine last night. He went to bed feeling perfect. About 4 AM, some premonition woke her up. She found Tom totally out—not breathing, not moving, cold. She rolled him over, shook him, but nothing. No response. So she started to pound on his chest and breathe for him, but still nothing happened. That's when she tried to get in touch with you. You had told her to call if anything happened again, so she called the service. The service tried to get you, then they told her you were already out of town."

At that comment, Darrell hesitated a second to let the effect sink in, choosing not to elaborate. I said nothing, my brain frozen. Stiles went on, "She then called 911. By the time the EMTs got there, Tom was gone—stone-cold blue, fixed and dilated. They went through the whole rigmarole anyway. Didn't want the wife to think they were giving up so easily. They intubated him in the field, then brought him here and the ER docs worked on him for another hour. But he was flat-line when he got here and never budged from there. I arrived about forty-five minutes into the code. It was hopeless. We finally pronounced him about seven AM. Probably was sleep apnea like you said. Or maybe an arrhythmia. Sorry, Miles. I know you must feel terrible."

Darrell stopped again, waiting, but I was just too stunned to respond. "Miles, you still there?"

I tried answering him. "Yeah, Darrell, sorry. I can't believe it. I saw Tom last week. He sounded like he had a similar type thing the night before he came into the office, though obviously not as severe. But he looked perfect when I saw him. EKG normal. Normal neuro exam. Blood work checked out perfectly. I scheduled the sleep study as quickly *as I could, but this Wednesday was the soonest I could get it. Damn. Shit. I can't believe it. I should have done something else."*

Darrell answered, trying to sound convincing, though I think he was mainly just glad he wasn't in my shoes. "What else could you have done? Sounds like you did everything possible. No sense beating yourself up for this."

"Not much sense to anything as far as I can tell," I said. Then I tried to rationalize my behavior to Darrell, making excuses for what I knew was inexcusable. "When Irene called last night, I thought Tom was just having another of his spells. I figured she could revive him with a few slaps on the cheek. Or at least the EMTs would. I was so exhausted. I'd been up the whole night before with that COPDer who didn't make it. Plus I had no equipment. I figured the EMTs would be a lot more useful and get there quicker than I could. God, this is a disaster."

Darrell tried to calm me down. "Nothing you can do about it now. I didn't tell Irene you were still in town. I guess I should have waited until you came back to break the news to you. But I thought you'd want to know. I'm truly sorry, Miles."

"My God, Irene. How is she doing? She must be beside herself."

"She left about ten minutes ago. She was OK. I gave her some Ativan. Plus her mother was with her. She had to go home to tell the kids. That task I do not envy her."

"Wow, this just sounds worse and worse every second. I better give her a call. Thanks for calling, Darrell. I'm sorry you got caught in the middle of this storm."

"Take it easy, Miles. Try not to beat yourself up. We all have tragedies like this. It goes with the territory. Try to forget about it and have a good vacation. You deserve it. You can deal with all this when you return." And he hung up.

I must have gotten out of the car in front of the 7-Eleven at some point, because I found myself wandering around in a daze, near the pond. I saw that family of ducks now comfortably ensconced, paddling in the only non-frozen area of the pond. They were wading in the pool with the mother duck in the lead. Single file, five ducklings followed a circuitous, winding route around their limited space, forming lazy, carefree ripples in the water. I remember thinking I had rarely felt such tranquility and ease. I wondered if, from then on, I ever would again.

I headed back to the car, concentrating on just putting one foot in front of the other, then went about the mindless task of pumping gas, staring out onto the road ahead, unable to focus. At that moment, Mandy, I swear, some divine, vengeful force intervened, transforming a terrible situation into an unmitigated catastrophe.

I was staring out at the intersection of Talcott Road and 183, where a thousand cars stop every day. Five cars idled quietly, waiting for the traffic light to change. There was a bright sun low on the horizon reflecting a glare off their acrylic sheen. Standing at the foot of my car, I squinted, trying to shield my eyes from the glare. At that exact moment, the front seat passenger in the slate-gray Camry, third car in line, turned her head toward me. It was unmistakably the tear-streaked face of Irene Mallory staring straight at me. For a second, I thought I was seeing some transmogrified vision of my mind in turmoil, a kind of visual representation of my own disordered thoughts. But then, as Irene's eyes fixed on mine, the change in her expression left no doubt. For, in the blink of an eye, Irene's grief-stricken face transformed from vacant sadness to one of unshielded, uncensored, complete contempt. We held each other's gaze, hypnotized for what must have been a full minute until the gas started overflowing from the tank, which made me look down. I shook off my hand and cursed and when I looked back up, the car and

Irene were gone. I was left standing there, the sickeningly sweet stench of gasoline filling my nostrils.

But ever since then, Mandy, that eye of judgment of Irene Mallory has haunted my every waking moment.

Asher collapsed out of his chair onto the carpeted floor and then fell into a dreamless deep sleep, his head resting on top of Zantay's manuscript.

YAD VASHEM

Finally, I had enough of passively visiting the museum. I was procrastinating. I needed to start on my true mission, one that would require me to access the vast databank dominating the center of the library. For there, I suspected, must reside the information I sought. If not there, then likely nowhere else on this earth would I uncover my heritage.

I approached the museum archives with the hesitancy one reserves for an unexpected encounter with a brown-wrapped, ticking package that appears on one's doorstep. First, I circled my goal by spending twenty-four hours submerged in the subterranean bowels of the Yad Vashem library, surveying its stores. Prior to investigating its databank—where I suspected might reside the secrets I sought—I spent my time rummaging. I randomly sorted through various and sundry documents—through this audiotape of damaged survivors or that video of mass graves, through piles of undelivered letters here or stacks of deceased victims' birth certificates there, through unrequited pleas for salvation and post facto photographs of damnation. I felt as an alien visitor from another planet might on sifting through the remains of a long-deceased civilization—unable to understand the complexities, unwilling to accept the verdict.

I scanned page after page of deportation journals, painstakingly maintained by the Germans, listing which railroad cars transported how many doomed souls to which concentration camp. The lists described in sickening detail the enormity of the Nazi crime— evidence that apparently cannot be produced often enough for the ever-present skeptics and deniers. But even more so, the lists provided damning evidence of the requisite collusion of thousands of "innocent" German bystanders, those who have long claimed ignorance of their government's sins.

I listened to the testimony, one hour and forty-three minutes worth, of Daniel G., a seventeen-year-old boy who, along with his twin brother Hezikiah, had managed to survive the torture of the camps, the subsequent liberation by the Russians, and the long *marches after. Finally, while both were in the hospital, wasted from dysentery, Daniel watched his delirious brother—hallucinating a vision of their deceased mother—jump through an open window to his death seven stories below. Daniel refused to speak for the next two years.*

Ultimately, I became numb from such information, such a catalogue of catastrophe. The vastness of the data sucked the emotion out of my soul. Unable to comprehend the totality of the crime before me, I shut down. I retreated. I empathized with all the others who may have shut down, withdrawn from the horror laid out before their very eyes. All who took part in this holocaust—both victim and perpetrator alike—must have constructed such a psychological cocoon. All must have numbed their sensibilities and frozen their hearts' circulation in order to endure. And in that brief moment of understanding, I managed to forgive some of them—surely not all of them, and not everything they may have done. But some who stood by and merely watched or those who at times poured just a bit more dirt onto the vast Jewish graves—those I began to forgive.

*

Later on, when I finally abandoned my procrastination, the microfilm databank in the center of the great lobby of the library awaited me. The first sensation I encountered on entering this vast, non-descript space was the odor. The dark wooden tables and chairs, the gray-tiled floor, the bright overhead lights held no compelling visual interest. For the purpose of this space was not to impress or stimulate. Its purpose was to promote exploration. And exploration was the odor it exuded. Like an underground cave, musky and dense. All else in Israel was dry, arid, and clear. But this spot smelled of aging mold and moisture, mixed with an undertone of smokiness, all reminiscent not of a reinvigorated Israel, but rather of a decaying, incinerated Europe.

The room was dominated in its center by ten rows of workstations, each containing seven square microfilm screens resting on desktops, all standing silent and tantalizing, enticing me to join them. During the prior twenty-four hours in the library, I watched dozens of explorers poring for hours over these screens, all in search of a past they had lost, a loved one who had vanished, an unsung ancestor who had perished in order for them to live. For contained in those rectangles of blue streaming data projected from twirling spools of film was the vast catalogue of accumulated information on who and where and when and how and what had become the fate of untold millions. Also amongst this array of concentrated, obscure data might be the secret to my father's fate.

First, I had to submit my request to one of a group of central librarians standing behind a tall counter built into the far side of the room. For an hour and a half, I waited on line with fellow researchers, each with his own agenda. Halfway through my wait, a man standing behind me—I had barely noticed him in my preoccupation—abruptly sat on the ground. He opened up a paper shopping bag and pulled out a large orange that he proceeded to peel. Seeing me staring at him, he broke off a piece of juice-dripping orange and offered it up to me. The man was maybe ten years my senior—high cheekbones, narrow nose, close-cropped gray hair and sporting an equally short salt-and-pepper beard, appearing almost like an aging movie star between jobs. Only the plastic prongs in his nostrils attached to plastic tubing leading to a small, green oxygen tank hinted at some suffering.

Seeing me hesitate before accepting his gift of the orange piece, he offered, after my non-response to his Hebrew, in heavily-accented English—eastern European gutturals and all 'w's replaced with 'v's, "Try some. Can't be bettered. The best oranges in the vorld. Jaffa oranges. Used to grow them myself ven I vas just a kinder. Here, take." And I accepted, reaching for the dripping orange, popping the entire half into my mouth at once, the juices dripping down my chin. "Very good," I managed to squeeze out between swallows.

"Sorry, they are too juicy I think these days." And he pulled a couple of square napkins from the bag and handed them to me. "In my day, they ver maybe half the size they are now. Kind of dried

out, every third one ve had to throw out because ov infestation or improper handling. Ve ver just learning to raise them at that time. Learning on our own, vit only one person on the whole kibbutz knowing a thing about agriculture. Now if you visit there, rows upon rows of deep green orange trees greet you, vit football-sized, plump oranges just vaiting to be picked. I myself vit mine own hands must haf planted a hundred of those trees now still producing fruit." He motioned for me to join him on the ground. "Going to be a long vait. Come sit down vit me." And I joined him on the tiled floor, not able to sit too comfortably with my bulk, but not wanting to be rude. He held out his sticky hand. "Stanislav Meyer here. People call me 'Slav.' Glad to meet you."

"Should be another twenty-five minutes or so before they get to us. Every request takes at least ten minutes to research. And the librarians, they never vant to miss a possible document or lead, so they often check two or three times. I can almost set my clock by them. See that white-haired von in green over there? She takes the longest, but she never makes a mistake. If you haf an inquiry, no matter how obscure, she's going to find out vhatever there is on the topic. Inside of ten minutes, she vill show you everything this library has, plus vhat's in the archives at the Moses Mendelssohn Zentrum in Berlin, and maybe too some leads in Belgium or Copenhagen or anyvhere you are asking about. Even still, eastern Europe is a mystery to us. But vit the fall of the Russians, ve hope to have new stores of information.

"Myself, I haf been coming here fifteen or sixteen years now. At least two or three times a month. Not that I hope to see any more information on my own family. I've researched them till my fingertips are callused. Though they keep coming up vit new documents all the time, so you never know. You might say fifty years later there vould be nothing new to discover, everything vould have been uncovered by now. But there are always new testimonies or hidden documents being brought to light and every vonce in a while, von seems like it could haf some information about vhat happened to my family. But always—how do the Americans say—always a dead end.

"But anyvay, I come to the library. This is a place very soothing *and stimulating and comforting all at the same moment. In just von morning, you can see all of humanity pass through here. People from every country in the vorld speaking a hundred different languages, all vit some question they hope to answer, all vit some mystery they vish solved." Slav gestured at a stooped, aging, dark-skinned couple whispering in the corner by a desk, deep in conversation. Though I have been steeped in languages throughout my life, I could not for the life of me identify which one they were speaking. Reading my thoughts, Slav said, "Ethiopians. Even the lost tribes in Africa ver not immune to Hitler's pogroms.*

"They all come to explore the past. It might be a question just academic and perhaps impersonal. Or maybe yet they are trying to find out vat happened to the baby they had to give up to some French family to protect him from the Nazis and haf never heard from him again since. But each and every one has his own reasons for being here. And most of the time, you can guess from their age and the looks on their faces and the anxiousness in their voices vhat they might be seeking. And even if you cannot, just vatching their reactions and their behaviors is a great lesson in human nature."

Slav saw me staring at his oxygen canister. "My von souvenir from my years spent smoking three packs a day. Should never haf picked up such a stupid habit. But on the boat over to Palestine everyone smoked and it vas a good vay to pass the time. I was only seventeen then and alone—vhat did I know from lung disease and emphysema?

"Looking back, I probably should never haf left Germany. But my parents insisted. It vas 1937, and my father saw vat was coming. He knew. But he could not gif up his life—he vas a respected university professor, my mother actif in synagogue. Plus, my two young sisters, just in their early school years and to disrupt all of that vas too much for him to consider. Two years later, it vas too late. But in 1937, I vas just done vit school and he vanted me out. He finagled a study visa for me in Palestine, and, vit only two days of warning, I vas gone. They hugged me goodbye at the train station and that was the last I ever saw of them. I haf five letters from them vhile I was avay

and then the letters stopped. Poof. Vanished into the air, like smoke or ideas or dreams."

The entire time he spoke, Slav's eyes never left mine. His hands moved in a hundred different directions, like he was gathering his story from the air. They appeared almost like one of the sculptures I had seen in another building, depicting five disembodied hands radiating from a central axis, each one holding a light against the darkness. But as much as Slav's hands could not keep still, his eyes remained fixed, studying my reactions, as if they alone could provide the emotional feedback he needed to re-energize a story he had likely told hundreds of times before. "Here also, I find I can sometimes comfort others. Efen support them on their search. As I might you. Vat is it you search for? Maybe I can help."

Despite myself, I began to tell my tale: my years in Latvia, the kidnapping of my father, my search for him on the bridge, our family's banishment and exile, our unending treks, our interchangeable sojourns amidst the camps, my mother's inexhaustible quest for her husband. I told him of our final journey to the U.S. and the occasion of my journey back to Latvia and now to Israel. I told all this to a stranger, a story I may have related at most two or three other times in my entire life. And during my tale, Slav nodded and frowned, grimaced and cringed, hearing anew a story he must have heard over the years with a million variations on the theme, yet still freshly able to absorb and emote. It seemed as if hearing another tale of sorrow and reclamation rejuvenated his soul and reaffirmed his humanity.

For just as I finished, Slav stood up stiffly, creaking his joints and brushing off his pants. "Come then. Let us search. Let us see what mysteries our library, our legacy holds for you and for your father." At just that moment, I arrived at the head of the line. Slav stood by my side, no longer involved in his own quest, repeated countless times before. Now alongside me, engaged as a kindred explorer.

At the counter, the white-haired, unsmiling librarian wearing a green uniform confronted me. No windows lit up this cavernous below-ground room, so the fluorescent light projecting off this woman's dead-white hair enveloped her in a spectral glow. I was met with a *sole question by this ethereal figure repeated three times, speaking first in Hebrew, then in German, while I was struck silent, trying to sort out the long-forgotten German in my head. Finally, she tried in English. "Yes, may I help you?"*

Amazingly, despite a lifetime to prepare, despite the hours, days, weeks, and years in which to formulate my request, I was dumbstruck, not yet ready to phrase my question. The librarian pushed a piece of paper and pencil on the counter in front of me. "Just write the topic or person you wish researched and I will return with the accessed sources on microfilm or bring to you the appropriate papers or books from the archive."

I was frozen to the spot, not able to pick up the pencil. I had been hoping to initiate a general exploration of Latvian prisoners or of displaced persons or of victims in the concentration camps that I might sort through by myself in a variety of documents. I thought I could gradually sneak up on the topic and if my father popped out, wonderful. But this third-party approach, after so long a wait, would provide me with perhaps my only opportunity for inquiry. I could not keep returning to this overwhelmed and overwhelming apparition with a new series of queries every several hours. I would have to make this one attempt my most direct. On the paper I shakily wrote only my father's name, 'Rudolfs Zantay,' and, without uttering a word, I pushed the paper to the librarian's side of the counter. Slav nodded in assent, encouraging me.

While we waited to the side of the counter with a half-dozen other petitioners, my white-haired librarian disappeared into a back room. She was replaced by a similarly dressed, somber woman who received the next inquiry from the person waiting in line behind us.

Within a few minutes, I began to sweat. I felt an electrical current run up my spine, setting off an eyebrow twitch I had never before possessed. Evidently, in spite of my hour-long wait on line, my two days in the library, my four days at Yad Vashem, my fortnight's journey to Europe, my forty-nine years of separation from my father, I was not yet prepared for the news of his fate. Somehow, I had not thought through the implications.

Slav, seeing my distress, steered me over to a seat by the bank of desks in the center of the room. He pulled out a cotton handkerchief from his front pocket to wipe the sweat off my brow and handed it over to me. Then he produced from his rear pocket a silver flask he may have kept for just such occasions. Without a word, he handed the flask over to me, gesturing for me to drink. I took a swig from the narrow mouthpiece, not used to hard liquor, choking and sputtering as the harsh liquid went down. Slav said, "That should calm you. Always does wonders for me."

After an endless wait, the librarian finally appeared and headed our way, holding a piece of paper and two plastic circular containers. I must have had a premonition of the nature of the news to follow, for again I felt the blood drain from my core. Seeing my ashen face, she hesitated a second. No doubt she had encountered such ambivalence and fear before. She advanced anyway and handed the containers to me.

In passionless recitation, she offered, "Here are two microfilms which contain reference to your Mr. Zantay. The specific location of the two references is written on this paper. I have a third reference which is documentary in nature and not available on microfilm. I will have to ask our archivists to search this last document in the basement files. I will bring it to you if and when they can locate the document." She hesitated then, trying to judge if I was stable enough to understand her message. Satisfied, she went on. "Have you need for assistance in the use of the microfilm machine?" While I was struck mute, Slav answered for me in indecipherable Hebrew.

Slav led me over to one of the Formica desks in the center and we sat down together, sharing a cubicle. I found myself trembling uncontrollably. To recapture control, I glanced around to see what audience might be witness to the scene that would next transpire before them. On one side of me sat a bearded young scholar with a half-dozen tomes resting next to the microfilm screen in which he was absorbed, oblivious to the world around him. On the other side was a near-bald, ancient woman, wearing all black—a wool sweater, skirt, and shawl—silently sobbing as she stared at the screen.

I had not the courage to look over her shoulder and eavesdrop on her just-discovered tragedy. I suspected she would be in no condition to eavesdrop on mine.

Slav held the microfilm canisters in his hands, suspended in mid-act, awaiting my signal. I barely nodded my head in his direction. He expertly placed the first spool of film onto the reel and waited. At that point Slav, had assisted as much as he was willing to. He sat still and patient, waiting for me to make the next move. Any further exploration would have to be initiated by me. We maintained such a tableau for minutes more.

Finally, I unfroze. Slowly, reluctantly, I turned the wheel on the side of the display to reveal the documents contained in the microfilm. Before me appeared a deep purple screen with white lettering in a continuous display of typewritten lines. There was no title or identification of the material other than a woman's name—Hannah Klieffer—at the top of the screen. This page was entirely in German and a mystery to me other than an isolated word that I recognized here and there—aufbudsen, mein sklunder, plessen—words possibly I had not encountered in fifty years, but which returned to my brain with a thud.

As I scrolled down, exploring, every third page or so a new name appeared at the top—Pavil Shranz, Mika Tollberg, Karl Passman— and a page or two of recitation would follow. Not all was in German; some in Polish, some French; some I could not immediately recognize the language, possibly Greek or Czech. Each contained a testimony of the author's experience during the war in his own words, maintained in the author's native language. So many testimonies, possibly two or three hundred on each spool. Occasionally next to the author's name appeared a picture—usually of the author at the age at which he gave testimony. Several times, the picture depicted a younger person, presumably the author at the age at which he suffered his trauma.

Once or twice, I stopped in my scrolling when I found a testimony in Latvian. I was compelled to read through each in its entirety, rediscovering my grasp of the language from a buried corner of my brain. Slav sat passively while I became absorbed by the scrolling purple screen, now as oblivious to my surroundings as those sitting in the adjacent desks. Finally, after maybe fifteen minutes or possibly an hour had passed, I took a deep breath, maybe my first true breath that hour, and sat back in my chair.

Slav leaned over, holding the paper in his hand and quietly said, "Your particular information is located on page 137." I was so absorbed that I was startled, both to discover him there, and then to recall I still had a further task to accomplish. I scanned the room, observing others in study or in transit or in wait, the fluorescent lights from above playing shadows on their faces. I realized I might not ever again see the world in the same light as I did at that moment. With a sigh of resignation, I scrolled down to page 137. At the top of the page was written the name Carla Biernstein. No picture accompanied the testimony, but I immediately conjured up the image of a teenager with a proud chin and a bandanna around her head.

The entire testimony was in German. First, I tried to follow on my own. I ran my index finger across the screen, stopping at each word, sounding it out and trying to roll its meaning from my tongue to my brain. I caught every fifth or sixth word, which I then repeated aloud in English. The meaning escaped me. Seeing my frustrated struggle, Slav hesitantly intervened. Initially halting, but with increasing confidence, he translated. Slav's gruff, tobacco-stained voice soon resonated in my head as that of the teenage girl, Carla.

"I was fifteen when the Germans finally found me and my brother hiding out in the convent. I was born in Brussels in 1928 and enjoyed a happy childhood there prior to the German invasion. My brother was two years older and much more adventuresome than me. During my entire upbringing, we spoke German in our house as the principal language. We learned French and Dutch, but German was our root. My parents had grown up in Germany, only coming to live in Belgium after they were married in order for my father's job. Every year on High Holy days, we would return to Frankfurt to celebrate with my grandparents the Jewish New Year. Naturally that stopped after 1936.

"When war broke out and the Germans occupied Brussels,

we were not as terrified as likely we should have been. After all, we were Germans too. But since that made no difference for real German Jews themselves, why would we have thought it should make a difference for us? *Das wunschdenken*, wishful thinking, I guess.

"In 1942, our parents were taken away on the way to work one morning. I was fourteen, Reuben sixteen. That's when we began hiding out, moving from convent to convent. Our neighbor's nephew was a priest who offered us sanctuary in a convent outside Brussels. There, we stayed several months, then moved on. The priests thought it was too dangerous to keep us in any one sanctuary for very long. Informants seemed to be everywhere. So we traveled at night, moving from convent to convent, changing our name each time, usually accompanied by a priest or several nuns. We received religious instruction at each convent so we could continue our role as students. Somewhere along these trips, I guess I became mostly Christian. Everyone we met was so kind. But to the Germans, I could call myself a Buddhist monk and I would still be Jewish.

"Then, in 1943, I think my brother could not take the hiding anymore, though he insisted our discovery was just an accident. He was always so full of action and hatred; I think hiding out was slowly destroying his spirit. He wanted to fight—to kill Nazis, to stand up and shout his hatred in their face.

"One night we were in a seminary in Louvain, living with six nuns. They were Carmelite nuns, ones who cannot have any contact with or even see any men. Well, the Gestapo came one night. And you know they could not care less about any rules of the convent. They broke down the door and barged into the convent. The nuns quickly tossed us both into big laundry bins and covered us with dirty clothes. We could hear the Nazis stomping around the convent, searching in this closet or that or under the tables, breaking dishes, pushing nuns on the floor, cursing them. They must have known about us because they were searching so determinedly. I myself wanted to jump out and fight them, so I can imagine what Reuben felt. But we held our breath as much as we could, not daring to make a sound.

"Finally the Nazis came to our laundry bins. They took cattle prods and began sticking them into the pile of clothes, trying to shock us, barely missing me. But they must have struck Reuben for he suddenly grabbed the prod and shouted, "You don't jab me, you stinking Nazis." And he jumped out and began fighting them. Naturally they beat him senseless. I was surprised they did not kill him. But I think they wanted to make him watch. For as soon as they found me, they stood him up and made him watch as each one raped me. In front of my brother and these nuns who had almost never seen a man, much less such a scene of brutality. At first, I was humiliated, but then I became too beaten down to feel much of anything.

"Afterward, when we were on the train going to Auschwitz, I asked Reuben to show me the mark where the Nazis had shocked him. But all he showed me was this tiny mark on his arm that could not have hurt but for a second. So I knew he just must have been fed up with hiding all the time. And I could not blame him."

Soon Slav's voice became more gravelly, breaking either from the strain or from emotion, I could not tell. He once more pulled out his flask offering me another swig and taking one himself when I declined. Thus fortified, he resumed.

"We arrived in the inferno that was Auschwitz. After the stripping and the spraying and the delousing and the waiting on lines for a shower that we did not know would clean us or kill us, I was assigned to laundry work, cleaning the Germans' uniforms. Much better than anything most anyone else in my barracks had, but still filthy, disgusting work. The German soldiers were pigs, drinking themselves sick many nights, vomiting all over their uniforms, soiling themselves in their drunken stupor. Cleaning after them made me retch. Yet, I considered myself fortunate.

"Reuben, I did not see or hear of him for the first two months of my stay in Auschwitz. I tried to find him, but could never discover where he had been taken. No one else knew of his whereabouts. I feared he was killed in the gassings. But then one day, as I was carrying a bushel of clothes across the yard, Reuban appeared from behind the barracks. He pulled me behind the corner and gave me a long hug. He was so thin and trembling. Only eighteen now, but with a beard and such a hollowed-out look to his face, he might have been forty. He tells me he wants to see me once before he dies; he must say goodbye to me. I tell him not to lose faith. We will survive, we will come out of this horror and have a life. I tell him not to give up.

"Reuben answers me that I do not understand. He will not live. There is no hope. He has been recruited to the Sonderkommandos—the 'Special Squads' of Auschwitz. They are the prisoners who run the crematoria. They maintain order among the new arrivals who have no idea they are to be gassed. They go into the gas chambers afterwards to extract the corpses, to pull gold teeth from jaws, to cut women's hair, to sort all the clothes and the shoes and the contents of all the luggage. They transport the bodies to the crematoria. They run the ovens, then extract all the ashes and dispose of them. For that they are kept alive and given some privileges—some extra food, as much alcohol as they want.

"But, Reuben says, soon they will all be killed. The Kapos, their guards, do not let them continue like this for more than several months. He knows because when he was first recruited to the Special Squads, at their initiation, the Kapos forced them to kill the previous squad and then burn the corpses. But he says he will not wait for such a thing to happen. He is only going along with them because he and the other members of their squad are going to rebel. They are collecting weapons, whatever they can gather. And they are going to overpower the guards and escape. He says he will come get me before he goes, so I can escape with him.

"I plead with Reuben not to do such a thing. He will be killed and I will never see him again. But he is adamant. He will be killed no matter what. At least this way he will die a man, not an animal. Not a victim and not a torturer, but a man."

Slav stops his recitation. He takes a deep sigh. It seemed no matter how many times he heard such stories, each one consumed another piece of his heart and tore at his soul. I had heard before of such squads, but not the exact details. I assumed they were men who had sold their soul to the devil in order to get privileges—an extra portion of food, better living conditions. I did not realize they were likely the most pathetic of all, suffering death a thousand times over.

Both Slav and I suddenly pulled in our breath at the same time. We had both been staring at the screen, I following along with him as he read, not able to understand the words but recognizing some here and there. In the middle of the next paragraph, as I scrolled the page both of us saw written out the name, "Zantay." Twice the name stood out like triple-faced bold type on the next page. Slav looked at me to make sure he should go on. I nodded silently, then held my breath as Slav proceeded to translate.

"Reuben says no matter what happens I should remember his story. To tell the story of what happened to him and why he came to be with the Special Squad. And he says to tell the story of the Kapos—the guards who are over him, who force him to do the basest, most terrible acts. These are Polish or Russian or Latvian vermin who give the squads a bone here or a scrap there, who laugh in their face when the Jews cry out or weep. Most of all he hates one of the Kapos—this Zantay, Captain Zantay they call him, though he's not German and they doubt he's even in the army. I remember that name because it reminds me of the French word 'sante'—to your health. The irony is too much."

Slav again stopped. He drew in a breath, not wanting to go on. I could not stop then. I urged him to finish.

"Reuben tells me to remember this name. This one is not the worst of the Kapos, but Reuban hates him the most, because the Captain Zantay should know better. He tells me, 'The rest are savages, animals who for punishment could just as well rip out your tongue as take away your food. They do not look at us as humans, not even as animals—more as despised insects worth only the effort to be squashed. But this Zantay, he tries to help the Special Squad when he can. Gives us extra bread to give to our families, sneaks an occasional piece of meat or once some cheese our way. But in the end, he is like all the rest. It was he who supervised us when we slaughtered the last squad of Sonderkommandos. He had us incinerate the bodies. I know he will do the same to our group when it is our turn, no matter how easy he seems now.' Reuben says if he is able to rebel, the first throat he will cut will be this turncoat, this half-human who is worse than a non-human. And if he dies, he wants me to remember this swine, so someone someday will bring him to justice."

Slav stopped again, his voice shaking too much to go on. He was the one now covered in sweat. He was the one trembling. I, on the contrary, was calm. I was suddenly overcome with inner quiet. Perhaps I was in shock. Or perhaps I was in denial. Or perhaps now faced with the most terrible of all possible scenarios, I could let go of all my stored-up hopes and dreams. For still, after all these years, somewhere in the recesses of my mind, I held out hope. Maybe my mother's never-relinquished, irrational hope had invaded my spirit. For I believe now that I had, up until that moment, never let go of the idea of connecting with my father. Maybe not in the flesh or in the physical sense, but connecting to him emotionally. I held out the hope that somehow across the years and across the continents, my father could again speak to me. He would show me by his deeds or by his memory or by his remnants that I was at the forefront of his life. That whatever had transpired to separate him from me, he would still communicate and guide me, that he was still and always would be with me.

But now I was released from such delusions. I was unburdened of such a false and juvenile hope. Like a boy who wakes up one day and realizes Santa Claus is just a fantasy, I realized my image of my father, the icon, was fabricated. Whatever motivated his acts, whatever governed his morality, I would never know. And whatever he had been or became truly had nothing to do with me. I was of a different age, a different spirit, maybe a different species. I was released.

Slav, though, could know none of this. He could only feel the horror of what he read and his supposition of what I felt. He assumed I would be, like him, mortified and disgusted. He placed his arm on my shoulder in sympathy. "I vould not go on at this time, if you like. Perhaps ve can read the rest another time. This information vill be here always. No need to explore into it now. Let us go."

But I had come this far. Nothing more horrific could confront me than what I had already heard, I thought. For his sake, I invented an option. "No, we should go on. I should and must hear this through. Maybe there is more than one Zantay. Maybe this is not my father at all." And in saying this statement, I gave myself a split second of false hope that again sent a rush of trepidation into my core. It took all of my self-control to suppress that hope.

Slav read silently to himself, first. Now wanting to absorb the news before he spoke it aloud, hoping he could cushion the next blow before it struck. He began to summarize. "There is not much left to Carla's story. She just describes what happened to her brother and then..." I interrupted. "Please, Slav, just read the words. I would like to hear them directly from Carla's mouth."

Slav complied. "My brother, he gave a hug and a kiss goodbye. He pulled two loaves of bread from under his jacket and presented them to me. A beautiful gold ring he had taken from some poor dead soul he had smuggled out and also handed to me. I have it still on a chain always next to my heart, so I will keep Reuben with me forever.

"After that day, I never saw Reuben again. A week, maybe two weeks later, one night late, we heard loud explosions and gunfire coming from the crematorium. We hid trembling in our beds in ignorance of what was happening, afraid whatever violence took place over there would come to more punishment here. The next morning, in the square in front of the barracks, maybe a hundred dead men lay on the ground, arms and some of their heads missing, their entrails hanging out. A sign above them, written in blood, said, 'Your brave rebels.' I searched through the bodies with a handkerchief across my face for the stench. But no Reuben there. Later I heard some of the Special Squad had cut through the barbed wire and escaped, but they'd all been hunted down and slaughtered. I guessed that must have been Reuben's fate.

"Part of me always held out the fantasy and the hope that Reuben had been able to truly escape. That he had run and run and somehow found sanctuary again. That he had escaped Europe and traveled to Australia. That he had found a wife and had babies and they had grown tall and proud and beautiful as Reuben. And that maybe his daughter, he had named her Carla. And someday maybe I would meet her and we would hug. Maybe still, you know. Maybe still."

Slav wiped his eyes. He asked to be excused, then rose to go to the bathroom. I sat still and quiet, unmoving, digesting what I had just heard, looking over the lit purple screen. The words now jumping out at me, taking on a new menacing quality, the letters themselves assuming odd shapes, appearing now as unnatural, violent symbols. I wished somehow to roll the reel before me in reverse, like rewinding a movie to the beginning. Maybe this time the story would end differently. Or maybe this time, I would more wisely chose not to view this scene at all and possibly return my life and my consciousness to what they once had been. Eerily, the letters began to run into each other on the screen, the words melting and dripping down the page as if a fire was consuming the monitor. And all became a purple blur of illegible smear, holding no meaning and no consequence. The words disappeared, and with the disappearance of the words, maybe their meaning and their reality disappeared as well. For they were only that, words, neither tangible objects nor flesh and blood—just words. I wiped the tears from my eyes and prayed such a view could be true.

I forced myself to look up from the screen to reconnect with a reality that was now preferable to the one I faced in front me. Immediately,

I found myself staring into the face of the bearded scholar in the next cubicle. His curiosity must have been aroused by the drama playing out next to him, for he stared right at me, reading the emotional turmoil written on my face. At the same time, I became absorbed in trying to read his expression. For a deep scar I had not noted before dominated the right side of his face, creating a dual image. On one side, he manifested high cheekbones, a glinting sharp eye, and a depth of sympathy. The other side sagged and drooped, his eye rheumy and tearful, manifesting disgust and disdain. Which view I accepted, with which verdict I would live, I now had to choose.

CHAPTER 23 ———————————

Having unburdened himself of his malfeasance, at least on paper, the next day Asher engaged his patients with an enthusiasm he hadn't felt in months. Confession might be therapeutic after all. That night, he eagerly retuned to his study to immerse himself in the twin tasks of reworking Zig's history and finishing his letter to Mandy.

He was drawn first to the latter.

We went off on the cruise, Mandy, and there was enough turmoil and fussing getting there and getting settled, I could fake my way through. The cruise itself was surreal enough that I thought I had entered another dimension. Watching the kids frolic with Chip and Dale and Mickey and Minnie on a sun-filled pool deck with a thousand other carefree sunbathers, I felt like a member of a different species entirely. So I withdrew. I hid behind a book. I used the excuse that I was just relaxing, trying to forget about the trials of life and death and my patients for a while. I told myself I didn't want to spoil your vacation, but more likely was afraid of your ultimate judgment about my behavior, so I said nothing about Tom and Irene. You gave me enough quizzical looks during the cruise, but I guess you accepted that I was just whipped.

The night after we returned from the cruise, you must remember. We were sitting at the dinner table, the girls finally upstairs in bed. It felt like our home life might return to normalcy. But for some reason you were agitated the whole evening. While making dinner, you snapped both at the kids and at me. I thought you were vacation-lagged. Then when we were alone, having some coffee, you came out with it. You said you'd heard from Leslie Catchings that Tom Mallory had died right before we left. You were distraught. Plus, you felt stupid that Leslie acted as if you should have already known. You wanted to know if I knew and how come I hadn't told you.

Though I had been prepared for your questions, I still felt my face flush, my heart pound. I fumbled out my prepared explanation as best I could, saying I had just heard about it that morning and didn't want to tell you until the kids went to sleep.

Naturally you were upset; you wanted more details. You knew he was my patient; you asked what could have happened to him. But I had laid out my course and would only go so far. I told you I had seen Tom about a week before we left and was working him up for sleep apnea. I said I just heard Tom had passed on in his sleep and that I felt terrible about it. But I was not willing to detail the extent of my crime. Thinking back, I guess you would have understood. But it was Tom and Irene. Screwing up is one thing… but over and above that, leaving Irene at her moment of greatest need and lying to her. Then, lying to you. How could a part of you not blame me, not lose your confidence and respect for me?

When you started to cry and worry about Irene and her kids and went to call her, I should have stopped you. But I would have had to explain the whole disaster. I knew I was compounding my crime, but felt passive, as if I were watching a movie, sympathetic but not in control. You spoke to Irene's mother who seemed inexplicably cold. She told you Irene was taking no calls and no visitors. You were grief-stricken and totally bewildered.

So I've multiplied my transgressions. I've treated my patients poorly, let down my associates, ignored the kids, lied to you, and sunk into a morass I've been unable to claw my way out of. To make matters worse, a couple of weeks after Tom died, for no apparent reason, I struck a woman in the face, a stranger no less—an act I still can't fathom or forgive myself for.

And now you've been watching me pore over this manuscript that's been carpeting our study, wondering what the hell is going on with me.

All I can say is that somehow in that story, in that manuscript, I feel like I can find redemption. I know it sounds crazy, but I'm nearing the end. I'm hoping you will bear with me. Not totally forgive me, but at least understand.

I love you and am sorry.

Miles

Asher folded the pages in thirds, carefully placed them in a plain white envelope, writing "For Mandy" on the outside. Then he quietly tiptoed into their bedroom and placed the envelope on Mandy's dresser next to the alarm clock, tucked her blanket in when she stirred and hurried back upstairs to finish Zig's story.

BRIVIBA

Slav returned from his leave, his eyes dry, now fortified. He was ready to go on with our quest, no longer a reluctant participant. For if nothing else, Slav was about truth. Unvarnished, unhomogenized truth. He may have been unprepared that day to delve into another tale of horror and disillusionment. But I realized, once he was confronted with the reality, like always before, he could not turn away.

Now Slav became the master and I the puppet. He handed me the next spool of microfilm, gesturing for me to insert it into the reader. I complied. This time Slav performed the scrolling. This roll of microfilm was much like the prior. Hundreds upon hundreds of testimonies of pain and torture and mayhem, and also of occasional triumph and ultimate survival, for these were the tales of those who had endured.

Slav wasted no time scanning the extraneous stories or reviewing the indirectly relevant. We now had a purpose and possibly the means to fulfill that purpose. Was this 'Captain Zantay' truly my father? Had he been the monster as portrayed? What had been his ultimate fate? My feelings on the matter, my desires, by then had become secondary, possibly irrelevant to Slav. We were to go on.

Slav scrolled to page 249, the indicated applicable page. The heading: "Leon Sonnenstein." This testimony was again in German. Others on the tape were in Italian or Greek or Romanian or Czech, some in English. All the languages in Europe contributed to these testimonies. Afterward I often wondered why this Sonnenstein picked German as the language of choice to record his story.

Aware that most of the narration of Leon Sonnenstein would not apply to my father, Slav skimmed the beginning of the page. He murmured the German to himself as he read down, not translating what he felt was immaterial. I sat passively, thankful my fate was now in another's hands. Finally he came to the appropriate passage. Slav again began to translate, now assured and unhesitating. I stared at his lips as he translated, the circuit formed from screen to brain

*to mouth to audible message turning Slav from human being into a
disembodied electronic transmitter.*

"I was finally unable to lift a hand to stop them," *read Slav.*
"Though it was my job and my duty, no different than much of
the activity that I had been performing over the two years before.
Something, though, finally stopped me, I cannot say what.

"For several weeks before, I had sensed an increased awareness
and heightened excitement of the prisoners. All around me there
was an air of anticipation and purpose, sensations that, up to
then in Auschwitz, had been totally absent. Before that, there
had been merely apathy—pain and disgust and apathy. No life,
no emotions, no caring—existence at its most basic.

"The men in the Sonderkommandos, the Death Squads, were
the most basic of all. They ate; they slept. When not working,
they got drunk so they could forget. At work they were solitary.
They communicated not with their fellow squad members, did
not look up from their work—I suppose they were too ashamed.
If they hid their faces from the rest, maybe they would disappear,
or at least be invisible. They made every effort not to see what
they were doing.

"We Kapos were not much different. We were maybe a rung
above on the ladder, but still we felt like victims. Even though we
inflicted all the pain, though we carried out all the orders. Even
though we were not going to be extinguished every three months
like the Sonderkommandos. Still, we could not bear to truly look
at what we did. We hid our eyes and our minds. Removing gold
from people's mouths, collecting their bones, the endless parade
of naked, shaved bodies turning into piles of naked, shaved
corpses. Who could look at such a sight? So all of our vision
became tunneled. We saw the half-meter in front of us, nothing
else. Our ears likewise shut down. When one of the other Kapos
yelled or threatened, we would close our ears, letting the violence
rain down on whomever this Kapos-beast chose. No one tried to
stop him. We chose not to hear. We chose not to hear the screams

of anger, the cries of despair, the last breaths of air escaping from a tortured victim.

"For two months I secretly watched while the Special Squad collected weapons. Anything they could find, they stole and hid. A shovel here, they stored away. A sharp rock there, they honed into a dagger. The metal tool used to extract gold fillings from the dead people's teeth, they smuggled out. Once sharpened, some of these metal rods could become truly dangerous. Usually the other Kapos kept a close eye and count of each instrument handed out to be sure they were returned. But by then, the rest of the Kapos seemed careless. They let things slip that six months before they would have slaughtered someone on the spot for. I saw all these preparations but did not act. I told no one. I stopped no one. Possibly I had been the only one noticing before and, now that I had become passive, no else took up the job. Maybe those years I had been doing my job too well.

"The best instruments the squad stole were the scalpels. Sometimes we forced the squad to slice off a finger in order to obtain the ring from a dead clenched fist after a gassing. They used a scalpel for this. Several other times, we made them remove the eyeballs from victims for scientific experiments. And once we forced several prisoners to slice out all the testicles from a group of dead males. I still retch at the memory of such an act. Anytime squad members thought no one was looking, they palmed these scalpels, hid them in cans or in their shoes. They were very clever and maybe I even missed some of the thefts. I knew they were planning something, I just did not know when or where. I wondered how I might react in such a rebellion. Then I too began to plan.

"Their most prized smuggled item was the *schwartzpulver*. I found out about this afterward from other rebels in the camp who felt betrayed by the Sonderkommandos. Some of the men in the camps were cooperating with outside partisans. They arranged with women working at *Weischel-Union-Metalwerke*— the munitions plant—to help them obtain the gunpowder. The women, I learned, hid the *schwartzpulver* in a secret compartment in their dresses at great risk to themselves. At one point, three of the women during a search were discovered. They were tortured and then killed, but did not reveal for what purpose or for whom the gunpowder was stolen.

"Later I heard that a Russian POW munitions expert, Timofei Borodin, used sardine cans to make explosives with the *schwartzpulver*. He gave the Sonderkommandos many of these devices to hide in the carts and lorries used to haul the corpses. The SS and Kapos never inspected these, they were too contaminated from thousands of dead Jews' blood."

Slav's voice became quickened and shaky. He began to sweat. He told me he had heard of the Sonderkommando revolt at Auschwitz but had never read a true eyewitness account. Reportedly none of the Special Squad survived. He went on translating.

"The revolt was supposed to involve many in the camp, plus the Sonderkommandos, plus the outside partisans. But somehow the Sonderkommando found out they were soon to be killed by us Kapos—no one on the Special Squads was allowed to live for more than three or four months. They found out their time was almost up. So instead of waiting for the other participants, they decided one night—October 7, 1944—they would blow up a crematorium and escape by cutting the wires during the chaos.

"I had an informant in the squad, Lothar Glassman. Like everyone in the plants, he had a price at which he could be bought. He came to my barracks and told me that night would be the night. The Special Squad would attack. I had to think long and hard. I would like to say that I felt sorry for the prisoners or that I was tired of the torture and the savagery in which I was engaged. I would hope to excuse myself that finally I had discovered once more in myself a trace of humanity, a glimmer of mercy. But day after day, month after month, year after year of brutality and evil had seeped into my soul. Whatever had been human in me had long since evacuated, leaving behind an empty hull of a man.

"No, I saw this rebellion merely as a chance to save myself. To escape the punishment I knew would inevitably come my way. I had knowledge of what was going on in the outside world then. We had bribed an SS guard with a victim's gold tooth to take out a subscription to *Volkischer Beobachter*, the most authoritative daily German newspaper of the time. I knew the war was going poorly for the Germans; sooner or later they would be defeated. Then I would suffer the consequences. Either by the wrath of the prisoners at the camp or at the hands of the conquering armies, I would be a prime target. This revolt might help me escape.

"After the revolt, I speculated the SS might assume I was killed with others of the Kapos. I knew the Sonderkommandos would target many of us for revenge. I decided I could take the place of a prisoner. One I knew, Leon Sonnenstein, had just been gassed that day. He looked like me. The daily roll calls were much less organized by then. I would just assume his role. I would take over his life. They would never find my body. They would assume I was blown up in the explosion or killed in the woods, chasing down the escapees.

"The hardest part was the tattoo, the brand. Again, I could bribe one of the special 'scribes,' whose sole job over the past two years had been to tattoo every prisoner at the moment of the new arrival's registration. I gave him the only remnant I retained from my prior life, the only vestige that linked me to my lost life and to my true self. I removed the amber necklace I had worn every day of my life and turned that and my heritage over to the scribe."

Both Slav and I stopped breathing; he to stare at my neck, I to finger the amber stone I have worn since childhood. He chose not to ask how I had come to possess this stone—the one I had rescued from the shop in Stuttgart—and went on.

"That day, I sat across from this stone-faced Pole, who must have branded a hundred thousand others at his table. No one before, I suspect, among those thousands had volunteered to be so marked. I had written Leon Sonnenstein's number on a piece of paper now resting between the scribe and me. Right before he was about to inscribe, his stylus in his right hand, holding my forearm straight and secure with his left, his face barely five centimeters from mine, he raised his head to look into my eyes. It was as if he was asking me, 'Are you sure you want me to do this?' I nodded my head, knowing this could well mean my death sentence. No longer would I be one of the favored Kapos. No longer would I be the keeper, but now the inmate. And with that tattoo—A77643—I would become a Jew, one of the nameless and numbered, doomed at some point sooner or later for destruction. I would become forever more Leon Sonnenstein.

"Every year on October 7, even to this day, I light a Yahrzeit candle. I learned about Yahrzeit as I learned about all matters Jewish after that day when I became an enlistee in that suffering army. I light a candle for the death of my benefactor, Leon Sonnenstein, who died that day so I might live. And also I light a candle for Captain Zantay, Kapo guard, Latvian prisoner, and exploiter of the helpless who also died that day. For this Zantay never again would be seen on this earth. With the candle, I mourn both of their deaths. And I celebrate my rebirth.

"As for today, I now have mainly shame. I wanted to live more than anything else. Maybe that is how it was for all those who survived. They had to want life for themselves above all else. Later on I read from a woman doctor who survived Auschwitz. 'How could I survive Auschwitz?' she said. 'I will tell you. My principal was: I come first, second, and third. Then nothing, then again I; and then all the others.'"

Across the library, a janitor sweeping the tiled floor dropped his broom, sending a loud, echoing gunshot throughout the room. Startled out of our trance, both Slav and I jumped. We looked around the room, stunned it remained as before—the other researchers quietly engaged in reading, the long line of interchangeable seekers patiently waiting along the far wall, the bustling librarians efficiently engaged. As always the world around us was unmoved, untouched by the upheavals enacted on its surface.

Slav resumed, "When the Sonderkommando assembled behind Crematorium IV that night after midnight, I hid in the shadows. I watched as they hurled the lit gunpowder cans at the crematorium. And then as it exploded into flames. I watched as the camp came alive with sirens and shouts and screams and gunfire. I watched as hundreds tried to cut the barbed wire fences and escape, many shot on the spot. Some became entangled in the wire and were left there by the SS like insects trapped in a spider's nest, the guards knowing they could come back and dispose of them later. I saw the guards chase the rest into the woods. Later on I heard reports that the guards had recaptured and killed every single one of the escapees—not one survived.

"Some of the Special Squad did not run, did not try to escape, though whether by a previous arranged plan or spontaneously, I do not know. But some stayed behind. Together, six or seven of them rushed into the SS barracks and dragged out a colonel who was still in his nightclothes. For them, he was the main goal—this Colonel Steinmetz. He was their chief persecutor, the man who ran the Kapos and the Sonderkommandos, the man who decided which prisoners would go to the ovens and which to the work details. He had no viciousness like the Kapos, no passion for the kill or delight in their torture. He had no emotion at all, as if no man inside truly existed. This Steinmetz remained ever apart, above the prisoners and the Kapos, but silently directing them all by his gestures and by his nods or just by his eyes. To a man, they feared him. He was reviled beyond all others, a symbol to all of the cold, stark cruelty humanity had inflicted upon them.

"That night, this Colonel Steinmetz became the object of the Sonderkommando revenge. By the light of the flaming building next door, I watched as they dragged him across the quad behind the building near where I hid. They tied him to stakes nailed into the ground and proceeded to disintegrate him. Piece by piece, bit by bit, while all around the cries and gunshots flew, they destroyed his flesh. First by kicks to every part of his body, then by tiny cuts made with the fashioned knives into his flesh. Then with their bare hands, they tore off his limbs. And finally with this same vengeance, they ripped the head off his neck, leaving behind a bleeding twitching torso, by then more a slab of meat than a man. Amazingly, before he lost consciousness, before he became no longer human, this colonel who had supervised such torture and brutality offered up no resistance, uttered not a word, succumbed silently to his fate. It was as if he always knew this would be his end and that he had been awaiting such an event for years. That it was not only to be expected but just. A demise he had more than earned.

"I, in turn, lifted not a hand to help him. I had chosen my side. That could have been my fate, ripped limb from limb and deservedly so. Instead, again I escaped. Again I survived.

"Afterward, I would finally walk away. I would join a new life. Move to new barracks and pretend I was someone else entirely. I would be reborn. I would act as if I was not someone who had compromised, not someone who had been both a persecutor and a torturer, not someone who forever more would hide his head in shame at what he had done and who he had become in order to stay alive. And this Leon Sonnenstein is who I have been for all these years. No longer Captain Rudolfs Zantay. For that man and his soul had already died.

"Later on, after we were liberated, after I became a free man, I again had a choice. I could admit who I once had been, accept my guilt, and return to the life I had before. I could try to return to my homeland, reunite with my family, and make us whole once again. All people in wartime performed acts for which they were ashamed; all compromised. Some stole food, some sold their bodies. Were my transgressions so much the greater? But I could not delude myself. I had crossed every boundary of civilization. I had embraced evil in a manner no human should be able to forgive. I had debased my name, my family, my heritage. There was no turning back.

"I moved to Argentina. I lived in a small city outside Buenos Aires. I attended shul. I fixed motorcycles. I reclused myself. No marriage, no family, no relationships. I did not deserve them. I no longer harmed anyone. This new life was enough for me.

"In time, I grew curious about the family and the life I had left behind. I thought about trying to find them, to make them aware I had survived. To ask for their forgiveness. To touch their lives—my young son, my beloved wife whom I had left behind. But I restrained myself. Such a reward I did not deserve. Such a life I could not reclaim.

"I did, though, begin to search. My search soon became a consumption. To what end, I had no idea. The search itself became an end. I spent a year trying to find out if my family had also lived, if they too had survived. The library in Buenos Aires had phone books from all over the world. How many Zantays in the world could there be? One by one, I searched the books for a listing of my wife or my son. First eastern Europe I searched, though I could not imagine them settling back there. Then Canada, for my wife had a cousin who had settled outside Toronto before the war. Then failing in those two, I researched America. How many towns, how many phone books, how many phones in America, I could not describe. Even in 1967, when I finally found my family, there must have been thousands of books left to go through. Finally in Greenwood, Massachusetts, I discovered Risa Zantay living at 145 Colebrook Lane. A month later I found Zigfrid Zantay living in Dover, Connecticut. How could they not be mine? My heart filled with a longing and a pride I had not felt for thirty years. My eyes filled with tears.

"Several times I have written letters to these distant Zantays, saying I had known their loved one long ago. That he had been a good man, that he had died honorably, that he had loved them both very much. I signed each of them 'Leon Sonnenstein.' But I could not send along such a lie. I could not dishonor the name any longer. The letters lie still in a drawer of my desk. There they will remain until I die.

"For the irony of ironies: my motivation throughout all my tortured years after being captured by the Germans—what kept me alive day after hellish day, what justified performing acts of atrocity that in my former lifetime I could not even conceive, was that someday, some way, I would return to my family, that I would again look deep into my beloved wife's eyes, that my lips would again graze the cheek of my adored son—what allowed me to endure the ultimate debasement would now engender such shame and self-loathing that I could allow myself to look upon them never again. Thus my very survival ultimately sealed my irrevocable sentence.

"So I tell this story which I have been afraid to admit for these many years. Afraid to admit to others and most of all, to myself. But a story that nonetheless is true. A story I will carry inside my soul for all eternity. A story to which I hope my descendants will never bear witness."

Slav took a long breath into his lungs and held it. He was not ready to exhale, not ready to release what he had just absorbed. He became mute as if all the words had been drained out of him. As for me, I was petrified—like fossil rock, ancient, bloodless, lifeless. Immobile and immovable, as close to inanimate mineral as any live human could ever be. Thus solidified, I might have remained forever.

One final discovery roused me. One discovery then settled all. Removed all doubt. If I could convince Slav there might be two Zantays from Latvia, two Rudolfs Zantays, why not myself? Alas, not to be.

With uncanny timing, the irrepressible librarian returned to our desk almost at the moment Slav finished his recitation. She had with her several photocopied documents which she immediately placed on the desk. They were faded white sheets of paper, smooth and shiny in the manner of photocopies twenty years ago. Again with a monotone that held now just a trace of harshness, "We located the final reference to your Rudolfs Zantay. Some documents rescued from Germany after the liberation. From Auschwitz. These have been copied. They are not the originals. The originals were pulled from a pile of papers that had been incinerated. You can see the burn marks on the edges of these. The Nazis tried to destroy all the evidence of their crimes. But we managed to recover some of the papers." As she walked away, though, she could hardly have missed our stricken expressions. She added, "I hope this particular person of whom you inquire was no relation."

We both stared at the two pages on the desk. Neither one of us could bring ourselves to touch them, as if they were still aflame or held a caustic substance that would incinerate the flesh on contact. Finally, accepting that this task would be mine and mine alone, I unfroze and reached for the papers. Slav placed his hand on my shoulder in support.

The papers were flimsy, porous, unweighty, in contrast to the leaden immobility of the microfilm monitor. The corners were dog-eared, the edges blackened from flames reaching over the margins into the text. Again the words were in German, yet this time I needed no translator.

Rudolfs Zantay, the heading read, followed by several lines of type. In the text I could pick out the only words that mattered, Lettisch *and* Auschwitz. *Page two was a picture—faded black-and-white, below it the caption—*Captain Rudolfs Zantay. *I pulled out a picture from my wallet that I had saved and carried with me over the past fifty years. Each time this photograph began to fade, I returned to a photographer's studio and had a reprint made. The only remaining picture of my father from 1941, just before he disappeared. Dark hair, a thick mustache, a serious expression with just a glimmer of humor in the eyes. I had carried that image of him with me always.*

The portrait now before me, taken three years later, showed my father little changed. His mustache was cropped shorter, the lines around his mouth and eyes furrowed deeper, much too deep for a man of just thirty-three. Most startling of all though, the eyes were not the same. In place of the deep-set, alive, dancing eyes staring at me in my photo, these eyes were now vacant, hollowed-out, lifeless orbs, unrecognizing and unrecognizable. That's what the Nazis had done to my father. Somehow they had stolen his soul and replaced it with a zombie's. And what was left may have had my father's shell, may have been supported by his skeleton, but had none of his lifeblood coursing through its veins, had none of his essence ennobling its spirit.

Was I tempted to seek out this Leon Sonnenstein who had overtaken my father? Of course. Would I do so, would I act on such an impulse? Never. For in truth, the father I had known and loved had died in Latvia long ago on that same day I searched for him on the bridge. The man who looked like him in Auschwitz could not have been my father. The man now called Leon Sonnenstein was a new being entirely, no relation to me or mine. And of no ultimate consequence to me. Or at least that is what I have told myself all of these years since.

I rose and, without a parting word to Slav, without a look back, I left that library and that memorial and that land. I followed my father's lead and removed my amber necklace forever. I was now a man transformed. No longer in unconflicted ignorance, no longer an innocent. But also no longer a victim of the past. No more a casualty of the ages or of circumstance. Now, I believed, a liberated soul able to chart a course of my own. Truly and finally a freed man.

Briviba. Die freiheit. *Freedom. The philosopher said, "Man is born free, yet everywhere he is in chains." And that unfortunately became my credo. For the freedom of knowledge did not free my soul as I would have hoped. It burdened me. It tortured me. For I had no means of atonement. I may not have committed the sins, yet how could I not feel responsible for them? If man is a product of his forbearer's legacy, if he inherits his riches, does he not also inherit his crimes, his guilt?*

So I withdrew, I self-interred. I sought oblivion from the tools available—tools that have been mainstays in my culture for a thousand years. I drank. I drank until memory and guilt were erased from my mind. I drank until I was lost, until my already damaged liver was beyond repair. My wife, who had grown up with the violent products of alcohol in her father, could not tolerate such a reaction. All else she might have understood, forgiven, and provided comfort—

were I to allow her to try—but drinking she could not condone. One day, after my third time failing at an alcohol rehabilitation program, she left a note on my dresser and never returned.

Thus I have endured my freedom alone. Freedom from the past, freedom from the present, and, finally, freedom from any future.

CHAPTER 24 —————————

Asher startled awake. After completing his letter to Mandy, he had returned to finish Zig's story. Exhausted then, he fell asleep, his head resting on the pages piled atop the mahogany desk in his study. Some spittle draining from his mouth stained the cover sheet of Zig's document. Asher quickly tried to dry it with his shirtsleeve while also hoping to erase the troubling memory of his dream. It was past midnight. Even as he became more and more alert, this dream remained glued to his consciousness.

Asher was sitting at a shaky, wooden table in a concrete, windowless bunker in the middle of a vast desolation. Sitting in the three other rickety chairs were Zigfrid Zantay, *his* father, Rudolfs Zantay, and, in the seat opposite Asher, his own father, Richard. Each existed in their current physical states: Rudolfs—a bent, brittle octogenarian, barely able to raise his head above his shoulders; Zig—emaciated beyond belief, deeply jaundiced, his yellowed eyes glazed and unrecognizing; Asher's father—a flattened, two-dimensional figure, the devastation of a locomotive having steamrolled his remains. Asher could not see himself, but felt his body equally degenerated, the flesh hanging loosely from his bones, his bony thighs in pain from mere contact with his metal seat.

Before them on the table lay a worn deck of cards, dog-eared from years of being played by the cell's occupants, no other means of entertainment available. The four were poised for yet another hand of Blind Man's Bluff, that card game where you held a card above your forehead so everyone else at the table but you could see what card you held, then you bet based on what you saw and what you surmised the others saw. The players stared at each other a moment, then, in unison, wearily picked up a card and placed it face side out atop his own forehead. Asher stared out at the cards of Zig and Rudolfs and his own father. Each face, instead of numbers or royalty, displayed a picture of its holder, not of the wasted soul as he was holding that card, but as the strapping young man he once had been, each about to enter his prime. On Rudolf's card above his youthful dancing eyes, Asher read the verdict "GUILT." Above Zig's square, solid, innocent face, he read the life sentence "SHAME." On his father's forehead, above the most penetrating eyes Asher had ever encountered—eyes Asher had forgotten once existed—was emblazoned "REGRET." And reflected off those black, black eyes of his father, Asher could see his own card—this one portraying a vibrant, dynamic Asher looking just a bit younger than he was now—the message read "REDEMPTION."

This frozen image shocked Asher awake. This prophetic, Dickensian vision finally mobilized him to realize what he must do before time ran out.

Prior to leaving, though, Asher was drawn to his bedroom, where Mandy lay sound asleep in their bed. He noted the letter he had written still unopened on the dresser table. Watching her even breathing, her body curled like a child's, Asher felt a tenderness toward her that he had not allowed himself to feel for months. He crept up to the bed and gently pressed his lips to Mandy's exposed cheek, whispering good night. Mandy stirred, aroused similarly a hundred times before, "Miles, is that you? Are you going somewhere?"

"Yes, hon. I have to go to out for a while. Sorry."

Mandy roused some more. "What time is it? You're not even on call?"

"It's after midnight. No, not officially but I have to take care of something. I'll be back. And then we can start again."

Mandy nodded, almost back to sleep by then, Asher sure she would not remember their encounter the next day.

Ninety minutes alone with your thoughts is a long time. Driving to Dobbs Ferry, New York on that dark, starless night, passing not a solitary other car on the road, feeling as if he might be the sole surviving occupant of the planet, Asher had ample time to rehearse his next lines. But narcotized by sleeplessness and overload, Asher's mind was dead—a blank, charcoal slate. As he drove, the three objects he had brought rested next to him. They shifted and rolled on the seat as the car raced ahead, slowed down, or turned, making a slight whooshing noise as they moved, as if the journey also filled them with anticipation.

*

Asher had not been back to his hometown since he had helped his mother move out of her home six months after his father died. With her children gone and husband dead, his mother felt the hollow rooms echoed with too many memories and had chosen to restart her life in Florida. Asher then had no reason to return. Now, though, he had twin destinations. The first one, he had visited almost daily for the first eight years of his life, until his mother stopped picking his father up at the train station after work every night.

Even in the dead of night thirty-five years later, the plank-sided, red-roofed building, sporting a cupola on top, looked unchanged. A solitary, yellow light penetrating the fog-filled night rendered the deserted building luminescent. One window on the building's side was shattered by what Asher surmised had been a teen's well-aimed rock. Asher was sure he was having an auditory hallucination when he heard a distant, lone dog howling at the night. Until that moment, Asher had not been consciously aware of his need to revisit this locale or that he'd spent all these years avoiding it.

Asher parked his car at the farthest end of the station, where the stairs led up to a platform only three feet wide. He uncoiled his reluctant body from the car seat, stiff from the unplanned ride, and then hobbled up the five steps, imagining his leg in a brace and his arms supporting a pair of crutches. He stood immobile on the cement platform, balancing on one leg while a cold wind whipped at his cheeks. Asher stared into the dark cavern that held the glinting train tracks, trying to recreate what had happened at this crossroad ten years before. Five minutes he froze there, his mind crawling into his father's.

First, he conjured up what he assumed must have been his father's initial lucid, wholly conscious calculation. Next, he envisioned his father growing an expanding, festering nidus of fear mixed with overwhelming despair. Finally, Asher imagined his father blanking out all emotions to become solely an instrument of action.

Suddenly, Asher felt the deep, earth-shaking rumble of a distant locomotive speeding down the tracks. He stared off into the horizon until he spotted the solitary light of the engine propelling toward him, knowing no train would stop at this tiny station in the middle of the night. The onrushing train took at most, thirty seconds from first sighting around a bend until it hit the station, slowing down not a whit. And as the train sped up to him and then plummeted past, Asher felt for the first time the enormity, and yes, the courage of his father's act that morning. Asher could not condone his father's course, but for that one brief moment while he envisioned himself launching off the platform and plunging into the path of oblivion, he grasped how impossible such an action must have been.

Then Asher transformed. He became one with his father. He felt the roar of the onrushing locomotive meld with the pounding of his heartbeat. He felt the ground fall away from his feet and the sudden freedom of being airborne. He felt the heart-rending, unexpected pang of remorse as he left all of his earthly consciousness behind. Finally, Asher suffered the instantaneous shock of searing pain as bulleted metal obliterated defenseless flesh. A hair's-breadth second later, he felt oblivion. Asher fell exhausted onto the platform. His face pressed into the cement, Asher tasted the gritty, salted concrete as if it were ingrained with his father's pulverized bones and fallen tears.

*

Maybe fifteen minutes later, Asher picked himself up and stumbled to his car. He turned on the engine. Then both his ungoverned car and streaming thoughts began meandering through the night. Into Asher's head flew a memory he had not recalled for the past 10 years. When Asher had finished his neurology rotation at Lenox Hill Hospital, as usual, he had received a written evaluation of his performance from his resident and attending physician preceptors. The evaluation was in no way glowing, just the standard platitudes about adequate knowledge and enthusiasm, and a suggestion to take more individual initiative. At the bottom of the page, written in different ink, instantly recognizable to Asher as his father's pen, Asher had read this unexpected and uncharacteristic missive: "You have a gift. You sense the feelings of your fellow man in a way few others can. Don't let the pressures of medicine or the pain of life deter you from using that gift." At the time, Asher could not tell if this statement was a compliment or an admonition. Driving away now from the site of his father's destruction, Asher realized he had not only forgotten about that comment, he had buried its message.

Jewish cemeteries are much like others. More Stars of David, maybe fewer grandiose monuments. Otherwise like the rest—dominoes of gravestones set into grassed lanes, punctuated by ancient trees and floral wreaths and, most of all, dominated by dead silence. Temple Eden Cemetery, technically in Hastings-on-Hudson just outside of Dobbs Ferry, was not much different. Of course, on a moonless, fogged night, no cemetery seemed different than any other, only that much more ominous.

Asher knew he might have a tough time locating a cemetery he had only visited once, at the time of his father's funeral. But he remembered playing baseball as a kid at a field on Mount Hope Road not far from the cemetery, and managed to find his way without too much misdirection. Locating his father's gravesite proved more of a challenge. After parking at the locked gate, Asher retrieved his flashlight from the trunk. He squeezed his way through a gap in the gate, no doubt made by curious teens, and began his search. He headed directly for the left corner of the cemetery, remembering a plot plan he had recently been sent by Temple Eden, when they had somehow found out his mother had passed on and inquired if Asher wanted her remains to be interred next to his father's. Asher had decided to leave his mother to rest in Florida.

Shining his light on row after row of fallen Levys and Greenfields and Moskowitzes, the rows of gravestones inscribed with "BELOVED FATHER," "DEVOTED HUSBAND," or "ADORED SON," Asher felt a flush of shame rise in his cheeks. How had he spent so little effort mourning the death of his father? What had given him license to harden his heart against his own flesh and blood? When his flashlight finally lit up the headstone with his father's name, Asher was both relieved and contrite. He read the simple inscription. "RICHARD MEYERS ASHER, MD 1925-1986, ALWAYS AND FOREVER AN INSPIRATION TO HIS PATIENTS, TO HIS CHILDREN AND TO HIS WIFE." An inscription that hoped to explain all, but in practice explained nothing.

With little forethought, Asher stood at the foot of his father's grave, a light rain beginning to mist his bare scalp and dampen his cheeks. He stared at the flat rectangle of grass and imagined his father perched atop, once more upright in his leather chair, once again holding court. Asher began. "Well Dad, I guess even anger fades with time. Must be like women forgetting the pain of childbirth soon afterward, otherwise they'd probably never have kids again. But I've been able to hold onto my anger toward you longer than most. I tried to bury that anger, bury it along with you; you left so quickly, leaving so much unsaid. When I found out three months ago that you did so deliberately, all that anger erupted. But it's hard spitting anger out at the dead, it seems to just blow right back into your face. And I must admit, I have been getting drenched with my own saliva of late.

"But *you* also might admit, you were pretty much a bastard. That father-as-autocrat role you heaved around has lost its luster. Maybe we've gone too far the other way these days in becoming best pals with our kids, but it seems far preferable to the parent-as-field-marshal scenario you set up. I assume you had your reasons for acting the way you did, and maybe I would have slacked off and become the ne'er-do-well you envisioned me as without your boot always up my butt. So for that I forgive you.

"But do I forgive you for cutting out the way you did? Then jumping out of your grave here after mom's death to throw that shitload of truth in my face? The first question is kind of moot. Does it take more courage and resolve to endure the land mines life places in your path—to fight through defeats and declines and humiliations—than to off yourself in the way you chose? Ever since I read your letter, I've assumed yours was the more cowardly way. But after standing on that train platform tonight, I am not so certain. In your mind, maybe you were performing an act of sacrifice. In any case, you made your decision and though all of us suffered the consequences, you suffered most of all.

"Why, however, did you need to tell me? Even if it helped you, how could it possibly help me? My knee-jerk response was that, in the end, you were a selfish SOB—first dispatching yourself to avoid humiliation, afraid to be knocked off your pedestal, and then unleashing that load onto me. Now look at me. Screwing up my patients, my friends, my career, and even my family.

Everything I've worked so hard to achieve is now circling the drain.

"Maybe I'm near where you were toward the end. You were swimming way over your head and I seem to be treading close to those waters. And maybe that was your message—sooner or later I was going to face something like what you faced. Now I have you to thank and also to hate for taking the path you did. I have your model to show me how my family would despise me if I followed it. The only alternative route, the one you chose not to take, is to fight back. To rededicate myself to those I have promised to care for and protect.

"So ultimately, maybe I should thank you. I guess a person can either be a model by example or by exception. In many ways, you are both. In the end, you are neither. You are just my dad whom I will always love, no matter what you did. And at least now I have the comfort of knowing you always loved me."

With that, using his car key and blunt fingernails, Asher began digging a hole in the soft turf. He dug until he made a foot-long rent in the sod, a couple of inches deep. Asher then rolled the letter his dad had willed to him all of those years ago and laid it, scroll-like, into the ground above his father's remains.

*

Asher drove the hour and a half back to Dover General Hospital at close to four AM, strangely exhilarated. He was but half done with his mission, yet felt more unburdened than he had in years.

On entering the darkened, eerie, silent hospital lobby, Asher stopped for a moment to check if Zigfrid Zantay was still a patient there. Could his nearly consumed liver have allowed him to linger this long? Amazingly, Zig was still in the same room as the last time Asher had looked, three weeks before. Asher hoped, prayed, and wrongly assumed his guide had not been confined continuously to this particular prison cell for that long. Better to have gotten back home for a time than spend your last days chained to a hospital bed.

The climb up the seven flights of dimly lit hospital stairs felt to Asher like an ascent to the mount. On nights such as this, the hospital was a ghost ship. Corridor and room lights were turned low so shadows played tricks in the vacant hallways. Scattered sounds echoed off the walls, a patient's monitor beeped erratically. A call bell went off in someone's room, summoning a nurse who never appeared; an occasional shout rang out from some demented patient screaming for his long-deceased mother. Asher's rubber-soled shoes screeched as he walked down the corridor to Zig's room.

This time, Asher bypassed the nurses' station and the chart room. He was no longer interested in the patient, Zigfrid Zantay, but rather the man. Asher waited outside room 712, screwing up his courage, listening for a moment to ensure that therein still resided a living soul. Other than the irregular sound of labored breathing, Asher could detect none of the sounds of medical paraphernalia that usually accompanied a hospitalized patient. Such an absence meant that either the patient was too healthy to really require hospital care, or that all sincere efforts to cure him had been abandoned, and he was soon destined for another state of existence. Asher hesitated at the door for a moment. He was suddenly aware he had met Zig face-to-face only once before—on the side of the road on a night such as this—and that he had never had a direct conversation with him, though Zig had been a presence in Asher's life for years and Asher felt he knew him like kin.

Asher knocked quietly on the door, then entered without awaiting a response. Lying in bed, covered to the neck in white, Asher found a body that barely made a dent in the surface of his blanket, as if the topography of the life hidden beneath had been ironed flat. Jutting out from the top of the blanket floated a pale, hairless skull, disembodied, resembling not at all the man Asher had rescued those ten years before. All that was left of Zigfrid

273

Zantay seemed to be this barely tethered balloon ready to ascend skyward.

No tubes or IVs connected to Zig's arms, his right hand outside the sheet unattached to any lifeline. No plastic prongs fed oxygen to Zig's nostrils. No monitor above his head recorded Zig's blood pressure, oxygen level, or heart rhythm. The room itself was otherwise unoccupied. No longer was there any evidence of the outside world's investment in his recovery. Only a lone, crudely drawn picture of a stick-figured boy holding a red balloon under a rainbow with a caption that read, "Get well soon, Grandpa," allowed the hope that someone else out there was still paying attention to the tragedy unfolding herein.

Zig was asleep, or comatose, Asher could not tell which. Asher pulled up the worn, vinyl-covered chair and sat by the bed. Zig's respirations were deep and sonorous, spacing further and further apart, then stopping for ten or twenty seconds, then beginning again with a start, slowly speeding up and then repeating the cycle all over again. Asher was well familiar with Cheyne-Stokes respirations, and did not necessarily assume them to signal that Zig's end was imminent. However, Zig's alien-like, yellow tinge, his body covered with huge, scattered purple welts, his indifference first to vocal attempts to awaken him, and then to shaking, and finally to forceful squeezes applied to his Achilles tendon, all testified to a body about to succumb.

Asher should have expected to find Zig in such a state—after suffering from liver failure for so long, how else might he be but barely hanging on? Yet Asher was still disappointed. He had hoped for a dialogue. But as was often the case when speaking with the eternal, Asher would have to settle for a one-sided conversation.

Asher pulled the chair up to the head of Zig's bed and leaned over him, not at all repelled by the smell of unprocessed bilirubin emanating from his pores. Asher began slowly, tentatively, his voice barely above a whisper, "Well, Zig, I finally made it here. I wonder if you might even have been expecting me. But I guess in your state, you can really only expect one thing. Though we've met in person only once before, you've never been far from my thoughts. I was shocked and grateful to find you also thinking about me even as your days dwindled down. When you trusted me with your memoir, maybe you knew you were throwing a drowning man a life preserver. Though I guess that might be giving you credit for being more of a mind reader than is humanly possible. But having thrown out your lifeline, maybe you knew sooner or later it would pull me back to you.

"After I came upon you on the roadside, you got me started on my career. You set me up, gave me the confidence to venture out on my own. Gave me the boost I needed. I never forgot the advice you gave and the faith you showed in me. You said, 'Just keep your patients first and foremost in your mind and in your heart, and you will do fine.' And I've tried to stay faithful to those words. Lately, though, I've encountered a few mountains blocking my way on the road. Of course, those obstacles would probably feel to you more like molehills compared to what you've been through in your lifetime."

While Asher spoke, he imagined Zig's breathing smoothed out some, became more regular; he even imagined Zig's eyelids fluttering, as if some electric impulses still swirled between his synapses. A nurse Asher did not recognize suddenly stepped through the doorway, holding a tray of medication. "Sorry, Dr. Asher, I didn't know it was you in here. I heard voices and wondered who could be talking. I'll come back later." Asher merely nodded in response, suddenly aware how strange he must look—disheveled, unshaven, holding a five-in-the-morning conversation with a comatose, near-dead patient.

Asher went on, undeterred. "With your help, Zig, I've come to realize we all sin. Against our loved ones, against our ideals, against our basic natures. The only irredeemable sin is the one that we never try to redeem. Shame and guilt are tough boulders to bulldoze over. They can take a sin and turn it into a mountain range instead of a hill. Your dad and I guess mine, too, chose to stop at the base. But as bad as your dad was, I suspect, had he chosen to, he could have returned to your mother and to you and confessed all, and you would have taken him back and forgiven him. He might have been a hollowed-out version of himself; he might have given you a worse model than the imagined one you carried with you all these years. But all that pain and doubt you lived with, all that legacy of guilt, might have eased up on you some. Maybe they would not have continued to torment you here at the end of your days.

"It seems too late now for you. But then again, maybe not. If your kids and wife could see and understand what you had to deal with—what you fought through and conquered—maybe you could still salvage something, at the very least your *own* legacy. Maybe your family might remember you, not for the man you have become, beaten down by life, but for the survivor you always were. If they read your testimony, they might understand."

Asher then rose and placed the exhumed document that had been resting on his lap onto Zig's nightstand and scribbled a note. "To the Zantay family. Zig wanted you to have this. I hope it will help explain him to you and to your children and on down the line. Your father was a man without equal. With all my respect, Miles Asher."

Asher sat back down, not yet finished. "My dad likewise threw in the towel. He judged and sentenced himself and then administered his own punishment. Never gave himself a chance at redemption. I have maybe half a lifetime left to undo my failures. But thanks to you, I have a chance to do better."

Asher placed his hand on Zig's and squeezed it for a moment, receiving no message in response. He rose to leave, taking one last look at Zig's unmoving form on the bed. Then he felt jingle in his pocket. "Oh, I almost forgot. I have one more item for you." Asher removed the amber amulet from his jacket pocket. "This is yours. Thanks for lending it to me. I'm not sure it carries with it much luck or supernatural healing powers. Its main quality seems to lay in its ability to foster insight, plus an unexpected measure of comfort."

Asher bent over and placed the object into Zig's upturned, inert hand, barely grazing his palm. Zig's hand twitched for a second, sending a shock through Asher's hand almost halting *his* heart. The amulet then rested in Zig's palm for a few moments, tangled up in a ball, as if that last jolt of electricity had drained dry whatever was left in his battery. But soon, slowly, minutely, Zig's hand stirred, then curled upward, finally grasping the stone. Zig's index finger and thumb gradually maneuvered the amber so that he could roll the jewel between his fingers, tracing the outline of his ancestor's noble face as he had done ten thousand times before. Maybe Asher only imagined the slight hint of a smile that crept onto Zigfrid Zantay's face this one last time.

Asher clasped his hands around Zig's, then rose and left his room, that floor and the hospital. He realized he had one further destination, a place where he could at last rest. On the drive home, Asher missed not a bit the three objects that had been his companions on the way out. Even his car felt lighter, more maneuverable, without the added burden of those talismans.

When he headed up the driveway to his home, the light was just breaking. A shaft of sunlight over the horizon lit the mountain opposite, sparkling the just-blooming trees of May in pointillist glitter. At the crest of his driveway, Asher was surprised to find Mandy sitting on the front steps for who knows how long, her hand clutching the letter he had left for her. Without a word, Mandy rushed up to the car and grasped him in a fervent embrace, the letter crushing between them. At that moment, Stacie and Emily, sporting huge smiles, opened the front door and, in unison, shouted, "Daddy's back!"

In response, for one time in his life, Asher felt his own face unite in a smile both broad and alive, a smile that stayed with him long after the four had ceased embracing, after the girls had headed off to school, and, finally, even carrying him back to his patients that day.